Ring Fire
The Fleabag Tril

The mysterious Ring F
protects the kingdom from evil. It might seem like magic but it is something different. And much stronger.

Now the Fire has been taken from the Ring. It falls to Gemma, a kitchen-maid, and Fleabag, a three-legged, humorous talking cat, to find it. It must be restored to its rightful place and a new King or Queen must be crowned. But the evil wizards of Porthwain are determined to overcome the Fire and take its power for themselves. Gemma loses her courage and, worse, is separated from Fleabag. In one final, terrible challenge the Ring Fire seems to be lost when it is betrayed by someone who was sworn to protect it. There is no one left for Fleabag to turn to – or is there? Who is the strange boy who plays the fiddle and seems so afraid of everyone?

In these three acclaimed stories, Beth Webb relates the thrilling series of conflicts over the Ring Fire as the unlikely accomplices struggle against the powers of destruction to save the kingdom.

'Fast-paced narrative laced with humour and magic.'
School Library Journal

'Opens the door to the heights and depths that fantasy can offer but with such a light touch and such a witty knowing edge.'
Philip Gross

BETH WEBB lives in Somerset with her four children and an entourage of pets. Her stories are mostly based on real places or events, intertwined with traditional folk legends.

For my children: Tom, Maddy, Gabs and John Ralls,
and for my great-nephew Zachary Dylan Walder Press.
With love.

Ring Fire

The Fleabag Trilogy

Beth Webb

A Lion Children's Book
an imprint of
Lion Hudson plc
Mayfield House, 256 Banbury Road
Oxford OX2 7DH, England
www.lionhudson.com
ISBN-13: 978-0-7459-4977-2
ISBN-10: 0-7459-4977-0

First published as individual volumes:
Fleabag and the Ring Fire (1995)
Fleabag and the Fire Cat (1998)
Fleabag and the Ring's End (2000)

First edition 2005
10 9 8 7 6 5 4 3 2 1

A catalogue record for this book is available
from the British Library

Typeset in 11/14 Aldine721 BT
Printed and bound in Great Britain
by Cox & Wyman Ltd, Reading

Fleabag and the Ring Fire

Contents

1

Strange Fire

The tongues of flame reached higher and higher. There was no sound or smell of burning, but Gemma could feel the excitement of the growing heat against her face. There were other people there too. She did not know them, but she could see their faces dimly reflecting the orange and yellow glow.

'One day...' she told herself. 'One day, I shall know what it all means...'

Gemma shook her head and rubbed her eyes. She usually saw strange things when she looked into the depths of the great milky opal. But what she saw was different every time.

The crimson fire that glistened in the heart of the Ring's huge stone seemed still to be burning in another world, far away. Yet it was scarcely a finger's breadth from the end of her nose.

Suddenly the Queen lifted her long, thin, tired hands from the bedclothes and touched Gemma on the shoulder. 'You must not look too long into the Ring Fire, little one. You are so young...' Her voice trailed away. Speaking was difficult these days. The old lady was failing. Gemma could feel it in her bones, though she did not want to believe it.

The girl always brought early morning tea to the Queen. She would sit by the royal bed and wait for the old lady to waken. It was during these silent minutes she had become fascinated by the strange fire burning deep within the great Ring on the Queen's hand. The glowing flame seemed to tell her so much, yet nothing she could describe to anyone who might have asked.

Gemma made herself come back to reality. 'Shall I fetch your clothes, ma'am? Today is the last day of the Great Festival. Perhaps you will find your successor before sunset.'

Queen Sophia raised her head and looked at Gemma with sad, grey eyes. 'And perhaps I will not,' she said slowly. 'To tell the truth, my dear, I have had enough of this festival. I have had wrestlers fighting to show how a monarch must beat all opponents, poets writing long and exceedingly boring elegies on the nature of royalty, runners bursting their lungs to exceed each other in speed to show that a sovereign must be... something else, I can't remember what...' She smiled wearily.

Gemma grinned. 'I liked the knights in armour, who wanted to kill dragons or rescue princesses to show how brave and strong they are.'

'Did you, my dear? Perhaps they did look brave and

strong. Unfortunately we have no maidens in distress in our good land and we don't seem to have any marauding dragons these days. In fact we haven't had one since, oh, about a hundred years ago. I was quite a young thing in those days. It was all terribly exciting...

'Anyway,' the Queen added miserably, 'They're all missing the point. None of them seems to have the remotest notion of what it really means to be a king or a queen. All anyone can think about is power – all that differs is whether it is in strength or wisdom or numbers of soldiers.' She sighed. 'Fetch me today's programme, will you, please?'

Gemma was dying to ask what *was* the point. But she was a timid girl and she did not dare. Instead she got up from her stool and went to pull back the pink cotton curtains. The morning sunlight flooded the room, giving the Queen's pale cheeks a golden hue.

It wasn't at all the sort of room one would expect a queen to sleep in. It was simply furnished and always bright and airy. Gemma resolved that should she ever have a bedroom of her own, she would make it just like this one.

From the top of the desk she drew a piece of white vellum embossed with the royal crest.

'Today, ma'am, we have jesters, more poets,' (the Queen groaned), 'some politicians,' (the Queen groaned again, even more loudly), 'a wise man and an historian. They all wish most humbly to represent to your Royal Highness their insights into what it means to be a monarch of this land... Oh, and there's one last entry here, in pencil at the bottom... your Royal Fire Welder...'

'The Fire Wielder,' the Queen corrected sleepily.

Suddenly she opened her eyes wide. 'Is *he* coming? When?'

'It doesn't say here, ma'am. But he's last. What does he do? Is he a fire juggler? Oh, I do hope so. I saw fire jugglers in the Great Hall last year at the Midwinter Festival. They ate roaring flames and threw great burning torches up into the roofspace. I was sure sparks were going to get caught in the rafters, and that the whole lot would catch alight. But it didn't. It was so beautiful, I almost cried.'

'No. No. Nothing like that. The Fire Wielder is important – without him, I am no queen.' The old lady sat up and slipped her feet out from under the bed covers. It was almost as if the last few years had suddenly been peeled away from her. 'Please help me dress, as quickly as you can.'

Gemma stared in amazement. The ancient, frail Queen Sophia was perched like a delicate bird on the edge of the bed, quite flushed and excited.

The girl lifted a sapphire-blue satin gown from the sandalwood cupboard.

The Queen shook her head and laughed. 'No, no, child, not that one. Get me my golden robes of state. I will wear my crown and my emeralds. Send for my hairdresser and my equerry and tell that pompous Prime Minister of mine to oversee the festival in my place. He will enjoy it much more than I would. Today I have more important things to attend to.'

The Queen clapped her hands in delight. 'Today is going to be a great day. Perhaps the greatest day of my entire reign!'

2

Just Look at Yourself!

The Royal Hairdresser was not hard to find and once Gemma had delivered all the other messages, there was nothing left for her to do, except to creep slowly and miserably down the back stairs to the kitchens.

Gemma had hoped to be allowed to stay and wait on the Queen for the day. She was longing to see this 'Royal Fire Wielder' who had caused Her Majesty to become so excited and alive.

But that privilege was for the daughters of lords and ladies. Gemma did not even know whose daughter she was. The Queen herself had found Gemma, a smelly, hungry ragamuffin, in the gutters of Harflorum and taken her back to the palace in the royal carriage. And as Cook reminded Gemma frequently, the gutter was where the likes of her belonged.

Cook was a fat, greasy-skinned, mean-eyed man who would always reinforce his comments on every subject with the back of a wooden spoon slammed hard on the nearest table. If it was a bad day, he would use the spoon on any of the kitchen servants who happened to be within reach.

Gemma knew today was likely to be such a day.

Cook hated festivals. They always meant extra work. This made him drink too much. Then he would get a headache. Headaches meant that everything anyone did would be wrong. And as this festival had lasted for three days, Cook's headache would be very bad by now.

The staircase down to the kitchen was not a long one. Gemma shivered. The warm glow of the fire she had seen burning in the Ring had gone. It had been only a dream. The excitement of seeing the Queen so happy was for someone else to share. Gemma descended each wooden stair one foot at a time, very slowly. Each movement brought her closer and closer to her nightmare. Two more steps and the stairs would twist to the right, bringing her to the bottom and into full view of the kitchen door.

Suddenly, she sat down hard and buried her head in her hands. She did not want to get shouted at today. She hated being beaten for nothing. Perhaps she would be better off going back to where she had come from, living off market scraps and sheltering in doorways. This was no life for anyone.

Just then a warm softness twisted around her legs. Absent-mindedly, she put her hand down and scratched the old black cat behind the ears.

'Hello, Fleabag. How are you today? I saved you some bacon rind; it's in the kitchen. When Cook goes out, I'll get it for you.'

The cat put up his ugly face and nuzzled into her hand.

'Let's go now,' he said. 'I have a little corner that needs to be filled.' He started to hobble downstairs on his three legs, but Gemma didn't move.

The cat stopped on the bottom stair and looked back at his friend. 'You don't want to go into the kitchen today, do you?' he purred in his deep, gravelly voice.

'How did you know, you old ratter, you?' Gemma laughed, scratching him under the chin with her toe.

'Dead easy,' growled the cat. 'You're sitting out here on the stairs instead of getting me my bacon rind. Don't worry, Cook is at market already. Manda and Jane have gone to help, and Harry and Tina are scrubbing out the scullery. It's quite safe.'

Gemma got up and crept stealthily into the kitchen. The great pine table had already been scoured and smelled wet and sweet. All around hung polished copper pans and ladles, moulds and shapes, bunches of herbs and baskets of eggs.

Suddenly Fleabag yowled and sprang across the room with fifteen claws unsheathed and razor sharp. The poor grey mouse that had been hiding behind the flour bin knew no more. Gemma turned her back on the scene. She knew it was most impolite to watch while the cat ate his prey.

After a few moments, Fleabag gave a small burp and a polite cough. 'Oh dear, excuse me. Um. A little chewy, but a good flavour. I must confess I let them get at the flour a little bit now and then. It does add to the quality of the final meal... Ho, ho, get it? The final meal?'

Gemma did not wish to 'get' such an awful joke and ignored him. 'Are you still interested in that bacon rind?'

'Later, thank you,' he muttered between licks at his

paws. He was always meticulously clean. 'That mouse has nicely filled the little space I did have. Perhaps later, though?' he enquired hopefully, his shaggy black head on one side. Without waiting for a reply, Fleabag resumed the examination of his fur and whiskers. Suddenly he stopped and looked up at her with his big golden eyes.

'To be honest, I'm more interested in *you* than in bacon rind.'

'What do you mean?'

'Just look at yourself!'

Gemma went over to the big mirror where servants were supposed to check their appearance before going upstairs to wait on the Queen or her guests.

She was thin, tall, with lank, fair hair pulled back into a pony tail. A few freckles spangled her long, straight nose. She was neither pretty nor plain, although she had a feeling she could look quite nice if she wore something other than the palace regulation brown gingham issued to all below stairs staff. But then, she was grateful to be out of rags and wearing something clean and mended.

Gemma could see nothing amiss. She straightened her apron a little, shrugged and turned round to look at the cat, who by now had sprung up onto the big table.

'Oh, you wicked animal!' she laughed, picking him up. 'Cook will cut your other back leg off if he catches you up there!'

Fleabag struggled free and landed heavily on all three paws. 'Huh, I'd like to see him try. Now, come and sit down. I need to talk to you seriously for once.'

Gemma sat obediently on the settle next to the huge open fire, and Fleabag sat opposite her, so the light from the flames caught his golden eyes. 'Now listen.

You know where you came from?'

'The backstreets.'

'Quite. Do you know where you are going to?'

'No, I'd not really thought about it… I'll stay here all my life, I suppose. I've often thought about running away and becoming a street urchin again, but I know that's silly. I can read and write now as well as do the basic kitchen work, so if Cook gets too awful I might be able to get a job somewhere else… But to be honest, I love the Queen. I don't want to leave.'

'How long do you think you will last here when the Queen dies?'

Gemma felt a huge lump swell up in her throat. She got up and poked vigorously at the fire until sparks rose into the black heights of the chimney. At last she looked over her shoulder at Fleabag. 'Do you think she'll die soon, then?'

'Don't you? This festival is putting a tremendous strain on her. I'd be very surprised if she lives a week. Then what will happen to you? Cook hates you because you're the Queen's pet. As soon as she's dead, you'll be back on the streets… or even worse, kept here.'

Gemma shuddered.

'What do you suggest I do?' she asked very quietly.

The cat stretched and rolled onto his back, his three legs sticking out at ridiculously odd angles. 'You could start by scratching my tummy,' he suggested. 'That always helps me think.'

Gemma knelt down next to the cat and felt the delicious roar of his purr thundering through his fire-warmed, barrel-like body.

At last he twisted round and sat up. 'That's enough,

thank you. Now, tell me, what would you like to do… if you could do anything?'

Gemma didn't need to think. 'I'd like to stay here and serve the Queen… or her successor, but you don't think that's possible, do you?'

The cat shook his head vigorously and a few dozy fleas landed on the hearthrug.

'No. But I have a few practical alternatives. First of all, and right now,' suggested the cat, 'you must make yourself scarce. I hear Cook coming through the back gate. Then you must go and answer the front door. I hear a visitor coming up the path and the butler is busy out the back polishing silver… Then you must wait and see what happens next.'

Just then, Cook's irritable voice roared for Jane and Manda to hurry up. Gemma jumped to her feet and ran out of the kitchen as fast as her legs would carry her.

Fleabag decided that Gemma should be given something of a head start. Deftly he tugged something out from a hiding place behind Cook's chair and then with one bound he landed in the exact centre of the kitchen table. Between the black cat's paws lay a fat, grey rat with yellow teeth. It was very dead and very ugly.

As soon as the huge bulk appeared at the kitchen doorway, Fleabag jumped down and started to rub himself around Cook's legs, purring and mewing for all he was worth to show his master the great prize, neatly laid to view.

As Fleabag had foreseen, the Cook took the cat's tail in one hand, and the rat's in the other. Then with a powerful swing, both animals were tossed right out of the kitchen door, to land in a heap in the middle of the herb garden.

Fleabag, whose tail was very tough, simply returned the rat to its hiding place. It was the same one he brought out on all special occasions to impress Cook or to annoy the butler. The rat always did the trick, although it was getting a bit smelly these days.

Fleabag then went back to the herb garden. There he blinked and twitched his tail in the sunshine, as he watched the front door opening to admit a very special visitor.

3

The Fire Wielder

The little man on the royal doorstep was completely round in every way. Round stomach, round head and, under his flame-red fez, there glinted big, brown, round eyes.

He stood quite still for a second, then with a wide, sweeping gesture, he plucked off his hat and bowed low. As he straightened he caught Gemma in his gaze, then suddenly, he opened a wide, tooth-filled grin which cracked his face into a million wrinkles and laughter lines.

'Oh, good,' he said. 'You're here.'

Gemma was so astonished, she just stood there, gawping rudely at the stranger who was left standing on the doorstep.

At that moment, Fleabag sprang over the threshold and pushed his silky fur against Gemma's legs. 'Pull yourself together!' he ordered. 'The butler is coming!'

The cat hobbled along the corridor into the dark gloom of the hallway with as much dignity as his three legs could muster.

With an effort, Gemma curtseyed and tried to clear her throat. 'Welcome, Sir. Whom do you wish to see, and who may I say is calling?'

The little man cocked his head on one side and looked at Gemma with a quizzical smile. He said nothing, but held out his hand to her. In his wrinkled palm was a tiny flicker of red flame. There was neither coal nor tinder nor match in his hand – the flame just hovered there, brightly.

Gemma gasped and looked at him wide-eyed. 'The Royal Fire Welder – I mean Wielder!' She curtseyed again, even more flustered than before. She felt herself going quite pink, then she lost her balance, stumbled backwards and landed very hard right on the butler's bunion.

The butler was a tall, thin, humourless man with a sour face the shape and colour of a lemon. With one motion, he picked Gemma up by the collar of her dress and deftly deposited her well out of sight in the shadows behind the great door.

With a perfect and obsequious bow to the visitor, he coldly invited the little man into the library to await Her Majesty's presence. As the butler closed the door, he managed to kick Gemma in the shins, hard and spitefully. He hissed: 'Get down below, and don't you ever let me catch you above stairs again. Ever! Get it?'

Gemma cowered back behind the door to wait for the visitor to pass, so she could slink off downstairs to cry alone.

But the Fire Wielder did not move. He stood dark and still, staring at the butler with a look that would have withered an oak tree. 'I wish to be attended while I wait,' he said firmly.

The butler bowed slightly. 'Of course, Sir. I will be at your disposal.'

'By that young lady behind the door.'

The butler glanced over his shoulder at Gemma's cowering figure.

'I'm sorry, Sir. You should not have been embarrassed even by the sight of her. She is a mere scullery maid and had no right to be above stairs at all. If you wish I will summon one of the ladies-in-waiting for you...'

The Fire Wielder stretched out one strong, brown hand and laid it firmly against the butler's chest. Then with his free hand pointing to Gemma he said clearly and slowly, 'I wish to be attended by that young lady there. I do not want a lady-in-waiting. I would like interesting conversation until Her Majesty can see me, not stuffy court pleasantries. And in the meantime I would like you, please, to go and arrange for two glasses of lemonade and a plate of Cook's best cakes to be sent up.'

Gemma wondered who this Royal Fire Wielder could be. This strange little man was obviously not the sort of person one argued with. The butler cast one deadly look at Gemma as he slid sideways out of the visitor's reach, and disappeared down the corridor.

Gemma stared hard at the floor. She dare not look up in case she giggled, although half of her wished that the Fire Wielder had not made such a fuss, because she now had yet another enemy in the palace. In his way, the butler was every bit as bad as Cook when it came to making servants' lives miserable.

Suddenly she realized that the strange little visitor was walking, or rather, waddling along the corridor ahead of her. Gemma pulled herself together and sprang to her place just behind him. As they reached the library, she opened the door wide with a flourish and a curtsey, just as she had seen the chief parlourmaid do.

At that moment there was a terrific crash from below stairs, followed immediately by Fleabag's agonized yowling and the butler's voice bellowing murderous threats at the animal. Gemma permitted herself a little grin. She could tell by Fleabag's voice that he was not really hurt, but had merely laid a successful ambush for his enemy, the butler.

The library was a bright room lined with oak bookcases and panelled walls. Tiny specks of dust floated lazily in the golden morning sunshine which streamed in from the open windows. The sweet smell of beeswax polish mingled with the scent from a bowl of roses on the table. It was a delightful place to just sit and be quiet.

The Fire Wielder sat down heavily in a big leather armchair and motioned to Gemma to pull up a stool. She hesitated. 'I'm not supposed to sit in the presence of visitors,' she said nervously.

The Fire Wielder leaned forward and smiled his big toothy grin which looked so startling against the dark golden-brown of his face. 'Then let us say... that I am not a visitor, but a long lost friend.'

Gemma curtseyed nervously and pulled up the stool so it was opposite the little man.

He leaned back in his chair and closed his eyes as if he

were very hot and tired. He pulled off his fez and ran his fingers through his grizzled, grey hair, until it stuck out at all angles. Heavy black eyebrows and a long, hooked nose gave him an air of solemnity despite his many smile lines.

After a while, when he opened his eyes, Gemma could see that they carried sadness as well as the warmth she had first noticed. At close quarters, he also seemed to be much older than she had first guessed. The Fire Wielder's heat and exhaustion were not helped by the long, heavy official robes he wore. These were made of glistening red, yellow and gold silk, stiffened and embroidered at every fold. They looked most uncomfortable, and he twitched at them miserably.

At last she realized he was peering at her from under his huge dark eyebrows. He was no longer smiling, but he still looked kind. 'Now, tell me, what is your name?'

'Gemma, sir.'

'A good name. Now, let us see if there is really any Ring Fire in this little Gem, shall we? When I opened my hand to you by the front door, what did you see?'

Gemma's mind ran wildly, trying to imagine what could be the right answer to such a question. In the end she swallowed hard and said simply, 'A tiny flame of fire, Sir. A bit like the one in the Queen's Ring…' She glanced up nervously. Had her answer been what he wanted to hear?

The old man nodded and smiled a little. 'Good…'

Just then a knock came at the door and the chief parlourmaid entered. She curtseyed and put the lemonade and cakes on a side table, giving Gemma a withering glance.

'Begging your pardon for interrupting, Sir, but Her

Majesty conveys you her deepest respect and says she will be with you directly.' The woman curtseyed again and hesitated.

'That will be all, thank you,' said the Royal Fire Wielder dismissively. The parlourmaid looked as if she was bursting to know what was happening, but she could do nothing except leave. When she had shut the door and her footsteps had retreated along the corridor, the Fire Wielder turned to Gemma again.

'Now where were we? Ah yes, you saw fire, did you? Like this?' He opened his palm again – but Gemma saw nothing.

Gemma looked up, confused. 'No, Sir,' she said quietly. 'Not like that.'

'Good.' He smiled with intense satisfaction. 'Now, something to eat and drink, I think. Help yourself, you look half starved.'

Gemma felt decidedly uncomfortable. But she was hungry – and thirsty. While they ate, their mouths were too full of whipped cream and chocolate topping to talk. Gemma tried hard to think. What did she know about the Royal Fire Wielder? What had she ever learned about this strange Fire?

Nothing. Was he a sort of king, or maybe a magician? Yes, that must be it. She thought of the fire jugglers she had seen at the Midwinter Festival, and the fire eaters who performed in the marketplace… He was not like any of them. Yet there was definitely something very mysterious about him. And most unnerving of all, was the way he seemed almost to… recognize her.

The little man cut across her thoughts. 'You say you have seen my Fire before?'

Gemma coughed as some cake went down the wrong way. Her mind raced. What had she said?

He sensed her anxiety and tried to help her. 'You said my little flame was like the Fire in the Queen's Ring?'

Gemma was relieved. 'Yes, Sir. I bring Her Majesty her morning tea, and sometimes, while I wait for her to waken... I sit and watch her Ring... it's...' Suddenly she panicked. How could she finish what she had started to say?

'Go on,' said the Fire Wielder quietly.

Gemma took a deep breath. 'It's as if I sometimes see things in it!' she blurted out. 'There,' she thought. 'Now I'll be sacked for sure. What must he think of me?'

But instead of shouting or being angry, the strange little man simply settled back in his big armchair, laced his hands over his ample stomach and closed his eyes. 'Ah!' he murmured softly.

And that was how the Queen found the pair of them: Gemma sitting bolt upright on her little stool, staring in amazement and awe at the Fire Wielder, who, in his turn was settled in peaceful contemplation.

Suddenly Gemma became aware of the slight rustle of the Queen's silk robes and she sprang to her feet. She blushed deeply and made her best curtsey, scurrying towards the door as fast as she decently could.

The Fire Wielder opened one eye and put out a hand towards Gemma. 'No, child, don't go. Stand by my chair.' Then with great effort, the fat little man rose and stood at his full height before the Queen.

But he did not bow to his sovereign. Instead, it was the ancient Queen who slowly and stiffly knelt before the fat little man!

'My Lord Fire Wielder,' she said softly.

'Sophia, my dear lady!' he replied, offering his hand to be kissed before helping her to her feet and gathering her in a big hug.

4

Learn to Eavesdrop!

Gemma stood nervously at her post by the door. She had her instructions. If anyone knocked, she was to send them away immediately. She felt shaky and scared, but she was comforted by the soft warmth of Fleabag who had hopped in through the open window and settled himself against her feet.

The warmth of the summer morning was filled with the hum of bees and the soft murmurings of the two old friends settled in their chairs, holding hands and talking intensely. Gemma rested her head against the doorpost and closed her eyes. Soon, she was drifting off to sleep.

Suddenly, she gasped. One of Fleabag's well-sharpened claws was picking at her leg. The cat was glaring at her. She bent down to push him away, but as she did so, he sprang into her arms and settled himself under her chin. Startled, she tried to put him down, but he hung on with all fifteen claws.

'Wake up, you duff-head. This involves you!'

'What?' Gemma whispered in horror.

'Eavesdrop, can't you? You really must develop the knack, you know.'

'I can't do that!' she hissed. But then she caught a glimpse of the Queen looking at her, so she whispered as quietly as she could, 'That's shocking, how could you even *think* of such a thing, you wicked cat?'

'If you're not meant to know what's happening, why do you think they told you to stay *inside* the room? If you weren't meant to hear they'd have posted you *outside*, or even better, sent you away completely. They are talking quietly so no one *else* can hear. Now wake up, you goose, and listen!' With which the impossible animal sprang to the floor and miaowed to be let out.

As Gemma shut the door silently behind the cat, she caught a glimpse of the butler leaning with his ear closely pressed against the other side of the wall.

Gemma pretended she had seen nothing, but listened with satisfaction as a yowl and a crash indicated that once again the butler had fallen prey to Fleabag's tactics.

When all was quiet once more, Gemma began to listen to the conversation between the Queen and her strange visitor.

The Queen's head was bent forward as she listened to the Fire Wielder. The sun glinted on her small crown, and dazzled in the emeralds at her throat. She looked very beautiful and seemed much younger than Gemma had ever seen her. Yet the Queen was saying she felt ill and old.

'I feel in my bones that there is much evil and injustice

in my kingdom, but I am too old and tired to do anything about it. I wish for nothing more than to sleep the Long Sleep and let all this slip away from me – and I have longed to talk with you, because I cannot let go until I am sure of my successor. There is no one in all my court that I can hand my Ring and my crown to. Although there are many wise and good people, none of them is the right one. I know it in my bones, and my great Ring grasps my finger with the firmness it did on the day you placed it there. It is not ready to leave me and go to another. I do not know what to do.'

And with a sinking heart, Gemma realized her beloved Queen was crying.

The Fire Wielder grasped the Queen's hand more tightly. 'I know,' he said softly. 'I have seen it. Now, tell me about this festival of yours.'

The Queen sighed. 'It was the idea of Hyrald, the Prime Minister. He thought that everyone in the kingdom should have the chance to come and say, in his or her own particular way, what it means to be the monarch. I think he hoped that the true successor would be found amongst them. It wasn't such a bad idea...'

'But it has yielded no one?' ventured the Fire Wielder.

'No one,' the Queen sighed. 'That is why I have been sending messages to you. Why did you take so long to come?' she asked sadly. 'I needed you.'

'Because I had to know what to say when I came.'

'But even your presence would have comforted me.'

The Fire Wielder smiled. 'I know. But I might have been tempted to speak words which were not yet ripe.'

'And are your words ripe now?'

The old man turned his head and looked out of the

window at the rose garden and the wonderful view across the green slopes of the South. 'I will speak the words, and together we will see if they are right or not.

'Firstly, you must know that I too am tired and ready to sleep the Long Sleep. My heart is not strong, and I think that when you surrender your Ring, I will follow you quickly into the Quiet Place. I too must find a successor. So listen to what I suggest, and tell me if it sounds true Fire Speech in your ears.

'I propose that you place your Ring into my hands...'

Without hesitation, the Queen began to tug at the jewel, but the old man prevented her with a gentle motion. 'Not yet. Listen first. See if you agree. Tonight we will perform the rite of severance which will remove the Fire from the Ring. The flame will remain here at the palace, for all to see, and the Ring will be hidden where only a king or a queen would ever dare to look for it.'

'Can the Fire survive without the Ring?' The Queen sounded worried.

'As you know, my dear Sophia, the Fire is not from this world. It will quickly fade if it does not have a place where it is welcome to dwell. I believe that if I hold the Fire, it will burn for a time without the Ring – but my strength can hold it no longer than a year and a day.

'In that time, your subjects high- and low-born, young and old may search for the Ring, and whoever finds it and brings it here may prove to be the new ruler of our land. If the wrong person finds it by accident, or if a rogue or villain takes it by force, the Fire will not acknowledge him or her.

'Thus all your subjects may see and know openly that if the Fire welcomes the Ringholder, that the person will be the chosen one. If the Fire burns the holder or fades in his or her hand, that person is a usurper and not to be acknowledged.'

Both were silent for a very long time.

At last Queen Sophia said, 'It is a terrible risk, my Lord.'

The Fire Wielder leaned forward and looked earnestly into the Queen's eyes. 'But is it a wise risk, my Lady? Is it the *right* one?'

The Queen eased her tired back into the chair's depths, and closed her eyes. At last she spoke. 'If, when the moment comes to perform the rite of severance, the Fire burns bright and clear, let us proceed. If it fades and seems sickly, let us wait and see what else may befall.'

With a sigh the old man smiled. 'Such were my thoughts, your Majesty.'

Just then, Fleabag once more reappeared on the window sill. He stretched his untidy, black shape into a long shadow which fell across the Queen's lap. She looked up and laughed, patting the chair arm beside her. 'Don't you dare sit on my best frock, you old Fleabag, you,' she said playfully. 'I suppose you have been listening, you wicked animal?'

Fleabag said nothing as he sprang up next to his mistress, but purred delightedly as she scratched behind his ear.

'Now, listen, you old rogue. I have an important job for you.' Fleabag stopped purring and sat to attention, staring at the Queen with wide, golden eyes. 'I know you understand every word I say and I'm sure you repeat most of it to your equally disreputable cronies below stairs. But this is a secret. I want you to look after Gemma over there. She will have a difficult time ahead, and two heads are better than one, even if one is filled with furry nonsense and fish scraps. Will you take on the care of a mere human, old friend?'

Fleabag did not answer, but jumped down and strode across the room until he reached Gemma's feet. There he sat and looked at her until she picked him up. But there were no claws this time. Just velvet paws and a deep, rich, rolling purr.

Gemma looked at the Queen in astonishment. What could she mean?

The Fire Wielder beckoned the girl over. 'Give me your hand,' he said. He laid his palm across hers and, when he took it away again, Gemma jumped, for there, burning brightly in the hollow of her hand, was a tiny flicker of flame.

There was a strange burning in her palms. But it made her feel indescribably happy.

Suddenly it was gone, and she felt quite lost and alone. 'Remember that little flame, whatever happens,' he said quietly. 'Now, go and call Her Majesty's Equerry and the Prime Minister. We have much to do before nightfall.'

5

The Ring and the Fire

'Just do as you're told, will you?' The cat looked most irritable. 'We have a lot to do before nightfall too.'

'But I've got work to do. I'm supposed to be in the kitchens. They'll miss me.'

'Let them miss you!' growled the cat, jumping up onto Gemma's bed. 'You're not going back there again. Now get on and start packing, will you? Not much, just the essentials. You don't want to be slowed down by *stuff*. Mind you,' he muttered, 'I don't see why humans need luggage anyway. Look at us cats – we're always immaculately dressed for every occasion, and we never carry anything.' Fleabag struck what he hoped was an artistic pose.

'Were you travelling light when you forgot to pack your fourth leg?' teased Gemma.

The cat bristled his long black fur in disgust and turned

his back. 'You're avoiding the real issue,' he said haughtily. 'We've no time for banter. Get packing, will you?'

'But where are we going?' asked Gemma. 'How will I know what to do next?'

'Oh, do stop pestering me with stupid questions,' moaned Fleabag. 'You'll find everything out in good time. But above all, make sure you're in the Throne Room at sunset. There's going to be a proclamation. Get there early, for the rest of the world will be there as well.

'Now leave me in peace, do. I need my sleep. You don't know what a hard life it is, being a cat.' And with that, the incorrigible animal curled up on his favourite cushion at the end of Gemma's bed, and went to sleep.

Gemma looked at him in exasperation. But what could she do? Once Fleabag was asleep, an earthquake would not shift him until he was quite ready to waken. In the end she shrugged and looked around. The attic bedroom was shared by all six of the youngest maids and a very little boy who blackened boots. Every child had a small cupboard for personal possessions and clothes. When she had arrived at the palace Gemma had had nothing but what she was wearing, and that was quickly burned. In its place she had been given two gingham kitchen-maid's dresses and someone's cast-off red skirt and white blouse for holidays.

Well, Fleabag wasn't intending to allow her to work here again – for a while at least – so she changed into her holiday things. Her underclothes and hairbrush she wrapped up into a bundle with her old grey cloak.

Just as she was tying a knot to secure it all, she heard her name being yelled by the under-chambermaid in a furious temper.

When she saw Gemma out of uniform, she screeched even more loudly and, without giving Gemma a chance to say a word, pushed her out of the door and down the stairs. In between the woman's tirade – how she had exhausted herself looking for the good-for-nothing guttersnipe all over the palace – Gemma gathered that the Queen was calling for her.

Standing outside the door of the royal bedchamber, Gemma breathed deeply and tried to collect her wits for a few seconds. At last she knocked and went in.

The Queen was sitting alone in the room. Her jewels were put away and her long grey hair was spread loose over her thin shoulders. She had been crying, for her eyes were damp and slightly red. But she looked calm and even happy in a strange way.

Gemma curtseyed and apologized for being late. The Queen shook her head and smiled. 'Please don't worry. There will be time for everything, I am sure. Now please help me change. I won't need these robes of state any more. I will wear my white linen gown and the green shawl.'

Gemma unfastened the Queen's robes and helped the old lady step free from the encumbrance of their folds. The linen dress was quite plain and light, and the warm pale green shawl was soft and comforting. Gemma brushed the old lady's hair and gathered it into a pink ribbon.

Suddenly the Queen looked no longer like Her Majesty. She was a granny – a friendly, loving, very old granny.

Impulsively Gemma sobbed and cuddled her. How she had always wished for a granny of her own. The Queen stroked the girl's hair and rocked her. After a little while she pushed Gemma gently away. Her eyes were damp again. Perhaps she had always wanted a granddaughter like Gemma.

'My dear, we will not talk again. Not this side of the Long Sleep. I want you to sit still and listen very carefully.' Gemma sat obediently on the little stool and took the Queen's hands in her own.

'Now, you heard my Lord the Fire Wielder and me making our plans this morning? Good. I want you to join this quest.'

Gemma looked up in surprise. '*Me*, your Majesty? You know I would do anything within my power for you, but what use can I be?'

The Queen looked serious. 'Listen. You have studied my Ring more than any of my subjects. Have you ever wondered why I picked *you* up from the street when there are so many urchins who need homes?'

Gemma shook her head. She had never understood why she had been chosen.

'It was because I saw you looking into my Ring as I passed. Not *at* it, as everyone else does, you understand, but *into* it. I knew we would need each other one day. Since then I have often watched you looking into the depths of the stone while you thought I slept.

'You of all people will recognize the true stone in whatever guise you may see it. You may be needed to protect it from an evil person taking it by force, or to prevent a forgery being foisted on my people.

'You alone can do this, Gemma. Will you do it... for me?'

Gemma swallowed hard. Suddenly she felt very small and particularly useless. 'Ma'am, I... I'm sure... but for you, since you ask it, yes, I will.'

The Queen smiled and nodded, patting Gemma's hand absent-mindedly. 'Yes, Gemma, do it for me. And look after my cat Fleabag, will you? He lost his leg in a great act of heroism and he holds a noble title and a great name. But it is more than my life is worth to tell you, so never let on you know... And,' at this the Queen leaned over conspiratorially to whisper in Gemma's ear, 'you probably won't believe this... but Fleabag is a *talking* cat!'

'Yes, ma'am,' Gemma replied, trying not to giggle.

The Queen straightened herself and sighed. 'I would very much like to give you a parting gift, but I fear that if anyone saw you with a jewel of mine they would not believe I had given it and would imprison you for theft.' Then she smiled. 'Take my shawl, child. Your clothes are hardly fit for the journey you must make. And your feet are almost the same size as mine, so take my good walking shoes from my cupboard. Just fetch me another shawl, please. It doesn't much matter what I wear now. My part is over.'

Gemma swallowed hard to try to rid her throat of the great lump that stuck in it. She wrapped a delicate pink shawl around the Queen's old shoulders. Then she dressed herself in the Queen's gifts.

Leaning on Gemma's arm, the old lady rose rather shakily to her feet.

'Now take me into the Hall of Light where the Royal Fire Wielder awaits me. There we will say goodbye.'

Gemma could not speak. She obeyed silently. The Queen seemed to have aged immeasurably since that morning. As they walked slowly down the long, dark corridors, Gemma held the Queen's arm firmly. The old lady moved more and more slowly with every step as age and tiredness seemed to descend upon her.

At the final turn, Gemma glimpsed Fleabag, watching his mistress open the door to the Hall of Light for the last time. He stepped out and rubbed his fur against the Queen's legs and she bent down and scratched behind his ragged ear. He purred and licked her hand, then she stood up straight, and entered the Hall.

'Go and get your bundle and meet me in the Throne Room. It's almost time. Hurry!' hissed the cat.

Gemma did as she was told. Strangely, no one seemed to notice or even recognize her as she slipped between the palace staff. They were too busy arranging chairs for the invited nobility and bringing up trays of refreshments for the guests.

Soon Gemma and Fleabag had possession of a small corner behind a pillar, where they would be able to hear and see what went on without being seen themselves.

'I almost didn't recognize you,' mewed Fleabag. 'You look posh in that outfit.' Gemma looked down. Of course, in her holiday skirt and the Queen's shawl, she looked quite different. That must be why she had slipped through unnoticed. She smiled and stroked the cat's ears.

'What's going to happen?' she whispered.

'Sssh! You'll see,' he hissed.

The room was quickly filled with throngs of all the nobility, royal advisers, courtiers and, of course, the knights who formed the Queen's Guard. Low voices buzzed with discreet concern and subdued excitement. Rumour had spread fast that this was going to be a momentous occasion. Everyone was dressed in glittering robes; the room was aglow with dazzling silks and satins, mingled with the gleam of polished dress swords and gold embroidery.

Gemma shifted to try to ease the cramp that was creeping up her leg. She would have loved to join the crowd, but she knew she would stand out like a sore thumb in such a company.

Just then a trumpet fanfare greeted the arrival of the Royal Fire Wielder, comfortable at last in a white linen shirt and loose white trousers. The Queen was carried in on a sedan. She was too weak to rise, but she greeted the people with a lift of her hand.

The Royal Fire Wielder stepped forward and addressed the crowd.

'My Lords and Ladies,' he bowed to left and right. 'Today, the Queen Sophia has surrendered the Ring of the Kingdom and now she goes to sleep the Long Sleep in the Quiet Place. I too will join her soon, but our successors have not yet been found. To this end, today, in the Hall of Light, I performed the rite of severance.

'This Ring,' he announced, holding the jewel high for everyone to see, 'is now quite simply an opal ring...' He paused, then he added, 'And the Fire resides with me.' At this point he opened his other hand and held his arm up high. Everyone in the Throne Room gasped, for from his palm leaped a great tongue of fire which blazed as high as the gold and white domed ceiling, casting its dazzling light all around.

Gemma clutched at Fleabag so hard he yowled. She could not describe her feelings – a tangle of joy, recognition and fear. But then the light was gone again, just as quickly. The Fire Wielder had closed his hand.

'The Ring will be sent by secret messengers to a place where only the true successor to our great Queen will dare to find it. The Fire I will hold here, in the Hall of Light, until the Ring is found and returned.

'When the two are truly reunited, the next queen or king will be known. Tomorrow, all those who will, be they noble, servant or farmer, may commence the search. If the Fire and the Ring are not brought together within a year and a day, the Fire will fade and slip back to the Other Place from whence it came and we will be left blind and lost.'

At this, the Royal Fire Wielder turned and walked out of the room, followed by the Queen and her bearers.

Silence hung heavily as the listeners sat stunned by what they had heard. At last, in twos and threes, the people began to drift away from the Throne Room.

Everyone was so shocked, the supper had barely been touched when the last visitors had gone. The girl and the cat stayed hidden in their corner until the room was empty. Then Fleabag gave Gemma a soft nibble. 'Time to move. But first things first: food.'

To Gemma's horror the cat jumped up onto the table and began to eat his fill. 'Come on,' he muttered through a mouthful of fishpaste sandwiches. 'This is good. Fill up and take some for tomorrow. You don't know when you may eat again.'

Gemma saw the point. She filled her pockets with dried fruit, and pushed hunks of bread and cheese into the end of her bundle. Just as she began to eat, a footman caught sight of them and chased them out of the Throne Room. With a flick of his tail, Fleabag leaped to the floor and sprang ahead down the corridor with something large and heavy in his teeth.

At last they reached the little back stairs behind the kitchen where they had often sat and talked. No one was about. A few more steps brought them to the boot cupboard where they could eat in peace. As they went in, Fleabag presented Gemma with his loot... a whole chicken! 'Waste not, want not,' grinned the cat. 'Wings or breast?'

6

The Hall of Light

After they had eaten their fill, Gemma sat licking her fingers and thinking hard.

'Are you asleep?' She nudged the recumbent cat with her toe.

'I *was*,' muttered Fleabag resentfully.

'What do I do now? I'm terribly tired, but I daren't go back upstairs to sleep. It's all right for you – you can curl up in a corner anywhere. I get the feeling that the sooner I'm well clear of the palace the better. I don't want to be here in the morning with both Cook and the butler after my skin. But I'm very scared. I don't know where to go or what to do.'

Fleabag licked a paw and looked at Gemma out of his big golden eyes. 'I thought humans were supposed to be the clever ones. You're asking *me*?'

Gemma sat quite still with her head on her fists,

staring into the gathering gloom of nightfall.

The cat jumped onto her lap and purred loudly. At last he rolled over on his back and stretched until he almost fell onto the floor. 'I know what I would do,' he said in an upside-downy sort of a voice. 'I'd go and ask the Fire Wielder.' With that, Fleabag made a smooth twist, landed on the floor with a soft thump and headed for the kitchen door.

He looked back at Gemma who had not moved. 'Well, aren't you coming? The Fire Wielder said he'd be in the Hall of Light. I don't see why you shouldn't go and ask him. He was very nice to you earlier.'

Gemma stood up and shook cat hair off her skirt. The incorrigible animal was already well ahead and halfway up the servants' stair. 'Are you sure this is a good idea?' she panted after him.

'I can't think of anything else to do, can you?'

The girl thought for a minute. 'No.' Then, 'You are coming in with me, aren't you?' she asked.

Fleabag hesitated.

Gemma coaxed him. 'A cat may look at a king.'

'But may he look at a Fire Wielder? He might singe my fur off!'

'But you've seen him before...'

'But not when he was... you know, *doing it*...' teased the cat.

Suddenly Gemma stopped in her tracks. She had never thought of what a Fire Wielder might *do* before... Would he be standing there actually wielding fire? It sounded very dangerous. They had reached the heavy carved door of the Hall of Light. She placed one hand on it and looked back at her only friend. 'Are you honestly scared?'

she asked. 'I don't think he's really fierce. He looked too kind.'

Fleabag slipped away into the dark shadows where Gemma could not see him any more. From there his rolling, laughing purr sang: 'No, I'm not scared. It's just that it's something *you* have to do. Not me.'

Gemma put her tired head against the door. The coolness of the wood calmed her racing brain. 'You're right,' she said at last. 'I've got to talk to him.' Then, with a small but determined push, she opened the little door that led into the Hall of Light.

The circular room was quite silent and almost dark. Its walls were plain white stone with tall, thin lancet windows set high and close together, forming a huge glass lantern in the ceiling above. Everywhere grey and purple shadows mingled with the soft, gentle light of the early evening stars shining in the indigo sky. The thin, white crescent moon was just rising over the lowest window ledge. The quiet and calm of the room invited Gemma to sit on the floor, where she stayed quite still until her eyes adjusted to the gloom.

As she looked around the room, Gemma noticed a tiny, flickering light in the very centre. She stood up quietly and stepped forward. 'Fire Wielder?' she whispered. 'Is that you?'

There was no answer. She called again. Although there was no reply, the silence seemed to be full and alive; it did not feel like an empty room.

She stepped gingerly towards the flame. It seemed to be very close. She reached out her hand towards it and called again.

There was still no answer, but this time she added, 'Fire Wielder, if you're here, help me please. I don't know where to go, or what to do next. In all the world I've only got Fleabag, the cat. Do you remember him? Oh I wish you were here. Perhaps you could come with us to find the Queen's Ring and we could give it to the right people.'

She was silent. A round, dark shape dissociated itself from the rest of the shadows as the Fire Wielder moved forward. As he reached the little table where the flame burned, his kind, wise face suddenly appeared, lit by the tiny gleam of golden light.

'My little Gem,' he said with a smile in his voice. 'I'm sorry I did not hear you. I was asleep.'

Suddenly Gemma wished she hadn't come. She felt silly. She wanted to run and find Fleabag and disappear into the night – to go back to the little street behind the market where she used to live. What business did a street urchin have here?

She turned to run, but the Fire Wielder's firm hand prevented her. 'Whatever you have need to know, ask, child. But don't ask me. Look steadily into the flame, and be sure the Fire Giver will answer you.'

Gemma did not notice when the Fire Wielder let her go. She was transfixed by the flame. She could not move. The light did not hurt her eyes, but once again, it made her intensely happy and terribly sad all at once.

After what seemed an age she whispered, 'Where do I go now? What do I do?'

Gemma never knew whether she heard the voice with her ears, or simply 'knew' the answer. But she knew it for certain. The Ring Fire had told her to go north by north-west.

She was so astounded she screamed and ran. Like a terrified field mouse caught in one of Fleabag's traps, she darted in panic-stricken terror from one side of the strange room to the other. At last she glimpsed the door opening slowly as the big brass handle caught the light of the almost fully risen moon. With one last effort, she bolted for the gap, only to collide with a very solid and firmly built figure which barred her way.

Strong hands caught Gemma under the arms and swung her round to face the centre of the room. Gemma felt the cold weight of chain mail against her face and leather gauntlets against her skin. The grip was one of iron and there was no resisting.

'What shall I do with this intruder, my Lord?' came a deep voice. 'Shall she be horsewhipped?'

'Certainly not!' came the Fire Wielder's indignant reply. 'Take the child to an inn. Feed her, give her a good night's sleep and in the morning listen to her story. She has much that will be useful to you. Remember that even guttersnipes are important in the eyes of the Fire Giver. And remember above all that you are sworn to defend *all* the Queen's people, whether high- or low-born, and whether washed or unwashed. Even kings and queens may come disguised in rags to see how their servants treat the lowliest of their subjects.'

'As you wish, my Lord.'

The Fire Wielder spoke again. 'My Lady Knight Rowanne de Montiland, I give you Gemma Streetchild. Gemma, I give you the Lady Rowanne. Now I must sleep again, for I am weary.'

And with that the dark, round figure lay back on his couch which was now visible in the strengthening starlight.

Outside the door, in the light of the torches which had now been lit, Gemma twisted in the unyielding grasp to try to get a look at whoever was holding her. All that was visible was a tall, muscular figure clad in leather and closely wrought chain mail. Over the mail shirt was a silk-embroidered tabard showing the arms of one of the Queen's Guard. A small, pointed helmet cast deep shadows across the wearer's face.

'Just let me get my bundle,' Gemma begged and the figure grunted, loosening her hold.

As they reached the gates the duty soldier saluted the mail-clad captor, but barred Gemma's way.

'What are you doing at this entrance, girl? The servants' door is at the back. Surely you know that!'

Gemma spoke quickly. 'I'm on an errand. I'm sent out with an urgent message.'

'Don't give me none of your lies! Brat!' and the man swung his arm as if to deliver Gemma a box on the ear.

With a swift hand Gemma's captor caught the man's wrist. 'It is a very important and secret message, Gordik. I am escorting her to make sure she comes to no harm.'

The sentry guard shook his arm free of the grasp and grunted, 'Funny messenger.'

'The ways of the Fire Wielder are mysterious and not to be questioned,' uttered Gemma's guard with authority.

Gordik shrugged and grunted. 'That's as may be. If she wasn't with you, my Lady, I'd send her to the sergeant. Goodnight.' And the man strode back to his brazier, where he very determinedly looked away as the two left the palace precincts and turned down an alley to the left.

A few minutes later a third shadow left the palace,

running with a strange hopping motion. The three-legged cat ignored Gordik's offer of a bit of meat, as Fleabag, too, left the comfort of his home for the dark of the city night.

7

The Queen's Cat

In the oak-panelled comfort of the inn the Lady Knight Rowanne de Montiland removed her corselet of mail. Gemma stared in amazement. Even without her armour, her Ladyship could never pass as an ordinary woman. Her long dark hair was coiled at the nape of her neck, and a fine, well shaped face showed annoyance and distaste. Her eyes and her whole demeanour were haughty; she made it quite clear that she had no intention of having anything to do with Gemma once dawn had broken. She would obey the Fire Wielder to the letter, but that was all.

Fleabag sat under the table and settled himself comfortingly around Gemma's feet. He had his eyes closed, but he was listening to every word.

'Well?' the knight demanded. 'What have you to tell me, guttersnipe?'

Gemma sipped from the pot of ginger ale she had been

given. The bread and meat looked appetizing but, after sharing a whole chicken with Fleabag, she was not very hungry. Anyway, she was too tired to eat. When the knight wasn't looking she would slip the food into her bundle for tomorrow.

'I'm waiting!'

Gemma looked at Rowanne de Montiland. Was she her saviour or her captor? 'What do you want to know, my Lady?'

'Whatever you have to tell. The Most Noble Fire Wielder told me you have important information for me. Why else do you think I have wasted good money on your bed and food? Now tell me quickly before I return you to Gordik and his friends.' The knight pushed her beer aside and sprawled forward on her elbows, until her glowering features were only inches from Gemma's face.

Gemma leaned as far back as she dared without falling off her stool.

'I... I really don't know what I must tell you, my Lady. If I knew, I would tell you without hesitation. You have indeed been most kind...'

At that moment, Fleabag crept out from under the table and sat down right in front of Lady Rowanne's nose.

With a most unknightly squeal Rowanne knocked her beer flying and sprang back three paces. As she leaped she grabbed her stool with one hand and drew her sword with the other.

'Cats!' she screamed. 'Someone's let a cat in here!'

Fleabag bristled his tail like a bottlebrush. 'Snobs!' he squealed. 'Someone's let a snob in here!'

This made the knight scream all the more loudly,

bringing three of the most burly men in the bar to her rescue, which did not please her at all.

Gemma was reduced to a heap of helpless laughter on her stool. Matters were made worse when the men, who thought they were rescuing a fair damsel from the grasp of terrible villains, realized what was happening and also began to laugh fit to burst.

Rowanne grew redder and redder until she could stand the embarrassment no longer. She rapidly hid her Queen's Guard tabard under Gemma's bundle so no one could guess her real rank, then she packed the girl off to their room. Ahead of them, like a royal equerry, strode the black shadow of the noble Fleabag. His head was high, his tail erect and his stride strong and brave.

At the bedroom door, Rowanne reached ahead and pointed the naked blade of her sword at the threshold. 'Come one paw stride nearer, puss, and by all I hold precious, I will have your fur for a collar.'

'No, you won't,' said Fleabag coolly. 'I've got fleas.'

The knight caught the pommel of her sword into a firmer grip as the blade touched the cat under his chin, bringing his head round so that they both glared at each other. His golden eyes met her dangerous, bright blue scowl. Neither blinked.

'Cat,' she said icily at last, 'I dislike cats of any description… unless they are fighting Toms, on whom I might have a bet. I concede such a bet won me the velvet cloak I wear… But unless you are such an animal,' here she ran the sharp blade along Fleabag's back, 'which, after consideration, I doubt… then fleas or no, I will have you dead at my feet unless you remove yourself NOW.'

At that moment she took a lunge at Fleabag. The cat

guessed her move and twisted round so that her sword pierced only the air where his fourth leg should have been.

'Missed!' he sang gleefully. Then with one bound he leaped onto a high beam which supported the door frame. From there he could survey his new found enemy more clearly. 'Guess what?' he spat, 'I don't like snobs much either. Not even fighting snobs. And what's more,' he sneered, 'I grew my own cloak. I didn't have to win it with a wager.

'Now,' he hissed, 'are we going to bed or what? We have a long day ahead tomorrow and I am quite exhausted!'

The Lady Rowanne turned with disdain to Gemma. 'Take this… creature out to the back yard, child!'

Gemma shook her head, suppressing a grin. 'I'm sorry, my Lady, but I can't do that. He was the Queen's cat, and I'm not sure whether he was given to me as *my* pet, or if I was given to him as *his* pet… but it appears we are together.'

Fleabag preened his fur and looked smug.

Even in the dim torchlight it was easy to see that the Lady Knight Rowanne de Montiland was quite puce with rage. She spoke very slowly. 'If that… cat so much as enters that room, I sleep here on the doorstep.'

Fleabag landed gracefully on the ground in front of his adversary and pushed at the door with both forepaws. 'Fair enough,' he said. 'Suits me.' And he marched inside.

8

The Paladin

Rowanne de Montiland did not sleep well. Military training had, of course, prepared her to bivouac under all conditions, but it was her fury at being defeated by a mere cat which kept her awake all night. Now, at last, dawn was breaking and its grey light was seeping under the thatch outside the window.

Rowanne got up stiffly from the corridor floor and eased her protesting muscles until she was more or less upright. Gingerly, she creaked the bedroom door open. That wretched animal was curled up and fast asleep on the girl's bed. She looked at the second, unslept-in bed. It was so inviting. She glanced at the cat. Not a whisker moved. If she just lay down on the bed for a few minutes she could close her eyes and ease her aching back a little...

When she woke it was almost mid-morning. The

golden sun was streaming in at the window with May warmth. Gemma was leaning over her with a tray of bread and honey and a tankard of fresh, foaming milk.

The Lady Rowanne flung back the covers in a rage. How could she actually have *slept*? She was meticulously disciplined and could wake or sleep as needed.

She grudged thanks at Gemma and took the tray. Before she ate, she tentatively glanced around the room, but the dreaded cat wasn't there. At least she could eat in peace. As she tore at the bread with strong white teeth, she absently watched Gemma tidying the room and remaking her own bed with fresh sheets. It wasn't her job, but she did it well and quickly.

Gemma finished the work, stood before the knight and curtseyed. 'I thank you for your care, my Lady. I would gladly tell you what you wish to know, but as I don't know what it is I cannot help you. Now I must be on my way, as I do in truth have an urgent task to perform for Her Majesty. If I can be of any further service to you before I leave, pray tell me, so I can perform it speedily.'

Rowanne spread some more thick, yellow honey on her bread. 'Where are you going?'

'North by north-west.' Gemma replied promptly as she picked up her bundle and sat on the made bed. 'Do you by any chance know where that is?'

Rowanne licked the dripping honey from her fingers. 'Yes. Go through the Beggar's Gate and keep on that road. But why are you in such a hurry to see what lies north by north-west? There's not much to interest a child along there. No fairs or entertainments for many long miles.'

Gemma hesitated and fiddled with the corner of her bundle. She pulled her mouth into a small, pink shape and thought silently for a few seconds. At last she decided that it did not matter if this strange woman laughed at her. She would never see her again, anyway. She looked up and kept her large, green eyes steady on Rowanne's face.

'The Ring Fire told me to go that way.'

'Don't be silly, child,' scoffed the knight as she took a long drink of milk.

Gemma flushed deeply and stood up. She pulled herself to her full height and stuck out her small, sharp chin. Looking down at the Lady Rowanne, she stammered, 'I may be only a child to you, but to Her Majesty, I was someone fit to send on an errand. And I will do it until I succeed or die. So there!' And with that she stamped her foot and ran for the door.

Rowanne sniggered into her bread as she took another bite. But she did not enjoy her food. Fleabag had suddenly appeared on the table right in front of his new enemy.

'That was ill done, ma'am,' he commented with gravity.

Rowanne did not scream this time. She merely picked the cat up by the scruff of his neck and went to the window. It was quite a long drop onto cobblestones below.

The cat merely twisted in Rowanne's grasp and sunk his claws so deeply into her skin she could not shake him off. As she bit her lip in pain and struggled in vain to release herself from his grasp, the cat spat at her:

'Fool! You asked to know the important message Gemma had to tell, and you laugh when you are told it. You are not fit to be a paladin on this quest.'

Rowanne balked at the cat's words and gingerly pulled him back over the window sill, dumping him on the nearest bed. His fur was standing on end and his great eyes glowed like watchmen's lamps. 'What did you say?' she gasped as she nursed the torn skin on her hands.

Gemma stepped back into the room and picked up Fleabag tenderly. 'He said, I told you what you wanted to know, though I don't know what that can have been, and you're not fit to be a... a something on this quest.'

Rowanne spoke coldly and precisely. 'A paladin – a knightly companion – on what quest? The one to find the Queen's Ring, you mean?'

'I don't know what anyone means,' replied Gemma unhappily. 'I just know the Queen told me to join in the quest. She said that I of all people would recognize her Ring when it's found. And it is my responsibility to make sure that no frauds are passed off as the real thing. That was the Queen's command and when I asked the Fire Wielder where I should start, he said ask the Ring Fire. So I did, and that's what I was told. North by north-west.' Gemma paused to catch her breath. She was not used to long speeches, especially in front of daunting people like this knight.

Rowanne sat down hard on a stool and leaned her head on her hands. Her long black hair was loose and her face was white. She looked almost ill. 'The Ring Fire really spoke to you?' she asked very quietly.

Gemma shrugged. 'I don't know, my Lady. I can't answer that. I'm just trying to do what the Queen asked me to do because I love her and I'd do anything for her. But it's so worrying and confusing that at the moment I wish it would all just go away!'

The girl spoke with such a firm conviction that Rowanne could not help but believe her. She sat quite still, then with a suddenness that made Gemma jump, the knight stood up and thumped the table with her fist.

'Then let us prove that abysmal cat wrong. Let us go north by north-west together. My squire broke his leg two weeks ago and may take a long time to mend. I noticed that, for a guttersnipe, you work well. If you will come with me as my squire or maid, or whatever you choose to call yourself, I will feed you and give you my protection on your journey.'

Still hugging her bundle tightly, Gemma watched the knight warily. 'And what about Fleabag?'

'Oh, he won't want to come. Cats never travel far from home.'

'This one does.' Fleabag jumped down to the floor and surveyed Rowanne de Montiland coolly. 'And I have sworn to stay with Gemma Streetchild for as long as she may need me.'

'I also wish to stay with Fleabag,' added Gemma. 'Her Majesty told me to trust him. But,' she added, looking Rowanne hard in the eye, 'she never said the same thing about you!'

Rowanne was furious at the insult, but she fought down her anger. If what she had heard was true, the ways of the Fire Wielder were mysterious indeed! There must be something very special about this child. And from her eyes and her whole manner, she was obviously telling the truth – every word. Although it did not make sense...

Yet, why shouldn't she take Gemma north by north-west? Her cousin Rupert had his palace there, and he was closely connected to the Queen's household. Perhaps the

Ring had been hidden there... and what if she should succeed in finding it, without mentioning the purpose of her visit to dear cousin Rupert? A simple test of showing it to the child might ensure... great things for her own future. She would reward the girl suitably of course, a purse of gold – or maybe silver and a job as under-parlourmaid at the palace. She could see it all!

Yes, she must go on the quest herself. The Fire Wielder had hinted as much. But she must get the child on her side – and get rid of that cat...

At last she spoke. 'If the cat goes, I stay here.' The knight puckered her dark eyebrows and glared at her opponents.

'Fair enough,' called Gemma, as she reached the door of the room again and slipped her foot around the jamb. Then, with a dash, she and the agile cat had sprung away along the corridor.

The Lady Rowanne's heart sank. How could Gemma possibly not be honoured beyond all imagining by her offer of escort? She had to get the child back and win her confidence.

Suddenly she realized there was quite a hubbub outside. With three long strides she crossed the room and leaned out of the window. Below, crowds were gathering in the streets, and people were howling and crying as if the end of the world were nigh.

With a feeling of dread, Rowanne gathered up her few belongings and ran downstairs. She paid the innkeeper, who was far too busy peering out at the street to take any real notice of the money she handed him.

'What's going on, landlord?' she asked.

The young man blew his nose on his apron and peered

at Lady Rowanne with puffy eyelids. ' 'Tis Her Majesty, my Lady. She died about a hour ago. Quiet-like in her sleep, they say. The funeral is to be next week, but now everyone is in mourning and turmoil, for 'tis said she named no successor. 'Twill be a worrying and tumultuous time ahead, by my reckoning.'

Suddenly, Rowanne was gripped with a clear-cut certainty. She must find Gemma. But a street child like that could slip away unseen in seconds. How could she ever find her in these crowds?

'Did you see which way the child and the cat went?' she persisted.

The landlord scratched his head, letting dandruff fall onto his shirt. 'Can't rightly say I did,' he said. I've been watching the crowds, you see, ma'am. Them's in an ugly mood and I'm worried, there's the truth of it.'

Rowanne clicked her tongue in annoyance and dashed out into the street. She did not have to look far. Rushing crowds had pushed Gemma hard against the wall of the Town Hall opposite.

With effort she waded her way through the mass of people until she was close enough to shout to Gemma. At last, Rowanne managed to catch her eye.

Gemma opened her mouth in a wordless cry. The girl's face was wet with sweat and tears. She was terrified, pinned by a surging, ever-increasing press of heavy bodies, pushing and shoving their way towards the palace.

With all her strength, Rowanne kicked and elbowed her way through. Gemma was pale under her freckles and her hair was loose and dishevelled. Suddenly her eyes stared wildly and her knees buckled as she fainted.

Rowanne forced her way alongside the crumpled figure, planted her legs far apart and braced her arms against the wall, making herself into a human cage protecting Gemma against the crowd.

Despite the battering of the crowds thundering along the narrow street, Rowanne de Montiland did not move. Something tickled her feet occasionally, but she did not look. She dared not even turn her head. It was only when she noticed that people sometimes shouted in pain and jumped away from them that Rowanne realized the tickle was Fleabag, squatting between her feet and scratching and biting at anyone who came too close.

Eventually the crowd lessened to a trickle. Rowanne scooped Gemma up and carried her back to their room at the inn. She paid for a second night for them both and left Gemma sleeping off her shock. Then, furnished with a tankard of good beer, she sat in the empty taproom and thought long and hard.

9

Round Two to Fleabag

Several hours later Rowanne peered around the door of the darkened bedroom. The cat was sitting bolt upright on Gemma's bed.

'Um...' ventured Rowanne, who really did not have the first idea of how to be polite to a person, let alone a cat. 'Um, Mr Cat – will you look after Gemma? Don't let her go until I get back, will you? I'm only going to get supplies, not a cage.' The cat stared coldly at the knight, but remained infuriatingly silent.

Rowanne tried again. 'Do you think she needs a doctor?'

Fleabag yawned and stretched, then turned round twice on the bed and settled down to sleep. 'No,' he said from the depths of his fur. 'Just get on with what you have to do. I'll keep her here.'

Downstairs, Rowanne met the landlord, still peering

nervously around the door into the street.

Rowanne held out two silver coins to the man. His eyes lit up. 'These are for you if the girl and the cat are still here when I return.'

The man shot out his hand for the coins.

Rowanne snatched them back into her fist. '*If* they are here when I return.' With that she slipped the money back into her pouch and stepped out into the street.

She was gone less than two hours, but Gemma slept until well into the afternoon. She woke when the chambermaid opened the door and brought in a tray with two bowls of hot stew and a fresh loaf of bread.

'Will you be wanting anything else, ma'am?'

Rowanne shook her head. 'No. We'll be leaving soon.' The woman curtseyed and shut the door behind her.

Gemma sat up in bed and rubbed her eyes. 'What's happening? What were all the crowds about? I was so frightened.'

'Her Majesty has died,' Rowanne replied simply.

Gemma felt her eyes stinging. 'How can you just say it as if it was the most ordinary thing in the world?' she choked angrily. She wished she could be alone for a while to cry in peace, but the knight was bustling around the room arranging piles of clothes and food into bags. Gemma swallowed hard. She would cry later.

Fleabag saw Gemma was struggling and decided to change the subject. He sprang up onto her bed. 'For once, this... cat-hater may have hit upon a good plan.'

'Thank you, mog. I can do my own talking,' Rowanne replied icily. 'Gemma, I have bought a pony for you and some travelling clothes. My horse is already in the stables and I have packed some essentials for us both.

'There is a great deal of unrest in the town: the lack of a named successor seems to have put everyone into a panic. The Prime Minister has declared a curfew at dusk to contain any trouble. I have managed to get permission to leave – but we've got to get on the move as soon as possible in case my captain changes his mind and recalls me to the palace. If that happens it will put paid to all your plans, for you won't get far without me.

'We must go now and ride through the night to be well away from here before dawn.'

'What do you think, Fleabag?' asked Gemma, scratching the cat behind his ears.

'I told you. For once old Miss Full-of-Herself is probably right. Without horses... and an escort, you will travel too slowly and be in too much danger. Whether we like it or not, we need to do exactly as she says... *This* time,' he added quietly, but with emphasis.

Laid out on a chair next to Gemma's bed were riding trousers, a cotton shirt and a squire's leather jerkin. They were rather large and loose and had to be tied with a belt but Gemma could see they would be much more practical for the journey than anything she might have had. Rowanne had put Gemma's own clothes, with the precious green shawl, into a canvas bag.

Once dressed, Gemma began to eat hungrily. Then a thought struck her. 'Fleabag *can* come, can't he?'

The knight stared hard at the cat, who simply smirked back in her direction.

'It seems I can't do much to stop him.'

The cat smirked even more broadly.

Suddenly a thought struck Gemma. 'Why are you doing this? I am an expense to you. Without me, you could have got out of Harflorum hours ago!'

Rowanne felt two pairs of eyes burning into her. She sighed. 'Oh well, you might as well know, I too have a mind to quest for the Queen's Ring. It is very dull at the palace. I was trained for adventure and fighting, not court manners and wearing silk costumes. I have taken leave of absence to find out whether soldiers will be needed to keep the peace in other provinces.'

She did not have the courage to say that the Fire Wielder's words about Gemma having an important message for her, made her think – even hope – that she might be involved in the Ring's finding. Or – perhaps – even find it herself!

She took a deep breath and blurted out very suddenly, so she would not have time to stop herself, 'Let's face it... I need you.'

'Ahh!' said Fleabag with immense satisfaction.

'Oh,' said Gemma, with a sinking heart.

'Why does my honesty offend you?' asked Rowanne angrily.

'Because what you are really saying is that I am your prisoner until I can identify the real Ring for you.'

Rowanne was flustered. 'No. No, not at all. You may leave my company any time you choose.'

Fleabag bristled his long, black fur into a huge mane as he sprang onto Rowanne's saddlebags. 'Swear it!' he demanded.

Rowanne swung a well-aimed kick at Fleabag's head. 'Get off, you louse-infested old hearthrug!'

But Fleabag ducked and began to dig his claws into the immaculate, richly worked leather of the bags. 'Swear it!' He glowered dangerously through his whiskers. 'Swear it, or I will scratch your posh leather to bootlaces!'

Rowanne narrowed her eyes into piercing blue points. Cat and knight once more began their dangerous game of out-staring each other. But this time, the cat had the added advantage of being able to make tiny little picking sounds on his exalted perch.

After a few seconds, Rowanne risked a glance at Fleabag's claws, poised right over her gold-tooled family crest. She swallowed hard. 'I swear it,' she whispered.

'Louder!' demanded the cat.

'I swear it.'

'Now bind that oath. Swear by your knighthood.'

Rowanne went quite white. 'I can't do that, that's the most sacred oath a knight can make!'

'Exactly!' grinned the cat, flexing his claws a little.

Rowanne looked at Gemma for help, but the girl was clutching her canvas bag and chewing nervously at the corner of it as she edged towards the door. If Gemma reached the door, she would be lost in a warren of backstreet bolt-holes within seconds. There were no crowds outside to delay her now. And if the girl ran, sure as eggs, the cat would follow like greased lightning.

Outside she could hear the town crier calling half an hour to curfew in the streets below. She had to make a decision. She swallowed hard and blurted out, 'I swear by my knighthood that Gemma and Fleabag are free to leave my company at any time and place of their choosing! But,' she added quickly, 'I also swear by the same oath that I will leave their company whenever I deem it good to do so.'

The room fell silent except for the buzzing of a trapped fly.

'Fine,' said Fleabag cheerfully, jumping down from the saddlebags. 'That's all I wanted to hear. Come on, Gemma. We must look lively now. Curfew starts soon and we must be well clear of Harflorum by then.'

10

North by North-West!

Horse-riding did not come naturally to Gemma. Fleabag didn't like it much either, but at least he could jump down for a run to stretch his legs occasionally, while Gemma sat like a sack of potatoes on Mistle, the little grey pony.

They had been on the road for only about an hour and a half, but Gemma was already so stiff and tired she kept falling asleep in the saddle. Several times, the knight prodded the girl awake so she would not fall.

Rowanne de Montiland was already deeply regretting having taken Gemma and the cat with her at all. She looked around and sniffed the air. The night would be short and mild. The blossoms on the May trees and wayside daisies glowed almost luminous blue-white in the fast waning light.

What was the best thing to do? She could easily give them the slip in the darkness and leave them. They were still very near home. They could go on or back as they chose. The child could keep the pony and the clothes. What did a few coins matter when so much was at stake? Alternatively, she could force a night ride. The going was good, and they would be well out of her captain's reach by dawn. Or they could just camp for the night and take what came on the morrow.

The girl looked awfully small in her heavy riding clothes, and there was that dreaded cat following close at the pony's heels.

'I was stupid to bring you here,' said Rowanne out loud.

'Perhaps *we* were stupid to bring *you*,' Fleabag retorted.

Rowanne sniffed disparagingly. 'I suppose you two want a rest now?'

'No, my Lady,' Gemma answered timidly. 'I will travel as long as you wish me to.'

Rowanne looked at the thin, tired face. 'We'll see,' she answered curtly. The more distance there was between them and Harflorum, the happier she would be. She would see how long the girl could keep going.

All night they rode steadily, until the first signs of dawn. Rowanne pulled rein and organized a camp in a clearing not far from the road. Gemma ate some bread and cheese, wrapped herself in a blanket and fell asleep straight away. Fleabag, who had managed to catnap on Mistle's back, offered to take the first watch. To his surprise, Rowanne agreed, and she too fell asleep.

He woke them when the sun was quite high. The faint sound of tack jingling had grown steadily closer. Horsemen were approaching. Rowanne buckled on her sword and squatted silently where she could watch the road without being seen herself.

'Why are you acting like this? Anyone would think we were in danger!' whispered Gemma.

'Look first, know later,' said Rowanne curtly. In truth she was still dreading the order to return to Harflorum, but she did not want to admit how much the quest for the Ring had come to mean to her. She merely added: 'There are always thieves about. It pays to be cautious. Hush.'

Gemma felt bemused by Rowanne's behaviour. She shrugged and peered through the undergrowth at the men on the road below. They were only farmers on their way to market. From their talk their only interest was the price of lambs and they soon passed by.

Rowanne suddenly chuckled and slipped her sword back in its scabbard. The captain had more important things to do than to fetch one of the Queen's bodyguards back from what was, after all, a perfectly legitimate mission.

'I think,' she said, 'it will be safe to travel by day. We are quite a way from Harflorum, after all. If we are challenged, however, never say you are on an errand for the late Queen. Simply say I am training you as my new squire. I took you on as a kindness to – your guardian who has recently died. It is all true, and your training would include much riding and learning to survive in the open. Say not a word else... especially nothing about the Ring.

'And as for you,' she pointed a threatening finger at Fleabag, 'if you value your fur, say nothing at all. Talking cats are very popular with circuses and I don't think you'd be happy there.'

The party travelled on, keeping the sun at their backs as they rode steadily north by north-west. Gemma had never left the city before and found the wide open spaces frightening. At first, she kept asking, 'Are we there yet?' It took Rowanne several days to realize that Gemma thought 'north by north-west' was a place, not a direction.

Rowanne tried to explain the rudiments of geography and orienteering, teaching Gemma how to use the sun and a stick as a compass, but quickly realized it was useless. She hoped that they would not meet any of her comrade knights on the road. If they questioned Gemma on her progress, it would quickly become obvious that the child was in no way cut out to be a squire.

Gemma did wonders, however, with camp-fire cooking. And Fleabag was an excellent hunter though he needed to be convinced that rat, vole and field mouse were not acceptable on the human menu. Even Rowanne had to give grudging praise to Fleabag's hunting skills.

The first time Gemma was shown how to skin and gut a rabbit, she was sick. After that she pulled herself together. To her surprise she spotted herbs growing wild that she recognized from the palace kitchen. She had never realized before that they came from anywhere other than the market. But Cook had taught her how to stuff thyme and ramsons into the rabbit's carcass, then roast it slowly over a low fire.

Gemma was also amazed to learn that milk came from cows, instead of from churns at the buttery door. Unfortunately, Fleabag could not be dissuaded from helping himself from a milkmaid's pail if he ever found one unattended.

Sleeping arrangements were less successful. Rowanne wanted to avoid the inns. She was worried that anyone talking to the guileless Gemma might guess that the child was somehow important and try to kidnap her. So they slept rough.

Gemma could not get used to always being a little cold, even on mild nights. Neither could she acclimatize herself to finding earwigs and woodlice in her blanket, or even worse, inside her clothes.

Luckily there was not much night rain and they did not get very wet. The local farmers were busy haymaking and were not pleased when lowering skies threatened rain and Rowanne asked if they might sleep in a barn; they were told in no uncertain words that barns were for hay, not for gypsies.

However, Fleabag enjoyed the journey, growing decidedly fat as small rodents fleeing the haymakers ran straight into his paws.

On the eighteenth day, Rowanne seemed particularly jolly and even spared a kind word and a scratch behind the ear for Fleabag. 'My cousin's palace is on the other side of this hill,' she told them at breakfast. 'I think,' she confided, 'there is a very good chance that the Queen's Ring may be there. Then we can all go home and live happily ever after.' She stretched and smiled up at the sun.

Fleabag sniffed the air and twitched his whiskers. 'Trouble ahead,' he said firmly.

'Nonsense!' chided Rowanne. 'It's a lovely day and we'll be sleeping in feather beds by nightfall. I don't know if I'll get you in, you flea-ridden old haybag, but you usually manage to come off best anyway.'

Fleabag twitched his tail contemptuously. 'I still say that all is not well.'

Gemma looked worried and glanced at Rowanne.

'What could go wrong as long as I am with you?' she laughed. 'But if it makes you feel better, I'll keep my sword loose in the scabbard. You're probably just smelling an overfed rat which has grown to twice your size and is waiting to pounce.'

Fleabag made a face behind Rowanne's back and settled in his usual perch in front of Gemma, with his paws on her saddle pommel. This time, instead of curling up for a snooze, he sat erect, eyes shining and ears pricked.

'It's people!' he whispered at last. 'I smell men, several of them. Their scent has got fear and anger on it,' he added. 'That knight is just too full of herself. Stick close to her, though. I think we're about to see if she's as good as she says she is.'

At that moment, Rowanne caught a tiny glimpse of sun reflecting on metal amongst the trees. It could be a drawn sword... or just a woodsman's axe. To be on the safe side, she reached for her little pointed helmet, spread its leather collar around the back of her neck and checked that her dagger was in its sheath at her waist. She decided not to give it to the child. If Rowanne lost her sword, she could still do some damage with the smaller blade, but the girl would just burst into tears and drop it.

The knight sat bolt upright and began to sniff the air like the cat. There was no apparent way around this wood. The road was bordered by a high stone wall on both sides. Either they had to turn back now and expose their backs to danger, or else they must go on.

Rowanne gave her mount a gentle kick in the flanks and began to trot. Gemma did the same to Mistle. The road swung round to skirt the hill in an easterly direction. The morning sun was still low in the sky, catching in their eyes and blinding them for a minute or two as they came to the black shade of the trees.

11

Fleabag the Battle Cat

Rowanne pushed her feet firmly into the stirrups as she braced herself to push her sword deep into the first assailant's throat. He could not scream as he died. He just gurgled as blood and air gushed from the gaping wound.

As she jerked her blade back, she saw another taller, thicker man come rushing at her from behind. She couldn't turn her horse quickly enough to use her sword effectively and she lost a precious second as she reached for her dagger. With a flick of her wrist it came free of its sheath and she caught the man neatly under his ear as he swung his arm back to strike a blow.

The sound of Gemma screaming made her turn her head. One of the men, younger than the others, had Fleabag by the tail and was swinging the howling cat around his head.

Rowanne almost wanted to let him get on with it. He

was doing her a favour. But Gemma's sobs made her move. Rowanne lunged under the cat's orbit and caught the man's body with the tip of her sword. As he swung round, heavy with momentum, the blade slashed through his clothes scoring across his chest and back. He hesitated and looked down in horror at the blood began to well and drip in pulsating splashes. As the pain reached his consciousness he lowered his arms and Fleabag bounded free.

In full battle-fury the brave cat then sprang, pouncing upon the last assailant who was trying to pull Gemma from her mount.

The cat clawed his way up the man's back and bit him on the back of the neck. In agony, the robber let go of Gemma and reached for a club which hung from his thick leather belt. Swinging the weapon over his shoulder, thinking that a man stood at his back with several knives, he missed the cat completely.

Instead, the club landed with a sickening thud on the side of Rowanne's head, felling her unconscious on the road.

It was then easy for the man to pull Gemma down and run off into the trees with the horses. It was a good day's haul for him. Two valuable animals, a well-beaten sword and two packs besides. What did it matter that his neck was bleeding and the others had died? All the more for him.

The first thing Rowanne knew was that she felt very sick. She could not think why she felt so ill when she was lying in the woods on such a lovely day. The birds were singing and everything was peaceful. What could possibly be wrong?

She turned her head to the side. It hurt terribly. By her hand, she could see something that looked like a huge cup. Shakily she grasped it. What was it? She knew she ought to recognize it. The object was metal and pointed and had a leather piece riveted to one side. Instinctively she pushed it onto her head. It fitted. A helmet. That was it.

She reached to her hip. Something was missing. Her sword.

Then she remembered everything. She forced herself to sit up and winced. She hurt all over.

Gemma, who had been cowering in the shadows, came forward gingerly, looking all about her. 'I think they're all gone – or dead.'

She looked at the two men Rowanne had killed and was sick. She had become used to rabbit blood but this was much worse. The younger thief lay quite still. He was bleeding badly and no danger to anyone.

Rowanne shifted her position. She was sitting on something hard. It was her dagger handle. At least she had that.

Fleabag walked unsteadily into Rowanne's painful field of vision. Gritting her teeth she flung the dagger at him.

Somehow he side-stepped it.

'What did you do that for?' he mewed pitifully.

'Wretched beast. If I hadn't tried to save your mangy fur I'd have got them all! Get out of my sight, for by all I hold precious I'll kill you if I ever set eyes on you again!'

Her head hurt too much to try to crawl after the dagger to have another go at killing the cat. She just collapsed backwards and allowed the dizziness to overcome her again.

Gemma took the helmet from the knight's head and loosened her clothing. Then she looked at the wounded robber. He wasn't very old, older than herself, but not yet a full-grown man. He had black down on his face and thick, dark, curly hair. His skin was a rich, clear golden-brown. She knew he must be from the southernmost part of the kingdom.

She bent down. Under his skin colour, he was very pale. Without thinking about whether it was right to save the life of someone who had almost killed her best friend, she picked up Rowanne's dagger, ripped his shirt into strips and used it to bind his sword-slash wounds.

When that was done, she felt thirsty. There had been water flasks in their packs, but now they had nothing. They had crossed a stream not far from the entrance to the wood so, picking up Rowanne's helmet, she ran off to fill it with water.

The cool liquid revived Rowanne, and Gemma made a cold compress for the lump on her head with a wetted handkerchief.

The young man groaned when Gemma began to wash his face. At last he regained consciousness and drank, but then both he and Rowanne fell asleep again.

Gemma went back to the stream and washed. To her surprise, Fleabag was there, with all three paws in the water.

'I thought you didn't like swimming,' she said, amazed.

'I don't,' he replied miserably. 'I just can't stand the taste of human blood on my claws.'

Gemma sat on the bank and stroked the cat slowly. 'What are we going to do?' she sighed.

Without answering, Fleabag pounced on an unsuspecting roach and quickly ate it. He shook his fur dry, almost like a dog and stretched out on the grass, washing himself carefully.

'Go on, I suppose.'

'North by north-west?'

'Where else?' replied the cat. 'Are you going to take that… woman?' he went on. 'She thinks I caused her downfall. I suppose I did, but I couldn't just sit amongst the trees and let her do all the fighting when I have fifteen sharp little daggers and several equally nasty teeth at my disposal. Now she's going to be more insufferable than ever.'

Gemma nodded. 'What's worrying me is that we still need her. One of the thieves is badly wounded, and we ought to try to take him to a doctor. I can't get him to the town on my own. Perhaps we could give her the slip when she goes to see this cousin of hers?'

Fleabag cheered up at this. 'Right, let's get moving, shall we? The day is getting on and I'd like to be away from here as soon as possible.'

When they got back, Rowanne was rousing. Her sickness had passed. She drank more water and noticed with relief that the cat was not around. Then she examined her helmet. It was badly dented where it had taken the brunt of the blow, and without it she would certainly have been dead. She took her dagger and started to clean it on the moss under the trees.

She tried to straighten her clothes, but they were torn and bloodstained. Her only comfort was the thought of dining in Rupertsberg that night with her cousin.

'We'll send Rupert's men back to collect the bodies and

see to this one,' she said, pushing her dagger back into its sheath.

'What will happen to him?' asked Gemma shyly.

'Oh, he'll be hanged, I expect,' she said in an off-hand manner, picking bits of wood and moss out of her hair.

'Ladies, I beg a favour,' the young man called weakly.

Rowanne went to him and looked down at him. She did have a sort of grudging respect for anyone who could best Fleabag.

'What is it? I'm not in a very good mood thanks to you and your friends.'

'Lend me your dagger so I can kill myself.'

'You won't have long to live, never fear,' Rowanne laughed.

He coughed, and more blood seeped though the bindings on his body. 'It is fear that I have,' he said. 'I make no secret of the fact that I am frightened of the scaffold. If I crawl into the woods I will die slowly. My fellows will never come looking for me – they daren't risk it: a sick man means slow movement and maybe even a betrayed hide-out. I beg that I may die with dignity of some sort.'

Rowanne crossed her arms and glowered. 'You're a fine one to talk of dignity, with the life you lead – or should I say, led?'

The boy shrugged as best he could. 'What else does an orphan lad do? My parents were unjustly put to death at the orders of that tyrant Prince Rupert. My only friends were the thieves in the shadows. No one else would spare me even a crust.'

Rowanne seethed. 'Prince Rupert is my much-loved cousin, pleb!' she said, kicking him viciously in the ribs.

She smiled at the bloodstain on her boot.

Gemma knelt down next to the boy. 'If he is caught, will he stand trial?'

'Of course.'

'Then shouldn't he be well enough to speak in his own defence?' she asked.

'He hasn't *got* any defence,' Rowanne replied curtly.

'What harm did he do you? It was Fleabag he went for!' Gemma ventured.

'Oh yes,' said Rowanne with a delighted grin. 'That's true. But he is still a villain who deserves to die.'

'He is no worse than you. You killed two men today; he killed none. You happen to be the Prince's cousin; he's only an orphan. You're a rich villain who has killed people; he's a poor one who hasn't.' Gemma felt quite exhausted after this speech and sat down hard.

Rowanne looked at her. Her face was hot and flushed with anger. She never much liked being told the truth. 'You sound like that infernal cat!' she said quietly and menacingly. Her dark eyebrows were pulled almost together and her head was thrust forward. She looked as if any second she might go for Gemma's throat.

'Please, I beg you,' whispered the boy on the ground, 'in the mercy of the Fire in Her Majesty's Ring, lend me your dagger and I will be no more bother to either of you.'

At these words, Gemma and Rowanne turned to stare at the boy.

Suddenly Gemma felt again that strange burning in the palms of her hands that the Fire Wielder had bade her never forget... But she *had* forgotten it. She breathed deeply. She needed all her courage now Fleabag was not here to speak for her. He would not be far away, she knew it. But this was *her* battle.

Holding that strange feeling of the burning Ring Fire clearly in her mind, she curtseyed formally and bowed her head. 'My Lady Rowanne de Montiland. I thank you most humbly for your assistance both in the past and today. If you will grant me one request, I promise that both I and the cat will be out of your sight and memory for ever.'

12

At the House of Aelforth

The knight and the child staggered under the weight of the young thief. It did not help that they were so unevenly matched for height. The walk down the hill into the city was not far and it would have taken less than an hour on horseback, but they struggled for the best part of the afternoon.

The lad had told them his name was Phelan, but Gemma was too exhausted to talk to him much, and Rowanne was muttering to herself. She was furious she had been talked into this crazy plan of helping the boy get down to the city, but the thought of being free of all of them for ever was worth the inconvenience – or so she kept telling herself. She carefully avoided thinking of Gemma's role in finding the Queen's Ring.

The city's pale yellow stone walls with open gates gleamed welcomingly in the late sunshine. The guards, wearing Prince Rupert's insignia on their shoulders, did not move from where they lolled as they watched the struggling group approach.

As they crossed the drawbridge, Phelan sank to the ground.

Rowanne stepped up to the sergeant. 'Why did you not run to help us, man? You could see we have a wounded boy here!'

The man laughed in her face. 'What? And get peasants' blood on our uniforms? That's a good one!'

Rowanne propped the boy against the wall and drew herself up to her full height so that she looked down on the soldier. 'I am the Lady Rowanne de Montiland, cousin to your Lord Prince Rupert. We were set upon by thieves, on a road you did not see fit to patrol. Look at this!' She held up her signet ring for the man to inspect. 'My ring bears the de Montiland crest. Now give me your assistance immediately or I assure you my cousin will hear of this!'

The man blanched and called to his fellow. 'Fetch a cart and take these people to the castle. Quick!'

Coldly Rowanne countered, 'Don't worry about them, these peasants are not with me. I met them on the road, they... suffered the same fate as I. Out of kindness I helped them reach the town.'

'Forget the cart!' yelled the sergeant over his shoulder. 'Just bring a horse.'

And so Gemma and the young robber watched the Lady Rowanne de Montiland disappear between the houses, mounted and looking very pleased with herself.

She did not even turn to wave farewell.

The sergeant scowled at them. 'I suppose you had your money pinched?' Gemma nodded miserably. 'And,' he added wearily, 'I suppose you don't know anyone in the town either?'

Gemma shook her head.

'We don't allow vagrants in this town. You must go to the hostel for poor travellers. Down there, on the right. House with a green door.' And with that, he turned and started laughing and joking with his companions. Gemma opened her mouth to ask if he could help her get the lad to the hostel, but she could see she had received all the welcome that she was going to get.

A warm push at her legs showed her that Fleabag had slipped in behind them. Remembering that she must not let anyone realize he could talk, she bent down and scratched him behind the ear. 'Hello, Fleabag,' she said. 'Nice to see you, puss.' She would sit and have a heart-to-heart with him later, in private. She still had to apologize to Fleabag for saving the life of his assailant.

The cat sprang onto her shoulder and nuzzled his face into her ear. 'You walk ahead. I'll see where you go and meet you there later,' the cat whispered and with a flick of his tail he had disappeared in the late afternoon shadows.

Gemma watched him go, feeling very lonely. Then she pulled the boy to his feet. 'I know this is going to be hard, but you will have to walk on your own. You can lean on my shoulder, but that is all.'

The two began to struggle down the narrow, smelly backstreet the soldier had shown them. Rubbish and mud clogged the open drain and the air stank.

The boy looked as if nothing mattered to him any more. 'Why didn't you just kill me back there? It would have been better for you and for me. You could have stayed with your mistress and slept in the palace.'

Gemma gave a short, hard laugh. 'I would rather sleep in the gutter than with her in a palace. Anyway, she wasn't my mistress. We were simply going the same way and she looked after me because it suited her.'

The boy nodded. 'I've met people like that.' Laboriously they staggered the length of the lane until they reached the green door. Gemma knocked hard, but there was no reply. She tried the handle, but the door was locked.

She let Phelan sink to the litter-strewn mud and knocked again.

Then suddenly from behind, a rather husky voice asked, 'Can I help you?'

Gemma turned to see a kind-looking man with a spiky, grey beard and wearing a long, homespun robe. In one hand was a large market-bag full of vegetables and in the other a huge iron key.

'It's a good job you came now,' he smiled, opening the door and putting his bag inside. 'Otherwise you would have been locked out until morning. Once I've collected what I can from the market leftovers, I usually bar the door for the night. It looks like this fellow needs a bit of help.' He stooped down, gathered Phelan up in his strong arms and took him indoors.

The hostel was a long, low, stuffy room with straw mattresses pushed closely together all along both walls. Men and women in various states of sickness and poverty sat staring into space or walking in a lost sort of way up and down the room. One or two were doing odd tasks, such as sweeping or peeling potatoes.

The man put Phelan onto a spare mattress. 'Wait here,' he said.

Gemma sat down on a bench and stroked Fleabag who had slipped in as well. The cat gave Gemma a wink and a nod then jumped onto the window ledge and disappeared into the street.

The man reappeared with a bowl of water and clean rags. He knelt down by Phelan and whistled in amazement as he eased the blood-caked rags from the boy's wounds.

'What happened?'

'We were set upon by robbers on the south road, just where the hill is crowned by woods.'

'I know the place,' said the man. 'It's notorious around here.'

Gemma looked at him. He looked kindly, but she had decided not to trust anyone, especially without Fleabag near. He always seemed to know what people were really like.

'My name is Gemma. I am from the city of Harflorum. My mistress died and I took to the road because I feared ill treatment if I stayed without her protection. I don't know this lad. I think his name's Phelan. He just happened to be... on the same stretch of road at the same time.'

The man shot her a sharp glance. He must have guessed what she meant. She did not want to lie, but she had no intention of telling the truth either. Anyway, Rowanne was far guiltier than the boy – she was malicious and unfaithful, only concerned with her own comfort and getting the Ring for herself. Gemma hated her at this moment.

'I must tell you I have no money,' she said quietly. 'But I am a good worker. May I work for our keep until the boy is better?'

The man sat back on his heels and surveyed her. She had clear eyes with a steady look, and her hands were obviously used to work. 'Thank you,' he said. 'That is a good offer. My name is Aelforth, and I am going to need a great deal of help in the next few days to get young Phelan here back on his feet. Now, this water contains salt and will hurt him a great deal, but I must bathe his wounds. You hold his hands so he can't struggle. With any luck, he will remain unconscious while I do it.'

That night, Aelforth would not let Gemma do any work at all. Instead he made her eat and rest to regain her strength.

She lay on a scratchy, thin little mattress and cried. Not because she had been betrayed by Rowanne – she shouldn't have expected much else – but, as much as anything, because she had lost the soft green shawl the Queen had given her.

13

Rowanne Washes Up

Fleabag stretched and rearranged himself under Gemma's chin. She moaned and struggled in her sleep. At last she began to awaken and gave the cat a sharp shove.

'Hey!' came the aggrieved whisper. 'I was comfy there.'

'Well, I wasn't!' Gemma retorted. 'I couldn't breathe with your tail right under my nose!'

'You could at least have asked me to move in a friendly way, instead of shoving me like that!'

'I couldn't talk with all your fur in my face.'

Fleabag stood up and arched his back in a big stretch. Then he sat down, stood up again and turned around twice. At last he settled, face to face with Gemma. She scratched him behind his left ear. 'I owe you an apology,' she said.

'What for?'

'For trying to rescue Phelan, the boy who swung you

by the tail. I hope you're still talking to me. I felt I had to do something. No one deserves to be left at the mercy of Prince Rupert... If Her Majesty had known what he was really like... Oh, but that's all past,' she sighed.

Fleabag licked her nose, then he rolled over on his back, leaving his three legs stuck up in the air at ridiculous angles. Then he began to purr his deep, rolling song. 'I *was* cross at first. But what he did wasn't against me personally, was it? It was the only way he knew how to live. When I heard his life story, I felt he deserved a chance to be different. I might just accidentally use his leg as a scratching post when I see him, but – well, let's see how he turns out before we judge him, shall we? I mean, if he's a decent sort, I might allow him to travel with us, but if he's a baddie then I'll feed him to a particularly unpleasant bulldog I met last night,' and Fleabag turned his head so Gemma could see that yet another chunk was missing from the cat's right ear.

'Wow!' she said. 'Does that hurt?'

'Nah!' sneered the cat. 'Once you've had one chunk taken out of an ear, the rest becomes kitten's play.'

But when Gemma tried to inspect the wound, Fleabag winced and presented his other side to be stroked. 'You're a fraud, cat,' admonished Gemma. 'Tell me if you need something on that.'

'You ought to see the mess I made of the other guy,' grinned Fleabag. 'He'll need quite a lot to soothe *his* aches and pains this morning. By the way, changing the subject to less interesting matters, how is Phelan?'

Gemma sat up, dislodging Fleabag who rolled onto the floor. She peered across the room. 'I can't see from here, but yesterday he wasn't being a very "patient" patient at all. We've been here four days now, and since his fever subsided yesterday morning, he's put all his effort into trying to run away. He doesn't believe that we're not going to turn him over to the authorities. He doesn't trust anyone.'

Fleabag climbed back onto his perch under Gemma's chin. 'Wait until I tell you how her Ladyship Rowanne Fancypants fared.'

Just then the woman on the next mattress stirred. Gemma pushed Fleabag gently onto the floor. 'Let me get dressed and we'll go outside. I don't want anyone knowing I'm with a talking cat. They'd put you in a cage and that would be the end of your adventures.'

'I'd like to see them try!' said Fleabag as he jumped lightly onto a window sill. 'See you outside,' he said.

The early morning breeze was very fresh and pleasant. The hot, city smells had not started to clog the air. The garden behind the hostel was used for growing food and hanging washing. Gemma sat in the shade of a dark green plum tree with tiny unripe fruit hanging in swathes above her head. She hugged her knees, her eyes bright with excitement.

The cat was stretched in full sunlight, with his eyes closed, and looking for all the world as if he were asleep. But in reality, he was speaking very, very quietly.

'Well,' he said, 'I have this on excellent authority. There's this very bright little tortoiseshell queen cat in the kitchen. Nice lass. Could get fond of a cat like her...'

Gemma twisted his long black fur between her toes and tugged. 'Get on with the story, mog!'

Fleabag took a friendly bite at her foot and settled back

to the tale. 'Well, this friend of mine saw the Lady Knight Rowanne de Montiland arrive at the palace gates, looking like something the dog dragged in, but pretending she was the Queen of Sheba... She stuck her pretty little nose in the air and presented her ring to the guards, like she did at the gate...'

Gemma nodded, 'I know! Like this,' and she jumped up and pranced around doing a very neat imitation of the knight.

'But this guard wasn't having any of it. He was a big fat man from the West, with muscles like barrels. He had our friend off her horse and threw her into prison, and I mean threw – down the steps head first, so I hear. This guard reckoned Rowanne was a thief who'd stolen the ring, and had her up on a charge of imitating a member of the de Montiland family, as well as suspected murder of the real Rowanne!'

Gemma leaned back against the tree and laughed. 'Oh, I like it! It serves her right! When's the trial?'

'Yesterday. Some Sheriff who'd never met Rowanne sat in judgment but, because they couldn't get the ring off her finger, he thought there might be a slight possibility she's telling the truth. The mark on her finger shows she's certainly been wearing it for a long time. Still, until her cousin comes back, the Sheriff's condemned her to menial work in the kitchens. It seems they can't keep staff there and so they have all the poor unfortunates doing the greasy jobs about the place!'

Gemma grinned. 'Better and better!'

Fleabag purred contentedly. 'I found the scullery where Rowanne works. She was washing up all day. I sat on a window ledge where I could see it all. I could have watched her for hours. I smiled and waved a paw of course, and she saw me, but she didn't seem to appreciate it. She threw a dishmop at me. That's the last time I'll try and be friendly to her!'

Gemma rolled over so she lay next to Fleabag on the warm grass. 'Meanwhile,' she said, 'I need you to do some thinking. People are only allowed to stay here for a week. They say it prevents anyone becoming dependent on the place or something. Anyway, Aelforth who's in charge says that's stupid. He gets people well and clean and almost ready to be able to go out and look for work, then the rules say he has to turf them out and they can't come back for a month. By the time people are allowed to come back, after sleeping rough all that time, they're ill and dirty again.'

'Who makes the rules?'

'Prince Rupert, of course. Anyway, a sergeant comes round every day and checks the entries, and makes sure the rules are followed. We're only going to be allowed to stay three more days – that's two more nights. What are we going to do? Are we going to try and take Phelan with us? His gang won't take him back. And what do we do about Rowanne? Should we try and rescue her?'

'Why should we?' snapped Fleabag. 'We promised her she'd never hear from us again.'

'I suppose, like Phelan, she's a human being who needs help.'

'Call that a "human being"?' sneered Fleabag.

Gemma looked serious. 'Well, it's more that she was sort of given to us to look after, by the Fire Wielder, if you remember. I get the feeling we are meant to stick together.'

Fleabag stopped purring and took a lazy swipe at a butterfly that came too close. 'Ummm,' he said doubtfully.

'I think she ought at least to have the choice – she ought to know we're here if she needs us. And that we're leaving on... let's see...' she counted on her fingers, 'Thursday.'

Fleabag said 'Ummm,' again, even more thoughtfully. He twisted his head round so he could see her properly and said, 'You look sort of Ring Fire-ish at times – and this is one of them.'

Gemma rubbed at the palms of her hands. They *did* tingle rather. She just said, 'This window you saw her near, is it one I could talk to her through? You'd better not get near her in case she cuts one, if not all three, of your other legs off.'

The window where Rowanne worked was barred and bolted, but a small pane was propped open for the scullery maid to throw vegetable peelings and bones out into the streets below. The heap of rotting rubbish under the window was slippery and evil-smelling. Fleabag climbed it lightly. He paused halfway up to whisper encouragement to his friend. Then, at the sight of a slim tortoiseshell cat rounding the corner, he was away.

Nervous and sickened by the smell, Gemma climbed to the top and peered over the sill. A woman was working at the sink, scrubbing pans. She was dressed in a none-too-clean peasant's dirndl. Her black hair was plaited in two braids and tied back in a greasy grey kerchief. Gemma knocked at the window, and a cross face looked up. It was Rowanne.

Gemma smiled. 'Are you OK?'

Rowanne scowled. 'No, I am *not*. No one could be all right in this hell hole. Anyway, how did you know I was here?'

'Fleabag knows one of the kitchen-cats.'

Rowanne made a face. 'Don't mention that animal's name to me... ever!' and she waved a bread knife wildly. Then she leaned over close to the window. 'Anyway, Rupert comes home tonight, and I'm to be brought before him.'

Suddenly there was a bellowing like a cow in pain, and a clatter of dishes being thrown or dropped.

'Quick, duck! Here comes the chief kitchen-maid. She's a fat pig and I hate her!'

For a few moments Gemma squatted on the heap of rotting vegetables and listened. She only heard a rough angry voice, and the clatter of more iron pots being put ready to wash.

'All clear!' whispered Rowanne.

Gemma leaned close to the window. 'Listen, I can only stay here two more nights, then I get chucked out of the hostel. I don't know what I'm going to do, so I'll be on my way, I suppose. Will you come too?'

Rowanne looked worried. She remembered she needed Gemma to identify the Ring. She made a conciliatory face. 'I'm sure I could get you a job and somewhere to sleep in the palace...?'

'No, thank you!' said Gemma with an inward shudder.

Suddenly a passing soldier yelled, 'Oi you, no begging at palace windows. Move along before I arrest you for vagrancy!' He picked up a rotten potato and lobbed it in her direction.

'If all goes well, I will send for you tomorrow!' called Rowanne, as Gemma slithered down the pile and ran for her life.

14

Fleabag Plays Marbles

Dinner with Prince Rupert was a grand affair at the simplest of times. Bathed and dressed for the occasion, Rowanne looked quite the part. She preferred the court dress of a Lady Knight to the flowing frills of a lady-in-waiting: rose silk pantaloons with white silk stockings, white satin shoes, a vermilion shirt and a white tabard with Prince Rupert's crest. Her long dark hair was loose over her shoulders and smelled of lavender.

She smiled as the guard who had arrested her was sentenced to ten years' hard labour. She dabbed at her pink lips with a damask serviette and nibbled at a little of the fruit set before her.

The man was led away, howling protests that he was only doing his duty and that he had a wife and children to support.

'Oh, very well,' yawned the Prince. The man turned with a look of relief on his face. 'Let them do ten years hard labour as well, then they can stay together.'

Rowanne closed her eyes for a second and imagined a picture of a lonely, frightened family. She winced involuntarily.

Rupert turned and bowed slightly to his beautiful cousin Rowanne de Montiland. He mistook her pale look of horror for anger.

'My dear cousin, does that not please you? How else can I beg your forgiveness for the terrible treatment at the hands of these ill-bred, misbegotten thugs I am forced to employ!'

Rowanne laughed lightly, but a tiny scratch caught at her silken stocking. She brushed it away. 'Consider it never happened. *Dear* Rupert, it is so good to see you. I can forgive any misunderstanding.'

'Should I have had him hanged?' the Prince mused, leaning on a thin hand and tossing a sweet white grape into his mouth.

Rowanne remembered the terrified thief boy looking up at her, begging not to be sent to the scaffold.

Just at that moment, two claws caught at her stocking and scratched her leg. It was that infernal cat!

She dropped her napkin on purpose and stared into Fleabag's accusing golden eyes.

'If you don't go away, I'll scream, and I'll have you flayed alive for clawing me!'

'No, you won't,' smirked the cat. 'You know perfectly well that a cat saved the Prince's life when he was little, and the attention of a cat is considered the highest honour in this palace.

'I'll think of something,' she assured him, and he smirked back at her.

'No, don't hang the man,' she said to Rupert. She hesitated. 'It was just a mistake, after all.'

The Prince lifted a thin, dark eyebrow and plucked at the bunch of grapes. 'Very well,' he lifted a hand to dismiss the soldiers.

A full set of claws now tore at Rowanne's stocking. She jumped. 'Er, he *was* only trying to do his job. It was not his fault – he had never seen me before and I was dirty and ragged after the fight... could he not just be...' the first set of claws on her leg was joined by more on her other leg... 'Could he not just lose rank and be sent back to work?' she ventured. She was not even sure it was her own voice speaking, but as the words were out, one set of claws lessened their torture.

Prince Rupert looked amazed. 'Oh, very well,' he yawned, 'I'm tired of all this.'

Rowanne smiled warmly. 'I do think your judgments are so *wise*, dear cousin.' At that moment, the second set of claws disentangled themselves from her leg, and a soft, warm feeling engulfed her feet in a comforting wrap as Fleabag began to purr loudly. The man was marched out of the room and the Prince smiled back at Rowanne. He loved flattery. 'I was wanting to talk to you anyway, dear cousin. I have much to discuss.'

'So have I.' She put her head on one side. She could feel the cat bracing himself for an attack if she spoke one word out of place. Why had she let herself be bullied by him? She wouldn't let it happen again.

The purr grew louder.

'What is that noise?' asked the prince.

'Oh,' Rowanne hesitated. 'There's a… cat under the table. I was just stroking him!' At the lie a sharp claw picked at her already sore leg.

'How nice,' the prince replied. 'I know how you used to dislike cats. It has been that which has prevented me from speaking out what burns within my heart… dear cousin, will you marry me? Now you have been honoured by a palace cat, I feel sure it is a sign that you will say yes…'

Rowanne blushed and went white in turns. This was the last thing she had expected. Before the Queen's death, she might have said yes, but now, things were different.

'My Prince, what can I say? It is such an honour! Before I can answer you, I must tell you something very important… something that may have a bearing on your request.'

'Speak on, my dear. We must have no secrets if we are to be wed.'

Rowanne swallowed hard and began to tell a very edited version of what had brought her to the city. In her story, she told how the Queen herself had sent her on this mission to find the Ring… and that should she, or even he find it, then they would be King and Queen of the entire land, not just Prince and Princess of the province.

The Prince's eyes opened wider and wider with delight, for he was every bit as ambitious as his cousin. He had heard of the quest, of course – every street corner was buzzing with gossip about it. As a relative of the late Queen, he had been officially invited to take part. But although he was greedy, he was also lazy. Consequently he was, as he told Rowanne, 'still thinking about it'.

Suddenly he sat up straight and clapped his hands to summon his valet. 'Call the palace jeweller,' he demanded. 'And make sure he brings me every box of trinkets I possess. I wish my intended bride to choose an engagement ring for herself,' he said with a broad wink. 'It must be very special. I think she should have... an opal.'

The poor jeweller spent long hours, deep into the night, bringing box after box of rings to his royal master. But there were very few with opals. With downcast eyes (for he feared for his neck) he informed the Prince and the Lady, 'There's been a bit on a run on opals since the Queen's death. It's funny,' he mused, 'no one seemed to like them much before.'

Time and time again he was sent back to the treasury to open more safes and rummage through ancient chests and boxes. At last, with relief and delight, the grey little jeweller presented a ring with three magnificent opals held in eagles' claws. But Rowanne still shook her head. 'I fancy,' she said with a look at the Prince, 'one with a simple band, and perhaps just one, large opal... with a fire in it.'

The jeweller looked frightened, for he understood the significance of what she had said. 'I am very tired now,' yawned Rowanne. 'But in the morning, I will draw what I have in mind for you.'

The jeweller bowed. 'Very good, ma'am. A drawing will help a great deal. If you will forgive me, I will go and look through my stock of raw stones immediately to see what can be polished and mounted for your pleasure.'

The prince waved his dismissal and the terrified little man scurried out of the room.

Rowanne yawned again and smiled knowingly at the prince. He nodded. She was clever. Very clever. He admired that. She would be a very useful consort.

Then she said, 'If I am to stay here, dearest, I would very much like my personal maid sent for. We were – separated at the gates when the misunderstanding took place. I heard tell she is at the poor travellers' hostel. Her name is Gemma Streetchild. I do not want the girl frightened, for she is new to my service and timid, so do not send for her until the morning. Would you mind if I retired now? – dearest…'

The Prince rose and bowed as she left the room. He blinked and wondered at the huge tears in her new silk stockings and the blood which trickled down to her shoes from raw claw marks…

Gemma Streetchild was not to be found when a servant from the Palace came to the hostel in the morning. For once, even Fleabag did not know where she was.

Aelforth just shook his head when the servant questioned him. 'The people come and the people go. They have no homes or addresses. If I asked them questions they would have no answers.'

He shrugged, and watched the servant step gingerly past the rows of elderly and frail guests. Aelforth stroked his greying beard and wondered how he could warn the girl. The place would be watched now, and he did not trust whatever was afoot.

He turned to start his morning rounds of the sick. It was then he realized that the boy, Phelan, was gone also. That troubled him, for there was something about the lad which was familiar…

Gemma had got up early to sit in the garden while the air was still cool and the streets were quiet. As she had passed by the beds where the sick lay, she too had discovered that Phelan was missing.

She slipped out of the back door and climbed the garden wall. Sitting on top, she could see along the street in both directions. Cat-like she jumped down on the other side and made for the town gate. It was still bolted. All the gates would be locked at this hour; it was scarcely dawn. He must still be in the city, but he had no friends or family – unless he knew some thieves, he must be hiding. Why had he run away when there was nothing to run away *from* and nowhere to go *to*?

She felt sad, hurt and a little lonely. She had not got to know Phelan well – he hardly said anything – but she wished him no harm. He had found life tough and he had grown up having to fight all the way, but he was nice enough for all that. Apart from Fleabag, he was her only friend.

Tomorrow she and the cat must leave the city and go north by north-west, on their own. She would have been glad of someone else to talk to – someone who wouldn't sneer at her all the time – someone who would not bring in dead rats before breakfast...

Slowly she wandered back to the hostel and walked straight into the arms of Rowanne's messenger. There was no use denying who she was. Aelforth looked like a man who could never lie and the shock on her own face was enough to betray herself.

She changed out of the hostel smock she had been loaned and put on her own clothes which had been washed and mended. Gemma asked leave to thank

Aelforth, and took the chance to whisper: 'He left very early. I don't know where he is.' She glanced at Phelan's empty bed and Aelforth nodded. The servant had asked nothing about the boy, and it was probably best he had gone before any connections between the two were made.

Gemma was given a small neat attic room. As the personal maid to the Prince's supposed fiancée she was given a pretty blue dress and treated almost civilly.

As soon as she had bathed and made herself presentable, Gemma was sent for. She was shown into Prince Rupert's library, where Rowanne sat at one side of a huge desk and the tall, thin, hook-nosed prince at the other. Gemma did not like the look of him. He appeared hard and cynical.

Spread on the table were hundreds and hundreds of rings. Some had opals, others had large round stones of other hues. In the corner cowered a small, grey little man with a huge watch-glass in his right eye. He looked for all the world like a rather moth-eaten old owl.

'My maid may not look like much' – she hesitated, the girl did look better nicely dressed – 'but she has a very good idea of the engagement ring I fancy. Come here, child…' Gemma approached her, but stood carefully at a respectful distance. Rowanne shot out an arm and pulled her closer. She thrust a pencil and paper into her hand, and said, 'Draw! Draw me the ring I have always hankered for, *dear* girl!' She reinforced her demand with a sharp kick from under the table with a new, long, leather, cat-proof boot.

Gemma felt her eyes stinging with tears. What could she do? She picked up the pencil and began to draw. How could she make it look enough like the royal ring to fool

Rowanne, but not enough to betray the Queen?

Just then with a magnificent rumbling purr, Fleabag appeared and jumped onto the table. With kittenish glee he began to roll the rings around and pat them with his paws, sending them skimming across the room in cascades of glittering light.

'Oh my rings! My gems!' squealed the jeweller as he bent his rheumaticky little knees and began to gather the stones into numerous leather bags which he pulled from every pocket.

At first, Prince Rupert began by being playful with Fleabag, but soon realized that the stones were rolling away and being lost between the floorboards.

Rowanne went quite white. That cat must be got rid of! But easier said than done. Her fingers itched to do the animal real damage.

Having pounced and danced across the table, sending papers and gems everywhere in a lively scramble, Fleabag then leaped onto the floor and skittishly skidded here and there across the polished boards, playing croquet with the crystals and marbles with the margarics. The moonstones he potted into mouseholes under the skirting boards.

Gemma crawled under the table in a pretence of helping to pick everything up. But instead she gently flicked the stones past the cat for him to pounce on.

After several minutes of this, even Prince Rupert no longer found the cat's antics amusing and Rowanne had found a sword. The knight lowered her dark eyebrows and cornered the cat, head down, every muscle in her tense body ready to pounce and slice Fleabag in two.

But Prince Rupert intervened. 'Don't kill the cat, my

dear, he's only a poor dumb animal after all...'

Rowanne turned on the Prince and glowered. She opened her mouth, thought better of it and shut it again. After all, she had need of the Prince's goodwill.

'Take the cat away, Gemma, and put him in the kitchen. Then come back here and clear up this mess.' Fleabag nestled contentedly in his friend's arms and stuck out his tongue at Rowanne as he was carried past.

Rowanne bristled but could do nothing except put up her sword. She had to keep Rupert's trust.

Gemma spent the whole day on her knees gathering up loose gems and rings of every imaginable shape and size. The next day, carpenters came to take up the floorboards and remove the skirting boards, until every last stone was found. Gemma drew a likeness of the Queen's Ring, but she comforted herself with the thought that the quality of stone could never be matched – and the fire was unlike anything else that had ever burned in all the world. No jeweller on earth could even begin to imitate it.

It was thus that Gemma found herself employed at the palace, with no prospect of resuming her travels for the time being at least. For a while it did not seem to matter very much. The summer was still young, and a royal palace seemed as good a place as any to begin looking for the Queen's Ring.

Her duties were to supervise the care of Rowanne's extensive new wardrobe of clothes and to clean her suite of rooms. But in her spare time, Gemma was sent out with a team of girls to 'spring-clean' the palace. Her task was to check in every nook and cranny in case, by any chance, the Queen's Ring had been hidden there.

This she did not mind. After all, she too wanted to find

the Ring, if only to make sure that Rowanne did not.

Fleabag wandered around at will and kept Gemma informed of all the gossip. One day, he had rather exciting news.

15

Gemma Speaks Out

'You remember I told you about Tabitha, the nice little tortoiseshell queen in the kitchen?' Fleabag rolled over on his back and smirked. Gemma scratched his tummy.

'Well, she's a good sort, is Tabitha. She told me something very interesting indeed. She says that about the time the Queen died, three black ravens landed on the palace roof. Now she likes the tiles, does Tabitha, we've often spent an evening up there... Anyway, she was about to try and catch a raven for supper, when she heard them talking.

'The first one said, "Here! Let's put it here. A king or queen is bound to find a royal ring in a royal palace – where better to find the new sovereign of our land?"

'But the second raven shook his head and said, "No, no. True royalty lies in wisdom, not in palaces and soldiers. A king may live in a palace, but without wisdom, he is no king at all."

'It was then Tabitha saw that one raven carried a large opal ring in its mouth.

'She was so amazed that she did not pounce quickly enough. The ravens smelled her near and flew off!'

Gemma picked Fleabag up and nuzzled his warm fur. His whole body shook gently with his deep purr.

'What are we going to do, cat?' she asked quietly. 'We have been here many weeks now. The summer is almost gone and in the marketplace people are beginning to lose hope that the Ring will be ever be found. I should have guessed that the Ring would not be hidden anywhere belonging to such an unwholesome creature as Prince Rupert.' She shivered in disgust. 'Rowanne is unofficially betrothed to the man and it looks as if I am going to be kept here for ever.'

The cat dropped to his feet and started to examine a few itchy places under his fur. 'At least the fleas die off in winter and I'll be a bit more comfortable for a while,' he mused.

Gemma took no notice. 'The Prince said something the other day about what would happen if the Ring were never found. I didn't understand it, but I didn't like it either. Something about seeing who was and wasn't fit to rule and getting his soldiers ready for a fight... Is this what will happen if the Ring Fire goes away?'

'I guess so,' replied the cat. Then he rolled over on his back. 'Scratch my tummy again!' he demanded.

Absent-mindedly Gemma did as she was told. 'Rowanne will never leave here. She has it made whatever happens next. Prince Rupert was the old Queen's nephew and Rowanne is his cousin. If the Ring isn't found, they will be the obvious choices for the throne. Especially if they are married.'

'What does the Ring Fire tell you?' purred Fleabag unexpectedly.

'The Ring Fire? I get a burning pain in my hands, if that's what you mean. I know I've got to do something fairly soon. But I'm scared… even with a mighty cat like you by my side. Humans… well… need humans. But I know it is time we went on again – north by north-west – with her or without her.'

The cat rolled over and sat bolt upright. He looked at Gemma. 'You must tell Rowanne your thoughts. You are right, she was sent to be with us. We need her – if she will come. If she has the choice, and refuses, then you and I will set off together. When will you have the chance to speak with her alone?'

Gemma put the cat down and leaned out of the window. The tower clock showed five o'clock. 'In about an hour, when I dress her for dinner.'

'Good!' Fleabag announced. 'While you wait, get yourself packed and organize yourself some food for the journey. I've got a few goodbyes to say myself.' And with that, the grinning cat slipped out of the room.

Gemma looked around. She had packed like this once before. She pulled out the squire's clothes she had arrived in: trousers, shirt and leather jerkin. She held them up. They did not seem as big as when she first wore them. She had grown and filled out while she had been at the palace. She looked at herself in the mirror. Her cheeks were pinker and rounder and her freckles had become alarmingly brown and multitudinous in the summer sun.

Her mousy hair was well brushed and tied back in a long plait that came halfway down her back. She straightened her blue dress. It was prettily made, with a white lace collar. It was the sort of thing she would have treasured before, but it would not fit her soon. Anyway, with winter approaching a cotton dress would be of no use whatsoever.

Instead she took out more trousers and a woollen jacket. The leather shoes the Queen had given her still fitted well. She had no winter coat, so she pulled a thick blanket from her bed and rolled it up tightly. She would need it at night and it could be a cloak by day.

Gemma glanced at the clock. Just time to grab something from the kitchen. If she told them she had to go on an errand for her mistress (which was true, she was still on the Queen's quest) they would allow her to take what she pleased.

At six o'clock she knocked on Rowanne's door. Of late the knight had taken to wearing the flowing robes of a courtly lady. They were fiddly and difficult to fit. Dressing Rowanne often took at least an hour and then her hair and make-up had to be ready in time for dinner at eight. Gemma thought all of this an extraordinary waste of time, but it meant she would have about half an hour alone with Rowanne before the hairdresser came.

When she went into the room, Rowanne was sitting at her dressing table in a cream satin underslip. Gemma curtseyed and went to the wardrobe. 'What would you like to wear this evening, ma'am?'

Rowanne did not look up. 'The turquoise blue. The jeweller has at last made a ring that looks... right!'

Rowanne smiled at herself in the mirror. The look was unpleasant and triumphant.

'Tonight, the Prince and I will announce our engagement and I will wear the Ring of the Land.'

She held out her strong fingers and imagined the pale, fiery-hearted opal already there.

Gemma stumbled on the hem of the turquoise silk dress. She did not know what to do with the feelings that rushed through her or the terrible burning pain in her hands. She covered up her clumsiness with a curtsey. 'Congratulations, ma'am!' she mumbled.

Rowanne swung round and glared at Gemma. 'You're not really pleased, are you?' she snapped.

Gemma closed her fists to hide the Ring Fire. It burned so fiercely that she almost expected to see the flame.

Since Rowanne had been living at the palace, she had become alarmingly selfish, like her cousin. Now her dark-browed eyes narrowed as fury built up. Gemma found she was frightened. But something had to be said. Now. The Fire Wielder was depending on her.

Suddenly she made herself open her hands so the fire could burn if it wished.

'No, ma'am, I'm not happy. Just look at yourself – all dressed in frills and laces like a courtier. You're not being true to yourself. You'll never be happy here!'

Rowanne shrugged. 'It's all a means to a very useful end.'

Gemma felt the Ring Fire burning even more strongly. 'And *what* end is that? It's not the real Ring – neither will it be the real Fire. I think you'll have precious little joy from either of them and you'll never forgive yourself if you go through with this nonsense. If you'll take my advice, you'll throw away those silly clothes you're wearing and come north by north-west with me. Tonight!'

Rowanne had her head down. Her nostrils were flared and she was flushed. The fury in her face was plain to see. With her right hand she toyed with the handle of her dagger. 'Get out of my room. Immediately!' she said very quietly and dangerously.

Gemma turned and fled. As the door slammed behind her, there was a heavy thud as a dagger hit the wood.

'Well,' said Fleabag consolingly, 'she can't have wanted to kill you very much...'

'Why's that?' asked Gemma as she ran up the servants' stairs two at a time.

'Because,' puffed Fleabag as he flung himself into her room and landed on her bed, 'the Lady Knight Rowanne de Montiland does not have a reputation for missing her mark.'

Gemma flung her blue dress onto the bed, changed into her travelling clothes and grabbed her bundle. Within seconds, she was shutting the bedroom door behind her. But for one moment she hesitated.

'What's the matter?' asked Fleabag.

'It's just – well, I always wanted a room of my own. It's what I longed for more than anything else in all the world. And now it's gone.'

But then she heard steps approaching. In case it was a guard coming to arrest her, Fleabag led her to the stepladder which went up to the top attic. Then they ventured out onto the climbing boards that the roof repairers used to check the slates. 'Don't look down,' he warned. 'It's quite safe for humans. I've often seen men with hammers spend all day up here.'

'I'm not a man with a hammer,' whispered Gemma, trying to keep her eyes on Fleabag's bottlebrush tail ahead.

At last the boards sloped down to a window above another part of the palace that Gemma had never seen before. The wall was thickly covered with ivy. Fleabag sprang lightly between the leaves, but Gemma found it more difficult. Not least because the ivy branches were brittle, shaking and snapping under her weight.

'Throw your bundle down,' the cat whispered. 'Then you'll have two hands.'

Gemma did as she was told and quickly joined Fleabag on the ground.

Swiftly they ran through the kitchen garden and out of the wicket gate at the back. Fleabag went ahead to see if he could find any soldiers. Then with a flick of his whiskers, he called her on. Trying to look as normal as possible they wandered through the backstreets of Rupert's city.

Gemma was worried. It would be dark soon and the gates would close. She would have been glad of a night's sleep before travelling. Facing a night alone – or almost alone outside the city walls was frightening enough... But which way was north by north-west?

It was then a firm hand gripped her shoulder.

16

Autumn and Porridge

They entered a tiny, hot room, with a very old lady seated by an open fire, stirring a pot. She looked just like a witch.

Gemma was pushed forward, nearer to a candle that burned on the table. She turned to glare at her captor. He was a tall, dark-skinned young man from the South. His beard was thin and his eyes were smiling.

Gemma gasped with delight and gave him a hug. 'Phelan! I'm so glad you're all right!' she said.

'Who've you brought in this time, youngster? Another waif and stray, or is it a spy?' the old woman croaked though empty gums.

'Auntie, this is the girl who saved my life – I told you about her,' explained Phelan.

'What's she doing here?' snapped the old lady.

'I brought her here. She looked frightened.'

The old woman snorted contemptuously.

'I *was* frightened,' Gemma admitted. 'But worst of all, I've lost my cat, he was in the street with me. I'd be a lot happier if he was here too.'

'If you mean this one,' said Auntie, kicking a black lump of fur with her toe, 'he seems to have found his own way in.' Sure enough, there was Fleabag, stretched out in front of the fire, toasting his paws.

'Yes, that's him. Everything's all right now.'

'Is it really?' asked Phelan. 'You looked worried sick when I saw you in the street.'

'I was,' she said. Then, pushing her fears aside, she told them the whole story.

Auntie scratched her hairy chin as she listened. 'There is good in the tale which I will not gainsay. She can sleep the night in front of the fire. But I have some advice.'

Gemma looked up expectantly. The old lady passed over a rusted pair of scissors. 'Cut your hair. The prince's soldiers are looking for a girl. You've got a lad's clothes already, but your hair betrays you. Close to, you'd never pass as a boy and your voice is all wrong, but if you shut your mouth and keep out of the way, there's a chance you might win through. In the morning the lad will help you slip out of the city unseen and set you on the road.'

With that the old crone slopped greasy stew into bowls. When they had all eaten, she climbed stiffly up the stairs to her bed.

When they were alone, Gemma whispered, 'I'm glad you found your Auntie. I thought you had no relatives.'

Phelan laughed out loud. 'This is a thieves' hide-out. She's sister, mother and aunt to us all! Now, you will need a proper night's sleep if you're going on the road. Goodnight.' Then Phelan slipped out of the room too, leaving Gemma and Fleabag alone.

Before dawn the boy reappeared and led Gemma silently through the dim streets to an easily climbed part of the wall where no guard stood.

Phelan pointed out the road and turned to go.

'Won't you come with me?' she begged. 'Even with Fleabag, I can't pretend I'm not frightened.'

Phelan shook his head and laughed. 'What have rogues and criminals to do with the Fire in the Ring? I would put it out as soon as look at it!'

Gemma felt the slight burning in the palms of her hands. 'No, you wouldn't. Not you!' she added with conviction. But he had already gone, so sadly she picked up her bundle and followed Fleabag down the fallen stones and onto the road.

The first few days passed comfortably enough, until the food ran out. Fleabag caught a rabbit, but Gemma could not cook it as she had neither knife to clean it nor tinder box to make a fire. She quickly found that too many nuts and berries made her stomach ache, so she survived by offering to scrub floors and do washing for farmer's wives, in exchange for a night's shelter and a square meal. The farmers were happier to give barn room now the hay and the harvest were safe. Perhaps too, they felt less threatened by a child and a cat than by a formidable knight.

Gemma soon learned to cope with this strange way of life, although she often had the feeling she was being watched or followed. But the leaves had turned rich gold and were falling fast. Autumn was coming to an end. The winds were beginning to blow cold. She was halfway though the year and a day allowed to find the Ring. She was quite alone in a strange part of the land, and she did not even really know whether she was doing the right thing or not.

Slowly but surely the days grew colder and Gemma's progress slowed. One night she had no work and no sheltering barn. Her blanket was damp and smelly from heavy rain and she felt ill. A shepherd's storm shelter kept the wind off her back, and Fleabag did his best to keep her warm. But it was a long, miserable night.

At first light, Fleabag brought Gemma two harvest-fed rats, but his efforts were not appreciated.

Gemma peered over the blanket with feverish eyes. 'I need water, but you can't carry it. Oh, I feel so sick.' Then she pulled the blanket up over her head and fell asleep.

Fleabag climbed up a dry-stone wall to watch the road for passers-by. He would just have to risk being identified as a talking cat. If Gemma did not get help soon, she would become very ill. She needed humans and cups of water and warm blankets. This was no time to think about what life might be like in a circus. He would just have to talk his way out of that one if it came to it.

He sat on the wall all morning. One farmer's lad gave Gemma a drink, but no one seemed to want to take her home. As night began to fall and the cold wind began to whip up the remaining autumn leaves into a dancing frenzy, a dark shape appeared on the road.

As Fleabag watched, the one shape split into two and then three. It was a man on horseback leading two ponies. Fleabag balanced indecisively on the wall. Something about the figure made him nervous. Should he run and hide, or stay and beg help?

He glanced inside the shelter. Gemma was shivering violently.

Plucking up all his courage, as the horses drew level Fleabag balanced himself and took a flying leap, right onto the pommel of the rider's saddle.

The rider jumped. He had obviously dozed off in the saddle. The horse snorted and swung round.

A deep woman's voice swore roundly. 'Fleabag, you wretched animal, you'll be the death of me if I'm not the death of you first!'

'Trust me to pick on *your* horse when I need real help. I'll go away and find someone I can trust,' and he tried to leap down.

Rowanne de Montiland's firm hand grasped Fleabag by the scruff of his neck. She reined in the horse and looked the cat in the eye. 'Listen, don't judge me by what you think you know. Where is Gemma? What's the matter?'

Fleabag knew that even Rowanne's help was better than none. 'Let me breathe and I'll show you,' he said, making it sound as if she were about to strangle him.

She let him go and sprang out of the saddle after him.

Within minutes, she had Gemma wrapped in dry blankets and astride the horse in front of her. Fleabag chose a gap between two bundles on the back of one of the ponies and they headed off up the road.

At the next farm, the farmer's wife regarded Gemma's fever suspiciously. Autumn fever was a dreaded illness. But she changed her mind at the sight of gold.

For three days, Rowanne sat by Gemma's bed, feeding her sips of water and gruel. For four nights, Fleabag watched, curled up at the end of his friend's bed, dozing lightly and opening an eye at Gemma's slightest sound.

On the fourth day she got up and ate well. She was still weak, but as she sat wrapped in rugs next to the farm fire, Rowanne told her what had happened since they had left Rupertsberg.

The night Gemma ran away, Rowanne had pleaded illness and sat alone in her room for a whole night and a whole day.

While she was alone, she began to see that Gemma and Fleabag had been right. Rupert was unjust and greedy, oppressing his people and helping no one except himself.

The next day, she made up a story that she had dreamed that the Ring Fire spoke to her, telling her she was not to marry until she had completed her quest – one way or the other – and that she must set off straight away. After many angry scenes and much persuasion, she convinced Rupert that the real Ring must be hidden in a place shown to her in her dream.

Better, she argued, to have one more go at finding the real thing, than to look foolish with the imitation. If the real Ring was not to be found, then they stood a good chance with the new one.

Rupert, who was cunning but not very clever, finally agreed and equipped Rowanne with an entourage of mounted soldiers, travelling clothes and money for the journey. But he refused to act quickly, taking as long as possible over everything. At last all was ready, but Rupert still would not let Rowanne leave until he had celebrated his birthday feast. She stayed, but only because she needed the supplies and the gold he had given her.

At last, with smiles and kisses she pushed the imitation ring onto Rupert's little finger so hard it would never come off again, and waved goodbye to Rupertsberg.

At first she had led her escort onto the southern road, then after two days, she got them drunk and slipped away unnoticed. Walking a horse and two ponies along the bed of a stream so they could not follow her tracks, she came north, travelling only by night and leaving false trails here and there.

For once, she seemed to be genuinely glad to see Fleabag, although her legs still bore the scars of long scratchmarks under her knee-high boots.

Fleabag treated her with caution. The sixth sense in his whiskers told him that she had betrayed them before, and although she seemed to have changed, she could betray them again.

The next day Gemma was well enough to travel and they set off. Rowanne gave her the plump little grey pony called Porridge and Fleabag rode perched on a pannier. The land was a wide, open plain, and the wind whistled mercilessly across the emptiness. The trees were now stripped quite bare and the days were very short. Ice formed on the horses' water pails in the morning and more and more often at night they tried to find a farm or inn where they could sleep.

'I've been thinking,' said Rowanne one morning. 'It's only a short detour from the road to the university town of Porthwain. It is still very much north by north-west of Harflorum, so we aren't really going out of our way... What better place to hide the symbol of kingship than in the seat of wisdom? It must be there. We will ask at the university!'

Fleabag and Gemma looked at each other. They had not reported what Tabitha had heard the ravens saying.

'Oh, great!' yawned Fleabag. 'You'll just go up to one of

the professors and say, "Anyone here got the Queen's Ring? Can we have it? Thanks!" '

Gemma gave his ear a quick tweak. 'Don't be rude!' she whispered. 'I don't want to get Rowanne's back up. I'm afraid we need her.'

Taking an easterly turning at the next crossroads, another day's ride brought them within sight of the walls of Porthwain. As it was no military base, the 'walls' were scattered remnants of broken masonry, though a fine example of ancient wrought iron-work gates was to be found hanging in one of the gaps. Behind these lay a sprawling collection of once-imposing buildings.

When they reached the town, they asked one or two passers-by for directions to an inn. One answered in the ancient – and incomprehensible – language of academics. Another leaned back against a wall and stroked his chin, then after a pause, began, 'Well, it depends what you mean by "inn". In the time of King Thributhious the Great, an "inn" implied a den of iniquitous living where brawls and gambling were to be expected. But in more recent times the usage has become changed to a house for business transactions to be worked out while the participants eat together late into the night. Now, if you want somewhere to gamble…'

Rowanne and Gemma looked at each other in horror. 'No, thank you, we just want somewhere to stay the night and rest our horses.'

'Ah!' said the man, with a gleam in his eye, 'you're taking the definition as proposed by Theumious in his erudite essay…'

But they never heard the rest. Gently they nudged their mounts to move off and left the man expounding to himself.

All the buildings were fine, but very old and in a poor state of repair. Everywhere they looked, the people seemed preoccupied with nothing, or just stood on street corners talking. But most people looked well fed and dressed. The town seemed to be suffering from neglect more than poverty.

At last they turned a corner and saw an ancient, very low building with a door which sat at a slant in a skewed frame. Over the door hung the sign of a bush. An inn!

They knocked on the door and a short, fat woman answered it. She had flour up to her elbows and a friendly face. Here at last was someone who might be a little more use to them.

'Do you have a room for two, please?'

'Yes, yes, come in,' smiled the woman. But as Fleabag sprang down to follow them inside, the woman's foot shot out. 'But no cats! Especially black ones. Bad luck, go away, ugh, shoo!' and she spat at him.

Fleabag sat in the mud and stared up in amazement. Rowanne shrugged and made to go into the house, but Gemma shook her head. Taking Porridge's rein, she turned away. 'I'll call for you in the morning, Rowanne. We'll find somewhere else.'

Rowanne cast a regretful glance at the landlady and sniffed at the sweet smell of freshly baked bread emanating from her kitchen.

The woman was still threatening Fleabag with her broom. There would be no room for negotiation. There was nothing for it – Rowanne dared not leave Gemma on her own again. They would have to find somewhere else.

17

An Invitation to the Great Hall

Everywhere they went, there was the same reaction. At the signs of the Bull's Head, the Two Lanterns, the Dancing Bear: no cats in the house… especially black ones.

At last, at a small hostelry bearing the sign of the Bush of Broom, Fleabag rolled in some ash to make himself grey and slipped off round the back to hide in the stable with the horses.

At dinner that night, Rowanne overheard several students talking about the death of the Queen and the great quest for the Ring. From what they said, it sounded as if there had been many questers on the road, who were considered fair game to be told a great many tall tales, relieved of their purses and sent packing again. The lads seemed to think it was all good sport. 'If they only knew the truth... If they only *knew*!' spluttered one of the voices gleefully.

'A fool and his money are soon parted,' quipped another and raucous laughter filled the taproom.

Rowanne bought several pots of honey ale and took the tray over to the students' table, asking if she could join them.

'I have been travelling for many months with my squire over there,' and she jerked a thumb at Gemma. 'We have only heard rumours of these happenings. What can you tell us that is true?'

One of the students, a gaunt-faced, narrow-eyed boy, looked hard at Rowanne and swallowed the honey ale in one gulp. Still staring hard, he wiped his mouth on his sleeve. 'More,' he demanded bluntly.

Rowanne ordered bread and cheese and more ale. Then, returning his stare, she sat astride the stool opposite him. 'Now,' she said. 'You were saying?'

The narrow-eyed lad licked his lips and began. 'There are stories of great magic and evil deeds. Only the Chancellor of All Wizards really knows of course. But it is said that the Queen was put into a trance and her Ring of Office was forced from her hand by that evil magician, the Fire Wielder. Then, by terrible spells which blackened the sky and froze the very blood of those who were near, the Fire itself was taken from the Ring. Until the two are brought together again, the land is in great peril.

'For,' he leaned forward and whispered, 'it is said the Fire cannot last without the Ring – or without some creature willing to let it live within it. But who could submit to such immense forces and live?

'Well, in Porthwain, we know that no human creature can carry the Fire without being consumed. The truth is that it is only his Holiness, the Chancellor of All Wizards, who keeps the Fire alive by spells...' and here he whispered even more quietly, '... which are too terrible to speak of!'

At this the boy sat up and looked very pleased with himself. Rowanne glanced around to see if the other students were laughing... was it a huge joke they dished out to every traveller? But there was not the flicker of a smile on any face. They had all turned pale and wide-eyed with terror.

Gemma sat silently in the shadows, well away from the speakers. She pressed her hands closed under the table lest the burning feeling in her hands should burst out and flare up with all the beauty of the Ring Fire. Her cheeks were flushed with anger at the terrible lies the boy was telling. But she sat alone in rigid silence, hardly daring to breathe.

The boy was looking hopefully into the depths of his ale pot again.

Rowanne did not order more. Instead, she compelled the boy's gaze one more time. 'I don't believe a word of it,' she said slowly and deliberately.

Gemma gasped and bit her lip. There would be trouble now, for sure.

The boy did not react, except to raise one eyebrow. 'Oh? Then perhaps you ought to meet the Chancellor of All Wizards to see for yourself how ill he looks with the effort of holding all our great land together with his spells and his will. Then you would understand how he casts his gaze around to seek the whereabouts of the Ring so that peace and justice may be restored... For truly, the small riots and unrest we hear of will soon turn into war if this thing is not quickly resolved, one way or another.'

The boy glared piercingly under his thin lashes and pushed his drinking pot across the table.

Rowanne ordered more ale, but did not pour it. Instead she watched the candles flicker their pale light across the lad's face. The other students had pulled back as if they sensed things beyond their control.

'Yes,' said Rowanne carefully. 'Although I am a mere knight who has no knowledge of these things, perhaps I should meet his Holiness, the Chancellor of All Wizards.'

The boy tapped the jug with his drinking pot, but said nothing.

When the pot was full, he said: 'Tomorrow night, you will be invited to dine at nine o'clock, in the Great Hall of the university.' And with that he drained the honey ale and left the inn.

After a few seconds, his silent companions got up and followed him.

The room was left in a chilling silence.

At last Gemma said quietly, 'I'm going to bed.'

'You're daft!' announced Fleabag, perched on the wooden rail at the foot of Rowanne's bed. Gemma was busy washing away the dusty paw prints on the window ledge where the cat had got in.

'I don't need your advice, thank you!' announced Rowanne in a chilly tone. She was sitting on a stool in front of a mirror putting eye make-up on. 'When you've done that, I want you to do my hair, Gemma.'

'Don't you ever say "please"?' complained the cat.

'She's not your servant, you know.'

Rowanne was about to say, 'Of course she is,' but she bit her lip and just mumbled 'please', under her breath.

'Why are you going to all this trouble?' Gemma broke in, surprised at her own daring. 'You're dressed in your best silk gown and you've ordered a carriage... it's obvious that the man hasn't got the Ring. And the boy could have been spinning you a tale just to get drunk for free...'

Rowanne mixed her eye colours vigorously in their little pots. She was angry. 'But he knows *something* – and I intend to find out what. And it is easier to get what I want to know from a man if I dress like a courtier rather than a knight.'

'But he will be most suspicious about what a lady like you is doing here. The curious traveller was a far better disguise.'

Rowanne winced as Gemma tugged at a stray loop of hair which did not want to sit in its place on top of her head. 'I can hardly go to dinner dressed in my leather trousers and coat, can I? I don't even have my formal knightly gear with me. No, don't worry. I know what I'm doing.'

Just then, a maid knocked on the door. Fleabag shot under the bed and hid. 'Your carriage is here, ma'am.' The girl stopped and peered at the end of Fleabag's tail which poked out from under the counterpane. 'Forgive me, ma'am, but I think I left fluff under your bed. I'll get a brush immediately.'

'No, no,' said Gemma in a hurry. 'It's my furry slippers. They're rather old and disreputable, I'm afraid, but I'm very fond of them,' and with that she kicked the whole of Fleabag's backside right under the bed. 'Please don't bother to come back tonight, I'm going to bed early.'

'As you wish,' said the girl and left the room.

Gemma helped Rowanne on with her soft, white angora shawl and watched her walk elegantly out of the door.

Turning back into the room, Gemma went to the dresser and picked up the cream vellum invitation that had arrived that morning. 'To the Lady Knight at the Bush of Broom. His Holiness the Chancellor of All Wizards requests the pleasure of your company for dinner tonight at the University Great Hall.'

'Perhaps she's right,' sighed Gemma. 'She would have looked out of place dressed in travelling clothes at a formal dinner. But I wish she hadn't gone. I have a bad feeling about this Chancellor. What do you think, Fleabag?'

But there was no answer.

Gemma knelt down and peered under the bed. Was he sulking because she'd described him as a 'disreputable old slipper'? Nothing there, except a trail of ash and a half eaten mouse. Really, he could have had his snack outside. She picked the poor thing up by what was left of its tail and threw it out of the window.

Fleabag, meanwhile, had slipped out of the back door while Rowanne was being helped into the carriage (she was never much good at doing anything when she had a skirt on). He had skilfully hidden behind her silks and crouched under the carriage seat, so stealthily that even Rowanne did not know he was there.

At the Great Hall, a footman stepped forward and opened the carriage door.

'I am the Lady Knight Rowanne de Montiland,' she announced, 'I have an invitation to dine with his Holiness the Chancellor of All Wizards.'

The footman bowed obsequiously and helped her down.

She was led up great white marble steps that fanned in a wide semicircle from a piazza up to a huge, pillared front entrance. At the top of the steps, enormous carved oak doors stood open, streaming golden light from candelabras onto the white stone. The footman led her through long corridors decorated with statues of great men and women of wisdom and learning. At last he stopped outside another massive set of doors and bowed again.

'The Lady Knight Rowanne de Montiland,' he announced pompously. As Rowanne stepped inside the room, the doors were shut behind her with a dull thud.

Left alone outside, Fleabag said something very rude in rat language. He had sprung from statue to statue, keeping well out of sight all the way up the corridor, but this last and trickiest manoeuvre of getting into the room with Rowanne had not worked.

He sat in the cobwebby recesses of the plinth that held the bust of one of the previous chancellors – a cross-looking old woman – and washed himself thoroughly.

'She's mad,' he said to himself over and over again. 'I can smell only trouble ahead. And what's worse, she's given her full name and title. Even kittens know that you never give your full name and title to a *wizard* – it only makes it easier for them to work spells on you.'

Once he had cleaned the ash from his fur well enough for it to stop itching, Fleabag curled up for a catnap. To get that stupid woman out of this was going to need brainpower, and that required sleep.

His Holiness the Chancellor of all Wizards was tall, slim and elegant. He had neither the white whiskers nor the pointed hat that Rowanne had half expected. Like all the people from the West, he was fair and broad-boned, and his beard and hair were immaculately cut. He was dressed in a vermilion silk robe, embroidered with gold and yellow flames from the floor-sweeping hem to the superbly cut collar at his throat.

He stood quite still in the centre of a round room. The walls were plain white stone with windows set up high, meeting to make a glass lantern roof.

With a pang in the pit of her stomach, Rowanne realized that he was dressed in a garb to copy the true Fire Wielder and that the room was a copy of the Hall of Light.

She curtseyed, as she felt it was expected. At this, the Chancellor's face lost its suave rigidity and loosened into a smile. 'My dear,' he said, in tones smooth as honey, 'welcome.'

He stepped forward and took her hand to kiss it.

As he bowed over her fingers, he glanced up at her with ice-pale eyes to enjoy the look of shock on her face, when she realized that his hand bore a huge, plain ring set with an opal – an opal with no fire at its heart.

18

Dining on Spells

Still holding her hand, the Chancellor led her to a table in the very centre of the room. It was laid for a formal meal for two, set with cut crystal glasses and exquisitely fine bone china plates.

With perfect courtesy, the Chancellor helped Rowanne to her seat. Another, smaller door opened and a tall, thin young man entered, dressed in a grey silk tunic and trousers. He bowed and kissed Rowanne's hand. As he stood, she knew she recognized him, but could not remember where she had seen him before.

'Allow me to present my son, Sethan.'

Sensing Rowanne's hesitation, the Chancellor continued, 'It was he, of course, whom you met at the Bush of Broom last night. He was so impressed by your generous hospitality to a poor student that he begged to be allowed to return the honour tonight. He will be waiting on us.'

Rowanne tried to murmur something about buying the lad a drink being a pleasure, but a sweet-scented clear white wine was already being poured and Sethan was organizing servants, approaching with trays of exquisite delicacies.

The courses came constantly, dish after dish. Rowanne was coaxed to taste everything. Each was accompanied by a different wine or cordial, all of which she was urged at least to sip.

Slowly, Rowanne became aware that she was unsure of the conversation. The Chancellor seemed to be doing most of the talking – mostly anecdotes about his time as a student and how hard it had been. He moved on to his rise to Chancellorship, how he had struggled against all opposition to prove himself worthy of the position. Then he started to talk about how it had been shown to him by various divinations that still greater things were within his grasp.

He told her that he had acquired the ring – he did not say how – to help him achieve this greatness for which he had been born.

'You see, my dear,' he smiled and patted her hand as Sethan passed a silver dish of fresh truffles for her to try, 'I am destined to be the next Fire Wielder. But unlike the others, with my mystical powers, I will reign for ever.'

Rowanne screwed up her eyes to try to see his face clearly, but it was swimming in and out of her vision. One second it was huge and lowering over her; the next moment he seemed almost to have disappeared.

She must excuse herself. She had to get some air and clear her head…

But try as she might, she could not move, and he was

still talking. 'Very soon, my dear, something wonderful is going to happen. As you know, in the past, a king or a queen needed a Fire Wielder to reign with him or her, but...' (here his face began to swim across the ceiling until Rowanne had to crane her neck right back to see. If only she could get out...)

'... but I will be both. I will be the perfect ruler. Complete in myself.' He pressed his fingertips together and smiled benignly.

Rowanne found herself struggling to say something, but she could not move. Her limbs had become as heavy as lead.

Sethan lifted one more wine glass to her lips with encouraging words to try this, the finest wine from his father's cellar. Rowanne did not want to drink it. She was already so dazed she felt she was slipping away to somewhere she did not want to go. But as soon as the glass was set to her lips, she drank as thirstily as if she had just crossed the Southern Desert.

Everything in her head seemed to shrink, until she was only aware of the tiny point of one candle flame.

The Chancellor slipped the opal ring from his finger and held it to reflect the flame so the fire seemed to burn from within it. Rowanne gasped and began to shake, her eyes staring wildly.

The Chancellor nodded to his son. 'She's ready,' he said. 'Help me carry her.' Rowanne was laid gently onto a chaise longue that had been hidden in the shadows. Servants removed the dining table and the bed was dragged into the very centre of the room. The opal ring was put on a little stand so Rowanne could see it, with the bright flame glinting through it.

The Chancellor drew up a chair and sat beside Rowanne. 'You will answer all my questions, Lady Knight Rowanne de Montiland. You will answer the truth completely and utterly.'

'I will,' she replied. Somewhere, deep in herself, a tiny part still struggled and screamed, but that soon faded to oblivion. There was nothing she could do to fight the drugs and magic that bound her. She was alone and trapped and there was no good sword within her hand's grasp. Not that she could have used it.

'What are you doing here?' asked the Chancellor.

'I am searching for the Queen's Ring.'

'Is this the Queen's Ring?'

'I do not know,' Rowanne replied dully.

'Who is with you?'

'A girl and a cat.'

At the sound of the word 'cat' two things happened. Firstly, Fleabag woke from his doze and realized it was time to take his favourite advice and do some eavesdropping and secondly, the Chancellor faltered and went pale.

'Where is the cat now?'

'I don't know. He was at the Bush of Broom, but he goes his own way. He turns up when he feels like it.'

'What is the cat's name?'

'Fleabag.'

'Is that all?'

'Yes.'

Fleabag smiled in his whiskers, glad that no one alive knew his real name. Only the Queen had known that, so no spells could be put on him very easily – as long as he did not eat or drink in this place.

The Chancellor said quietly to his son, 'As long as the cat is not black, we have nothing to fear. I am sure the time of our downfall cannot be yet. The prophecy spoke of times of glory before the end...'

Then he turned back to Rowanne. 'Who is the girl? What is her name?'

'She is known as Gemma Streetchild. She is a guttersnipe. She travels with me and acts as my maid.'

'Of no importance, father,' said the boy. 'I saw her last night. She was a scared child who sat in the corner and shook at the very sight of me. I am certain she cannot possibly be the Fire Maiden of whom we were warned.'

Again Fleabag sighed with relief. Gemma had never known her real name. 'Streetchild' was a nickname given to her at the palace.

'What do you know about the Ring?' the Chancellor persisted.

Mechanically and with a dull voice, Rowanne told all she knew about the Ring and about the taking of the Fire.

'Why did you come here to look for it?'

Fleabag held his breath. What would she say? Would she explain about Gemma hearing the Ring Fire speak? At the moment the Chancellor was asking all the wrong questions to get the truth from Rowanne. As long as he kept off tack, all might yet be well.

'I came here because it seemed to me that if the Ring is not kept in the houses of royalty, then it must be resting in the halls of wisdom.'

'Why did you come here tonight?'

'Because the boy in the inn made me suspect that the Chancellor might know something to help me find the Ring.'

'By the Quenching of the Fire! She doesn't know!' The boy stamped in fury and frustration.

'I'm not so sure. I think the truth drug is fading. Her mind is bound with strong spells which will hold, but we will not get much further tonight. More of the truth drug might kill her and I don't want that yet. Not until I've drained her of what she knows, and I'm sure she knows *something*.

'I have just not touched on the right trigger question. What have I missed?' The Chancellor paced up and down the circular chamber, stroking his well-trimmed beard. For several minutes the swish of his silken robes was the only sound.

'Father,' said the boy at last. 'She has fallen asleep.'

The man strode over to Rowanne and lifted one of her eyelids. He clicked his fingers a few times, but there was no response. He sighed. 'That's it for tonight. I cannot help but feel we are terribly close to the answer…

'In the morning I must supervise the Convocation of the Wise. I may be able to slip away in the afternoon…'

Then he smiled. 'No. What I will do is to cancel the dinner with the professors of philosophy in the evening. They will be so busy worrying about what is meant by "dinner" they won't notice anyway. During the day, make sure she is comfortable. She will only sleep, I am sure. At dusk I will say the spell that will enable me to take her mind from her into my own.

'We can arrange for her body to be found dead at the bottom of a wall or something. There won't be any problem there. Take her away and get some sleep, boy. Tomorrow will be a long day.'

Fleabag soon found a way out of the Hall. Doors had been left open all over the place. Although the kitchen rubbish bin looked most tempting, he could not risk eating anything in case it was magic or drugged.

First he must get back to Gemma with a report of what had happened. Because he had travelled blindly beneath a carriage seat, he had not been able to see or smell the route, so it was almost dawn before he found the Bush of Broom. All the doors were locked, and Gemma's window was fastened against the night's chilly wind. There was nothing to do except curl up in the stable. But even deep in the warm straw, he could not sleep. Finally he went out again.

Gemma did not sleep well either. She had expected Rowanne back late, but somewhere at the back of her mind, she knew that the knight had not come in at all. She woke, stiff and unrefreshed, and went to the pump in the yard to fetch herself some water – she never saw much point in waiting for a maid to do what she could perfectly well do for herself.

Once again she shivered with the strange notion that she was being watched. She had not felt it for a long time – not since Rowanne had found her ill in the shepherd's hut. She told herself not to be so silly, and the feeling went with the first splash of icy water on her skin. She fed the horses and kicked Fleabag awake with a friendly toe under his black pelt.

But it didn't feel like Fleabag.

She looked closer. It was a human head, hidden under the straw. For a second, she hesitated. Should she call the innkeeper? What if it was someone on the run? Her hands tingled just a little as she pushed the straw aside.

The person was lying very still, perhaps pretending to be dead? It was a man… would he pounce? She stepped back and grabbed a pitchfork. Then she called as quietly and as steadily as she could, 'Stand up. I want to talk to you. If you do as you are told, I will not hurt you.'

The figure slowly stood on his feet and risked looking at his captor.

'Phelan?' she whispered, lowering the pitchfork. 'What are you doing here skulking like a thief?'

He grinned, showing his strong white teeth. 'I *am* a thief, in case you'd forgotten.'

At that second, Fleabag sprang into the stable, wet, cold and in such a panic he made the horses start. Phelan turned and quietened them with a sure hand.

'Quick, quick,' howled the cat. 'Grab what you can and get out of here. The whole town will be after us soon.'

'I know which horses are yours,' Phelan said. 'I'll get them saddled, you pack what you can. I'll meet you in the courtyard.'

'If I value my fur I must get out unseen!' Fleabag wailed.

Gemma had never seen the cat really ruffled before.

'Come with me,' she said, 'I'll pack you in the luggage.' With that, she scooped him up and carried him in under her towel.

Inside the room, Gemma flung clothes into their bags, while Fleabag stalked the room uneasily, recounting the night's adventures in the Great Hall of the university.

'… I got back here at dawn, but couldn't sleep. I knew Phelan had been following us for some time, so I went and found him and told him we really needed his help. I had hoped to get back here in time to warn you, but you know this place has a thing about black cats?'

Gemma nodded as she pushed Rowanne's riding boots into the recesses of her bag.

'Well, I gathered last night that there is some sort of prophecy that a Fire Maiden and a black cat will be the downfall of this particularly evil Chancellor.

'I couldn't resist it, could I? It was too good a joke to miss. I simply had to give them all a scare and have some fun. So as soon as it was really light I went back and I climbed the roof of the Great Hall. I started parading around with my tail in the air, declaring at the top of my voice the imminent demise of the Chancellor and his followers.

'You would never believe the commotion I caused. I'd have kept my whiskers and tail to myself if only I'd known what the result would be... I soon had archers shooting at me, wizards chanting at me and lawyers yelling legal clauses – (though my clawses were better than theirs!) – everyone telling me not to be a bad puss and to come down.

'At first I just laughed at them but then they set the dogs on me... not just nice little lap doggies like the ones at the palace – you know, the sort you say "meow" to and they turn pale and run. No. These were *proper* dogs.'

He stopped talking and cocked an ear. 'And I think I can hear them a few streets away. Is that Rowanne's perfume? Good, smother me in it so I don't smell of cat quite so clearly.

'I got away by jumping into a pond at the back of the library. The dogs lost the scent completely, then I crept round the outside of the city. Oh, I thought I would never see you again!' and he jumped up and gave her a big lick on the nose.

'No time for being daft,' she laughed as she pushed him down on top of a load of dirty washing she had meant to tackle that morning. 'This lot will help to cover your cat smell, too.'

'Pooh!' said Fleabag from under the leather bag flap. 'I see what you mean.'

'Shut UP!' she warned him, pushing him down. 'And whatever happens, lie still.' She snatched at Rowanne's purse, left some coins on the table for payment, swung the bags over her shoulders and went out into the courtyard.

Phelan was there already with the horses bridled and saddled.

He looked at her roughly cut hair and squire's clothes, then handed her a dollop of mud. 'Dirty yourself and keep mum. I'll do the talking.' He mounted a horse lightly and trotted out into the street.

The sounds of dogs howling on leashes could be clearly heard only a few streets away. They obviously had a cat in their sights. There were plenty of the animals, even in Porthwain, but was this a black one? Gemma hoped not.

19

Fire Maiden

The town did not have a proper garrison. A few raggle-taggle soldiers kept some sort of order, but they were not trained like Rupert's men, or the Queen's Guard.

A thickset, fair woman, dressed in the university colours of dark- and light-blue, challenged the fugitives with a raised sword. Even Gemma could see that she did not know how to use it.

'Halt!' she demanded. 'Who goes there?'

'Cough loudly,' Phelan whispered. 'And keep coughing.'

Phelan put on a thick Southern accent. ' 'Tis only a poor man from the South, Phelan Muckraker and his brother Gorthrod. We have been to see the good doctors of this town, but they cannot cure him…'

At this point Gemma coughed until she felt her lungs would burst.

Phelan leaned across the horse's neck and made sure he spat when he spoke. ' 'Tis sad, my brother seems to have the plague and...'

But he could not finish his sentence. The woman stepped back and wiped the spit from her face as she screamed, 'Plague! Plague! Get them out! Plague!'

Gemma buried her head because she could not stop giggling. She hoped her convulsive shaking would be taken for fever instead of uncontrolled laughter. Several passers-by hit the horses with sticks to make them run faster. Galloping wildly they fled past the massive dogs who strained at their leashes, but the cry of 'plague' had gone before and the dogs were pulled back.

In the depths of his saddlebag, Fleabag chuckled as he heard the dogs howling to their masters that there was a cat with the horses. But the masters were either too stupid to understand the dog-speech, or too frightened of the plague to do anything. Within minutes, Phelan, Gemma and Fleabag were riding free as birds down the hill and away from the town.

At the first wood they came to, they pulled rein and stopped to water the animals. The horses had a few cuts where they had been beaten with sticks, but nothing too bad.

Fleabag climbed out of his prison and rolled on the grass to rid himself of the stink of perfume and dirty clothes.

'Clever Phelan. That was almost worthy of a cat's wit!'

Phelan grinned and bowed. 'Sir Cat, I am honoured.'

Gemma clambered down and faced the boy. 'What are you doing here, Phelan? It's not that I'm not pleased to see you, but where did you spring from? And how did you know which horses were ours?'

Phelan grinned 'I was worried when you left Rupertsberg. I wanted to go with you, but – well, I am only a common thief, fit for the scaffold and you are on the Queen's business. You have had dealings with the Ring Fire… As I said, I would put it out as soon as look at it!'

Gemma shook her head, 'But…'

Fleabag put up a paw. 'Let him finish,' he said. 'We'll talk about things being right and wrong later.'

'Well, I followed you. I must have missed you somewhere, for I lost you for several days. I guessed you might be heading for Porthwain and I had some luck with a lift on a farm cart. I thought I had lost you completely until I saw you arriving two days ago. I met up with old Fleabag in the market yesterday and he told me everything you've been up to. He said he had a feeling you might need me, so I wasn't surprised when he came and got me this morning.'

'I'm glad you did.' Gemma smiled, stroking the cat. 'I couldn't bear to think of my best friend as dog-meat.'

Fleabag shivered. 'Don't say such things please, even in jest!'

'At least it explains the horrid feeling I've had for ages that we were being followed. I just wish you'd told me who it was, you wretched cat. I've been really quite scared at times.'

'You never asked,' replied Fleabag coolly as he began to wash.

Gemma took a low swipe at him but turned it into a scratch behind his left ear. 'I forgive you, this time,' she laughed. 'But now we are sitting still for a few moments, you must tell Phelan what happened to Rowanne.'

Fleabag stopped washing and, for once, cracked no jokes.

When the story was told, Gemma bit her lip. 'I had a feeling she was walking into something dangerous, but she wouldn't listen. The only question now is, how are we going to get her out? Facing danger is one thing, but surely we would need the Fire Wielder himself to stand up to the Chancellor?'

'Are you sure you *want* to rescue her?' Fleabag muttered, rolling onto his back and letting the wintry sun warm his tummy.

'Of *course* we are going to rescue her!' replied Gemma indignantly. 'She may be a cat-hater, but she was sent on this quest too... by the Fire Wielder no less.' She paused. 'But what frightens me most is that if the Chancellor of All Wizards says the spell to take Rowanne's mind from her, then he will know everything she knows. Then he may follow us and we may lead him to the Ring. We must rescue her to protect the quest, if for no other reason.'

'True,' mused the cat in his upside-downy voice, as he scratched at a wandering flea. 'But don't you think everything would be easier without her?'

'No!' replied Gemma firmly. 'Bother it, we need her!'

Fleabag wriggled hard, rubbing his back on the fallen pine cones. He had a look of intense concentration on his face. But he could not stay serious for long. At last he chuckled, 'You win! I was only teasing. We'll rescue that cat-hater, but I beg you, never tell any of my relatives what I'm about to do, or I'll be called a poodle for the rest of my days.'

'I am glad,' Gemma said mischievously. 'If Rowanne

wasn't with us you'd have to annoy me instead. I don't think I could face that.'

'Mind you,' Fleabag added, 'if she threatens me one more time after this, I'm off. You can come with me if you like, but a cat can only take so much... Now, let me get some sleep so I can think.'

No one spoke for a while. They sat wrapped in blankets listening to the wind rattling the bare branches of the trees.

The clouds grew thick and heavy early in the afternoon, making it almost dark. Phelan found shelter for the horses in a dip in the ground, more or less out of the wind. The cat snoozed in one of the saddlebags. Phelan lit a small fire and they huddled in blankets while a rabbit roasted.

'Why did you run away at the hostel?' Gemma asked. 'You didn't even say goodbye.'

Phelan shrugged. 'Why should you want me to? My friends and I tried to kill you. I was the cause of your arguing with the Lady Rowanne and not sleeping in luxury in the palace. I had done you nothing but harm. Anyway, being caught in my company is no great honour. If I'd been recognized and put in prison, they might have taken you as well. As I told you before, Prince Rupert has no great reputation for justice.'

'I was lonely when you went. Oh, I know I've got Fleabag, but he's not always there and I need as many friends as I can get.'

'Why do you stick with the Lady Rowanne?'

'Well, she may be difficult, but we were told to help each other. We've just got to find a way of getting on together if possible. Anyway, in an odd sort of a way I'll miss her and – and we can't just let her die. That's just not the right way to do things, is it? It's just like we couldn't let you die. For the moment at least, we belong together. And she has been quite nice to me lately.'

Phelan pulled the blankets closer. The day was getting colder and he could sense the night would be worse. 'For what it's worth, I'll help in whatever way I can. Now look, I don't know what sort of idea that fur-brained cat of yours comes up with. We'd better know what we're going to do if – I mean when we escape. We won't be out of the town until after dark and I think I can smell snow in the air. We'll need to have somewhere we can run straight to and be able to rest. Especially if anyone gets injured.'

Gemma climbed to the lip of the hollow and surveyed the countryside beyond the wood. 'There are farmhouses with barns and sheds further along the road. But a lot depends on how fit Rowanne is. If she can ride we'll make it, but if there's a hue and cry after us or if she's still unconscious, we'll need somewhere closer to hand. Here's as good a place as any, I suppose,' she added, shivering.

'It's going to be a chilly night, I think,' said Phelan.

'I'm freezing already, and I can smell perfectly good rabbit burning,' moaned Fleabag as he jumped down to the ground, stretching his back, tail and all three paws.

'Now,' said Fleabag, his mouth full of food. 'As I told you this morning, there seems to be some sort of prophecy about a Fire Maiden and a black cat which terrifies the wits out of this Chancellor. I pushed my luck a bit this morning, by acting the black cat part, but what I really needed was a Fire Maiden with me. So what we will do is this…'

Phelan left the horses in a small side-alley near the Great Hall. They were good animals and he knew they would come when he whistled.

As there were few guards of any sort, they managed to reach the main door before they were challenged. Gemma held herself tall and tried to imitate Rowanne's 'imperious' voice. 'I have had a dream. I need to speak to the Chancellor immediately. There is great danger for him at the very door of his house.'

The guard bowed and swiftly led the young woman and her attendant to the doors of the small round chamber.

'You may leave us!' said Gemma, waving her hand dismissively.

The guard looked surprised but obeyed. As soon as he was out of sight, Phelan opened the satchel on his shoulder and let Fleabag jump down to the floor. Gemma then threw her cloak back to show the flame-red silk dress she had borrowed from Rowanne's baggage. Phelan lit the two large torches that Gemma had smuggled in under her cloak, and knocked on the door.

There was no answer, but low voices could be heard within. With heart pounding Phelan threw the doors open and announced, 'The Fire Maiden has come with her black cat to claim your life. Tremble and fear!'

At first the Chancellor threw back his head and laughed scornfully. 'Don't be silly children,' he snapped. 'Go away, I am busy. Go and play your games somewhere else.' But Gemma did not move. Fleabag jumped up on the table where a great book of illuminated texts lay open with phials and plants neatly arranged next to it.

Meanwhile Gemma could hear Phelan stealthily

making his way around the room to reach Rowanne lying on her couch in the shadows. Once he had managed to get her out, all they had to do was run... *all* they had to do! She could feel the fear tightening in her chest and the noise of blood pounded deafeningly in her ears.

Abruptly the Chancellor stopped laughing. He took a swipe at Fleabag with a stone pestle. But his erratic movement missed the cat and sent some of the glass phials crashing to the floor.

Sethan sprang forward and grabbed Fleabag, who twisted in the boy's grasp and scratched his face and eyes again and again, until blood flowed profusely. In agony he dropped the cat who sprang back to the table and faced his foe, spitting hideously.

But the Chancellor seemed to be ignoring everything. He was intent on making signs in chalk on the floor and chanting an ugly sounding rhyme.

'How... how did you get in here?' sobbed Sethan, nursing his face.

'There were hardly any guards,' replied the cat.

'But we don't need them. The place is ringed with magic. Only the Ring Fire itself could get past the spells we have placed...'

'Shut up!' yelled his father. 'A spell must have slipped somewhere. Probably one *you* made. I'm always telling you to be more careful. It *must* be your fault. The Ring Fire could not come this far north without me knowing. The Fire Wielder's every step is watched and reported to me daily. At this very moment he is asleep in the palace at Harflorum.'

With that the Chancellor lifted his arms high and began to chant out loud.

'Watch out!' yelled Fleabag, as bright blue flame sprang from the chalk lines and surrounded the Chancellor. From the centre of it came an arc of greenish light that reached out for Gemma.

The girl was too scared to move. She just held onto her torches and thought very hard of the day the Fire Wielder placed a little Fire into her palms.

'I won't forget,' she whispered. 'I won't forget!'

As she did so, the green light faded, but the blue flames around the Chancellor rose even higher.

Again he threw an arc of light, but this time it was purple. Again Gemma thought of the Fire in her hands and again the purple light faded.

Drawing all his strength and power to himself, the Chancellor summoned lightning from the sky.

This time Gemma was so terrified, she dropped her torches and grabbed the big book from the table to hold over her head.

With an immense crack of thunder, the lightning hit the book, setting it alight.

'Not my precious book!' screamed the Chancellor, jumping through the flames to grab it back. But as he did so, the long trailing skirts of his robe caught in the blue flames and he fell to the floor, screaming.

Sethan rushed to his side, but he too was caught in the hungry pool of cerulean heat.

Gemma could not bear the sight of their agony. She had not meant to hurt anyone. She reached out to help them, but both father and son cowered back at the sight of her. 'Not the Ring Fire! Take it away, the sight burns us...'

By this time the chamber was filled with attendants bearing water and fire brooms. But no one could get near the raging blue flames which roared and towered high above them until they licked the glass lantern roof.

'Run!' yelled Phelan. 'The whole place will be alight soon. We can do nothing.'

Rowanne was draped across his left shoulder, so Gemma took her other arm and between them they dragged her out of the room and along the corridor.

In the smoke and confusion, no one noticed them leaving. Fleabag soon appeared by their side and the four of them ran out into the night.

20

A Cottage in the Rocks

Everything was in turmoil when the three shadowy figures and the cat reached the flight of stairs down from the Great Hall to the piazza below. Snow was falling, making the steps slippery. Hundreds of people were pushing and shoving – some trying to get inside with pails of water, others fleeing the burning building in panic.

The four were buffeted and trampled. Gemma and Phelan dragged the all but lifeless Rowanne between them while the cat went ahead to bite the ankles of any who got in the way. The hubbub was so great that Phelan's piercing whistle could not be heard by the waiting horses and slowly the roar of the flames behind them was coming closer.

'Wait here,' called Fleabag as he dashed between the thundering, crushing feet, risking life and paw to reach the little alley where the horses stood quietly.

With one leap, he gained the mare's saddle. Try as he might, he could not whistle, but he managed to cajole and bully the two ponies into following. They had to pick their way gingerly through the seething confusion, but it did not take long to reach the steps of the Hall where Phelan and Gemma were framed against the flames and smoke. Behind them masonry was beginning to crash down.

A kindly man helped to heave Rowanne onto the back of one of the ponies.

When he saw Fleabag seated grimly on the back of the horse with Gemma behind him, the gold of the flames reflected in their wide eyes, he looked from one to another in amazement and shook his head. 'So it is true: the black cat and the Fire Maiden have come at last. All speed to you!'

Phelan took the rein of the pony carrying Rowanne. Carefully they eased their way through the team of fire-fighters and made for the north road.

The snow was falling faster as they left the noise and flames behind them. Fleabag jumped down and led the way down to the little hollow where they had camped earlier. Dismounting, Phelan coaxed the banked fire into life again, and they made camp as best they could. But it was a long, cold night.

At first light they struck camp. The snow had stopped, leaving only a light sprinkling, but the sky was still lowering blackly. Gemma wanted to get on the road again as quickly as possible.

But there was something she had to do first.

'Phelan, I want you to believe me when I say this. We all need you. I know what you have been, but that doesn't make you too bad to be a friend. Please don't disappear again. Without you, I won't get to wherever I'm supposed to be going. I can't look after Rowanne without help – she needs you too. And Fleabag needs someone to insult. Say you'll stay with us?'

Phelan was inspecting the ground and kicking at the snow with the worn toes of his shoes. He was quiet for a few moments. 'Very well, just until the Lady is well enough to look after you all... and to make sure she's not going to desert you again. I'll not stand for that a second time. But I'll have nothing to do with the search for the Ring if you don't mind. All that sort of thing makes me... feel ill.'

Gemma nodded. 'I can't pretend I understand, but I'm grateful.'

Phelan helped Gemma heave Rowanne over the back of Pudding, the fat little pack pony, then he mounted the mare and took Pudding's rein. Gemma was glad to be back with Porridge again. Fleabag chose to walk. He said he wanted the exercise.

'What we need to do first,' suggested Gemma, 'is get back on the main road north by north-west. I should have realized things would go wrong when I heard Porthwain was slightly out of the way.'

They rode with the watery sun at their backs for several days. The winds became increasingly bitter, but the snow turned into icy, cutting sleet. Slowly the ground rose ahead of them into the foothills of the Gwithennick Mountains which lay solidly across the path as far as the eye could see, from the north-west to the north-east.

One miserable morning they were camping in a barn

which was about as waterproof as a net curtain. Gemma was trying to make Rowanne drink a little, when Fleabag came and sat in front of the pile of spitting damp sticks that passed for a fire.

'It's no good. I hate having wet fur. We have to stop somewhere warm for the winter.'

Phelan was sorting wood, looking for something that might be burnable. He stopped and looked out of the door at the terrain. 'I've never seen mountains before. What are they like in winter? Are they warmer than here?'

Fleabag shivered and shook his pelt. 'No. Worse. Much worse.'

'Then my vote is with Fleabag. We need to stop to get Rowanne better if nothing else... and with all due respect to Gemma, I think you have to sit and think about what you are doing. Hearing voices that tell you to go north by north-west sounds a bit potty, if you don't mind my saying so. It doesn't mean it's not true, but you need a practical plan as well. Rest, warmth and food will help.'

Phelan stamped on a dry branch and it snapped with a loud noise. Gemma jumped, but Rowanne did not so much as flicker an eyelid. She was not improving.

For the first time, Gemma began to question why she was on this strange journey at all. In the beginning, while the memory of the Queen and her loving care were so fresh in Gemma's mind, everything had been simple. She had obeyed without question. But now it seemed so long ago – and as Phelan said, it sounded a bit daft.

But if her quest was real, dare she stop? They had wasted valuable weeks at Rupertsberg. Since Rowanne had become caught in the Chancellor's spells at Porthwain they had been travelling painfully slowly. Already it was early November, and the year and a day was slipping away. If they rested for the winter months it would mean they would have to turn back as soon as the snow melted – having found nothing.

Here they were, at the foot of the Gwithennick Mountains. Snow would block the north by north-west road before they could reach the mountain passes. They could neither go on nor go back. She looked at the others. She owed it to them to rest – and to think.

She nodded. 'I agree,' she said. 'But where shall we go?'

Phelan stood up and sheltered his eyes against the cutting winds. He peered all around. 'What do you fancy? A farm where we can beg work for the winter and earn our keep, or a place of our own?'

Gemma looked worried.

'The farms around here are terribly poor and run-down,' Phelan continued. 'They are all owned by the University and it seems nothing has been done to maintain them for years. I don't think we'd find anywhere which could afford to keep us for the winter – however hard we work.'

'Then it must be a place of our own,' Fleabag said decisively.

Phelan put down the branch he was breaking. 'If you will lend me the horse for the day, I will ride ahead and see what I can find. You might as well rest here. It's as good a place as any.' He looked at the huddled group and felt sorry for them. Everyone was so cold and wet.

'Take her,' said Gemma. 'But try and be back by nightfall, or we'll worry.'

Phelan brushed himself down and saddled the mare.

Gemma handed him a thick blanket and some food. He turned the horse's head to the road and shivered. Everywhere looked so grey and miserable. The trees were bare and more rain was coming. These days the sky seemed to be perpetually weeping. Squeezing the horse's flanks with his heels, Phelan urged her into a trot and set off.

'You know what Rowanne would say, don't you?' said Fleabag unhappily.

'What?'

' "You'll never see that horse or that boy again. He'll ride away, sell it and go his own way." '

'Do you believe that?'

'No. Do you?'

Gemma shook her head. 'No. I always get a fierce burning feeling in my hands when something's wrong. I don't get that with him.' She poked at the fire and wished she had left it alone, for the charred twigs fell apart and the flames went out.

'I wish you could do something useful with your burning hands like light us a real fire,' moaned Fleabag.

'That'll be the day. But it would be nice, wouldn't it?'

The hours dragged on in their grey, damp, unhappy way. In the early afternoon Gemma took the ponies for a run to warm them up a bit. As she returned, she saw a rider in the distance, coming in their direction very fast.

As the heavy thud of hooves approached they began to slow, as the horse was eased to a standstill.

Phelan swung down to the ground and ran down the little slope to the derelict barn.

'I've found just the place!' he proclaimed breathlessly. 'It's a bit tumbledown, but it's perfect. It's a deserted goatherd's hut in a small cleft, sheltered from the wind. If we hurry, we'll just get there by nightfall!'

Taking a cloth from his saddlebag, he rubbed the mare down and gave her a handful of bran. Then he helped the others pack. Heaving Rowanne up and across Pudding's saddle was a struggle and she had to be tied into place. At last the mare was cool enough to have a drink, after which they set off as fast as they could.

The weather held dry for them. A biting wind cut across the barren landscape and seemed to want to drive them back from the foothills. As they went on, sharp rises of rocky outcrops suddenly dipped into marshy flats, then rose steeply again. But the road was fairly good and kept north by north-west, much to Gemma's relief.

A few crofters' cottages were dotted across the landscape. Skinny, chilled-looking cattle and sheep huddled in the lee of anything which afforded shelter. As the light began to fail, Gemma became increasingly worried. The road was rising well above the plain now and the rocks were becoming slippery with evening ice. There were no buildings at all within sight.

Phelan caught the expression on her face and gave her a hearty slap on the back.

'Not far now. Look!' He pointed ahead to where the road seemed to detour around a rockfall. There was still no sign of a dwelling of any kind. Gemma bent her head doggedly to go on, patting Porridge's neck and talking gently to her. The pony was very tired.

Secretly, Gemma was beginning to wonder whether they had missed the cottage in the evening shadows.

Suddenly Phelan gave a whoop of delight and sprang to the ground. He led the mare away from the road and across a short grassy slope. Then he disappeared. 'We're here!' he yelled triumphantly. 'Come on!'

Fleabag jumped down from Pudding, where he had been curled up on Rowanne's back to help keep her warm. The pony followed the cat and Gemma came next leading the tired, patient Porridge.

The cottage was certainly 'a bit tumbledown'. It had been invisible from the road because it was little more than a roof across a wide split in a rock. The front was built of dry-stone walling with a wooden door. But as Phelan had said, it was at least better shelter than they had been used to.

The cottage was roughly triangular. The door to the first room was still more or less on its hinges, but had little roof left. It was big enough to shelter the ponies from the wind. Behind this, a second, smaller room was built deep into the rock. It was very dark, but dry and just about big enough to let everyone lie down comfortably.

Phelan managed to get a small fire going. Bread and water were passed round and, for the first time in over a week, everyone was warm.

Soon Phelan and Fleabag were asleep, but Gemma's night was disturbed by dreams. They were not unpleasant. In fact they reminded her of something far off – something, some time which had been good. They seemed to be echoes of the things she used to see when she watched the Fire in the Queen's Ring.

When she woke, she found her hands were burning more fiercely than ever.

Carefully she climbed across Rowanne and went to build up the fire, which was slowly falling to ash.

She sat staring into the flames until dawn. Phelan was

right. What was she doing on this quest? Did she only *wish* the Queen had sent her? What possible use could she be to anyone? What did she know about the Ring or the Fire?

As dawn began to lighten the corners of the little shelter, Phelan woke. 'Did you know you were thinking aloud?' he asked quietly, squatting down beside her.

Gemma hung her head. 'Sorry.'

Phelan laughed. 'Don't be. I didn't want to make you doubt what you are doing, I just felt you needed time to rest and think. With winter coming on, it seemed like a good time to stop.'

Gemma looked at him through hazy tears. 'But I don't *know* what I'm doing or where I'm going, or why. I don't know how anyone could ever hope to find the Ring in all this wide land. Rowanne might know some answers – but she's in this strange magic sleep. Ever since we left Porthwain I've been worried sick that we came too late and that the spell to take her mind from her has already been said. Are we just carrying the shell of Rowanne? Can we do anything?'

Phelan turned to look at the knight. She was very pale and breathing in a slow, shallow rhythm. He lifted her wrist and felt the throb of life in her veins.

'I don't know,' he said. 'I have some knowledge of herbs and fungi I picked up while living in the woods. I can try and rouse her. But I think it's going to need something stronger than potions to heal her.'

'You mean more magic?'

Phelan shook his head. 'No. Something stronger even than magic.'

He left Gemma looking wide-eyed and worried as he

got up to go and fetch water. He found Fleabag devouring a rather scrawny rat outside the door.

'Awful hunting around here,' he moaned. 'Couldn't you do better than this? I ordered the best hotel with room service and milk on a saucer every morning. I'm not paying for this!' he grumbled, 'I'm complaining to the management!'

Phelan paused and went back. He picked up the cat by the scruff of the neck and looked him in the eye. 'I bested you once, cat. I can best you again. Watch it!' he grinned, giving Fleabag a friendly cuff as he put him down gently.

Fleabag looked as sheepish as a cat can. 'Would you care for some rat's leg – or maybe a nice bit of ear? A bit chewy but very tasty – sir?'

21

Fungus Soup

For the first few days, they divided their time between repairing the cottage and looking for food. Fleabag caught some partridges and a hare and Phelan bought vegetables and hay from one of the nearby crofts.

Much of the roof-support timber was still usable. It just had to be pushed back into place and held firm with narrow wedges of stone. The roof itself they remade with flat fir branches covered with cut turfs. They twisted ropes from heather stems to lash the roof down and weighted it with small boulders.

There was plenty of dead wood for the fire and the cottage soon became warm and pleasant.

Everyone began to feel better – except Rowanne.

One day Phelan came back with a large piece of bark and a bag of toadstools. Banking up the fire so it smouldered rather than burned, he began to scrape some greenish-grey slime from the bark into the cooking pot. This he mixed with water and let simmer for several hours. He would not let Gemma cook the evening meal, as the fire had to be kept at a steady temperature and there was only one cooking pot.

Fleabag was not too bothered – he had caught a trout in a nearby river and was quite happy to eat it raw. Gemma chewed dried fruit and scowled.

'What are you doing? I'm famished, and that stuff stinks. I wouldn't eat it if I was dying of hunger.'

Phelan concentrated on stirring the pot. 'You're not *supposed* to eat it. It's a potion I'm making out of a powerful lichen which stimulates the mind. Its effects are dramatic. I've seen people jump over cliffs after drinking the juices, because they think something terrible is after them. There's never anything there, except perhaps a mouse. It makes everything bigger and louder and brighter. I thought a few drops might do something for Rowanne.'

'Shock her out of it, you mean?'

'Sort of.'

'Well, can you give her a nice mentality while you're at it?' enquired Fleabag. 'Turn her into a cat-lover so she can treat me with the respect I deserve.'

'She already *does* treat you as you deserve,' observed Gemma. 'Can you eat that fish in the other room with the horses or, even better, outside altogether? I can't stand the sound of you chewing when I'm so hungry!'

With a 'humph' of disgust, Fleabag picked up his particularly juicy fish head and stalked out, tail erect and fur fluffed. The reception he got from the horses was fairly similar and he ended up behind the woodpile in disgrace.

'What happens if she goes and does something daft and we can't stop her? She's very strong.' Gemma was worried.

'I don't really know. I reckon in her state it will need quite a lot to waken her at all. She's been like this for almost three weeks now. She's hardly moved and her muscles will be weak. She hasn't eaten much either, so I reckon we could hold her down.'

Gemma wasn't happy. 'How long does it take for the effects to wear off?'

'Usually about a day, but you can get flashbacks for up to a year.'

'Is it worth the risk?' Gemma asked quietly. 'Is there something a bit milder in your bag? Something a bit less drastic?'

Phelan spread out the pile of toadstools. 'It's very difficult to find anything once the snow falls, but there's a small wood in a hollow over the ridge. It's sheltered from the mountain wind and feels a lot milder.' He picked up a white puffball that looked soft and delicate. 'This one is called "Dreamcloud". It's a sleep inducer. And this,' he held up a thick liver-like fungus about the size of his hand, 'is delicious if fried, especially with fish, but it won't help Rowanne today. These orange ones I can dry and we can eat them at a pinch. They aren't poisonous, but they're very chewy and taste like old socks. It depends how hungry we get.'

'Oh look, that one on the floor! I know that, it's a mushroom. That's clever of you to find it at this time of year.'

'Er...' his thin hands grabbed towards the small brown fungus which he had tried to keep out of sight. '... don't touch it. It's "deathcap".' Then he said nothing else.

'What does that do?' asked Gemma doubtfully.

'There's enough poison in that to kill half of Prince Rupert's army and make the other half very sick.'

'Ugh!' she jumped back. 'What did you pick that for?'

Phelan hung his head. 'In case... in case of a lot of things.'

He went back to stirring the pot vigorously. At last the lichen was reduced to a smooth, greyish sludge in the bottom of the pot. He put two drops of the stuff into a cup of water and stirred it. 'Feed her this on a spoon. If she starts coming to, then stop straight away. I don't want her going crazy.'

Gemma took the cup and picked up the spoon. Suddenly she had such a stabbing pain in her hands that she dropped everything.

'Hey, watch out!' moaned Phelan. 'I had to climb a difficult tree to get that bark, then it took me hours to get that mixture just right. Don't go flinging it around!'

'What's the matter?' enquired Fleabag, sliding his sleek fur around the doorpost. 'Pooh! what's that stink?'

'That "stink",' Phelan said, huffily, 'was the potion I've just spent hours brewing to try to revive Rowanne. Now Gemma's just flung half of it away.'

Gemma hung her head. 'I'm sorry. It's just that something seemed to stab right into my hands.'

'Let's have a look,' said Fleabag, climbing into Gemma's lap. She opened her palms, but there was nothing there – no mark or swelling. Fleabag sniffed her hands and licked them a little.

'Never mind,' said Phelan. 'I have more. Just be careful this time, will you? Pass the cup.'

Fleabag put a paw on Gemma's arm. 'Wait. When Phelan passes you the mixture, just hold the cup for a minute and see what happens.'

Gemma looked at the cat. 'You're odd,' she said.

'Not as odd as I suspect *you* are,' he retorted. 'Just do as you're told, will you?'

Phelan mixed the potion again and passed Gemma the cup. Nothing happened.

'Now, bring the cup slowly towards Rowanne...'

'Ouch!' Gemma jerked her arms back, again spilling everything. 'I felt as if I was being burned!'

Fleabag sniffed at her hands again. 'I know what it is,' he announced triumphantly. 'It's the Ring Fire. That's what it is. The little bit of Fire the Fire Wielder gave you is warning you not to give that stuff to Rowanne. It's wrong for her.'

Gemma and Phelan looked wide-eyed at the cat. Then Phelan looked wide-eyed at Gemma.

'You mean you have the Ring Fire, and I've been treating you just like – just like *anyone*! I... I've even been rude to you... I'm sorry, I'm so sorry!' And before Gemma knew it, he was on his knees.

'Oh, don't be stupid!' Gemma was frightened. 'I *am* "just anyone". If a street child can't be friends with a thief, what good is anything? I'd have no friends then, except this disgusting cat who keeps trying to make me eat rat...'

'It was a very *fresh* rat,' muttered Fleabag.

'... and what good are friends on their knees? I need people who are rude to me. Get up and insult me again, for goodness' sake! Can't you see I'm frightened?'

Fleabag curled up under Gemma's chin and purred.

'What are you getting upset about? You often get a burning in your palms when something is wrong, don't you? So why shouldn't it be the Ring Fire warning you not to give the potion to Rowanne?'

'Because the Ring Fire is back at the palace with the Fire Wielder.'

'Except for the little bit that I saw him give you. The bit he told you never to forget.'

Gemma opened her cupped hands and looked at them. They looked like ordinary hands, stained and callused from hard work. Indeed, they *were* very ordinary hands – except that in her palms there burned a tiny speck of flame!

22

Ring Fire!

As everyone stared at the tiny flame in Gemma's cupped hands, it seemed to fade slightly as her hands began to tremble.

'Hold it! Hold it steady!' commanded Fleabag. 'Think of the Fire Wielder… Think of the Queen… Hold it!'

Gemma's hands steadied, but tears began to stream down her cheeks. 'I'm scared,' she whispered. 'Help me!'

'The Ring Fire only stays where it is welcome,' said Fleabag quietly. 'Do you want to hold it?'

'Yes.' Gemma's voice came choked and hoarse. 'It is so beautiful and calm. I want it, but I'm scared of it as well.'

Phelan and Fleabag held their breath, staring with wide eyes as the little flame in Gemma's hands grew stronger and steadier. Even Rowanne had her eyes open. She seemed to be aware of the tiny light. Gemma brought it closer for her to see.

Rowanne opened her mouth as if she was trying to say something, but couldn't.

'There,' said Gemma. 'Would you like to hold it?' She opened the knight's hand and tried to place the flame in it. The little light would not stay; it slid like a bright jewel back into Gemma's palm. But where the flame had touched her, Rowanne's hand began to move.

'Look at that!' gasped Phelan. 'Do it again, Gemma...'

This time Gemma placed the flame into Rowanne's other hand. The same thing happened. Rowanne's eyes opened wide with longing.

Fleabag said very softly, 'It was her mind he tried to take. Try putting the flame onto her head...'

The room was heavy with silence. Trembling with anxiety, Gemma lifted the flickering little light to Rowanne's face and moved it gently across the knight's forehead to rest in front of her eyes. 'Wake up, Rowanne, wake up,' she said softly.

'As I said,' murmured Phelan, as Rowanne stirred and sat up, 'it needed something greater than magic.'

23

King of the Castle

Over the next few days Rowanne quickly regained her strength. From the moment they had left the burning Hall, she had been aware of what was happening all around her, but she had had no ability to move or respond. She had spent almost three weeks trapped inside the cocoon of her own body – a terrible situation for one so accustomed to command.

She had lost a great deal of weight, having only taken soup and water for all that time. Fleabag celebrated the return of his arch-enemy by leading a small mountain goat and her kid to their cottage, so Rowanne had milk to drink as well as the usual rabbit and fish.

It was not long before she was up and about, and taking her share in the daily tasks.

One day, Rowanne and Gemma came toiling up the steep slope to the cottage with huge bundles of firewood piled on top of the branches of what looked like half a tree they were dragging home. They were rosy cheeked and laughing as they struggled along, singing an old song in the afternoon sun. Heavy snow clouds were gathering in the sky around the mountain tops; the tracks they were making would soon be covered by snow.

As they came nearer, Phelan could see that Fleabag was riding on top of the wood, clinging on for dear life. 'I'm the King of the Castle!' he proclaimed.

'Get down, you dirty rascal!' laughed the others. Gemma tried to shove him off and Rowanne wiggled the boughs until Fleabag lost his balance and fell upside down in the snow.

'Is that the way to treat your future King?' asked the cat. 'Little do you know I've been hiding the Queen's Ring under a knot in my fur for months. Tomorrow I will produce it and astound you all. Then I'll have your heads cut off for insubordination, then you can all come to my coronation feast.'

'We won't be able to eat much if we've had our heads cut off!' complained Rowanne.

'That's the idea, of course. All the more for me.' At this the laughing cat gave an enormous jump in the air. But the somersault did not work and turned into a flop into the snow.

Having completely lost his dignity, Fleabag began to chase his tail, spinning round and round and making the soft snow fly into a small blizzard.

'You know,' Phelan said thoughtfully, 'I think Fleabag ought to be King. He'd make people laugh and forget their worries. Everyone would be happier. Too many people went in fear of Prince Rupert and his henchmen, and I'm glad the Ring wasn't found in his palace. He rules by fear and force – that's not what being a king is about.'

As soon as he stopped speaking he realized he had insulted the cousin and fiancé of the Lady Knight. Half of him wished he could have swallowed his words. The other half was glad it had been said.

Rowanne went very pale and still. For a few seconds he was quite afraid that she would lash out at him.

Then she breathed deeply. 'You're quite right. While I couldn't speak or move, I did a lot of thinking. I'm so ashamed that I was a part of all that once. I'm sorry, Phelan – for everything: for the things I have said to you, and about your parents. When we get back, I'd like you to work for me. I have a great deal to do in Rupertsberg. You know what's most needed there. Will you help?'

He felt a lump come into his throat and pretended to be too busy to talk as he tugged the wood inside. 'Hurry up,' he called, 'Let's get this wood in the dry before the snow starts again.'

That evening Gemma made a venison stew. The onions and turnips they had bought from the nearest croft were rather bruised and soft, but the taste was heavenly after a hard day's work collecting wood. Everyone agreed the gravy needed a good hunk of home-made bread, but that was not to be had, so they all drank the juices from their bowls and felt content.

'What will happen when the Ring is found?' asked Gemma. 'Will the finder automatically become the King or Queen at once?'

Rowanne shifted her position and looked thoughtful. 'I don't think so. The Fire Wielder told us it had been hidden where only a King or Queen would dare to look, so it is unlikely that anyone else would find it. But the Ring will have to be taken back to the Hall of Light to be formally identified by those that know it.' (Here Gemma's face burned, but she said nothing.) 'Then the Fire will have to be put back in the Ring. It won't go into a Ring that isn't the right one, and if the wrong person is holding it, the Fire will fade. The Ring doesn't *make* a monarch – it just confirms the right person for everyone to see.'

'What *is* the Ring Fire?' asked Gemma nervously.

To everyone's surprise, Phelan started to speak. 'It comes from somewhere else – not another planet, just another place. It is more than goodness and truth and all that sort of thing: it is alive as well. I heard tell once that it is the heart of the Fire Giver, watching over us. Who knows?'

Rowanne looked at him curiously. 'Where did a thief-lad learn that?'

Phelan hung his head and mumbled, 'Nowhere. I just heard.'

And he would say no more.

Fleabag did not like the uneasy silence that followed. 'When I am King,' he said loudly, 'I shall have Gemma come and cook for me every day. Since we have had her in charge of the cooking pot I have almost gone off mouse.'

'Only almost,' chuckled Gemma, 'I saw you this morning with a nice fat one you were having for breakfast.'

'That wasn't mouse. That was shrew!' roared Fleabag indignantly. 'I'll make a rule about everyone having extra lessons in telling a mouse from a shrew. Vitally important, that will be. Yes, I must make a note of that,' he muttered, as he licked some gravy from behind his whiskers. Then he settled into a more comfy spot, wrapped his tail around his head and went to sleep.

Rowanne was watching Phelan out of the corner of her eye. She could see he was upset and she desperately wanted to make him feel better: 'I meant what I said earlier, you know,' she said. 'I really would like your help to put things right.'

Phelan felt confused by her offer. 'I'll think about it,' was all he would say.

'Will you marry the Prince?' asked Gemma, changing the subject.

'Goodness me, no!' laughed the Lady Knight. 'I think I knew I wouldn't as soon as he asked me. Although,' she hung her head, 'I was taken with the idea for a while...'

'But if you don't marry him, how will you bring about all these changes you are planning?'

'Ah!' said Rowanne with great satisfaction. 'That's the really good part. As a close member of the family, I have the right to challenge him to his title.'

'What sort of challenge?'

'It's usually sword fighting or wrestling, but it could be chess. Any contest of skill, really. Three challenges are held and the winner of two out of the three may take the title.'

'And what if you don't win?' asked Gemma, quite pale.

Rowanne looked serious. 'If I can't beat an idiot like him, then I don't deserve to rule the city. But if I do win, it can go back to its old name of Erbwenneth. I'll have none of this Rupertsberg nonsense when I'm Princess. And another thing, I can't believe that Queen Sophia knew what was happening there, for I'm sure she wouldn't have stood for it. So I'll insist that the monarch comes to visit at least once a year.'

'It'll be a pleasure,' came Fleabag's fur-muffled voice from next to the fire.

24

Phelan Turns Back

Now that Rowanne was well enough to look after Gemma and to help with hunting and repairs, Phelan became more and more quiet and withdrawn. The snow was becoming thicker and each fall lasted longer. Wolves could be heard howling in the mountains behind the cottage.

'Doesn't "Phelan" mean "wolf"?' asked Rowanne one night.

Despite the warm crackling fire, Phelan shivered. 'Yes, but it's not a name I'd have chosen. Wolves are yet another thing that I'm frightened of. I think I had a different name when I was a child, but I can't remember it.

' "Phelan" was what the thieves called me when they took me in – I was grey all over with dirt and had long matted hair. I'd been living rough for quite a while.'

'Would you like to be called something else?' Gemma asked kindly.

'Like Catslayer!' chipped in Rowanne mischievously.

'No. Phelan will do fine – unless I discover who I really am one day… I don't think I'd answer to anything else.'

'What do you mean about discovering who you really are?' Gemma asked.

Phelan shrugged. 'I know my parents ran a shop that sold bits and pieces – old furniture and junk, I remember that. I don't mean I'm anyone special. Far from it. It's just that when they were killed, I was forced to become someone I'm not. I didn't *like* being a thief; it was just the only way I could survive. At first it was fun – being big and brave and macho like the others. But I think we all ended up unhappy.

'One of the men had been a goldsmith. He'd been muddled up in a fraud and although he realized what he had done was wrong, he didn't dare go back. All that skill wasted. He was utterly miserable and frustrated.

'Another was a farmer – and a good one by all accounts. He was chased off his land by Rupert's soldiers. The Prince wanted the land to build a pleasure garden, of all things! The farmer had nowhere else to go but the woods. It turned him strange. He had been a decent bloke once but he became the most vicious and mean of the lot. He was convinced that everyone was out to get him, and that we were all after the bits and pieces he had put together over the years. It was frightening to watch.'

'But what about *you*, Phelan?' urged Gemma. 'Who would *you* like to be?'

He shrugged. 'I don't really know. Most of all in the world I want to get a job and find friends. I want to be able to live without hurting people.' He thought for a moment. 'I could do something like Aelforth at the hostel, maybe. Then I'd feel as if I was being useful for once, instead of destroying all the time.'

Rowanne was about to make her offer again, but she felt that now was not the time. If he wanted to be her steward in Rupertsberg, he would when he was ready.

Fleabag jumped into Phelan's lap. 'I'll employ you as tummy scratcher if you like. You will be paid in dead rats and a few fleas when I can spare them!'

Phelan laughed and pushed the incorrigible cat back onto the floor.

Long after the others were asleep, Phelan lay awake thinking. What was worrying him most was that he felt uncomfortable. Suddenly he was in the company of a Knight of the Queen's Guard who wanted him to work for her, a highly intelligent talking cat and worst of all, someone who carried the Ring Fire. He did not *belong* with them. They were special and important. He felt small and out of place.

By dawn he realized he wanted to leave. Now Rowanne was strong again they did not need him. He knew he could no longer follow them at a distance. The icy winter closing in all around meant that he would not survive in the mountains on his own.

He would have to go away and never see them again.

Phelan sighed and stood up. He went to the outside door and looked out into the night. By starlight he could see where the hills became mountains. It all looked very lonely and forbidding.

He would have to go at dawn. If he left before they got up, he could walk to one of the villages on the plain by nightfall. There must be a farmer or a workman somewhere who needed another hand. He would work for his food and shelter and wouldn't ask for money.

When spring came he could think again. He crept back into the room where the animals were stabled. He milked the goat and drank the warm sweet liquid. He tried to think. There was nothing he needed to take with him. After all, he had nothing anyway. He knew Rowanne would not begrudge him the cloak she had given him. That was all.

Then he remembered the deathcap toadstool he had left to dry in a gap in the wall. He slipped that into his pocket. He would rather eat that than be caught by wolves; its effect was very swift.

He went back to the fire and sat in a corner. There he dozed a little until the first pale streaks of light coming under the door roused him.

Softly, Phelan stepped over the sleeping Gemma and Rowanne, but he had not counted on Fleabag having a pre-breakfast nibble so early. The cat was just washing his paws and talking to Porridge, the more intelligent of the two ponies, when Phelan stumbled over him.

'Where are you off to?' challenged the cat.

'I... I decided to try to go down to one of the farms to buy hay for the horses. There's no grass worth speaking of now. And while I was out, I was going to try to buy a bag of flour. Gemma was saying how she missed bread.'

Fleabag picked at a flea for dessert and said, 'You'd better take the horse and the pack pony for that lot. How much money did Rowanne give you?'

'Bother that cat,' thought Phelan. 'Why does he never mind his own business?'

'Er, oh, I forgot the money.'

Fleabag immediately went to call Rowanne.

Phelan considered just bolting out of the door, but he would not get far, even with a horse. He stayed where he was.

The inner door creaked open. Rowanne was standing in front of him, stiff and bleary-eyed. 'How much do you need?'

From the depths of the cottage Gemma called out, 'A sack of flour and two bales of hay will come to about 19 groats. If you can buy some vegetables as well, it would be good. We're getting low and I've bought everything the crofters have for sale. Give him three silver pieces, Rowanne.'

The knight counted out the money. Phelan did not want to take it. But he had been caught out by his own lie. He calmed himself. Once he was out of sight, he could stop and think.

'None of the farmers between here and the marshes has anything to spare. They scarcely have enough to keep themselves alive. I will go further afield today – I may even ride to one of the villages – so if I am not back at nightfall, don't worry.'

And with that, he led the horse and the pack pony outside.

It was a glorious morning. The sun was shining in an intensely blue sky. Everything was clean and brilliantly white after another fall of fresh snow. The horses danced a little, glad to be out of the cramped stable.

Hiding the turmoil of his feelings, Phelan turned and waved cheerfully at the others.

The horses picked their way gingerly down to the road below. With one more wave, Phelan turned southward.

Gemma went back inside and sat by the fire. She began to poke at it miserably.

'What's the matter?' purred Fleabag, rubbing his fur against her leg.

'I shouldn't have let him go.'

'Why's that?' asked the cat, jumping into her lap and curling up.

'He's miserable. I'm sure he thinks we don't need him and can't possibly want him. I'm scared he won't come back.'

'Are your hands burning?'

'Not yet.'

'Well,' Fleabag stretched out to get the most heat on his tummy fur, 'I suggest you stay just where you are for a bit, so I can have my between-breakfasts doze. Then, if and when your hands start warning you something is wrong, we'll go and see what's what!'

Gemma lifted the cat from her lap and put him onto her blanket. 'Oh, you're useless,' she moaned, and went outside to stare blankly at the tracks in the snow.

25

Trapped!

Phelan rode for about two miles. The snow was not deep except where it had drifted in great frozen waves against hedges and walls. Everywhere was dazzling white in the brilliant sunshine. Far ahead, he could see where the rough land gave way to marshes and then to tamer country. A few poor crofts lay scattered across the wild terrain. They had bought supplies there before, but the land was poor and people were heavily taxed on their produce. Even gold could not buy what wasn't there.

As he made his way further and further from the cottage, he began to worry. The others would be depending on these supplies. Could he get them, leave them outside the door and slip away again? No. Daylight was too short. It couldn't be done in the time. And tomorrow he might not have the courage.

Anyway, now Rowanne was strong again, she could go and buy what was needed.

He reined the mare to a halt and looked around. Soon the land would become easier. He could ride fast – faster if he left the pack pony here. If he took her with him she would slow his progress but, on the other hand, he could sell her. She must be worth something.

Just then he heard the sound of hoofbeats behind him. Cantering down the steep road towards him were Rowanne and Fleabag on Porridge. The pony was thoroughly enjoying the run. Her sturdy legs were sending a cloud of powdery snow high into the crisp sunlit air.

Rowanne waved enthusiastically. 'Wait for us!' she called. Then she caught sight of his miserable face and hesitated. 'I hope you didn't mind us coming. It is such a glorious morning for a ride and we gave you so many errands it didn't seem fair to make you do it all.'

'What she means,' chimed in Fleabag, 'is that she didn't want to miss all the fun of a day out.'

Phelan shrugged. He began to think quickly. He could lose her easily enough. But perhaps he ought to play along just for today. They did need a lot of things and goodness only knew what the next two months would be like. The others would need plenty of supplies. How could he live with himself knowing he had left a carrier of the Ring Fire snowed in with little or no food?

He smiled sheepishly at Rowanne. 'Sorry. Just lost in my thoughts. Will Gemma be all right on her own?'

Rowanne turned round in the saddle and shielded her eyes against the glare of the snow. 'She's just coming. She shouldn't be long, it's not far and it's all downhill.'

Within a few minutes, another large black dot high up the road showed that Gemma was on the way. Fleabag jumped onto Pudding's back and whispered a few words of horse speech into her ear. Without hesitating the pony began to clamber back up the slope to meet Gemma.

'Why can that cat make Pudding do as she's told when I can't?' Phelan wondered out loud.

'I suspect he makes terrible threats involving finding new homes for his fleas under Pudding's saddlecloth or something,' Rowanne replied. 'Anyway, here they come.'

The four of them rode downhill for about an hour. The road was slippery where snow had thawed and refrozen in patches. The sun was getting high and they stopped to eat. While the others were chewing dried meat and laughing at Fleabag's plans for when he would be King, Phelan sat unhappily on a rock and surveyed the landscape. Any other day, he would have said how beautiful everything looked. Today he just measured the distance between himself and the nearest village.

They had passed two or three small crofts on the way down, but the next stretch of road was rocky and uncultivated. Crossing that would take another hour or more. Then there was the marshy area with a few buildings fairly close to the road on a little rise. Everything looked very tumbledown and poor. The crofters probably had nothing to sell.

Phelan vaguely noted it would be a good place to aim for when he did run away. There might not be food or work, but at least he could get shelter. He would have to take his chance when he could.

He was prodded from his reverie by Rowanne's boot.

'Time to be on the road again. We don't want to risk being out after dark.'

He shivered at the thought. Taking a deep breath, hoping it would give him courage, he jumped down from his rocky perch to where the horses were waiting. But the snow had an underlayer of ice. As he landed, Phelan slipped and fell, catching his foot in a crack in the rock.

For what seemed like a long time he lay there, feeling the pain throbbing through his body.

After a while he opened his eyes. Rowanne eased him into a sitting position. 'Are you all right?'

Gemma knelt by his foot and gently tried to ease it from the cleft. It was tightly jammed. She reached down and loosened the thongs which tied his shoe. If he could get his foot out, it did not matter if he lost the shoe. But that did not work either. For what seemed ages, they tugged and wriggled at his foot until he cried out in pain.

Rowanne rummaged in her pack until she found her dagger – the same one that Phelan's gang had missed – and tried to gouge some of the looser chunks of rock free. But she only succeeded in snapping the blade.

'Bother!' she hissed. 'Look, I'll go on to the next farm and see if I can borrow a hammer or a crow-bar – or preferably both. There's only a few more hours of daylight left, and we don't want to get caught here. I've seen a lot of tracks in the snow; I fear the wolves are running low.'

'Well, tell them from me that the cat is running high!' replied Fleabag, fluffing out his chest fur. 'I used to be known as "Wolfbane" in my youth!'

Gemma grinned at Fleabag's bravado. 'I'll stay with Phelan,' she volunteered.

'So will I,' added Fleabag. 'He might need someone to protect him.'

'I can't think of anyone I'd less rather have if I were in a spot,' Rowanne jibed. 'You're all quips – and no equipment!'

Fleabag pretended that he hadn't heard, but his tail twitched irritably.

'Come on, cat!' called Gemma. 'Help me find firewood. At least we can keep warm while we're waiting.'

Alone at last, Phelan sat still and closed his eyes. In his imagination he saw snarling wolves with saliva dripping from pointed teeth. He opened his eyes again and concentrated on looking up at the sky. The sun was well past its zenith and heavy clouds were beginning to blow across the sky.

He could think of nothing but the cold, and the fear of what would happen when night fell. He mustn't endanger the others. If he were dead, then they would *have* to leave him and go home.

He felt in his pocket for the deadly toadstool. Nothing. He rummaged in the other pocket. Still nothing... Yet he remembered picking it up and putting it in there. Had he dropped it? Please, no... if someone thought it was a shrivelled mushroom and put it in the pot for tonight's supper... No, he mustn't let himself think like that. It must have fallen out onto the snow.

The important thing was that the fungus wasn't there. He was well and truly trapped and the others would be bound to be heroic and stay with him. When night fell, the wolves would get them all.

The sunlight had gone. The day was growing colder and darker. Phelan sat up and looked around. Dusk was several hours away. The darkness came from more snow clouds. He was getting very cold. Even his thick cloak was no real protection from the wind.

Once more he wriggled forward and examined his ankle. He had hoped that if he stayed still and did not tug at it, the swelling would go down so he could ease his foot out. He was pretty sure it was only sprained. If only he could get it free, they all still stood a chance.

Taking a handful of snow, he rubbed it as far down his leg as he could reach to reduce any swelling. But the touch of the snow burned him painfully and his foot remained as stuck as ever.

He swung his arms wildly and rubbed himself all over to keep warm. The wind was beginning to whip up and he knew that if the wolves did not get to him, the cold would.

Once more he searched his pockets, vainly hoping that amongst the dusty lint and bits of string there might be something useful. Nothing.

Phelan closed his eyes again and told his fears to go away. He must think of something good. He must not let his last hours be filled with horror and regret.

He thought of the Ring Fire dancing in Gemma's hand. It made him feel as if there might be hope.

Suddenly it occurred to him that if the Ring were not found, the Fire would fade. That would mean the end of hope, and not only for him. There would be utter misery throughout the land. Without it everyone would feel as empty and desolate as he felt now. It must be the Ring Fire that made sure a good king or queen sat on the throne. Without it, there would be war and tyrants everywhere.

It was then that he made a decision. If he got out of this alive, he *would* stay with his friends and help them find the Ring. Perhaps he *could* do something – even something as mundane as helping them survive the winter or fight off other robbers. He would do what he could to help. Even if he was just a thief, for once, Phelan was going to be someone who *did* something instead of running away all the time.

He pulled his cloak around himself and wished the others were back. Brave decisions needed brave friends to help keep courage alive.

It was not long before he heard Gemma and Fleabag cheerfully poking fun at each other as they hauled sticks and brushwood back to where he sat.

That was something. Wolves were frightened of fire.

He helped to snap the wood into kindling and twigs while Gemma went back to gather more. He selected a few strong, straight branches and rubbed the stick ends against the rock until they had sharp points. At a pinch the sticks could be jabbed at an animal's eyes. He would fight as long as he was able to.

He must not let himself be afraid. Wolves could smell that in a man's sweat. If he concentrated on good things, the fear smell might not be so bad and they might not come.

For once in his life, Phelan knew he must not let himself be afraid.

26

Wolf Pack

The sound of the wolves howling in the foothills behind them mingled with the whistle of the wind as the beginnings of yet another blizzard swept down to the plains below. Daylight would soon be gone. An unhappy greyness hung in the air.

Rowanne led the mare by the head and bowed before the blast, clutching her cloak around her. The horse stumbled through the soft, ever-deepening snow. Bundled on the animal's back were faggots of wood collected on the way.

The crofter had no tools he was willing to lend or sell. He had given Rowanne short shrift. Now they were left with nothing but their wits to keep Phelan alive in the teeth of a mid-winter blizzard. Painfully cold, she struggled the last few steps to where Gemma, Fleabag and Phelan sat huddled under their cloaks.

The two ponies had been tethered under a small overhang behind them. It was not close enough to share warmth, but one good fire should keep the wolves away from them all.

To Rowanne's surprise, although there was a good pile of wood ready to light, it had been left cold and wet, with the snow-spotted figures shivering miserably next to it.

'Thank goodness you're here,' mewed Fleabag pitifully. 'Phelan forgot to bring a tinderbox and Gemma has worn her hands raw trying to get the wood to light with a spindle.'

'I'll be with you in a minute,' called Rowanne, as she threw the new wood down and led the horse away to shelter with the others. When she came back, Gemma pulled a few bits of kindling out from under her cloak where she had been keeping them dry.

Just then snuffling and heavy breathing made the horses rear and whinny in terror.

'Light something, Rowanne,' hissed Fleabag from his depths. 'Light it quickly!'

The first sparks from her tinder box failed, but soon a small flicker of orangey-yellow light caught in the tiny twigs. The first glimmers of fire caught the bright gold reflections from the eyes of a young wolf.

Rowanne pulled out her handkerchief and let it catch light. Then she wound it around a stick and jabbed it in the direction of the animal until, with a flurry of snow, it turned tail and ran into the blizzard.

With the last remains of the fire she began to coax a few larger twigs alight until there was a small but comforting blaze. 'Keep it going,' she instructed Phelan. 'I'm going to get some things from the saddlebags.'

Gemma went to help unsaddle the animals and pulled blankets over the horses' backs. Rowanne carried the saddles back to the fire. It was warmer sitting on the well worn leather than the ice-cold stone. She had no real supplies with her. After all, they had not expected to be out after dark.

From the position he was in, Phelan could not sit on a saddle, but Rowanne managed to feed a log underneath him.

'My ears are cold,' moaned the cat.

'You'll be nice and snug in a wolf's tummy in a minute,' muttered Rowanne. 'Try sorting out small twigs. That'll keep you warm.'

Gemma pulled a nicely burning stick from the fire and peered all around for signs of wolves, holding the torch high and letting its yellow light toss in the wind. But a strong gust, heavy with wet snow, quickly put the flame out.

Only a few strides away, a wolf-shadow stopped and stared at the smoking stick. It hesitated and stepped backwards. As it turned to run, Rowanne lunged after it and caught it in the belly with her sword. Swiftly she dispatched it and flung the carcass further down the hill. Now the smell of blood would bring the rest of the pack. She did not know whether they would feed on the flesh of one of their own and be satisfied, or if they would seek human, horse- or even cat-flesh...

She did not have long to consider the matter, for out of the darkness came more long, low shadows with the distinctive musty smell of wolf-kind.

The dusk was deepening every second. Rowanne turned to the fire, which seemed to be losing the struggle for life in the teeth of the ice, cold and wet. One by one the tiny flames winked yellow, orange, then red as they cooled and died. Phelan was leaning sideways, holding his cloak as a shelter from the wind. But it was not enough.

Gemma's benumbed fingers struggled again and again with the tinder box as she tried to light the last few dry wood-shavings. 'It's no good!' She flung it down, almost crying. 'I can't get the kindling to catch!'

'Let me have a go,' offered Phelan. 'Hold the cloak up, will you?'

For several minutes he struggled. 'I think the flint must be wet. I can't even get a spark.'

Rowanne swore angrily. 'Gemma, take my sword. I'll do it.' But everything was getting colder and wetter by the second. Her fingers reddened and swelled until she could hardly bend them.

'Rowanne?' Gemma called nervously. 'I think the wolves are coming closer.'

'I can smell them,' Fleabag added. 'They are frightened. They always smell strongest when they are scared. We must get the fire going.'

'Easier said than done,' Rowanne hissed as she renewed her efforts with the flint and iron.

Suddenly she lost her grip completely and the little box rattled down the crevasse which held Phelan captive. 'Oh!' she gasped. 'Oh, I'm so sorry!'

No one could see down the black gouge of the crack. It was now almost completely dark. Even the intense white glow of snow had faded in the eternal grey smudge of the blizzard. Fleabag sprang forward and pushed his paw down the hole. 'It is too deep for me,' he said.

Phelan leaned forwards and pushed his fingers down. 'I think I can touch it, but I can't pick it up. It's fallen to one side, so I can't poke it out with a stick or anything. Can you have a go, Gemma? You have the smallest hands.'

Gemma, who was trying very hard to say nothing harsh to Rowanne, slid her achingly cold fingers down the crack, but she could feel nothing except burning ice. How she wished she could feel the comforting warmth of the Ring Fire again. She sat up and wrapped her hand in the folds of her cloak. She bit her lip and rubbed her skin gently, but the pain throbbed relentlessly, and her fingers would not even bend.

Rowanne passed a small flask of spiced cordial around in silence.

'Why don't you three ride back to the cottage?' urged Phelan, trying to be brave. 'You still stand a chance if you go back now, but none at all if you stay here.'

'We couldn't do it in the dark and snow,' Rowanne replied. 'If I'd realized earlier on in the day just how difficult it was going to be, I'd have gone back for all sorts of things. But our only chance now is to stick together.'

'Are your fingers warm enough to have another go at finding the tinderbox yet?' asked Phelan.

Gemma tried, but was met by the most painful aching cold she had ever experienced. She sat back on her heels and squeezed her hands under her armpits, rocking with the burning agony and trying not to cry. Tears would freeze on her face and make things even worse.

Rowanne was glad no one could see the worried look on her face. She was a trained knight. She had been sent to protect Gemma. Somehow they must survive – it was her responsibility. 'Has anyone got any weapons of any kind?' she asked.

'My fifteen claws are the sharpest in the kingdom,' Fleabag announced proudly. 'They have put out the eyes of many of the Queen's foes!'

'I've got some sharpened sticks,' offered Phelan. 'If we sort through the firewood for the strongest, straightest boughs, we could make some more. Has anyone got a knife?'

Rowanne handed over the broken dagger blade. 'That's about all it's fit for now,' she said, peering into the deepening gloom where the low, dark shadows of wolf pelts seemed to be ever multiplying. The beasts were crouched quite still. It was as if they knew their moment would come. All they had to do was wait.

As the scent of wolf grew stronger, one of the ponies whinnied and began to tug at her rope. Gemma got up and pulled a rug across the pony's back, talking gently to the animal all the time. It crossed her mind that if she took the rug from the pony, it might help keep Rowanne and Phelan warmer. But she couldn't bring herself to do it. Poor Porridge was shivering with cold and terror as it was. And should they find a way to free Phelan's foot, they would need all the ponies to be warm and alive to escape from the wolves.

Gemma smoothed her face against the animal's neck. It made her feel better and warmer. For a while she stayed that way. Perhaps they could all take turns to warm up like this during the night. It might keep them going – except for poor old Phelan.

Reluctantly she left the shelter of the horses to return to the slowly growing snow drift that gave them some protection from the night. Just then a long, dark shadow cut the narrow distance between her and the others.

Crouching low, the animal snarled at Gemma, trying to steer her away from the horses. If they got her a little further back, there would be high rocks behind her and a sheer drop to her left.

She glanced around in panic. The heavy smell of wet wolf hair mixed with its foul breath as the beast began to close in on her.

'Rowanne!' she whispered hoarsely, too frightened to scream in case the animal pounced. 'Rowanne! Help!'

But the howling wind carried her words away.

Just then the mare whinnied and shied, lashing out with her forehooves. After a few seconds, Porridge and Pudding did the same. But they were too well tethered to do any good.

The noise was enough, though, to rouse Rowanne from her icy state of near-exhaustion. Fleabag leaped out too and bristled his fur so he looked about three times his normal size. But between Gemma and her friends was a semicircle of deadly hunters, merciless and hungry.

Gemma took a step or two to the side. The wolves swayed that way too. Then she took a step back. The black, stinking bodies began to crowd in closer.

The horses began their cacophony again. They tugged at their ropes as they tried to flee in panic. But all they could do was roll their eyes and scream horribly.

Rowanne threw back her head and yelled as she drew her sword and began to lunge at the wolves from behind.

But as she did so, Phelan flung the first of his wooden spears in the opposite direction.

They were surrounded.

Gemma froze with horror. No one could help her. None of them could help any one else. The wolves had succeeded in separating the travellers from each other.

She felt sick as she heard Pudding howling in pain as one of the wolves sank his fetid, yellow teeth into her leg, or perhaps it was her neck… who knew?

Anyway, it was too late.

27

The Burning

Suddenly Gemma became very, very angry. Without knowing how or why, she flung her arms open wide and yelled: 'Go away! *Go away*! How dare you attack us?' Red faced and furious, she stamped her foot very hard on the snow-covered rock.

Rowanne and Phelan watched open-mouthed. For from Gemma's hands, great plumes of orange and yellow fire streaked up into the night sky.

With howls of dismay, the whole pack of wolves turned and ran off into the night.

The snow had stopped falling and the Ring Fire had gone. Now the night was everywhere, pressing in on them with a silent blackness from which there seemed to be no escape. Gemma was still standing alone on the rocks, shaking with fear and astonishment. Fleabag ventured out from under the blanket and caught hold of her trouser leg, drawing her back towards the bivouac. 'Come into the warm. I will go and see what state Pudding is in.'

Rowanne, who had run a little way after the wolves to kill any she could reach, came panting back up the hillside. 'I'll come with you. If she is badly wounded I can kill her quickly. I won't let her suffer.'

Pudding had only a shoulder wound. Rowanne packed clean snow onto it to staunch the flow of blood. If the wolves did not attack her again she stood a good chance of surviving.

The knight cleaned the wolf-blood from her sword with snow. She dried it meticulously on her cloak and slipped it back into its scabbard.

She called Gemma to help her shift some of the wolf carcasses further away from their camp, but the girl did not answer. Rowanne called her again.

This time Phelan's voice replied: 'I think you had better come here.'

Rowanne gave up on the carcasses and climbed back to the others. Huddled under vegetable sacks and half of Phelan's cloak, Gemma was staring blankly at the pile of wood they had not been able to light.

'If – if I can make fire come – just like *that* – ' she said hesitantly, ' – then why shouldn't I light *this* fire?'

'Why not?' Rowanne encouraged her.

Tentatively, Gemma stretched out her hands to the pile of small twigs and thought hard about heat. But nothing happened. Then she screwed her eyes tightly closed. 'Come on, Ring Fire!' she said. 'Burn!'

She could feel the nervous, quiet breathing of the

others next to her – but that was all. No crackle or snap of a burning twig.

After a while she opened her eyes and looked at the wood, then at her hands. She could just see them in the pale luminescence of the snow. But that was all. No Ring Fire.

Angry and embarrassed, she said nothing, but snuggled between her two friends and tried to go to sleep. Numbing cold was creeping up her arms and legs and she was very tired.

Slowly the time wore on into the pitch-black, colder-than-ice dead of night. The four of them sat almost silently, taking turns from time to time to comfort the horses and warm up a little at the same time. Phelan quietly whittled at sticks to make more lethal-tipped spears, but after a while he could hold Rowanne's broken dagger no longer. He let it drop in the snow next to him.

They knew the wolves were still there in the silence of the dark, although further away than they had been. Occasionally a shadow shifted, or they heard a slight scuffle in the snow.

From time to time, Rowanne took up Gemma's spindle and socket to try to revive the fire. But apart from a slight whiff of smoke, nothing happened. They passed round the last of the food and spiced cordial, but there was still most of the night to go before dawn.

After a while, Gemma found herself dozing and dreaming about the Ring Fire in a way that was real enough to actually warm her – but she guessed it was that dangerous state of exposure when the snow begins to feel welcoming and good. She sensed that Phelan was at that stage already.

With an effort she shook her head and arms and forced herself awake.

Fleabag opened his eyes and stretched. 'What d'you do that for?' he moaned.

'What?'

'Put the fire out. We were all just beginning to get warm at last, and you put it out.'

'What are you talking about?' she asked, quite bemused. Suddenly she realized that she really *had* been warm. She put her hand out to stroke the cat's fur and that too was pleasantly hot.

Gemma shrank back into herself. This frightened her. 'What do you mean, I put the fire out?' she asked suspiciously.

'Just now,' Rowanne began, 'while you were sitting quite still, there was a warm fire glowing at your feet. It wasn't the bonfire – it just burned. No twigs or anything, just fire. But then you stirred and sat up and it was gone!' She clicked her fingers. 'Just like blowing a candle out.'

Gemma closed her eyes and shook her head. She felt so confused.

'Go on,' urged Fleabag. 'Think of the Ring Fire one more time.'

'Must I?' pleaded Gemma, terrified of failing again. But the sight of a wolf shadow shifting closer answered her own question. She looked at a space on the ground a little ahead of her. Slowly a tiny glowing light appeared. Then it grew bigger and bigger.

Slowly and gingerly, Gemma carried the precious golden flame over to the pile of wood. 'Please, burn,' she said quietly, 'or we are all wolf meat.'

Suddenly with a soft roar, the wood caught and orange

flames leaped high into the night sky. With a cheering crackling and hissing noise, warmth and light began to chase the darkness backwards. Shadows retreated into themselves and the wolves howled and ran as flying sparks caught in their shaggy coats.

Rowanne and Fleabag stared in amazement and awe at Gemma's tired, pale face. She looked terrified and exhausted.

She looked at her two friends. 'Did *I* do that?' she whispered.

Neither of them answered. Then softly from behind them, Phelan said, 'The Ring Fire did it – you just allowed it to happen.'

'But why couldn't I do it the first time?'

'Because you wanted it to obey you. You were trying to force it as if you were a wizard. It's the sort of thing the Chancellor would have done. The Ring Fire obeys no one. It burns when someone allows it to do so, not when people try to *make* it happen.'

Gemma closed her eyes and remembered the Fire Wielder in the Hall of Light, giving the last bit of his strength to enable the Ring Fire to burn even though it was separated from the royal ring. 'Because it is welcome,' he had said.

Gemma turned to Phelan, wide-eyed. He alone of all the companions did not look happy. Caught as he was by his foot, he could not run, nor even turn away. 'How *do* you know so much?' she asked gently.

There was a long silence. Phelan looked sadly into the firelight. At last he spoke, with a visible effort. 'When I said that no one would take me in after my parents died, it wasn't true. I lived with Aelforth at the Rupertsberg hostel for a while and he tried to teach me. He is a wise man. He understands things like the Ring Fire.

'But I made friends with street kids who were learning to be thieves and pick-pockets. I wanted to be big and tough like them, not quiet and gentle like Aelforth. So I ran away and lived rough until I could prove myself as a thief – then they took me in. But I really was grey and filthy. That part was no lie!'

Suddenly he smiled as he looked into the rich, warm, living gold of the flames. 'Since then I've done a lot of running away. But tonight I've promised myself that if I get out of this, I'll stay with you and help you as best I can.'

Softly the fire crackled and roared and rose up in the night sky. Phelan did not say anything else. He just leaned his head on his knees and sat quite still until dawn.

As the first light crept across the snow to the east, the flames began to die. Phelan stirred, looking around him. At last he stood up and stretched. It was then he glanced down. 'Just look at that!' he said.

The swelling on his foot had gone down. He was no longer caught in the rocks. He could stand.

Before the sun had risen the companions had re-saddled the horses and were well on their way back along the narrow road which led towards their home.

The journey back was slower because of the uphill climb. The wind had dropped and there was no more snow, but still it took them almost three hours to struggle back.

Gemma sagged on the pony's back in a state of almost complete exhaustion. As soon as they got home, she sank into a corner by the very ordinary fire Phelan had lit with his tinderbox and slept.

Rowanne fussed over Phelan, trying to make him get some rest as well. But he did not want it. He simply sat on the doorstep, wrapped in a blanket and stared out across the empty snow. He said nothing. There were no words left to say.

Fleabag went on a little hunting trip, more because he couldn't stand the silence than out of need. He sensed that now was not the time to crack jokes. Rowanne tended to the horses, then she slept as well.

It was late in the afternoon when Phelan roused them all with a bowl of hot broth. When Rowanne asked him how he was, he just shook his head and said, 'It's funny, but I feel as if for the first time I'm really myself.' He looked up and smiled warmly. 'I can't tell you how good it feels.'

Gemma smiled a little from where she was still half asleep in a corner. She was glad he was happy, but everything that had happened the night before had terrified her. She ate the broth and slept again.

Two days later there was a lull in the biting northerly wind and Rowanne and Phelan went together down to the plain to get the hay, flour and vegetables they would need to see them through the long weeks ahead. Phelan said almost nothing the whole way. As they approached the place where the burning had happened, he reined in the horse and stared at the spot for a long time. 'Gemma doesn't want to believe she's carrying the Ring Fire, does she?' he asked.

Rowanne, who was riding the mare, stared at the spot and felt uncomfortable. She said nothing. Gently she urged her mount to follow in the horse's tracks and gave Pudding a tug on the leading rein.

She was not sure whether she hated or loved what was happening. One thing was clear, Gemma was more than just some street brat who would be able to identify the real Ring when she saw it.

She knew that she, the Lady Knight Rowanne de Montiland, was jealous of a street child. She wanted to be someone special too. But perhaps her importance was yet to come to light... Perhaps she would find the Ring – or at least be present when it was found. She must have been sent on this quest for a reason.

Anyway, her training told her there was no room for jealousy. They would have to be cooped up in two tiny rooms for another six weeks or more, and they would have to work together in order to survive. So she pushed her feelings aside and concentrated on keeping to the path in the treacherous snow.

28

The Warming

Phelan took to sitting in the morning sunshine leaning his back against the rough stone wall of the cottage. His golden-brown skin had become even more tanned with snow burn and his black curly hair and beard were getting rather long. But he carried an air of contentment that reminded Gemma of the way the old Queen had looked the day the Fire Wielder came.

One day, after sitting like this in silence for a while, Phelan leaned back and closed his eyes. Then, taking a deep breath, he began to sing. Gemma had never heard him sing before, but in rich tones, he sang an old folksong about the hope each season brought; how, at the centre of all the turning year, the Ring Fire always burned.

Gemma had been fetching water from the stream. She stopped, put the bucket down and stood transfixed, for she had never heard such a song before. It was so beautiful it brought a lump to her throat.

Even Fleabag managed to be silent for a while and listen.

When the song was finished, Phelan did not move, but opened his eyes and smiled.

Gemma found she was staring very rudely with her mouth wide open. Coming to herself suddenly, she wiped her eyes and picked up her bucket. The song had made her feel as if she was hearing the Ring Fire speak – something she had half imagined in the days when she was still the Queen's maid.

But despite the beauty of the song, Gemma did not like it. Every little reminder that she was carrying the Ring Fire in her hands worried her. She felt so small in the face of something so great that, like Phelan once, she wanted to run away from it.

She busied herself with any and every little task she could find, and even did several things twice but, however she tried to shut her feelings out, the words of Phelan's song went round and round in her head.

She was very unhappy.

The next day, Fleabag managed to get Gemma away from the others on the pretext of asking her to pick off his fleas – a task he always preferred to have done in private. It was a chilly, grey day, but the cat had carefully chosen a spot in the lee of the woodpile where they could sit in relative comfort.

Gemma patted her lap and Fleabag jumped up. But instead of immediately rolling on his back and purring as she combed through his tummy fur, he sat bolt upright and stared hard right into Gemma's eyes.

'OK,' he said sternly. 'Spill the beans. What's the matter?'

'Nothing,' said Gemma, tugging at his fur. 'You'll have to shift, I can't comb you if you don't co-operate.'

'And I can't help *you* if you don't co-operate!'

'You can't help me,' she said flatly.

'Who says?' asked the cat, head on one side and blinking his golden eyes at his friend.

Gemma began to tug the comb through the cat's neck fur. 'You don't seem to have many fleas,' she said.

'Course I haven't. I ate them all for breakfast. I just needed an excuse to get you alone.'

'So what are you going to do now? Eat me too?' Gemma was cross. She did not like being cornered. Suddenly she stood up and tried to push the cat off, but he clung on with all fifteen claws.

'Sit down!' he commanded. 'And listen! You are unhappy. A blind, half-witted field mouse could see that if he looked out of his hole backwards. And it's all because of the Ring Fire. Right? Now spill. Tell me what you are feeling, because none of this is going to go away.'

Gemma shrugged. 'It's just that... Well... You of all people should understand... After all, you're like me, a nobody. We're both strays. We came from nowhere and after this is done, we're *going* nowhere... Or so I thought. Suddenly I seem to have been given the most important thing in the whole world to carry... I could cope with being timid little Gemma Streetchild who had to go on an errand for her Queen. But suddenly, I feel as if *I* have to do something as well. I don't like it. It's not me – it's too much.'

Fleabag ignored a small shrew that scuttled past

Gemma's feet. 'How do you know it's not you?' he demanded. 'Who *says* you're only Gemma Streetchild? Who says I'm only a mangy old street cat? No one in the whole wide world is made to be "only" anything. Perhaps one day the Ring Fire will be given to everyone to carry – then we wouldn't need queens and laws. Wouldn't that be nice?'

Gemma laughed at this. She hadn't noticed that Phelan had come quietly round the woodpile and was watching them.

Silently he knelt in the snow next to them. Then he said, 'Bring the Ring Fire to light, Gemma. Do it now. It will cheer us all. Let it burn in your hand a little and you will feel better.'

Heart thumping, Gemma opened her hands and watched as the tiny flame flickered in the cup of her fingers. Everyone was silent for a long moment.

'It's funny,' she said softly, her head on one side, 'I had always thought of it as burning for right or wrong, or for getting rid of horrid things – but I never realized before how warming it is just to look at it. It's almost as if, in a strange way, it loves me.'

The weeks wore on slowly. The closeness of the confinement, especially on days when the weather was very bad, meant that tempers became frayed. Rowanne became increasingly officious and Fleabag took great delight in winding her up more and more every day.

Phelan and Gemma began to talk for long hours. He told her all he knew about the Ring Fire and she told him about the Queen and how kind and good she was and how it would have grieved her deeply if she had seen the oppression and injustice of Rupertsberg, or the neglect and poverty around Porthwain.

'She knew she was just too old to rule in the end. But she just didn't know how to find a successor.' Then a new thought struck her. 'Do you know how *she* was chosen? It must have been a long time ago.'

'It was well over a hundred years ago. She must have been very young then, and very old when she died. I don't know what she did to be chosen, but I believe it always has to be an action that only a king or queen would dare to do.'

Gemma nodded. 'In the same way that the Ring will be found where only a king or queen would dare to look? I remember at the Festival that the Queen said everyone was so busy trying to do noble feats they were forever missing the point of what it was all about...'

She hesitated. 'Phelan, what will they do if no one is found? What if the Ring is lost for ever?'

'I know Rowanne fears a lot of problems if a successor is not found within a year and a day. There will be unrest everywhere. The Prime Minister is very old too, and with no Fire Wielder or monarch either, we could be into a very dangerous situation. I doubt if the old ways will be followed – there's really no one left to ensure that a monarch is chosen properly. I'm afraid it's more likely to end up as an unsightly scrap between the various noble families of the six provinces.'

'But what will happen to the Fire?'

'Without the Ring it will fade back to where it came from, and who knows what will happen then? But in the end it's got to be all right.' Phelan paused. 'The Fire Giver would never desert us, even if there's a long struggle ahead.'

Gemma sighed. Suddenly she remembered the Fire Wielder. How was he? Would he live to proclaim the new king or queen? He had longed to hand the Ring Fire to his own successor and, like the Queen, go to the Quiet Place in peace.

Soon everything would be settled one way or another. But what would happen to her and to Phelan? She knew she could not face going back to the kitchens, and he had no skill or trade except thieving. He would never work for Rowanne, however much she pleaded.

Fleabag would be all right. He always was. There must be many a cook who would employ his excellent ratting skills.

If Rowanne did not win the Princedom of Rupertsberg, she could go back to being a knight at court. The life suited her. It was obvious that long months cooped up in a tiny cottage with a talking cat, a thief and a guttersnipe had been a miserable experience for her.

Gemma gave up thinking about the future. It was too depressing.

But after the long tedium of endless snow, one morning came when the companions were wakened by a steady dripping. Fleabag was the first outside and minutes later he returned with wet paws and a large fish.

'It's a thaw!' he declared gleefully. 'The trout are swimming and there are birds in the sky. Spring is on its way!'

The easing of the temperature did not last long and soon fresh snow had fallen. But the thaws became more frequent and lasted longer. Phelan scraped a patch of snow away for the horses to nibble at early grass, and everyone began to feel better.

Eventually the day came when, apart from the higher hills, all the snow had gone.

The companions sat on the sun-warmed grass and watched early bees searching for nectar. High in the air an eagle soared, and the earth smelled rich and loamy.

'Time to be on the move!' announced Rowanne in her best 'campaigning' voice. 'If we leave straight away and don't stop anywhere, we'll be back in Harflorum by May with a little time in hand before the year and a day is up.'

Gemma stared at Rowanne in disbelief. The woman was standing in her riding clothes, arms folded across her leather jerkin and dark hair bound up in the woollen snood she wore under her helmet. She looked every inch the knight.

But she was looking the wrong way: back across the marshes to the plains and the way they had come.

'No,' Gemma said firmly. 'How can you even suggest going back? We go on – north by north-west.'

29

Dire Warnings

Rowanne looked at Gemma incredulously. 'But how can you even think of going on? It took six months to get from Harflorum to where we are now; there are only about nine or ten weeks left of the year and a day.

'We will get back in time if we go now – but if we go on we will have lost everything. I know you meant well, going north by north-west, but we haven't had so much as a sniff of the Ring. No sightings – not even rumours.'

Gemma stood up. She was still a lot shorter and skinnier than the knight, but she felt she could not argue sitting down. The wind flapped at her hair. She pushed it back and climbed onto a small rock so she could look Rowanne in the eye.

'I don't care if you think of me as a silly child. I did what the Ring Fire told me to do. And I will keep *on* doing it. I will go north by north-west until I can go no further. By the oath you took on your knighthood in Harflorum, you are free to leave us whenever you choose. But I will go on. Alone if necessary.' The girl's green eyes were blazing and she felt her face going red. But she had spoken and that was all that mattered.

Rowanne blinked and looked quite taken aback. Gemma had always been so timid before. 'But you can't go on,' she protested. 'You are needed at Harflorum to identify the real Ring. What happens if you don't come back in time?'

Suddenly Fleabag sprang up beside Gemma, hissing as he rubbed himself against her trouser leg.

Rowanne looked hard at the cat. 'What do *you* want?' she demanded.

The cat sat up straight and glared at his old adversary. 'You want to be in at the proclamation of the real Ring so you can be sure of getting a good position at court for yourself... Furthermore, you know that without Gemma there will be no proclamation at all, because the Fire Wielder might not be alive when we get back. You're scared of missing out for yourself! That's why you want Gemma to go back with you now!'

Rowanne lowered her head and glowered under her dark brows. She pointed a firm finger straight at the cat's head. 'I have sworn to have your pelt for a fur collar, and by all I hold precious, one day I will keep my vow!'

Fleabag just looked up at Rowanne and smirked. 'I'd like to see you try!' he said.

Just then Phelan came out of the cottage. 'What's all the noise about?' he asked.

Gemma and Rowanne both started talking at once. He could not understand a word either of them said, so he and Fleabag went down to the stream for an intelligent conversation about what was happening.

When they returned, Gemma and Rowanne had all their things spread out on the grass. They were sorting and packing furiously, but in deadly silence.

Phelan stood and watched them for a few seconds. Then, 'I'm going with Gemma,' he announced suddenly.

'So am I,' added the cat, sitting down firmly on Gemma's saddlebag to strengthen his point.

Gemma straightened, clutching a pile of clothes in her arms. 'Rowanne, we need you. The quest for the Ring needs you. Please don't leave us.' Gemma was no longer defiant, but looked up at the woman with a child's eyes again.

The knight stopped packing and stared around at the others. Inside she was struggling. At last she sighed and bowed slightly.

'I have seen you holding the Ring Fire, Gemma. It is my duty to stay with you. If we move now, straight away, we may have enough time to go a little further.

'But there will come a day when I will spend the rest of the money Prince Rupert gave me to buy a swift horse and gallop ahead of you all back to Harflorum. It is also my sworn duty to defend the peace of this kingdom. And there will be trouble when a year and a day is up, I guarantee it. The Ring Fire will lead you as it may, but I must be at the palace for that day. Whatever else happens. On that day you will be penniless and on your own. Do you understand? I can do no more.'

'How much further can we go?' Phelan asked.

Rowanne scratched some figures on a rock with her broken dagger. 'I will accompany you for two more weeks.

On the day of the vernal equinox, I must leave you.'

'Which way is north by north-west, anyway?' asked Gemma, sitting on a bag so Phelan could tie it more tightly.

'On through the mountains,' Rowanne replied, lashing a bundle of blankets onto the pack pony's pannier. 'I talked to one of the crofters the other day. He reckons the pass will be open by now and it's not a bad road anyway. We should be in the province of Beulothin within a couple of days. Apparently they have a spectacular Spring Festival and we might get to see it if we're lucky.'

'How far does north by north-west go on for?' Gemma sounded weary, despite the long months of enforced rest.

'Beulothin extends from the mountains to the sea. There's nothing else then, unless you take a ship.' Rowanne stopped tugging at cords and looked hard at Gemma. 'You're still convinced that's the way to go? How long will you keep going?'

Gemma shrugged. 'I'll keep going until I know I must stop, I suppose.'

'The Ring Fire will tell you when to stop,' said Fleabag.

Gemma smiled uncertainly. 'Maybe. I still find the Ring Fire is something too big to even think about. Sometimes the only thing I'm certain of is that I'm going on because I promised the Queen I would. I'm doing it because I loved her.'

No one felt they could say anything after that, although Phelan longed to try and be comforting. He wanted to tell her she must let the Ring Fire burn *inside* her, not just hold it at a distance in her hands... But now was not the time. They had to get on the road.

The road across the mountains to Beulothin was not a long one, but the travellers took it slowly because there were still many icy patches. The first evening they could still see the foothills where they had wintered.

The second night was spent in a bivouac at the top of the pass, under a canopy of blankets because it was raining. No one slept and they found nothing to eat. Miserably, they started off again very early. The road was fairly level, but wound tortuously between rockfalls and mountain streams. Before noon the path began dipping downward, then twisted and turned out of a steep-sided rift until suddenly a misty plain spread out far below them.

As the days wore on, the ground was softer and greener and the air became warmer, until they reached the plains of very rich and fertile land. Forests lay to their left and to their right was mile after mile of well-tilled fields, fat hedgerows and plenty of wildlife. They were cold and tired, but passers-by told them the city of Beriot lay straight ahead – north by north-west.

Gemma was greatly cheered by this news. She wanted to go to the city to buy good food, but she did not want to leave the right road again.

Everywhere there were signs of people preparing for the Spring Festival. Garlands were being hung from windows, bunting slung across village streets. Yet the people did not seem excited. In fact they looked terrified. They scuttled in a frightened way between houses and shops, and at the sight of the travellers they turned their backs.

Eventually they did manage to find a farmer's wife who was willing to take them in for a night. She fed them well and provided beds for all.

The thin, grey-looking woman cooked them a good breakfast and Fleabag was given cream. She seemed friendly enough, although, like everyone else, very sad. As she cleared away the plates, she asked them where they were going.

'We've come to see the Spring Festival,' replied Phelan enthusiastically. 'We've heard it's wonderful.'

The woman pulled herself up straight and looked at her visitors. 'Don't!' she said tersely. 'Don't ask why, just clear off in the other direction as fast as you can.'

The travellers looked at each other in amazement.

The woman leaned on the table and looked each of the friends in the eye. 'It's a bad business. This is no place for those who do not belong. Come to the *last* day of the festival, if you must – the day of the equinox, when there will be parties and rejoicing. But for now – take my advice if you value your lives, and *flee*!'

She stood straight again, clutching her teatowel to her thin chest.

'But what's wrong with now?' Phelan asked, disappointed.

The woman clicked her tongue and finished clearing the breakfast things noisily. Phelan paid her for their board and lodging and tried to coax more information out of her with an extra silver piece. Although she looked hungrily at the coin, she would say nothing further. She just scurried into the kitchen, from where she called out into the street that if they kept going 'steady-like' on the north by north-west road, they would surely make the festival in good time.

'Good day and good speed to you,' she added, shutting the door firmly in their faces.

Bemused, they gathered up their things, loaded the horses and set off.

Fleabag jumped onto Porridge with Gemma. 'Something is very wrong here,' he said. 'You've seen how miserable and frightened everyone is? Even the animals are in terror. Do you think we should turn back?'

Gemma shrugged. 'Well, *I* can't. You can do what you like.'

'If I was King,' muttered Phelan as a man pulled his child inside a house as they approached, 'I would put this place right first. Perhaps even before Rupertsberg. Something very strange is going on.'

They made the city of Beriot late that afternoon. Rowanne's money was beginning to run low, but she bought everyone a good meal and a night's lodging at an inn. 'This is my last treat,' she said. 'We will have to sleep rough after this – I have to keep the rest of my money to buy a swift horse to return next week.'

Soon the smell of hot pie and roast potatoes filled the little inn. Through the crowded room came a young boy pushing a wooden trolley laden with enough food for twice their company. With a great deal of difficulty he managed to elbow his way through to the travellers' table.

'Compliments of the management,' he said, with a worried look on his face.

Rowanne caught the lad in her iron grip. 'What do you mean, boy?'

'Nothing to pay, ma'am. The landlord says so. Ow!'

Rowanne gripped him even tighter. 'Landlords don't give away food like this to complete strangers. What's happening?'

Just then she caught a glimpse of the fat landlord in

his white apron peering into the room.

She let the boy go. 'That looks very nice indeed, thank you,' she said loudly. 'Will you bring me some pepper?'

The boy scurried off and returned quickly with a small earthenware pot.

As he put it in front of her, he whispered, 'Please, my Lady, go away, back where you came from. As soon as you've eaten...' When Rowanne tried to grab the child again, he slipped away like an eel in a stream.

Gemma could not eat, but sipped unhappily at her tankard of ginger ale. At last she said, 'I feel in my bones it will be dangerous to go on, but I simply can't do anything else. If anyone wants to turn back, I shan't think the worse of them.'

Rowanne bristled. 'We've been through all this. Can't we just eat in peace for once? Unless you would *rather* I went?' she added icily. 'Then you can find the Ring and keep it for yourself!'

Fleabag glared over the tabletop from his place on Phelan's knee. 'How *dare* you?' he spat. 'Watch her, Phelan, I don't trust that so-called knight the length of a fishbone.' Then he ducked down under the table again and measured how far he would have to spring to catch Rowanne's knee with a particularly well-sharpened claw he had been nurturing just in case...

Phelan bent down and spoke softly in Fleabag's ear. 'Forget Rowanne for the moment. She's just frightened, like the rest of us. Would you go and slip into the kitchen and see what the local cats say about these people? I've got a funny feeling and I don't like it. I wouldn't desert Gemma for the world – as long as she says we're going the right way, I'm there beside her –

but I'd like to know what we're walking into.'

Fleabag slid with a black silken smoothness from Phelan's knee, but before he could emerge from under the table, the inn door swung heavily open and a troop of soldiers marched into the room in rigid formation. The sergeant, a tall, dark-haired man in immaculate bright blue uniform and sporting a huge moustache thumped the bar and roared: 'Well, are there any volunteers this year?'

The travellers looked around in astonishment. But apart from themselves and the soldiers, the room was suddenly quite empty.

30

Prison!

The prison was extremely cold and depressing. The perpetual drip, drip, drip of fetid water seeping from the ceiling of the vault combined with the musty smells of rotting hay and stale urine. But the worst of it was not knowing why they were there or if they would get out. So much seemed to depend on their freedom, yet how could they explain it to anyone? Who would believe them anyway?

All night long they sat in a huddle and wondered if they had been wrong all along. Gemma felt guilty because she had brought her trusting friends so far on the say-so of a voice in her head.

Rowanne felt she should have been able to prevent their arrest if she had had her sword in her hand.

Phelan worried whether someone had recognized him from his thieving days and they had all been arrested on suspicion of being like-minded criminals.

The only faintly happy one amongst them was Fleabag who was having excellent sport with a family of rats and had killed three of them in less than an hour.

The night was long, dark and frightening.

At dawn, bolts were drawn back on the cell door. Then came a screeching, grating sound of keys in an ancient lock. The door opened slowly and heavy footsteps heralded a thickset, bald man with no teeth.

He kicked the door shut behind him and put a loaf and a jug of water on the floor, right where the drip from the ceiling landed.

The man straightened and grinned. 'So you're the volunteers. Well done. Most public-spirited of you, I must say! Congratulations! I hope you have a nice time at the festival.'

Phelan struggled to his feet with difficulty, because of the weight of iron manacles on his wrists. 'What is happening? Volunteers for what? Why are we here when we haven't done anything wrong?'

Rowanne also tried to get to her feet, but her chain was too short. 'I demand you tell us what's happening. I am the Lady Rowanne de Montiland of the Queen's Guard. You must release me and my companions immediately!'

The gaoler grinned and bowed. 'Pleased to meet you, I'm sure, my Lady. Now I'm sorry, I must go and see to the other lords and ladies in my care. "So much to do, so little time", as they say.'

As he was about to go out of the door he caught sight of Fleabag's hunting trophies. The man's face lit up and before the cat could move, he had caught Fleabag up and tucked him under his arm. 'Now you are what I call a useful sort of a cat. I'll keep you. He won't get *you*, no, he won't, puss.'

To everyone's amazement, Fleabag did not protest, but purred and snuggled up to his new master. The key turned in the lock and they were alone again.

Gemma sniffed and wiped her nose on her sleeve.

Phelan said quietly, 'Fleabag would never desert us. He probably thinks he may be able to help us best if he is free.'

'I'm sure you're right,' Gemma replied. 'It's just that it felt so awful to see him go off like that without even a lick goodbye.'

Rowanne started to examine her chains. 'If I had my dagger, I'm sure I could force one of these links,' she said. 'They're heavy but not particularly well made.'

'If I had a dagger I could pick the locks,' muttered Phelan. 'I'm quite good at that. In fact, I could probably do it with a hairpin...' He looked hopefully at Rowanne.

She rummaged under her woollen snood and pulled one out triumphantly. 'Will this do?'

'Perfect!' and he set to working on Rowanne's manacle. 'I'm starting with you because you're the best fighter. I'll do Gemma next because she is the most important. If you get a chance to run before I'm free, then go. And may the Ring Fire light your way.'

Gemma did not know what to say. She couldn't imagine running away without her friends.

For a long time Phelan worked in silence. The only sounds were the scratching of wire against iron and the dripping of water right onto their breakfast bread.

'Almost got it!' he whispered triumphantly at long last, but before he could snap the lock open, the thump of feet along the stone corridor made him drop the pin.

Seconds later, a sharp command halted a column of soldiers outside the door. The keys jangled again and the door swung reluctantly on its hinges.

The bald gaoler came and undid the chains. 'Time to go now, boys and girls,' he said cheerfully. 'You didn't eat the breakfast I cooked for you so loving-like. Tut, tut, that's a waste now, isn't it? Still, you won't need it where you're going.'

Next to him the sergeant barked, 'Get up!' and Gemma and Phelan found themselves jerked to their feet. Reluctantly Rowanne stood next to them and was about to demand her rights again, when she caught sight of Fleabag in the open doorway. He looked right through her, warning her to silence.

As they were marched out, he slipped between their feet unseen by the gaoler, who was left calling, 'Puss, puss? Nice bit o' fish I bin and bought for you. Here, puss!'

Fleabag skilfully matched his step with the soldiers and managed to leap into Gemma's arms. She buried her face in his warm fur. 'I'm scared, Fleabag.'

'So you should be,' replied the cat. 'I had a long talk with the gaoler's dog and I've found out what's going on.'

The prisoners were bundled into a covered wagon. Bars were put up to prevent their escape, and a thick oilcloth was thrown over so they could see nothing of the outside. The wagon began to move and they could hear the iron-clad wheels clattering over cobbles. Soon the noise gave way to a softer sound. 'Mud,' said Rowanne. 'We're out in the country again.'

Gemma put Fleabag down and he wriggled to the middle where they could all hear him. 'Now, this is what I have found out. It seems that there is a beast in these parts – I don't know what it is exactly, but many years ago it used to devour all the sheep and cattle for miles around. It is said it was lured into the depths of an ancient cavern and chained there. But by evil magic it slowly began to regain its strength. A few years ago it broke out and returned to its old ways.

'The Prince of this province pleaded with it to go away, but it would only do so if it was given humans to eat instead. However, in return, it now only feeds once a year – at the beginning of the Spring Festival. It is also content with less, usually only one adult or two or three children. The people of this land seem to prefer this to having all their cattle and crops ruined at the beast's whim. Apparently more people used to die from simply being in the beast's way, than by the annual meal.

'That's terrible!' gasped Rowanne. 'Let me at it with a good sword and I will rid the land of this plague!'

'No good,' replied Fleabag. 'It is plated all over with scales like steel, greased so thickly with slime that no sword can catch in it, let alone pierce it. But let me finish before we plan.

'It seems that before the Spring Festival, lots are drawn to choose that year's victim. Many people have lost loved ones.'

'No wonder everyone is so sad,' said Gemma.

'But the worst of it is, if there are any strangers in the land, they are put at the top of the list. The people are not inhospitable, but obviously they want to protect their own friends and families.'

Phelan whistled quietly. 'So we walked right into it. It all makes sense now.'

A strangled silence filled the wagon. Suddenly the friends were thrown together as it jerked to a halt. Fleabag hid himself under Gemma's cloak.

The black oilcloth was pulled back and dazzling daylight streamed in. Guards in blue uniforms tugged at the iron bars and tail-board until the trio fell back with a clatter. 'Out!' ordered the sergeant. 'Quick about it.'

They found themselves outside a small grey stone building with tiny, high windows. Phelan's heart sank, for to one side there were carpenters, busily constructing what could only have been a scaffold.

Phelan did not have long to look before he was pushed and shoved through a dark doorway and down steps. Once more they were in prison.

The room was small and square. Food, water and a bucket had been left for them. In the corner was a pile of blankets. Gemma handed one to everyone then wrapping herself up, she curled up in a corner.

Phelan came and sat next to her. 'We're not dead yet,' he said gently. 'Show us the Ring Fire, Gemma. We all need it.'

She opened her hands, though they were trembling.

There was no flame!

There was little time to think about their predicament, for the door opened again almost immediately.

'Which one of you is the Lady de something?' demanded the sergeant's stern, military voice.

Rowanne jumped to her feet. 'I am the Lady Rowanne de Montiland, and I demand to see your Prince.'

The man looked her up and down. 'I don't know about

you seeing *him*, but he'll see *you*. You're first. Tomorrow at dawn.'

The man looked at the others. 'If the beast goes away after that, the rest of you will be free. If he doesn't, it'll be you, then you,' he jerked a thumb at Phelan and Gemma in turn. Then he looked down at Fleabag. 'We'll even use the cat if we have to.' He turned his sad face to Rowanne again. 'Because if he's not full after that, the lot has fallen on my little son.'

He turned smartly on his heel and left, slamming the door behind him.

Gemma lifted her head from her blanket. 'Once the old Queen told me that there had not been a dragon in the land for a hundred years. I wonder if it's the same one and people only thought it was dead.'

'I bet she became Queen because she was the one who got rid of it for them,' said Fleabag. 'It's just the sort of thing she would have done.'

Just then, Rowanne was violently sick in the bucket.

After a few moments she lifted her head. 'It's funny,' she said at last, 'but before a battle I'm nervous but never frightened. I've never known what it means to be really frightened before. I... I think it's because this time I have no weapons in my hands. Before, I always had my sword and my skills – it was an even match, if you like. But the thought of being chained up... out there, just waiting... I can't stand it.' And she collapsed into hysterical sobbing.

The others sat in silence, just watching and listening. There seemed to be nothing left to say.

31

A Bad Night

Whether Rowanne was asleep, or lying in a terrified stupor, Gemma did not know. But the grey shape against the opposite wall did not move all night.

Gemma did not sleep either. She would have welcomed oblivion for a few hours to make the inevitable come more quickly, but she was too cold. A few hours before dawn, Phelan pushed his old jacket over to her.

'Take it,' he whispered. 'I don't feel the cold as badly as you do.'

Gemma pulled the coat over her shoulders and leaned back. But sleep still did not come. She was almost warm enough now, but there was an uncomfortable lump against her back and, however she twisted, she could not shift it.

At last Fleabag, who had been asleep on her lap, got up in disgust. 'A cat's got to get beauty sleep!' he moaned.

'Even a condemned cat.' And he curled up under the table.

Soon the dull blue-grey of first light began to creep into the cell from a small grating above their heads. Phelan stood and went over to Rowanne. Gently he pulled the blanket back from her face, then let it drop again.

He sat down next to Gemma.

'Are you awake?'

'Yes.'

'I'm going to take Rowanne's place. I'm sure the beast won't care whether he gets a knight or a thief. I'm taller than her and there's a chance I might fill him up better.'

Gemma looked at him with wide eyes. She did not know what to say.

'Rowanne can't do it. I have never seen anyone look as terrified as she does. If I go, it gives you three another full day to think of a way out of this mess.' Phelan held out his hand to Gemma. 'Goodbye. Thanks for everything.'

Gemma shook his hand.

At last she managed to find her voice. 'But you've always been frightened of beasts – wolves and things... And the scaffold was your worst nightmare because of the way your parents died!'

'That was dread – it eats into you so you can't function any more. It's funny, but the dread has gone away quite suddenly. Now I'm just scared. That's different. I'm not being brave. It's just that I've got to do it – Rowanne can't. And I keep thinking about the other people, like that soldier's boy, who will be next. I might at least be able to give them another year.

'All I ask is that you'll take any chance to escape. Don't

martyr yourself in memory of me or anything stupid. You of all people must get back. Who knows what crook or tyrant may be holding the Ring at this very moment? You must be sure the holder is a true king or queen. And Rowanne – she must get back too. She must speak for the people who are suffering across the land. So run the second you can. Promise?'

'I promise.'

Phelan hesitated. 'I've got two more favours to ask.'

'Anything.'

'Will you light a little of the Ring Fire for me when I'm out there? It will help me go through with it.'

'If the Fire will burn at all, I will burn it until I drop, like the Fire Wielder.'

'... And the last thing...'

'Yes?'

'Can I have my coat back? I'm freezing.'

Gemma laughed, although she wanted to cry. She pulled the jacket from around her shoulders and passed it across to him. 'There's a funny lump in the lining at the back. It kept me awake all night.'

Just then the sound of footsteps echoed along the passageway. 'Light the Fire now,' whispered Phelan. He watched the tiny glow glimmering between her fingers, then he stood to attention next to the door, waiting for the moment it would open.

32

The Wolf Prince

On the first morning of the Spring Festival every man, woman, child and animal was safely barricaded in cellars and basements. No one moved or even breathed lest the beast should come their way.

The stench of its breath was beginning to seep under doors and through loose windowframes. Dawn had come, but a thick cloud hovered across the face of the sun. Slowly the cloud grew blacker and denser, until at last it took the shape of a serpent-like creature with blood-red scales and two pairs of huge leathery wings, beating the air with a singeing, searing heat.

The land was empty. There was no one to see the monster approaching except the tiny figure of Phelan, chained to his scaffolding, and Prince Tomas of Beulothin, watching from one of the upper windows of the prison. The Prince was a thin, grey old man, dressed in funereal black and unashamedly weeping to see yet another victim go to his death. In the last few years the beast had been taking more and more people. Would there be enough prisoners in the dungeon to satisfy it this year?

He knew in his heart that one day there would not. On that day he must at last take off his crown and step forward himself to prevent the whole land being laid to waste.

The Prince was not cruel in letting the others go first. He was just scared – like everyone else.

As Phelan waited, the Ring Fire burned in Gemma's hands. Suddenly Gemma realized she could see pictures in the flames, just as she had done in the Queen's Ring all those long months ago. Of course – it was Phelan and Rowanne she had seen!

But now she saw only Phelan, chained and alone. Suddenly she wished she had given him a tiny flame, to comfort him. But perhaps that couldn't be done. It was too late now, anyway.

The monster had landed. It scraped its rattling metallic scales across the fields, leaving the stench of burning slime behind it.

Slowly it approached the scaffold, snarling and glaring hungrily at Phelan. But it did not attack straight away. It seemed to be considering its prey.

Gemma held her breath. She was concentrating on Phelan so hard that there was no room for anything else, even her fear. Suddenly she realized that, for the first time, the Ring Fire was burning *inside* her. She had become one with it, and was surrounding Phelan with the Fire glow.

She saw him standing straight and still, but she could feel dread pulsing all around him. 'Don't let the dread come back,' she whispered. 'Or you won't be able to think.'

'No,' she heard him say. 'I must be able to think.' Then he did a strange thing. He seemed to be rummaging in his coat pocket.

At last he pulled out something small and knobbly. He held it in his hand and watched the beast approaching. It had stopped in front of him, sniffing and flicking its lurid green tongue as it stretched its sagging neck towards its prey…

Gemma held the picture of Phelan surrounded by the Ring Fire. She dare not let it waver for one moment. His dread must not return.

Phelan seemed to be measuring the distance. Waiting. Calculating.

Suddenly the beast opened its maw and engulfed its victim in a cloud of asphyxiating smoke. Phelan choked and retched, but he swung back his arm and threw the small knob right into the cavernous mouth.

The creature swallowed it and looked surprised. Then it flung back its head to roar. But the noise caught in its throat. It looked down at Phelan and opened its mouth again. But this time, scalding black blood belched out.

The beast swung its head from left to right as if it was in agony. It arched its back high and crashed down onto the scaffold, splintering it from end to end.

Phelan was left hanging like a puppet in his chains.

But still the beast did not attack. Instead it writhed and flung its huge body from side to side, rolling and crashing until it finally lay on one side, lashing its tail and howling with a terrible bellow that echoed in all the hills for miles around.

After what seemed an eternity the steam and stench subsided and the creature lay quite still.

A word from the Prince, and soldiers swarmed onto the field. They all drew their swords and tried to hack the beast's head off, but to no avail.

Then Prince Tomas himself was at Phelan's side unlocking the chains that bound him.

Phelan was dazed and sick. Dizzily he sank to the ground and sat staring at the body of the beast.

'Deathcap.'

'What?' asked the Prince.

'Deathcap toadstool. I lost one in the lining of my coat months ago, but I found it this morning. I thought that if the beast could not be killed from the *outside*, than perhaps I could kill it from the *inside*.'

He shook his head and whistled. 'I didn't realize the effects were *that* quick.' Then he grinned.

'Good job they were, though.'

And with that, he fainted.

Soldiers came and flung the prison door open. Gemma dashed out, with Fleabag hot on her heels. Daylight had never felt so real or so welcoming. The sun was beginning to come out again, as everywhere the poisonous blackness thinned and blew away in the morning breezes.

Gemma ran over to the beast's head and looked into its dead eyes. Carefully, she placed a flame of the Ring Fire onto the greasy head. Then she leaped back, for with a great roar of flame the whole creature caught light and began to burn.

When Phelan woke, he was in the Prince's own bedroom in the palace at Beriot. Gemma and Rowanne were seated next to him. They had bathed and eaten well.

Fleabag had begged to be excused because he preferred his fish raw, and did not think the Prince's bedroom was quite the place to eat it.

'Try and eat something,' coaxed Gemma as soon as Phelan opened his eyes. 'There's no deathcap amongst the fried mushrooms. I've checked.'

Phelan grinned weakly and sat up. 'Ow! Why do I hurt so much?'

'You've got bad burns from the beast's breath, but you'll be all right,' Rowanne replied. 'But first of all, I want to thank you for doing what you did. I never realized I was such a coward before – or such a snob. To think I once wanted you hanged!'

Phelan shook his head. 'Each to his own. I'd be useless in battle. I just suddenly found my dread had gone, and I could meet the monster. I'd forgotten about the deathcap until the last minute. I don't know where I got the courage – or how I remembered the fungus.'

'Gemma kept the Ring Fire burning all the time,' Rowanne told him. 'She *willed* you through it.'

'I know. I could feel it. I think the real thanks go to you, Gemma.'

Gemma smiled. 'No, to the Ring Fire and the Fire Giver. Now eat up, someone wants to see you.'

Phelan ate a little, then a servant came and dressed him in a loose silk robe that would not chafe his burns. Painfully he eased himself into a chair and the door opened. In walked Prince Tomas himself, attended by all sixteen of his advisers.

As the Prince approached, he knelt and took off his crown. He handed it to Phelan.

'Twenty years ago, when the beast returned, I begged it to go. It told me it would leave for ever if I would let it take me. I thought it was a trick to get me to leave my land unprotected. I never told anyone, but I convinced myself I was needed to rule the province. Really, I was too frightened to dare to look death in the face, even for the sake of my people.'

'I am no longer fit to rule. In the name of our departed Queen, and whoever her successor may be, please be Prince of this province.'

Phelan stared at the Prince, and the crown that had been placed in his hands. He turned it over and looked at it. 'I – I don't know what to say… is this your will also?' he asked the advisers standing behind the Prince.

A tall, dark-skinned woman stepped forward and bowed. 'Our Prince has served us well and faithfully for many years. But if he feels he must abdicate in favour of one who is braver and will serve his people better than himself, we can only agree. We vow to serve you as well as our skills permit.' She bowed again, and stepped back, pulling her emerald silk gown around her.

By this time, Fleabag had finished his supper and returned, licking his whiskers contentedly. 'Now there's an offer you can't refuse. The food here is first-rate. I'll stay and be your chief adviser if you like.'

Phelan laughed. Fleabag had given him a moment to make his mind up. 'Two wonderful offers,' he said. 'I am indeed a rich man! But I cannot accept, because we must leave very soon. My friends and I must return to Harflorum, for the year and the day is almost up when the Queen's successor will be presented. For many reasons we must be there.

'But more importantly, although I am deeply honoured, you must realize that just because I had an old toadstool in my pocket it does not mean that I would be a good prince. You understand your people. You know their needs. Please – keep your crown.'

Prince Tomas was not to be deterred. 'But I have *not* served my people faithfully. I am no prince at all.' He offered the crown again.

Phelan thought for a moment. 'If I accept, may I go away to complete my other tasks first?'

The advisers conferred for a few moments. 'Of course, Sir,' they agreed heartily.

'Then I accept,' Phelan said, inclining his head. 'But on condition that I have a good regent to rule in my place. Is this good in your eyes, my Lords and Ladies who advise the Prince?'

Again they agreed.

'Then, Prince Tomas of Beulothin, I appoint you as my regent.' And he leaned forward and placed the crown firmly back on the thin grey hair of the Prince. As he did so he whispered, 'You will be a much better prince from now on. You won't forget today, will you?'

'Never, my Lord.'

'Then get up. You have work to do.'

Prince Tomas no longer looked so grey and old. Years seemed to have fallen away from him. He smiled at all the company. 'We will have a banquet tonight in your honour. The people have many gifts to give to you. Please rest until then, my Lord and Ladies.'

'And Cat!' purred Fleabag from the place of honour he

had claimed for himself on Phelan's lap.

The Prince bowed to Fleabag and left the room with all his counsellors in tow.

Gemma and Rowanne looked at each other and whistled.

'Well, I never,' said the cat. 'Prince Phelan – the Wolf Prince.'

'I'll present Rowanne with that catfur collar she's always wanted if you ever call me that again,' Phelan laughed, pretending to cuff the cat around the ear.

Then he looked at Gemma. Her face was long and miserable. 'What's the matter? Don't worry, I'll come back with you and then after that – who knows? But at least I always have a home and both of you are welcome to be part of it for as long as it pleases you. Gemma will never have to peel another potato as long as she lives – and Rowanne, what would you like? To be Captain of the Guard?'

Gemma shook her head. 'It's not that at all. It's just that I have this awful feeling that I have to go soon – very soon. I'm sure you'll think me terribly rude, but I can't help it – the Ring Fire is calling me. It's urgent. We may not have found the Ring, but I am needed.'

Phelan looked from the cat to the knight, then back to Gemma again. 'You're right. I feel it too.'

Fleabag jumped down from Phelan's lap. 'Shame,' he said. 'The dustbins here are superb.'

33

Return to Harflorum

The hours before the banquet were very busy with preparations for the journey. Prince Tomas gave Rowanne and Phelan good horses and Gemma a sure-footed pony. Fleabag was given a special pannier where he could sleep like a king on a soft new fleece.

Supplies were packed onto the backs of three strong horses, but as time was of the essence, only two soldiers were sent to protect and speed the party on the road.

It was almost dark when everything was ready. Gemma wanted to ride through the night as soon as the banquet was over, but Rowanne persuaded her that the horses might stumble which would slow them badly. It had to be daylight travel as much as possible. On top of that, Phelan really needed a night's sleep; he was far from well after his encounter with the beast.

Fleabag permitted his fur to be washed and combed

dry, then a scarlet silk ribbon was tied around his neck. He sat on a fat satin cushion at the end of the high table and held court with all the admiring palace cats.

Rowanne dressed in formal knightly dress. She wore white silk stockings and knee length breeches, with a loose lawn shirt and a cloth-of-gold tabard. Her short cloak was of scarlet satin edged with gold. For once she let her hair fall loose and tumbling down her back.

As she entered, everyone gasped. Even Fleabag admitted that he had never quite thought of her as *beautiful* before.

Gemma had her hair cut properly. It had never looked right since 'Auntie' had hacked it in the thieves' kitchen. Now it was neat and shiny. Phelan had given orders that she should wear a long robe of flame-red silk. Gemma did not think it was really her colour, but she did not like to turn it down.

Phelan himself would only wear a plain white linen shirt and trousers, with a blue woollen waistcoat. He too had his black hair and beard cut short, so it curled tightly around his dark face. To please Prince Tomas, he wore the small golden crown of the princedom, but he took it off again as soon as he politely could, on the pretext that it kept slipping to one side.

The four travellers looked at each other in amazement. None of them would have recognized the others, they were so transformed. Phelan took Rowanne and Gemma in to dinner, one on each arm, and they were seated at the High Table.

After the food and the speeches there was dancing and merriment. The whole city was alive with music and fireworks. Flashes of bonfires and squeals from rockets brought the night sky to life all the way across the province.

At last Gemma felt she really *had* to go to bed. She wanted to be on the road at dawn and there was little enough time left for sleep as it was.

As Phelan went to follow the others to the sleeping chambers, the Prince caught him by the arm.

'We must give you our gifts,' insisted the Prince. 'All the people have brought you tokens of their gratitude.'

'But quite apart from making me a prince you have given us these beautiful clothes and equipped us for our return. That is more than enough,' protested Phelan.

'No, no, not a bit of it,' laughed the Prince. And he led him into another room which was piled high with boxes and packages of every conceivable shape and size.

Phelan blanched. 'I can't possibly… I mean, what would we *do* with it all?' he muttered.

'Please,' begged the Prince, 'take *something* as a token of our love and gratitude, otherwise the people will be offended.'

Phelan sighed. 'I will take one small thing as a token. My friends may also take what they will, but I beg you, take everything that is here and give it to the poor in the land. There is more here than any man could even *look* at in one lifetime – let alone *possess*.

'Show me where the smallest gifts are to be found, for I cannot take anything bulky with me.'

A servant led Phelan to a table at the back of the room, where blue and purple velvet cases containing the rarest jewels of the Kingdom were laid out. He walked past them with barely a glance. At the very end, tucked almost out of sight, lay a little olive-wood box carved with the symbol of the Ring Fire on its lid.

'What is this?' He picked it up and turned it over.

'I do not know, Sir,' replied the servant. 'None of us has been able to open it. Maybe it is just a carving. It is nothing.' He shrugged.

Phelan smiled. 'Then I will take it. It is very small and light and it will fit easily into my pocket. It will remind me that it is only the Ring Fire which has brought me here. Thank you.' And with that he bowed to the Prince and went to bed.

As the first light softened the black curves of the countryside, Gemma was up and dressed in new travelling clothes. They were very much like her old ones but warmer and with no holes. The Queen's shoes still fitted her, but they leaked terribly, so she had them packed with her other gear as she could not bear to be parted from them.

Rowanne appeared at her door. She too had fresh riding clothes but best of all, she had a bright sword slung at her side and a finely wrought new dagger. 'Personal gifts from Phelan,' she grinned. 'I think we're even now.' Then she caught sight of Fleabag, who had made a special effort to get his fur comfortably matted again.

'Don't look at me,' he said. 'You'll never have my hide round your neck. I've acquired some particularly itchy fleas here. Would you like one?'

Prince Tomas waved the friends off, but there were no lengthy farewells; Gemma's sense of urgency would not permit it. Rowanne was a little grumpy. She was greatly enjoying the fuss that was made of her and would have liked to spend time in the Prince's stables and working out with one or two of his knights in the practice yard. Her sword fighting had really become rusty of late and she doubted if she could still unhorse an opponent with a lance.

She looked longingly at the archery butts as the horses wheeled out of the yard, but then she turned her attention south by south-east.

Day after day, they rode with the sun in their eyes all morning. The soldiers accompanying them set up strong canvas tents at night, so no time was lost looking for accommodation, except when the spring rains came. Then they were forced to stop in a small village as floods swept across the low-lying ground and cut them off for a whole week.

Gemma fretted and wouldn't eat. She sat morosely looking out of the upstairs window of the cottage where they were staying and watched the waters swirl endlessly.

Rowanne champed at the bit. She paced up and down the short muddy street asking every inhabitant how long the floods usually lasted and how deep the draining ditches were. She drew up calendar after calendar, deciding that each one must be wrong. They had left several days before the equinox, but every day was precious. At last, the tops of grass shoots appeared in rough patches here and there amongst the smooth yellow-grey flood water. The next day muddy banks appeared. Rowanne tried to find the road with her horse, but she could not locate the bridge they needed to cross the swirling submerged river.

Two days later they were on the road again.

Slowly the days lengthened and warmed until blossom

and leaf filled the air with the rich smells of early summer. They had only a few days left when at last they reached Rupertsberg.

Rowanne reined in her horse and looked silently for several minutes. 'We must go round it. I must not even ride through, or we may never make it in time.' And with that she urged her chestnut stallion along the wide road that ran along the foot of the walls. With every bit of speed they could muster the party galloped up the next hill and through the wood where Phelan's gang had first attacked. But the ex-thief looked neither to his right nor to his left. He bowed his head over his horse's mane and rode.

The city of Harflorum was situated on a small hill overlooking wide plains which rolled to the south. The approach road from the north-west wound between hills and woods, then opened out suddenly on the view. Everywhere the scent of May blossom filled the air. Gardens were springing verdant with strong young seedlings. Everything looked peaceful.

Until they reached the gates.

The soldiers admitted the party as they were obviously visiting dignitaries, but everywhere the streets were crammed with people from every corner of the kingdom.

Everywhere stank of bodies pressed together. People jostled and crammed and pushed. Thieves plied their trade, as did pedlars with trays of imitation opal rings and fire jugglers breathing 'real Ring Fire' from their noses and mouths. Mothers struggled to get frightened children home through the crush. Everywhere was turmoil.

Gently, the friends eased their horses through the

throng until they reached the palace gates. Rowanne leaned over and gave her name to a guard who did not know her.

'I don't care who you are, you take your place with the rest. The queue goes on right round the palace. Be patient and you'll get your turn.' And with that he turned her horse's head and slapped the animal on the flank. The frightened horse swung badly from left to right, but Rowanne controlled it with a tight rein.

'This is hopeless,' Rowanne yelled above the hubbub. She called to the guards who had accompanied them. 'Take the horses and find somewhere for yourselves to sleep outside the city. This is no place for the animals – nor for anyone who doesn't need to be here. We will send for you in a few days.'

The soldiers saluted and led the horses out of the city. Gemma kept close in behind Rowanne. The crush frightened her. Crowds always made her feel as if she could not breathe, but she must not faint this time. Fleabag jumped up onto Phelan's shoulder so he could be carried.

'What do we do now, clever-clogs?' the cat asked rudely.

Rowanne scowled at him. 'Why can't you be useful for a change? Jump down and see how we can get into the palace.'

The cat scrambled down, inadvertently scratching Phelan as he went. Swiftly he dodged the many feet and disappeared.

'What do we have to queue for, anyway?' asked Phelan out loud.

A short fat woman with a water bottle and a cup was

shoving her way through the masses. 'You want to know what this is all about? Don't you know? Goodness me!' she tutted, 'where have you been for the past year? These are all people who are wanting to show their opal rings to the Fire Wielder in case they have found the true Ring. Trouble is, he's very weak. He won't live much longer, and he's certainly too frail to see anyone, so we're all just sitting here. Only got to wait until tomorrow though, then the year and a day's up! I'm doing all right, though. Would you like to buy a drink, dearie?' she turned to Gemma.

'No, thank you. But what happens at the end of tomorrow if he still can't see anyone?'

The woman shrugged and her three chins wobbled. 'Dunno. There'll be a big fight, I suppose. I won't stick around for it, though.' She turned to the next person behind them. 'Buy a drink, dearie?'

Just then Fleabag came panting back and leaped into Phelan's arms again. He looked quite exhausted.

'I've found a way to get into the palace, if you don't mind going through the kitchen. Cook left the door ajar. But the bad news is he's there and in a filthy temper.'

Gemma winced at this, but Rowanne, who had heard all about Cook's ways, pulled herself up to her full height. 'Come on, cat!' she said, 'Let's have him for supper, shall we?'

Carefully they edged their way through the people, until they reached the wall of the kitchen garden. As Fleabag had said, the gate was slightly ajar. Phelan pushed it open and they all slipped inside.

Cook, who had been beating one of the kitchen boys, stopped and looked up at the intruders. He dropped the poor unfortunate lad into the sage bush and turned on the others, brandishing his rolling pin.

Fleabag took good aim and leaped with all fifteen claws splayed and caught Cook on the face. At the same moment Phelan wrested the rolling pin from his fist.

With a strong hold, Rowanne caught the greasy man's arm behind his back, and marched him along the path, opened the garden door and pushed him firmly outside so he fell right into the gutter.

Phelan pushed the door shut and locked it with a satisfied sigh. 'It'll be a long time before he's able to get back in *here*!' He grinned.

All the kitchen staff were crowded around the pantry door, watching with open mouths what had happened to the tyrant. As the travellers stepped into the kitchen, they were all applauded. Fleabag excused himself and went to have a quick look at his favourite dead rat, to see whether it was ready to eat after having matured behind Cook's chair for a whole year.

Gemma led the way from the back stairs where she and Fleabag used to talk. Without pausing they ran straight past the butler, who did not dare to stop them, and into the main hall. There they turned left and went up the next flight of stairs to the top of the palace. At the end of the next corridor was the Hall of Light.

There Gemma stood still.

'What are we going to *say*?' she asked, looking at the others with a worried frown. 'We have nothing to show him.'

34

The King and the Fire Wielder

'Well, at least let's see him and tell him we tried,' said the cat practically.

Gemma put her hand against the door and gave it a gentle push.

'You can't go in there,' yelled a stentorian voice from behind them.

Rowanne swung round. It was the Captain of the Queen's Guard. She stood to attention and saluted smartly. 'Sir!' she said, 'I have escorted this lady for many miles at the Fire Wielder's request. I am sure that he will want to see us.'

The Captain relaxed as he recognized Rowanne, and said very quietly. 'I'm sorry. It's impossible. Don't you know he's dying? It won't be much longer.'

'But he expressly ordered me...' began Rowanne.

While they were arguing, Fleabag pressed both front paws on the heavy carved door and pushed it open. 'Psst, leave them at it,' whispered the cat. 'Rowanne likes a good row – she'll be fine.'

The three of them crept into the Hall. Phelan stood uncertainly on the threshold, but Gemma beckoned him to follow. The room was silent, and filled with the soft light of an early summer evening.

Asleep on the chaise longue, apparently just as they had left him a year ago, lay the Fire Wielder. He had become very thin. His round face was sunken now and the once golden-brown skin was pale and sallow. His hooked nose looked huge against his wasted features. He seemed unutterably tired.

On the table next to him burned a tiny, weak flame, not much bigger than a glowing match head. All that was left of the Ring Fire. 'I must have used it all up,' said Gemma. 'I do hope it's not too late.'

'Quick,' said Phelan. 'I hear more guards coming.'

At this, Fleabag jumped onto the Fire Wielder's chest and licked his face. 'Wake up, Sir,' he said. 'We're back!'

The old man moaned, opened his eyes and smiled. 'I had been dreaming you were on your way,' he said weakly. 'I hoped it was true. Now, give me the Ring. We will put the Fire back straight away.'

'We haven't got it, Sir,' Gemma said, hanging her head. 'Everything went wrong. Either that or I misheard. Anyway, I failed you and the Queen.'

'Nonsense!' snapped the old man, lifting his tired grey head from the pillow. He waved a finger at Phelan. 'You there, let's see what you've got tucked away.'

Bemused, Phelan pulled a penknife, some string, a candle end and the little carved wooden box from the depths of his trouser pocket. 'I've only got these and a dirty handkerchief.'

'Open that!' said the Fire Wielder, pointing to the little box.

Phelan was about to protest that it *wouldn't* open, when he noticed a narrow gap in the side. Carefully he eased the crack further apart and there, on a bed of sea-green velvet, lay the Queen's Ring.

'Give it here, boy. Gemma, pass me the Ring Fire. Gently, it is very faded.'

Gemma picked up the tiny flicker of flame. For one awful second she thought it had gone out, but it steadied between her fingers.

The Fire Wielder lifted his tired hands and tried to hold the Ring and the Fire, but he was too weak. His thin fingers fell uselessly back onto the quilt that covered him.

'You'll have to do it for me, child. Just let the Flame flow into the Ring. There, that's right! Now,' his voice had almost sunk to a whisper, 'put it on the boy's finger. What's your name, lad?'

'Phelan, Sir.'

'Phelan, do you swear to be a good King and to serve your people faithfully all your days?'

Phelan opened his mouth and looked aghast.

'Go on! Do you?' Fleabag prompted.

'Yes, Sir, I do.'

'Well, that's settled.' The old man let his head rest back in the pillow, but his bright eye held Gemma in its gaze. 'And you, Gemma by name, Gem by nature, do you swear to carry the Ring Fire so that Phelan here will always have light to see by as he rules the land?'

Gemma swallowed hard. '*Me*?' she gulped.

'Of course, child, you! Who else? You've carried the Ring Fire all year. No one else has had any practice at it. It's *got* to be you! Gemma Fire Wielder, the latest of our line. Carry it well.'

Phelan nudged her.

'Yes,' she replied quietly. 'I swear.'

'Even better,' he said, closing his eyes and smiling. 'That's everything seen to now.' And he went to sleep.

Gemma held the old man's hand and felt his breathing slow until it was scarcely a flicker in his chest.

'He won't waken again, I'm afraid,' Phelan said softly.

'But what happens now?' Gemma asked.

'I think you ought to speak to your visitors,' Fleabag interrupted. 'There's lots of them.'

With a jump, Gemma and Phelan turned to see the room was full of people, mostly court officials – the Prime Minister, the Captain of the Guard and, standing in front of them all, the Lady Knight Rowanne de Montiland.

Suddenly, the knight pulled her sword from its sheath and knelt before Phelan, offering the hilt to the young King.

'My Lord,' she said. 'In more ways than one, my life is yours.'

There was a murmur of steel and a rustle of clothes as one by one, everyone in the room followed suit. Gemma started to kneel as well, but Fleabag stopped her. 'Don't, you silly girl. *You're* the Fire Wielder. You hold the flame high for everyone to see.'

Gemma lifted one thin arm and let the Fire burn until it filled the evening-darkened room with a glorious light.

When she looked around, even Phelan was kneeling.

'All homage to the Ring Fire,' the King said, 'in which we live and move and have our being.'

The next few hours were a blur to Gemma. Everyone wanted to make a fuss of her – especially the butler who had kicked her so viciously when she had been a mere kitchen-maid.

She and Phelan were taken away by lords- and ladies-in-waiting, bathed and dressed in the finest robes. Fleabag made himself scarce when a maid came in his direction with a flea comb.

The next day, Gemma looked ruefully out of the palace windows and watched the children playing in the gardens. At that moment she would have given anything to be with them, running free and scruffy across the grass.

When she saw the heavy red and gold embroidered over-garments she was expected to wear all the time, she winced and bit her lip. She remembered how hot and uncomfortable the old Fire Wielder had looked the first time they had met. Suddenly she turned to the servant who was dressing her.

'I'm not going to wear these,' she announced. 'I've been carrying the Ring Fire for a year and a day, and I never needed heavy robes – so I'm not going to start now.' With that she ran from the room and disappeared down the servants' stairs and into the garden.

As she ran she was grabbed by a dark figure who had been hiding behind a tangled rambling rose. It was a miserable-looking Phelan.

'This means the end of all our fun – all our freedom,' he said unhappily. 'You ought to see the *stuff* I'm expected to wear! And worse than that, they've been lecturing me on how a king is expected to behave – all these *rules*. I won't be able to stand it. I wish I'd known before I made my vow to the Fire Wielder. I would have said "no".'

Gemma squatted next to her friend. 'I know,' she replied. 'I feel exactly the same.' Then she shifted suddenly as she felt the rose thorns pricking her back. But it wasn't a rose. It was Fleabag.

'Who do you think made the rules in the first place?' the cat enquired. 'Who thought of all those silly clothes and stuffy rules?'

'Other kings and other Fire Wielders, I suppose.'

'So who would have the authority to *unmake* the rules?' Fleabag persisted.

Phelan sprang up and looked at Gemma with glee. 'Why, *us*, of course!' He grabbed her hands and swung her around three times until they tripped and fell into a dizzy, rolling tumble all the way down the steeply sloping lawn.

When at last they stopped, all muddied and grass-stained, they were met by wide-eyed children staring in amazement to see the King and the Fire Wielder acting in this way.

Within seconds the lords- and ladies-in-waiting came swooping down from the palace armed with sponges, towels and royal robes, all clicking their tongues.

'Oh, go away!' Phelan laughed. 'From now on, when we're not doing something important, we're just going to be ourselves!'

Gemma did agree to wear a heavy gold and red embroidered robe for the Fire Wielder's funeral, as a mark of respect for the office she held.

Solemnly she led the procession from the palace to the graveyard on the sunny slope behind the city. Although she was sad at having lost someone so special, she knew he was glad to be sleeping the Long Sleep. The old Fire Wielder had been so tired.

After the funeral was over she sent her servants away and just sat quietly stroking Fleabag, smoothing his silky fur between her fingers. He was as dear and as ugly as ever. He sprang into her lap and they cried together until a flame-red sunset burned the evening sky with livid fire.

It was there that Phelan found them. He had taken off his royal robes and told his attendants in no uncertain terms that he wished to be left alone.

He sat quietly with them until the crimson and gold sky faded to indigo. At last he stood up.

'It is over now,' he said gently. 'Tomorrow we have other things to think about.'

The coronation was not held in the great Throne Room – or anywhere in the palace. Phelan insisted that if he were to be King of the people, he must be crowned amongst them.

On the last day of June, when the sun shone most strongly, an ordinary wooden chair bedecked with scarlet and yellow ribbon was carried to a large field outside the city. Phelan walked so he could hold the hands of the city children as he came. Behind him, Gemma rode a white pony. On her lap was a white silk cushion, bearing the crown of the land and a plain opal ring with a strong red flame burning at its heart.

She smiled and looked at the thronging crowd.

Everyone wore flowers in their hair and dressed in bright-coloured robes. Music sounded at every corner as buskers and court musicians joined together to play dance music for the procession.

Soon the city was quite empty, for everyone had gone to the field to see the new Fire Wielder place the Ring on the hand of the young King, and then crown him.

When the simple ceremony was over, Fleabag (who had permitted Gemma to comb him a little) came and sat and stared hard at Phelan.

'Well, you verminous hearthrug, you. What do you think you are doing?' asked Phelan.

'A cat may look at a king, mayn't he?'

'If he really *is* a cat, but I've been looking for a fur collar for my friend Rowanne de Montiland and I think you might just do,' grinned Phelan.

'Oh, *her*,' sneered the cat, jumping up into the King's lap. 'I hear she's off and away soon, anyway.'

Rowanne, who was just bringing Phelan a glass of wine and a large piece of coronation cake, almost tripped on the hem of the long dress which Gemma had persuaded her to wear for the occasion.

'What lies are you spreading about me, cat?' she laughed.

'Only that I hear you're leaving us.'

'I have decided, and my Lord King has given his permission, to challenge my disgusting cousin Prince Rupert to face me in fair fight for his Princedom.'

Fleabag scratched himself vigorously behind one ear and looked thoughtful. 'I'm coming with you.'

'What?' Gemma couldn't believe her ears. 'I thought you were going to be supervising the installation of central heating in the palace so you'd have warm radiators to sleep on all winter.'

'Plenty of time for that later. Summer's still young.'

'So why do you want to go with Rowanne to Rupertsberg?'

'Well, if she's going to be challenging that poor, defenceless little man to a contest, I think I'd better go and ensure there's fair play, don't you?'

'Come off it!' laughed Rowanne. 'You can't expect me to believe any of that tosh. And since when did you know anything about fair play? You cheat at every turn!'

Fleabag looked at the King's Ring, which was burning gently with the glorious sheen of restored Ring Fire.

'Oh well, I suppose telling a lie ill befits a day like today.' Then he blushed (as much as a black cat can). 'The truth is, I received word from Rupertsberg this morning that the nice little tortoiseshell in the Prince's kitchens has at last consented to be my bride.'

Gemma grinned. 'I know just the wedding present for you!'

'What?' asked the cat warily.

'A can of flea powder!'

Fleabag and the Fire Cat

Contents

1

Blue Lightning

Blue lightning flashed in terrifying sheets across the darkened sky. Everywhere the oppressive air was uncannily still. The rain had not yet closed in behind the storm. The world seemed to hold its breath between flashes. Everything was waiting for the thunder… which never came.

Fleabag stretched as he climbed out from his nest under the lavender bushes. He turned his black furry face this way and that, swivelling his ears to catch sounds of his grandkittens playing somewhere in the undergrowth at the back of the palace gardens. He yawned and began to call their names. He would have to get them in. Their mother would have his fur if the kittens got wet or frightened.

He *was* supposed to be kitten-sitting, after all – although his idea of supervising the little ones consisted mostly of finding a warm, dry patch of earth and having a catnap for an hour or two with just half an eye open until lunch, or tea or elevenses or whatever excuse for eating he could think of next.

He had spent the morning dreaming about his heroic adventures on the quest to find the Queen's Ring, two years before. Sometimes his thoughts were full of how bravely and nobly he had carried out the quest. But at other times, like today, he felt more afraid, remembering how real the danger had been. Tales were all very well, but they were scary when they were actually happening. They really made a cat's fur stand on end.

Rather like this eerie, thunderless storm.

He balanced on his three legs and stretched as he called the kittens again. As he waited for their answering calls, he looked up at the sky. The strange lightning was becoming more frequent. The rain would pour down any second now. The heavy blue-black clouds were stacked up into gigantic, ominous-looking towers, ready to pour torrential waters onto the earth below. It did not need a great deal of imagination to see fearsome faces leering down from above.

Suddenly the rain *did* come, as fiercely and totally as Fleabag had feared. The huge raindrops caught in the black cat's golden eyes and made them sting. In the walls of the palace behind him a window clattered open at the mercy of the frantic wind. A hand reached out to pull it shut.

Fleabag was about to call the kittens again but what he saw made his voice stick in his throat...

Not far away, Gemma the Royal Fire Wielder was sitting with her desk pulled up to the window so she could look out over the garden. She liked to day-dream between reading official documents. From here she would watch her old friend Fleabag the talking cat, playing with his grandkittens. Their games made her laugh.

Gemma was scarcely more than a child herself, and had once been a street urchin. Now she held the highest office in the land, higher even than her friend King Phelan. She was the Fire Wielder. It was her job to look into the flame of the Ring Fire and understand the ways of the Fire Giver, to protect the Kingdom from all evil and give wisdom to the King. But she never felt comfortable in her job. Although she loved the Ring Fire she served, she never felt she understood it properly. She never seemed to really grasp how to be the carrier of the great eternal flame. Surely it was too great and awesome for someone ordinary like her. She always seemed to get everything wrong. The Ring Fire never flared when she called upon it, but always roared to life spectacularly at the most embarrassing moments. All her ceremonies went wrong, and she was sure everyone was laughing at her behind her back. She was miserable.

She longed to be a street child or even a kitchen-maid again. Then at least no one would expect her to be something she wasn't...

Official duties hemmed her in. It was bad enough having to sit inside most of the day reading difficult books or signing papers, instead of being amongst the familiar bustle of the stallholders in the market, or laughing at Fleabag as he performed his ludicrous antics. Life had been hard when she was younger, but at least she had been free.

Gemma sighed. She could not escape her duties but at least she could watch the world and laugh at the kittens, even if she couldn't join in.

But today, she was sitting with her thin face in her hands, staring out of the window for a different reason. The lightning bothered her. It flashed again and she shivered. It was too similar to something she had known, something from not so long ago. Something she had hoped never to meet again.

Absently she scratched the itching in her palms, then jumped as the Ring Fire flared between her fingers. It did not burn her – it wasn't that sort of a fire – but the shock of its golden, exuberant flames leaping against the eerie blue lightning outside made her gasp and go cold. Its presence meant she was right: this was no ordinary storm, and *something* was about to happen!... But what?

Gemma swallowed hard as she turned her gaze back to the ominous skies. She watched the brilliant blue flashes skimming across the slate-black clouds. They seemed to be illuminating the world while an evil mind was searching for something down below.

'I thought the Chancellor and his son were dead,' she muttered to herself. 'This is the sort of magic they used. I could never forget it...' For a few moments her mind drifted back to the day when Phelan, Fleabag and herself challenged the terrible power of the Chancellor of All Wizards in the imitation Hall of Light at Porthwain. At the time she thought she was merely acting a part to scare the Chancellor. She had not realized the true power of the gift in her hands. If she had, she would never have dared to do what she did that day.

She shook her head and sighed. Perhaps part of her

problem now was knowing that she really *did* carry the Ring Fire. The thought daunted her.

There was another flash of eerie blue light. She closed her eyes tightly, but she knew it would not make it go away. Normally Gemma loved storms, and had been known to climb up into the attic and out onto the roofs of the sleeping apartments so she could get a really good view.

But today she merely sat very still and watched. Her breathing was shallow and fast. She did not like what was happening. She did not like her memories. What was worse, the Ring Fire was burning in her palms. It would not go away. It was a warning. Maybe there would be another battle like the one they had fought at Porthwain, or the time she had beaten the wolves back...?

Gingerly she shook her sleeves back as she raised her hands, and let the Ring Fire blaze out properly. If there was to be a battle, she knew better than to get in the way of what the Ring Fire chose to do. She felt very small and alone and wished that Fleabag or Phelan were with her. They always knew what to do, but there was no time to go and get help. Whatever had to be done, had to be done now. As she raised her hands, a tremendous gust of wind caught the palace buildings. Doors rattled everywhere. Her window tugged on its catch and swung wide.

As she did so the heavy blue-black clouds seemed to swoop down and engulf the palace in sudden rain.

Gemma leaned out to pull the window closed. At that very second the thunder came at last – crashing with an unbelievable noise that shook the ground. Blinding lightning flashed, but this time, instead of the harmless eerie sheets of searching light, a five-fingered fork of lightning darted towards her. Then another. Then another, each groping closer and closer to where she stood.

She jumped back, but not because of the lightning. Something much worse had frightened her. Something inconceivably terrible…

For as she had reached out to catch the window, the rain had caught the Ring Fire that still burned in her palm. As the water touched the flame, it went out! The unquenchable Ring Fire that gave life and meaning to everything, had failed while *she* had been holding it!

Gemma forgot the clattering window and fled her room, running blindly down the darksome corridor. She did not stop until she reached the familiar safety of the broom cupboard. She fumbled with the wooden latch and slipped inside. Years ago, when Gemma had been a kitchen-maid she used to shelter here from the wrath of the drunken cook.

It was a tiny, circular room at the top of a small, spiral staircase. There was one window in the place, a small, vertical slit which admitted enough air and light to make the hiding place tolerable for several hours.

The violent wind that had come so suddenly was now buffeting the palace like a petulant giant. A blustering draught slammed the cupboard door behind Gemma. It was difficult to open from the inside, but she did not care. Instead she curled up very small under a pile of rags and dusters, closing her eyes to the all-pervading blue lightning.

She was too dazed to cry. The last time she had seen anything that eerie blue colour it had been in the hands of the evil Chancellor at Porthwain. She had not been so frightened then. But the magical blue fire had not felt this powerful, and she had not been alone, for Fleabag and Phelan had been there too. More importantly, then the Ring Fire had flared high and wide from between her fingers. It had been glorious, defeating and swallowing the threatening evil with a burst of golden flame. It had been exhilarating and exciting! It had worked!

But now, what she had always dreaded more than anything had happened. In *her* hands, the Ring Fire had failed. It had died. She had seen the strange wind and rain quench it. There was nothing more she could do. She must have weakened it by her ineptitude. It was *she* who had brought it to this pass!

At last Gemma managed to let her feelings out. She buried her face in her hands and sobbed silently. Outside the cupboard she could hear Fleabag pacing up and down the corridor calling her. She stopped crying and held her breath. How she wished she could rub her face into the cat's knotted flea-ridden black fur and feel his thunderous purring against her cheek. She wanted to hear his impossibly awful jokes and just laugh with him. He would comfort her and say something kind and warming.

But her friend could not help her this time. Alone she had to face the fact that she was no good as Fire Wielder. Fleabag must never know that the rain from the strange, evil clouds had quenched the Ring Fire. Everyone in the land would be in deadly terror if they knew this evil menace was stronger than the Ring Fire.

The whole land was at the mercy of the blue magic until she could find another Fire Wielder, one who was worthy of the office. Someone who would know what to do.

Tentatively she lifted her head a little to listen. Had

Fleabag gone? Was it safe to cry again?

Gemma could hear nothing. There was always a hope that she hadn't allowed the blue magic to kill the Ring Fire completely. But she knew a real Fire Wielder should be able to stand with Fire blazing before whatever danger threatened the land. And *she* didn't know how to do that!

Whatever was happening outside felt stronger than the Fire.

'Please let me go,' she whispered. 'Let me be plain Gemma Streetchild again!'

Below in the kitchen, a sodden Fleabag lined up six bedraggled kittens in front of the fire to dry their fur. He was very worried. He had only glimpsed Gemma's outstretched hand reaching for the window. The Ring Fire had been dancing on her fingers as she reached out, then it had faded as the blue power gathered to strike.

But suddenly Gemma had pulled her hand back, leaving the loose window clattering in the wind. Fleabag had run upstairs as soon as he had brought the kittens inside, but he couldn't find her. Instinctively he knew something was very wrong, but Gemma had been so withdrawn of late... She didn't seem to want to know him any more. He couldn't *make* her talk to him. He would talk to Phelan. He might know what to do.

But there was nothing more Fleabag could do for now except make the kittens presentable again, so he turned his attention to washing a struggling little black miniature of himself. 'I wonder what will happen next?' he thought.

2

Fleabag is Uneasy

Fleabag twitched his whiskers. Something had brushed past his face, disturbing his dreams. Lazily he stretched out a claw and took a sleepy swipe. He missed, but who cared? Let the mice get bold. The more careless they were, the easier they would be to catch. He turned over and put a loving paw around his wife Tabitha, then went back to sleep. He was tired. Yesterday's strange storm had left everyone feeling exhausted.

Suddenly he sat bolt upright. There *was* something in the room, and it wasn't a mouse!

He got up stiffly and balanced himself on his three legs, smelling the air and turning his huge tattered ears this way and that, scooping at the night, trying to catch the slightest sound. What *was* it? He felt the fur on his back begin to rise. But why? He could not smell or hear anything strange, but ever since the storm a peculiar feeling had stayed hanging in the air…

The royal palace was silent except for the usual pacing of the guards outside and the sniffings and scratchings of the guard dogs. In the next room King Phelan was snoring loudly. He was only a young man, scarcely in his twenties, but his snoring could shake the window panes if he had curry for supper. But the 'something' was not Phelan.

Tabitha turned over sleepily. 'What's the matter, dear?' she purred (unlike Fleabag, she could not use human speech).

'Nothing, dear. I'm just going to stretch my legs for a while. Go back to sleep.'

'I can't,' she replied sleepily. 'Something keeps brushing past my whiskers and disturbing me.'

Fleabag did not want his wife to be worried. She was pregnant with what looked like an enormous litter of kittens. She needed her sleep.

'I felt it too,' he said. 'I think there's a mouse that needs teaching some manners. I'll catch it,' he promised.

Tabitha rolled over and stretched the length of the velvet-lined cat basket, glad to have the extra space to herself, and went back to sleep.

Fleabag did not like the feeling that was running up and down his spine. It was not good. He drank some water and slipped out into the corridor. He sniffed all along the bottom of Phelan's door. No one except the butler had come in or out since the King had gone to bed. Yet something… something… was… *behind him*!

He jumped and twisted 180 degrees in the air, landing with a thump! Nothing. Only the midnight shadows on the walls. Shadows he had known since he was a kitten.

Nothing strange… Yet there it was again! He jumped high this time, clawing halfway up the wall as… *something* went past.

'This is ridiculous!' he told himself. Once again he felt compelled to leap and pounce, attacking somewhere above his head, then behind him, then all around, just beyond the end of his own tail. He found himself jumping and thudding along the corridor – yet there was absolutely nothing there! He had no idea what he was after, he just had to do it. He was acting like a demented kitten. This was ridiculous – it was so undignified!

Tabitha called out sleepily, asking him either to go out and play in the garden or to come back to bed – he was keeping her awake.

Fleabag turned and growled warningly at the something-that-was-nothing. 'I'll be back!' he warned, as he slipped back into the bedroom and curled up next to his beloved. But sleep eluded him.

At breakfast a grumpy Fleabag asked Phelan if he had slept well. The young king shook his head and pushed his dark curly hair out of his eyes with marmalady fingers. 'No, you woke me up with your mousing in the middle of the night. Couldn't you let the poor little things live until morning? Honestly, it sounded as if coal was being delivered, the way you were jumping around.'

Fleabag did not think this was the right time to discuss the matter of the strange 'something' with the King. He wanted to have his thoughts clear first, so he selected a fat herring from the tray the butler was holding and took it out into the garden. There he could crunch the bones without Phelan throwing a slipper at him for being disgusting. There was only one way for a cat to think, and that was to eat a very substantial breakfast and follow it with a mid-morning nap.

He had a funny feeling about what was happening these days. Last night had not been the first time he had been woken by this strange 'something' that he just *had* to chase. He sometimes woke and found his fur on end. Some of his children had been acting rather strangely of late too, jumping and chasing at shadows in a frenzied way, just as he had.

But since yesterday's storm, the feeling that hung in the air was definitely worse, and he did *not* like it. He was suspicious, but he wanted to be certain of what he was suspicious *of* before he spoke to Phelan. Then there was Gemma. She had been so withdrawn and unhappy lately. She was no longer her old fun self, and she certainly didn't have time to see to really important matters of State such as rubbing his tummy and picking his fleas out. He felt in his whiskers that something was very wrong. In fact he felt uneasy all the way to the tip of his scraggy tail.

He finished the herring in the shade of a purple lilac tree, donating some of the chewier bits to a passing kitchen-cat. Then he had a leisurely wash in the morning sun. There was something very familiar about what was happening. That was more worrying than anything, for he could not remember *why* it was familiar. He longed to get up and *do* something, to find an answer, to solve the mystery, but he knew that if he acted without the proper preparation and enough catnaps, he would miss a vital clue. He curled up where he was, with the sun dappling through the trees, and fell asleep. But he did not get much rest, for the sound of voices woke him.

It was Gemma. She was striding along the gravel walk, dressed in her full robes of state (she was rarely out of them these days), giving orders to a group of tired-looking acolytes and acting like one of the arrogant nobles she had always despised.

But the effect was sad, rather than awe-inspiring. Gemma's heavy white robes, thickly embroidered with gold and red flames, made her look swamped rather than dignified. Her straight mousy hair had been dyed flame-red and piled high, and she wore thick make-up. Her tired face was beginning to show small, irritable-looking lines. She was nothing like the timid scullery maid who had been befriended by a mangy old kitchen-cat called Fleabag. Only three years had passed, but power and authority had changed Gemma – and not for the better.

Now was his chance. With the speed and agility of an acrobat, the fat, lazy Fleabag managed to dash to a plum tree a little further down the path, and scramble up it. He flattened himself on a branch that hung out over the walkway. He lay panting, gripping the bark with his claws. 'Where did I find the energy to do *that*?' he wondered.

Just then Gemma came almost level with him. He tightened his hold on the branch with his three paws and allowed his bottlebrush tail to tickle Gemma's nose.

She looked up crossly and pushed the offending tail to one side. 'Don't *do* that!' she snapped. 'It makes me want to sneeze, and you're *filthy*!'

Fleabag grinned and landed deftly on Gemma's shoulder so he could whisper in her ear. 'It never used to bother you, Miss High-and-Mighty. Come and sit down with me for a minute. I'll share my fleas with you and I'll even pounce on bits of grass if you twiddle them for me!'

'No!' she said, removing him from her shoulder and putting him firmly back on the ground. 'Not now. I'm busy. I'm off to an important meeting.' She stood up and brushed dust and loose petals from her robes. 'Look at me, I've got muddy paw prints all over me!'

'Sit down and I'll lick them off, I'm good at that,' the cat volunteered as he trotted alongside her. 'It's time we had a talk anyway.'

Gemma stopped for a second and looked down at her friend's huge golden eyes. Despite his teasing he looked worried. 'What about?' she asked suspiciously.

'About lots of things, but first of all there's yesterday's storm.'

'What about it?' she snapped. She could feel herself going pale.

'I was in the garden when the rain started, and I heard your window blow open. When I looked up, I saw something you ought to know about…'

Gemma was almost sick. *He knows! He saw!* she thought. Swiftly she gathered her skirts and put her nose in the air. 'This is ridiculous. I told you I'm in a hurry – I've no time to discuss the weather!' She had to protect him from the truth. She had to pretend she didn't know what he was talking about. When she had found a new Fire Wielder she would sit under the trees and scratch Fleabag's tummy and apologize. But not now. She dare not say anything *now*…

Fleabag could do nothing to make her listen, so he darted off after a butterfly, pretending he didn't care. But from the corner of his eye, he watched her over-dressed figure disappear between the trees. His heart sank. Why was she treating him like this? They had been through so much together; they had been such good friends. She really understood how to get the fleas out of the awkward places in his fur that even Tabitha could not manage with her excellent rough tongue. But most importantly of all, whether she liked it or not, he *had* to find a way to talk with her soon. She was in deep trouble. They needed to discuss the strange things that were happening, and most of all what he had seen…

Something evil and frightening was coming close. And it was Gemma's job to know what to do about it. He wanted to talk to her, but he knew she would not listen. Fleabag was not sure what the matter was, but her message was plain: he was only a cat and she was the Fire Wielder. In other words, he had to mind his own business.

He lay on his back and rubbed the warm earth into his matted fur, making it even messier. Something was very wrong, and things wouldn't get any better with Gemma acting all high and mighty. Rolling in the deliciously scratchy warm earth was much more helpful to a worried brain than attending meetings. He waved his three legs in the air in a most ridiculous manner, although not even the boldest shrew would have dared laugh at the sight. For he was Fleabag the Magnificent, sire of over twenty kittens, and grandsire of at least ten more (and five or six more on the way!), defeater of the evil Chancellor of All Wizards…

Suddenly he righted himself and sat alert, every whisker stretched in anticipation of hearing or feeling something close by. But no, it was gone again. Troubled, he resumed his rolling in the lovely, prickly earth. Where was he? Oh yes. He was the defeater of the Chancellor who had intended to claim the throne for himself, saying he was both Fire Wielder *and* Monarch…

Fleabag's fur rose again at the thought of the great Battle of Porthwain when he and Gemma had fulfilled the ancient prophecy that the Chancellor would be defeated by a black cat and a Fire Maiden. The Chancellor had raised terrible blue flames to try to destroy the Ring Fire. But he and his son Sethan had been burned to death by their own terrible magic. Indeed, Fleabag had brought about a great victory for the Ring Fire – Phelan and Gemma had helped a little too, of course!

Suddenly Fleabag rolled over and sat bolt upright. He was amazed at his own stupidity. That was it! Somehow the Chancellor's blue magic was awake again! He began to wash vigorously as cats always do when they are embarrassed. How could he have been so *stupid*? Perhaps Gemma had made the connection too, perhaps she was frightened, but why? The Ring Fire had defeated the blue magic before; it would do it again.

Things were dire. There were no two ways about it; with or without Gemma, he would have to find out what was happening.

3

Gemma Makes Plans

Her Eminence, the Lady Gemma of the Sacred Fire, Fire Wielder to the King, longed to take off her heavy robes and sit on the ground next to Fleabag. She would have loved to spend the morning scratching his ridiculous furry tummy, listening to that great deep rolling purr of his. It would be so good to tell him all her worries and fears.

But she didn't dare. No one must know.

She felt ill and weary. Knowing the terrible truth, that the blue magic could put the Ring Fire out, was a weight she found intolerable. On top of that, her shoes hurt and she was late for a reception to meet the new Chancellor of the University at Porthwain. A young man, she had been told, very anxious to meet her as he wished to be instructed in the ways of the Ring Fire. That was certainly a change from his predecessor, who had also held the office of Chancellor of All Wizards – an evil, destructive man, who had been intent on destroying the Ring Fire and claiming power for himself.

But Gemma did not feel like instructing anyone, even a keen student. After all, what could she, who had failed so badly, say to anyone? But there was always the very slim chance that he might prove to be the man to succeed her. Who knew? More than anything in all the world she wished that she had never heard of the office of Fire Wielder, so that she could be plain, ordinary Gemma Streetchild again.

'Bother the Ring Fire,' Gemma muttered, scratching the palms of her hands under the long sleeves of her formal robe. Her hands had been itching badly since the strange rain had put the Ring Fire out. She had put soothing cream on the reddened itchy places and her wardrobe mistress had tactfully chosen a gown with very long sleeves. Gemma was certain the Ring Fire wasn't dead; she had spotted a glimmer of a flame while she was dressing. But at least it was unlikely to flare up in her hands this morning, if it ever did again.

She was glad that the rain had put the flames out while she was holding them. She hated it when the Fire appeared. She never knew what to do. The responsibility was too great. She was no Fire Wielder, she was just a street urchin-cum-kitchen-maid.

Gemma was angry with her life. She had never had a childhood. She had never had *fun*! When she was little she had to fight in the streets to survive. Then in the palace kitchens she had to work until she dropped. Then the Queen had ordered her to go on the quest for the royal ring. Now she was the most important person in the land – even above the King. People expected her to be something she wasn't, and it wasn't fair!

But now she had failed the Ring Fire she felt better. With a clear conscience, she would find a successor and run off to the little cottage in the rocks where she and her friends had stayed one winter when on the Ring quest. Life had been good then. She could find that cottage again, and live there with some hens and a milking goat. That was all she needed. She hated having to be the Fire Wielder. She got things wrong all the time and the Ring Fire never did what she thought it was supposed to. She dressed in these silly robes and tried to look dignified. But it didn't help. If anything it made her feel more hot and cross and stupid than ever!

She wiped away a tear surreptitiously. Her palm was burning hot! Quickly she let her sleeve drop over the reddened skin. Danger was near, she knew it; but she dare not try and do anything in case it went wrong. The best thing she could do was to have this audience with the new Chancellor, then set her mind to the task of appointing another Fire Wielder. Once that was done, the land would be safe and she could go away and never come back!

Just the thought of living in the cottage in the rocks again made her feel easier. She'd want a cat with her of course – it needn't be Fleabag, although she would love to have him. He probably wouldn't want to come now he was married and had a huge family. She'd ask for one of the kittens – one of the talking ones. The ordinary cats weren't nearly so interesting…

As Gemma day-dreamed, she began to cheer up. She forgot the burning in her hands which should have put her on guard. In her head she was far away, in the foothills of the great mountains beyond Porthwain… In fact she was so deep in her thoughts she did not look where she was going. She tripped on a step and hit her head on the banister. The pain brought her back to reality. But now she had a headache as well as too-tight shoes and sore hands.

She sighed as she climbed up the rest of the steps into the palace from the gardens. She promised herself that before she went, she would sit out in the sun with Fleabag under the lilac tree and tell him the truth.

But today she had to pull herself together. She gathered up her skirts, entered the hall and walked up the main staircase. Suddenly she smelled burning. She looked down. One of her sleeves was scorched! In her right hand was a tiny, steady golden flame of fire! Why did it choose to burn like that? The flame rarely caught things alight. It was usually more of a glow… She brushed at the scorched cloth and the flame went out.

Oh, why did it all not go away? She did not want this. She had failed the Ring Fire yesterday and now it was back to mock her! Why did it not understand that it was not right that a mere street child should become the bearer of the living flame of the Ring Fire – the heart of the Fire Giver, watching over the people of the land? She clenched her hand tightly and bit her lip to stop herself crying out. But it did no good. She longed to run all the way back to Fleabag and cry into his fur. But it was too late. She had reached the top of the stairs and the heavy carved doors of the Hall of Light were already swinging open.

The white stone walls of the circular chamber were

bright with the morning sun which streamed in from the octagonal lantern set high in the middle of the ceiling. Here eight great lancet windows rose out from the roof, curved over and met in the centre, letting the sunlight stream across the great silk carpets that lay end to end across the floor in a glorious celebration of colour and design.

Gemma blinked. The light in the Hall always seemed to be intensely bright, but it was probably because the corridor outside was so gloomy.

When she was able to see clearly once more, her heart missed a beat, for across the room was a figure she had thought she would never see again.

4

The Chancellor's Offer

The young man standing in the centre of the Hall was tall, slim and fair, with a wide-boned face, typical of people from the West. He was suave, elegant and immaculately turned out in a grey silk tunic and trousers.

But what made her blood run cold was the realization that he was the image of a nightmare from her past – Sethan, the son of the evil Chancellor of All Wizards, whom she had seen die with his father in terrible blue flames in the imitation Hall of Light at Porthwain.

Gemma felt herself go pale. The burning in her right hand increased until it seared her in a way she had never felt before. So today at least, she *was* still the Fire Wielder! She was determined to keep calm.

She did not offer her hand to be kissed as the young man stepped forward and bowed to her.

The Chancellor's equerry bowed too as he said, 'My lady, may I present the Lord Domnall of Porthwain,

Chancellor of the University. He presents his respects and humbly requests to be instructed in the great and sacred truths of the Ring Fire.' The equerry stepped back. Once again the young man offered to take Gemma's hand.

Keeping her arms stiffly by her sides she silently thanked her wardrobe mistress for her long sleeves. Lamely she nodded towards a chair. 'Welcome, Lord Domnall. Would you care to sit?'

As she calmed her mind and looked hard at the Chancellor, Gemma sighed with relief. The man who had died was quite a bit younger than her visitor, even allowing for two and a half years since that day. The two young men were similar, that was all, and the grey silk suit was commonly worn by university officials on formal occasions. She was just feeling twitchy. She promised herself that this would all be over very soon.

'He seems very young to be Chancellor,' she thought. 'But then I suppose I am young to be Fire Wielder.' She settled herself in an ornately carved chair opposite her visitor. Mechanically she began the formal recitation of the Holy Writings.

After about ten minutes of polite listening, the Chancellor raised a finely boned hand. 'Forgive me for interrupting, my Lady, but these writings have been familiar to me since my youth.' He leaned forward with intense enthusiasm written across his face. 'It is real knowledge and the wisdom of the Ring Fire I seek.'

Gemma stared blankly at her visitor. How was she going to answer him? Somehow she knew, just by looking at him, that he was not the longed-for replacement. She might be exhausted and miserable, but she would not betray the Ring Fire by telling its secrets to everyone who asked. After a few moments she shrugged and rose to her feet. The young man looked up anxiously then stood as well.

'I'm sorry,' she said, 'what you ask is secret. The ancient wisdom belongs only to the Fire Wielders.'

Domnall kept his composure. He had expected as much. He had not imagined Gemma would simply tell him how the Ring Fire was passed from Fire Wielder to Fire Wielder, and how he might take it from her to become the next and greatest of all – both Monarch and Fire Wielder in one. Once he had the Ring Fire, disposing of the King would be easy. He was the sixth son of a sixth son of a sixth son after all! It was his birthright to claim the crown *and* the Ring Fire. All he needed was just a little more knowledge…

His father had planned this glory for himself, and he had died for his presumption, along with his younger brother Sethan. They had perished as they deserved. Usurpers!

And this Fire Wielder was weak and a mere child. What was more he could sense that she did not *want* the power she had. This was going to be easy. The secret goal of the Ancient Order of Wizards was within his grasp. But he knew he must be careful.

The girl was watching him intently, waiting for a reply. He had been silent too long and was in danger of being ushered out of her presence. He smiled and bowed his head. 'Of course, my Lady. My enthusiasm for sacred knowledge is greater than my wisdom. Forgive me.'

Gemma smiled. 'Of course.' She had to keep her composure. She was scheduled to be with this young man for three whole hours. How was she going to cope? It was so airless inside as well. Then she had an inspiration. 'I do find the palace stuffy on a sunny day like today, Lord Chancellor. Would you care to walk in the grounds?'

Domnall bowed in response. 'Madam, I would be delighted.' And he stood back to let her pass.

Although Domnall was fairly sure the ceremony of Giving the Fire had to take place in the Hall of Light, he had only met this slip of a girl a few moments ago. There would be plenty of time...

The formal gardens were a blaze of spring colour, laid out in intricate designs between covered walkways, supported by beautifully carved and painted pillars and arches. Each area of the palace was in a separate building. The Great Hall, the Hall of Light and the library were in the main building, but dotted around the gardens were guest quarters, children's nurseries, sleeping halls, smaller dining halls and kitchens, and a wonderful ballroom. Here and there tall, elegant trees shaded patches of green lawn and children played or did their lessons in the shade.

As Gemma took her visitor along a gravelled path between the bathhouse and the guest quarters, a kindle of kittens darted out, chasing each other wildly.

Domnall stopped dead and blanched, making his already pale skin paper-white.

Gemma turned and smiled. 'I know the people of your city have a natural dislike of cats, but these are quite harmless.' The memory of how she, Phelan and Fleabag had stood against the terrible Chancellor of All Wizards, and met his evil blue flames with the Ring Fire was forever fresh in Gemma's mind. She was grateful that this young man was only the Chancellor of the University. The Order of Wizards had been disbanded by royal proclamation after the Battle of Porthwain. She did not know what she would have said if this Lord Domnall had been one of them – probably she would have refused the audience.

As they watched the kittens, Fleabag appeared from a large clump of blackcurrant bushes and ushered his grandkittens away. Domnall stared hard at the venerable grandsire and made a slight gesture with his left hand. Fleabag and his kittens suddenly darted off amongst the shrubs chasing, or being chased, by *something*.

Gemma was so wrapped up in her misery that she did not notice.

Fleabag found himself in a breathless heap amongst the wild strawberries and began to wash himself hard, to cover his loss of dignity. 'This,' he muttered to himself, 'has got to stop!'

Gemma and her guest sat to drink tea at a little table in the rose garden. Fleabag soon caught up with them, but kept well out of sight, pricking up his wide, black ears as he began to listen intently. Almost immediately Domnall jumped, then sat stiffly with his head on one side as if he was listening. But in his intense blue eyes was a far-away look that betrayed a flicker of hate, or was it fear?

Gemma raised an eyebrow. 'Are you well, my Lord? Is something the matter?'

Domnall shook his head and relaxed again. 'I am sorry, Madam; I am just not used to the presence of cats.'

Fleabag smirked at this as he silently promised himself that this young man would have to get used to the presence of cats. 'I'm afraid from now on, a cat will follow you wherever you go,' he promised silently. He would have a chat with his eldest daughter, Cleo. She was highly intelligent and an excellent sleuth. What's more, she had kept her ability to talk a secret. He would ask her to follow him. She would enjoy the game and was less obvious than himself. Any visitor from Porthwain would be nervous of being followed by a three-legged, black scrag-bundle with a reputation as a slayer of wizards.

'Let's face it,' Fleabag muttered smugly to himself, '*I'd* be scared of me if I saw me coming.'

After discussing the garden and sipping mint tea for a while, Domnall skilfully turned the conversation back to the Ring Fire. Gemma let her head drop a little and sighed.

Domnall did not press the point, but, feigning sympathy, gently enquired whether carrying the Ring Fire was burdensome, for her Ladyship seemed very weary whenever the subject was mentioned.

'Yes, indeed I am weary,' she confided. 'In fact, I am planning a holiday. Things will be different after that.'

Better and better! Domnall laughed to himself. This girl was like a ripe plum about to drop into his lap!

'My lady, I own an excellent lodge in the north of Beulothin, not far from the city of Beriot. It overlooks the sea and is not troubled by neighbours. The city itself is only half a day's ride away, yet in my lodge, you would think yourself alone in the whole world! It is very beautiful, set between two great hills and with a small sandy beach below. Please, allow me, as your humble servant, to give you the use of it this summer.'

The young man smiled so warmly and genuinely that, although Gemma felt worried by the pain in her hands and a burning tingling down her spine, she found herself quite taken by the idea. It would give her time to think about what to do next, and most importantly of all, the journey would mean passing her beloved little cottage in the rocks.

'That sounds wonderful!' she enthused. 'But I fear I will not make a good guest. I have little conversation these days.'

Domnall brushed her fears aside. 'I will not be there, my Lady. I would not dream of imposing myself when you obviously need space and peace for a while to recover from the strains of your work.'

Gemma looked into the young man's eyes. Their intense blue reminded her of the blue flames raised by the evil Chancellor she had helped destroy. But now she was being silly! He looked so honest and kind, she found herself smiling warmly in response. 'Thank you,' she replied quietly. 'I should like that.'

Domnall could hardly contain his glee. He stood up and made an over-elaborate bow to hide the fact he was grinning widely. He had won the first stage in his victory!

'Then, my Lady, it is agreed. No more talk of the Ring Fire, as it wearies you so greatly. Simply a month by the sea with whatever friends you care to bring. You will be my guest but left completely alone. I will provide food, servants and everything you could possibly require.

'Meanwhile, I will take my leave of you, as I fear I am trespassing on your time.'

Then, before she could answer, he swept another bow and strode smartly away towards the gatehouse, closely followed by his equerry.

Gemma leaned her head on her hands, trying to ignore

the burning throbbing that would once have warned her of great danger.

Fleabag took his cue. With one bound he landed on the table in front of her, knocking the delicate china cups flying and smashing them on the gravel below.

Gemma turned to glower at the impossible cat, and stretched out a hand to shove him away. But he just sat there, head on one side, great golden eyes wide. 'You're not going to Beulothin, are you?'

Staring in the direction her visitor had gone, Gemma shrugged. 'What's the harm? I've got to have a rest!' and with that she sobbed and sobbed into his fur.

The black cat looked wistfully after the disappearing figure of Lord Domnall. There was something seriously wrong with Gemma if she had not sensed the blue shimmering danger that the Chancellor seemed to wear like a cloak. What was worse, Fleabag was angry with himself for not managing to set Cleo on that evil man's tail. Bother!

5

Sir Fleabag

To Gemma's surprise, Phelan thought the idea of a few weeks by the sea an excellent one.

He had been worried about Gemma for some time. The king had listened while Fleabag had tried to describe what he had seen the day of the strange blue storm. It troubled him deeply. He did not want her to go so far away without being near her, just in case something was seriously amiss. Phelan decided he would accompany them as far as Beriot in the hope that Gemma might confide her worries to him while they were riding.

It was no lie that Phelan wanted a holiday too, but he did not want Gemma to feel crowded when they got to the Chancellor's lodge. He decided to leave her there and visit his friend Prince Tomas, the Regent of Beulothin. Phelan would only be a few hours' ride away if he was needed.

So messages were dispatched. The company would make their first official stay with Rowanne de Montiland, the Lady Knight who had accompanied them on their quest to find the royal ring. She had challenged her spiteful, greedy cousin Rupert to the Princedom, and had won. As Princess she had changed the city's name back from Rupertsberg to its ancient title of Erbwenneth. It was over a year since they had seen Rowanne, and a night or two in her palace was sure to cheer them all up. She had excellent cooks and usually followed her feasts with plenty of storytelling and music.

After seeing Rowanne, they planned to ride north by north-west as they had done on the Ring quest. The snows were thawed and the spring rains were over, leaving the roads open and dry. It should be an easy ride, taking three weeks at the most.

During the next few days, Gemma dismissed her maid and packed her own things. She did not want anyone to guess she was not planning to stay long at the lodge by the sea, but to escape as soon as possible. Her luggage was mostly filled with seeds and basic farming tools, oilskins and blankets – things she would need for living alone in a rough place. She did not pack a single robe of state.

She felt sorry for her acolytes. They would have to bear the burden of official duties until someone came to take her place. She told them simply that they must oversee all the Fire ceremonies until further notice. She gave no explanations and made no excuses.

She felt better for doing what *she* wanted for a change. The day they were to leave she pulled on her leather jerkin and riding breeches and smiled properly for the first time in many long months. First, she would have a short holiday by the sea; then, when she had thought of how to find her replacement, she would simply disappear. It would be easy to hide in the mountains. She would be the Fire Wielder no longer.

Fleabag did not wait to be invited. As the horses and pack ponies drew up outside the stables for loading, he simply hopped onto a spare saddlebag (making sure first of all that his daughter Cleo was safely hidden *inside* the same bag), then they were off.

The journey to Erbwenneth was pleasant, but Phelan winced at the top of the last hill where he and his gang of thieves had once hidden and ambushed Fleabag, Rowanne and Gemma.

The Fire Wielder rode past the spot, head down, as if the memory meant nothing to her.

Fleabag jumped onto the King's saddle and made as formal a bow as a cat can manage. 'Sire,' he chuckled, 'I think you ought to dub me knight for my famous deeds in the late Queen's name on this field of battle.'

Phelan laughed out loud. 'Nonsense, I ought to cut your stringy tail off for daring to bite the flesh of your future liege-lord and King.'

'Well, it was your fault for pouncing out like that. Anyone would have thought you were a thief!' the cat pouted.

'I *was* a thief!' the King replied, reddening. 'And you are quite right, you should be dubbed knight on this field of battle.'

And with that, the King dismounted and drawing his sword, pointed to the grass at his feet. 'Kneel, noble cat!' he commanded. But then he regretted it, for three-legged cats cannot kneel very well and it was hard for Fleabag to remain dignified because he kept losing his balance and falling over. In the end Phelan said, 'Just stand still, Fleabag!' and he touched the cat lightly on both shoulders with the gleaming blade. Then he pronounced very solemnly, 'In the name of Queen Sophia of beloved memory, I command you to arise Sir... er... what would you like to be called?'

Fleabag stretched up and said something very quietly, so only Phelan could hear.

The King bowed his head and replied equally quietly, but with great dignity, tapping the cat on both shoulders again.

Then he stood up straight and said, so everyone could hear, 'Arise, Sir Fleabag Scrag-Belly.'

Everyone clapped and cheered, and the King gave the cat a golden earring as a token of his new status.

Gemma turned in her saddle as Phelan remounted. 'He's not really Sir Fleabag Scrag-Belly, is he?' she asked, quite horrified.

'No,' the King replied in a voice full of awe. 'He told me his real name.'

Princess Rowanne was delighted to see them. They were feasted and fussed over, but in the middle of the party, Fleabag sat right under Rowanne's chair, and prodded a not-too-sharp claw into her leg. Before Rowanne and Fleabag had made friends, this had been his way of making her listen to him. Since then she had always worn knee-high boots when he was around.

This time Fleabag was careful not to hurt, but Rowanne knew exactly who was under the table and that he required an audience with her. She dropped her napkin and bent down, glowering at the cat hidden in the gloom below.

'Listen, *mog*!' she hissed, 'why don't you come up and talk to me like a human being?'

'Because I'm *not* a human being!' Fleabag grinned.

'Well, why don't you come and talk to me properly, then? I could have you arrested for scratching my leg, you know.'

'But you won't, because you like me too much,' Fleabag retorted smugly. 'Now, this is secret,' he said, serious for once. 'I need to talk to you urgently and in private.'

'Talking like this isn't very secret or private.' Rowanne made a face. 'And I've eaten too much dinner, so if I don't sit up straight in a minute, I'll be sick all over you.'

'And spoil my luxurious black fur you've always coveted as a collar? Never! I'll meet you at midnight in the bell tower. Don't be late!' he demanded, and stalked away under the table, nibbling at a few fallen scraps as he went.

Rowanne righted herself, smoothed her hair and continued her conversation with Phelan.

The bell tower was a tall, thin, circular building, with a spiral staircase inside, ascending for three hundred steps before reaching the bell platform at the very top. From there all of Erbwenneth was in view, as well as a wide sweep of the countryside beyond.

Rowanne had once been very fit, for she had been a Lady Knight in the late Queen's Guard. But she had not been in action since fighting off some of her cousin's supporters after she became princess. Now she was quite out of breath when she reached the top. Fleabag, of course, was calm and composed, staring out of a small window towards the north-west, his bottlebrush tail neatly curved over his three paws.

'I'm a grandfather, and I'm much fitter than you!' he mocked. 'You ought to be ashamed of yourself, puffing like a pensioned-off mole!'

'And you're an alley-cat who doesn't know how to address a princess!' Rowanne retorted.

'I would if I met one!' Fleabag would never let Rowanne best him, even though they were friends these days.

Rowanne decided against dropping him out of the window for his cheek. She knew from experience that he would scratch her hands badly, and besides, it would make a mess in the courtyard below. For now, she was more interested in hearing what he had to say than in vengeance.

'Why have you dragged me all the way up here?' she complained. 'Why couldn't we have had a nice chat in my room over a flagon of ale?'

Fleabag looked out across the rolling countryside again. 'Because I want to be sure that no one in the whole world knows what I am going to say. I wanted to be sure we would be quite, quite alone...' The cat hesitated as he looked down at a row of dead bats and mice lined up across the floor. He patted one of them that he thought he saw twitch a little. 'I don't trust anyone except you to know this...'

'Know what?' Rowanne was getting exasperated.

'I think Gemma has either lost, or forgotten, the Ring Fire. Normally there is always a little flame hovering about her wherever she goes. I suspect that humans can't always see it, but I can. For at least two weeks it hasn't been there. The flame has gone, whether by her own choice or some other reason, I don't know. She will not talk about it.'

There was silence for a few moments. Rowanne tightened her grip on the handrail, and felt her fingers become cold and sore as she squeezed the iron. This was unbelievable. It was more than dreadful, it was...

Suddenly, above their heads came cawing and clattering sounds. Rowanne and Fleabag leaned out of the little turret window to see a crow flapping its great heavy wings laboriously as it flew off into the midnight skies. 'I forgot there might be birds listening,' he said. 'Still, with any luck, it's an ordinary stupid bird, or one who is loyal to us.'

Rowanne sniffed. 'Don't be daft, Fleabag. Would a bird care about the Ring Fire?'

'It has been known,' Fleabag answered nervously, remembering the ravens who had given a clue as to the whereabouts of the royal ring three years before. Then he went on to tell her what had happened to Gemma, how she had changed and how she had accepted this strange invitation for a month by the sea in Beulothin from this new Chancellor who smelled and looked and moved like the long-dead Sethan of Porthwain.

Fleabag did not tell Rowanne about the strange disturbances, the 'somethings' that drove all the cats silly with distraction. Neither did he try to explain what he had seen on the night of the storm. She would just have laughed and said it was normal for cats to jump around like half-witted lunatics.

'The long and the short of it is,' Fleabag looked up at the Princess with urgent gravity, 'you have got to come with us. I think Gemma will need help.'

Rowanne leaned on the window sill next to the cat and looked out across the landscape they had travelled before. 'When do we leave?' she asked.

6

The Voice

Gemma was delighted when Rowanne asked if she could come for a few days by the sea as well. The princess never tried to discuss the Ring Fire. She was more interested in telling tales of battles whilst downing a pot of ale. She made Gemma laugh, and never once alluded to the storm or the blue magic.

Phelan was relieved Rowanne had come. He realized that Gemma either would not, or could not talk, and he found riding next to her very wearisome.

As the company neared the mountain pass, and the little cottage in the rocks came closer and closer, Gemma became more silent than ever. Fleabag sat on the pommel of Gemma's saddle and tried to joke with her, but she did not even smile. In fact she scarcely spoke to anyone. Fleabag took to annoying a small dog that Rowanne had brought with her as a gift for Prince Tomas. But the animal was so stupid, he found it meagre and unsatisfying sport.

When they came to the bottom of the grassy slope below the stony outcrop where the tiny cottage was wedged in a cleft, Rowanne and Phelan jumped from their mounts to go and look at the place. Gemma pretended she wasn't interested, and called it a 'smelly dump'. Every part of her longed to go and sit in that tiny back room and to rekindle a fir-cone fire, as they had so long ago. The bright flames had transformed the damp little hovel to a warm home filled with golden light and soft brown shadows. Once the Ring Fire had glowed there as well, making the whole place feel joyful...

Gemma found she was aching to know whether the cottage was still standing after two bad mountain winters. Had Phelan's repairs held good? She so wanted to go and stand quietly on the earth floor and remember how good it had all been. Most of all, she wanted to remember how it had felt to hold the Ring Fire in her hands, and not feel frightened or inadequate, just loved.

As the others came back from the hidden place, slipping and stumbling down the slope towards her, she knew by their laughter and chatter that all was well. She had to feign disinterest. They must never think of looking for her there.

They camped just below the mountain pass before nightfall. Within a couple of days, Gemma's spirits lifted as they saw the wide fertile plains of Beulothin spreading out before them. Phelan ordered all royal insignia to be hidden. Three years before they had saved the land from a terrible flesh-eating monster. If their presence had been known, they would have been thronged by cheering crowds.

It was not until the travellers had reached the Chancellor's comfortable little lodge near the sea that Phelan turned back. He felt he could do nothing to help until Gemma felt like talking. Meanwhile he would make sure she had peace and quiet for as long as she needed it. With the cats and Rowanne to guard her, she would be safe enough.

'You keep an eye on her, Fleabag,' Phelan had told him. 'I'll come to see you all as often as I can, without seeming rude to Tomas. Probably quiet and sea air will do Gemma good. Then we can all sit down and talk. Meanwhile, try and relax a little and have a holiday yourself. Worrying won't help. And I suspect the Ring Fire will do something to help Gemma fairly soon.'

Fleabag wasn't so optimistic. 'Come back as soon as you can, Phelan. I've had an uncomfortable feeling about this holiday since the Chancellor suggested it. Something is badly wrong. I don't know what it is, but I can sense it in my whiskers and I know I saw what I saw! In my heart of hearts, I don't trust anything that comes out of Porthwain.'

Phelan looked at the lodge. It was a whitewashed thatched chalet, perched at the head of a pleasantly wooded valley that ran down to the sea. Everything seemed perfect for a peaceful holiday.

'It seems safe enough, but I do trust your instincts, you old ratter. I'll post sentries secretly in the woods all around. Send Cleo to them if you are worried. I know she can't talk, but tell her to carry a feather in her mouth if I am needed.'

Fleabag grinned. The King did not know that his daughter could out-talk any cat – or human – he had ever met. And what was worse, she had a great partiality for fresh game. That dear, innocent golden cat usually had *several* feathers in her mouth… along with the feathers' owner, half eaten. She rarely missed her prey.

'Don't worry Phelan, we'll get a message to you,' the cat assured him. 'Take care. May the Ring Fire light your path.'

The King picked up Fleabag and scratched him behind a tattered ear. 'Thank you, my furry friend. We can't know what the Chancellor's real intentions are, but I know the Ring Fire will be burning, with or without Gemma being there to watch and listen.'

'True!' the cat jumped down. 'And we must learn to listen to it for ourselves. But I'm still frightened for her. I am sure she is in danger!'

Phelan left after giving Gemma a warm hug. As he disappeared between the trees, an elderly manservant stepped out of the lodge to help the travellers carry in their luggage. Gemma refused the housekeeper's offer of help with her unpacking. What she carried had to remain a secret.

Soon everyone had washed and eaten. The servants bade the guests goodnight and left Gemma, Rowanne and the cats alone.

Fleabag was still nervous. The 'somethings' seemed to have gone when they left the King's palace at Harflorum. Neither he nor Cleo had been troubled by them since. But his feeling of doom and the troublesome memory of the storm had not lessened. He chewed at his claws while he sat by the fire in the cool of the evening. How he wished Cleo had had a chance to follow the Chancellor that day he had come to the palace.

Cleo was at that moment following Gemma round the

house. The sleek golden cat had not remained hidden for the whole journey – just long enough to make it too far for her to go back alone. After that she had ingratiated herself with all the travellers with her deep tuneful purr and willingness to be stroked.

Gemma's room overlooked a river that tumbled down towards the ocean. The sounds of water sang pleasantly all night, and she smiled as she fell asleep with Cleo purring gently at the foot of her bed. As soon as Cleo was certain all was well, she slipped back to sit by the fire with her father.

'Gemma is sound asleep, Dad,' she whispered as she stretched out to toast her tummy fur. 'She's as peaceful as an overfed kitten. We can relax until morning.'

But Gemma's dreams were far from peaceful. Something, someone was behind her, talking hypnotically in a low voice, suggesting the very thing she wanted with all her heart, to lay aside the Ring Fire. All night she tried to turn around and see who was talking to her, but she could never quite see who it was. It was only a voice, not a person. But what a wonderful voice – so kind, so gentle, so understanding of how very, very tired she was.

In fact she was so tired, she dreamed she fell asleep. Then she dreamed, within the dream, that the same voice was speaking to her again, and again she fell asleep within her dream. Soon she was under so many thick layers of suggestion that if anyone had seen her, they would have thought her dead. Only no one did see her, for Rowanne was just as deeply asleep herself, and the cats were not there...

7

Swept Away!

Fleabag and his daughter Cleo were walking by the shore. Once the humans were asleep, they had spent most of the night enjoying catching small fish in the pools and caterwauling at the moon as loudly as they liked without having boots thrown at them.

At first light, they were both still in fine voice, when they spotted a figure walking slowly down towards the sea. Although the sun was not yet fully up, there was enough light to know it was Gemma, by the way she stood with her hair blowing in the wind. She looked very small and lonely on the thin stretch of sand between the rocks, her long, loose night-robe tugging against her legs in the chilly morning breeze.

Gemma did not seem to notice the cold. She just stood staring out to sea, without turning to greet the cats as they ran towards her, calling happily.

Suddenly Fleabag hissed to Cleo to stop, and tugged at her tail with his teeth, pulling her back behind a rock. 'I don't like this,' he whispered. 'Something strange is happening. I'm sure Gemma is sleep-walking. My fur is all on end.'

Cleo nodded her agreement. 'So's mine... What's that, Dad?'

She pointed a paw out to sea where the grey rocks and even greyer water were tinged with dawn light. The sky was streaked with gold and rose, promising a glorious sunrise. Out at sea, a small boat was heading towards the shore. In it stood a tall, thin figure. He used no oar or sail, yet the boat seemed to move with perfect control. As sand and shingle scraped the keel, the figure stepped into the shallows and ordered the little craft to stay close. There it bobbed as surely as if a strong hand were holding it.

The figure reached Gemma's side, although she seemed quite unaware of his presence. He moved behind her and seemed to speak in her ear.

Gemma shook her head, and the cats could hear her replying faintly, although she seemed to remain asleep. Neither cat could hear what was said, but whatever it was, it had not satisfied the man. He pointed to the boat and, unprotesting, Gemma got in. Then, with a blast of blue flame that made Fleabag shudder, the little craft skidded right over the waves towards the open water.

The man stood on the shore, tall and dark in the very early morning light. For several minutes he watched the boat spinning and bobbing as the blast of blue magic faded, and the current took over, tugging the little vessel further and further away from land.

Then he laughed softly, turned, and vanished into thin

air. High above, a black crow flapped slowly away...

The cats stared wide-eyed. 'Cleo,' Fleabag whispered, 'run back to the house as fast as you can and get help. It doesn't matter what you have to do to waken Rowanne, but do it. Gemma's life and my fur depend on it!'

'Shall I summon the King's soldiers as well?' Cleo asked.

'No, they could be anywhere in those woods. I need help *now*!'

Cleo was gone – a streak of rusty gold in the early light.

Fleabag gingerly took a few steps towards the sea. The icy water made his fur hang in heavily sanded points. He jumped back. He did not *like* water, but the sight of the ever-retreating little boat made him take another step, then another, deeper and deeper into the swirling sea, until the next little wave caught him under the belly, and lifted his paws off the bottom.

Cats can swim, but they do not like it. On a hot summer's day, even Fleabag might almost have enjoyed a splash (although he wouldn't have admitted it to anyone). But in this freezing cold sea, with a stiff breeze blowing from the east, Fleabag was not a happy cat.

It was only the thought of Gemma, alone in a small boat heading for the ocean, that kept him going. He was frightened for her. She had seemed so strange and unaware of everything. That man must have been Lord Domnall. He was the only person who knew exactly where Gemma was, and he wielded the blue flames as the other Chancellor had done. It was obvious to Fleabag that Domnall was a member of the Order of Wizards. He shuddered. Simply banning them had done nothing to stop their evil work. It had only made them more secretive. Now they had some sort of hold over Gemma, and the danger he had seen threatening her in the strange blue storm was becoming a reality.

Fleabag's neck was aching as he lifted his head to keep his black nose above the water. The salt was in his eyes and he admitted to himself that he was very scared. He longed to turn back to shore. But he had to keep swimming, for Gemma's sake. He *had* to reach her and waken her.

He could sense they were all at war now, and it wasn't going to be the sort of battle that could be fought with swords and armour. Rowanne was going to find this hard to understand.

Fleabag spluttered as a wave caught him full in the face. He must stop worrying and concentrate on swimming. The lack of one back leg made his steering difficult, but Gemma's boat was still in sight, so he kept on trying. Suddenly a much bigger swell caught him, lifting him onto the glassy green curve of its back, so for a second or two he could take a good look in every direction. The shore was a long way off, and the boat seemed no closer. The size of the waves told him he was now in the open sea, and he was very frightened.

But, catfully, he kept swimming. The sun was now gleaming above the horizon, and the waves were rising higher and higher all the time. He was swallowing more and more water. His fur was completely sodden; even the tiny soft under-hairs next to his skin were drenched, making him heavy and ungainly.

He managed to breathe, but he had to close his eyes, for the salt stung them terribly. He had water swilling around his wide ears, making glugging and whistling sounds deep inside his head. For no sensible reason, he opened his mouth and mewed 'Help!' As the waves grew bigger he could feel himself being dragged under. Desperately he struggled to keep afloat, expending precious energy as he fought the sea. He was now so stiff and cold he could hardly move.

Then another wave lifted him high again. He could no longer see the boat, but there was something that gave him a glimmer of hope. It was a piece of driftwood, a branch from an old tree. With the last dregs of his strength he steered himself towards it, hoping it was not some sort of a mirage. To his relief his claws sank into something very solid indeed.

Cleo, meanwhile, was struggling to waken Rowanne. The servants had disappeared. She was alone with the sleeping Princess. She did not dare try to run for Phelan's soldiers; it would take too much time to find them. But nothing, not even a specially sharpened claw, honed to perfection as Fleabag had taught her, could rouse the sleeper. Once or twice Rowanne reached for her sword, waved it and shouted 'To battle!' but then sank down into the pillows again, still fast asleep.

The golden marmalade cat sat firmly on her victim's chest, licking the Princess' face long and hard with a rough, warm tongue. By noon Cleo managed to get Rowanne to open her eyes.

Rowanne turned over and tried to shoo the cat away, threatening her with battlefield oaths.

But Cleo did not budge. Now, she decided, was the time to reveal that she could talk. She had kept her secret from humans, because it was the best way to gather information. She always followed her father's advice of eavesdropping whenever possible. She had noticed how people fell silent when Fleabag or one of her talking brothers came into sight. By remaining mute, she had discovered a great many useful palace secrets.

But this was an emergency of unbelievable magnitude! Gemma would be far out at sea by now, and her father was in real trouble. So Cleo dug her claws a little more deeply into Rowanne's chest, then stood, raised her tail and stretched her back into a glorious, marmalade arch and said, very politely: 'My Lady Rowanne de Montiland, I beg your forgiveness for disturbing your sleep, but Her Eminence the Fire Wielder has been kidnapped. My father may at this moment be drowning, and the servants have fled!'

Then Cleo lowered herself to glare, golden-eyed into the princess' bleary face. She was no longer polite, simply determined. '*Get up*!' she ordered, displaying her special claw. 'Get up immediately, your Highness, or I will be forced to use this, my ultimate weapon, on the fancy leather saddlebag you prize so highly!' Fleabag had done this before to make Rowanne listen, and the anecdote had been a favourite tale amongst his kittens.

At last Rowanne raised her head and managed to say, 'If you get off my chest, you walking dog food, I will get up. While I am dressing, I would like a sensible explanation of what you have just said, and why you are waking me at such an unearthly hour.'

Cleo sprang lightly down and sat on the window sill where the thin shaft of sunlight caught the glossy golden hues of her coat to best effect. She looked up at the chink of bright blue summer sky. 'It is now past noon. I do not know what time it is your habit to rise, but I do not call *this* unearthly. Furthermore, I have been trying to rouse you since dawn.'

Rowanne struggled over to the window, almost tripping as she tried to pull her breeches on at the same time. She tugged the curtain back and gasped. 'No! I have never slept this late in my life... except when I was under a spell, but that was different.'

Cleo turned her golden face to look at Rowanne. She was an honest-looking cat, with a neat white triangle around her pink nose. Her expression was serious. 'Your Highness, I don't think that *was* different. My father told me the story of your enchantment by the Chancellor of All Wizards, and I think this may be more of the same.'

Rowanne did not reply. She pulled on her shirt and buckled her sword by her side. Then as the two ran out of the house down the track towards the beach, Cleo told Rowanne what had happened in the early hours.

It was then that they saw the branch of driftwood bobbing near the shore, with the black, unmoving shape still clinging to the sodden bark. The cold, stiff little bundle of fur that was washed into the bay on the afternoon tide would not have been recognizable as Fleabag, if it hadn't been for a golden earring.

8

Flotsam and Jetsam

Rowanne gently lifted the cat's cold body and wrapped it in her overshirt.

Before she became a Princess, the brave Lady Knight had seen many heroes die, and had never been known to cry, but now she did not stint her tears for her old enemy and friend, the redoubtable Fleabag.

Cleo followed Rowanne up the path back to the house. She was too stunned and confused by what had happened to know how to cry.

Rowanne went inside to collect her saddlebags and a cloak. She called Cleo to jump into one of the bags, but she tied Fleabag, still rolled in the woollen shirt, across the back of her saddle, like a great warrior slain on the field of battle. Then Rowanne sprang up onto her horse.

She looked down at the frightened little ginger cat cowering in the leather bag behind her left knee. 'We must go and find Phelan. He may think of something he can do to help Gemma, and Fleabag will be buried with full honours as a knight and a hero.'

The journey was not long, for Rowanne rode like the wind. But to Cleo, hiding in the saddlebag, it seemed to go on for ever. Sometimes she stayed low, feeling very sick, curled up in a ball and at other times she looked out of the flap and watched her father's untidy black head bobbing up and down in time to the horse's pace. Sunlight glinted on his golden earring as water trickled from his nose and mouth, and his fur dried in untidy sandy tufts under Rowanne's loosely tied shirt.

By the time they reached Beriot it was scarcely four hours past midday. Phelan met them outside the gates as he returned from a ride across the countryside. He waved cheerfully and called out to Rowanne as soon as he saw her, but she did not reply. She simply rode, cold and stony-faced, until she was so close to him that no one else could hear.

'Gemma has been kidnapped and is drifting out at sea in a small boat, and I have brought the brave Fleabag to you for burial.' Rowanne spoke hurriedly and softly. She could not risk her grief overwhelming her, and she dare not let anyone else know that the Fire Wielder was in danger. Phelan went pale and turned his horse so he could call his equerry to his side. 'I want my most senior sea captain in my study in one hour.'

Then with a heavy heart he beckoned to Rowanne to follow him through the streets until he came to the royal residence of Beriot. This was a fine, stately building, but more like a large country house than a palace. It was built of warm-coloured red bricks and its roof had a hundred different little gables and slopes to it. Set high on a hill at the northern edge of Beriot, it overlooked the city on one side, and the sea on the other.

The private study Tomas had set aside for the King's use had a wonderful view over the sea. Phelan leaned on the window sill, peering out, as if trying to catch a glimpse of Gemma's forlorn little boat. Cleo had told him everything she could. Now everyone had fallen silent.

At last Phelan sighed. 'Thank goodness you can talk, young lady. We'll bury Fleabag in the royal cemetery at Harflorum. As soon as we have found Gemma we will take him home in a gold coffin.' The king spoke quietly, without turning away from the window.

Stretched out on the settee next to him, Fleabag lay in the warm afternoon sun, looking for all the world as if he were asleep.

Cleo put a paw up to the king's knee. 'If you please, your Majesty,' she said, 'he would far rather be buried in the strawberry patch or under some brambles. He was never a cat for being formal about things. He would much rather be somewhere a little wild and untidy…'

Phelan nodded. 'I know what you mean, but he was a knight of the realm and a national hero. He was of a noble family. He told me his real name when he was knighted. My predecessor, Queen Sophia told Gemma that he had a pedigree many times longer than his venerable tail. The people will expect a proper funeral in a proper place.'

Cleo wanted to cry. 'I wish my Mum was here. She would agree, I know. He needs to be buried somewhere open and free…'

Just then a deep voice not far away murmured, 'How about you don't bury me at all? I'd much prefer it!'

'Fleabag!' everyone shouted at once. The black cat stretched a little and opened one golden eye. He smiled under his black whiskers. 'Hello,' he purred. 'Did I give you all a scare?'

'You did indeed, you incorrigible rogue!' Phelan leaned over and stroked the cat's doormat of a head. 'What happened?'

Fleabag grinned and rolled over, as Cleo jumped up next to him and began to lick his ears with delight. But the effort of moving made him cough badly. 'I felt like a little attention and I had nothing better to do at the time. Did you find Gemma?' He coughed again.

'No, I'm afraid not,' Phelan sighed. 'It appears she was swept out to sea.'

Rowanne took a few seconds to realize that Fleabag was really alive. Then without further hesitation, she flung the study door open and bellowed, 'Fetch the royal vet!' into the face of an amazed-looking chambermaid who happened to be passing at that very moment. '*NOW*!' the Princess screamed as the girl stood there with her mouth hanging open.

The chambermaid dropped the pile of sheets she was carrying and ran as fast as she could. Within minutes, she returned, leading a fat little man puffing and panting up the stairs behind her, straw and hay dropping in a trail behind him as he ran. Wiping his bald, shiny head, he bowed as he tried to dust down his clothes. 'My apologies, your Majesty... In the middle of delivering a foal... no time to change...'

'Please do not worry yourself,' Phelan assured him, 'This is too urgent to stand on ceremony.' He ushered the vet over to the settee where Fleabag lay, dazed and bleary-eyed. 'Our friend nearly drowned in the sea this morning; in fact we thought he was dead. But it appears he is very much alive!'

After a short examination, and a few drops of medicine, Fleabag fell into a healthy sleep. There were no more plans for his funeral. His chest was rising and falling steadily, and his fur was warm.

'He will be all right in a few days,' the vet announced. 'He must have taken a deal of water into his lungs, as well as getting hypothermia. Any longer in the sea and he would not have survived. Probably the ride on the horse saved him – the jolting must have revived his circulation and warmed him up. Putting him across the saddle with his head down must have helped to drain the fluid from his lungs. He is a very lucky cat indeed. Tell me,' the vet went on, 'how many lives has he had? Seven, eight?'

Phelan smiled. 'Many more than that. I have seen him use all nine at once before now, and he still comes out with his whiskers gleaming.'

The vet laughed and promised to look in again that evening. 'Just keep him quiet and warm. Plenty of rest and a little good food at regular intervals. Above all keep him well away from the sea and he'll be fine.'

The next visitor was Captain Marcus, of the King's flagship, the *Flora*. He was a lean, dark-skinned man, probably from the south like Phelan himself. His long black hair was scraped back into a tight pigtail, and his black eyes seemed to take in everything at once. He seemed to be perpetually scanning a distant horizon rather than letting his gaze rest anywhere. He said nothing when he entered but dipped his head in a short bow, and tugged off his faded blue cotton cap. A fine woollen captain's cloak trimmed in gold braid had been hastily draped around his shoulders, but Marcus looked uncomfortable under it, as if he were unused to such clothing. The man stood quietly, legs apart, as if he expected the floor to heave like a deck at any moment.

Phelan liked him immediately. This man was watchful and aware. He would be glad to trust his precious mission to a man like this.

Cleo explained things as best she could, and Captain Marcus listened quietly, asking a few questions here and there. Then Fleabag, disturbed by the voices, awoke and told his story before eating a little lightly steamed fish and going back to sleep.

The Captain unrolled a chart he had been carrying under his arm. Rowanne showed him the bay and the lodge where they had been staying. Then he pointed out the way the tides ran, and where Gemma's little boat had probably drifted.

'Why did Fleabag not get swept out to sea too?' Rowanne asked.

Captain Marcus stretched a strong brown hand across the map, pointing to the two rocky arms of the bay. 'As long as he remained within this area, he would be carried back to shore with the flotsam and jetsam of the tide. But the Fire Wielder's boat may have been swept further out and caught in the ocean currents. I have a rough idea where she may be floating. The currents follow a fairly regular pattern around these waters.'

Phelan stood and looked at Captain Marcus. 'I must warn you, Captain, there are dark powers involved in this. There may be no regular patterns for you to follow and you may be sailing into a trap. This is a dangerous voyage. You may never return to your loved ones.'

The Captain rolled the map carefully, keeping his eyes down as he did so. 'Sire, five years ago I lost my wife to the monster you killed before you became High Prince over our Lord Tomas, and King over the land. What you did was too late for her, but a great service to all of us. I am prepared to do what I can for you in return. I am not frightened by evil magic, and I have no more family to leave behind. She was all I had.' And with that he bowed stiffly and left the room.

Phelan turned his gaze to the sea again, and Fleabag muttered under his blanket, 'I resent being called "flotsam and jetsam"!'

9

Adrift!

Gemma did not wake until night had almost fallen. The layers of unnatural sleep Lord Domnall had woven around her gradually slipped away over the hours.

During that time she dreamed many dreams of carrying something very, very heavy. Too heavy. Then someone came to her from behind, always from behind, and offered to take the burden from her. It was a man, she knew that. He was so understanding, so helpful. She wanted to give him whatever it was that weighed on her so badly, but she could not… *ought* not.

He told her she was being silly and obstinate, but she wasn't. She did not know why. She was so tired, she did not know anything, only that she still carried whatever it was that was too heavy.

Then there were flames, and a feeling of flying, or was it sailing? The flames were not warm and golden; they were bright, vivid cerulean blue, and ice-cold. As they licked her skin, they burned by freezing. They were unkind flames. They brought fear, and that voice again.

Only this time it was no longer asking gently. Now it was telling, insisting… *ordering* her to surrender whatever it was she was carrying. She was crying. Gemma would have given up her burden if she could, but it seemed to be a part of her. She could not let it go. She tried to pluck it from her hands, but it was so tiny, she could not find it. Odd, she thought, how something so heavy could be so small.

Her dreams went on. The voice from behind begged and pleaded, cajoled, wheedled, commanded, threatened. All day long it went on, until Gemma was so exhausted, she simply decided to wake up.

And when she opened her eyes at last, she found herself in a small boat, surrounded by sea, with the rain pouring down her face and neck. An oilskin had been roughly pulled over her. She was thirsty, so she scooped a little rainwater from between the folds of the cloth, and drank.

Some instinct told her that she might need the water that was left, so she carefully arranged a part of the oilskin so rain could collect and form a good-sized pool at the end of the boat. This left her feeling cold and wet around the shoulders, but she huddled down as far as she could and shivered.

Hiding under the heavy cloth, Gemma tried to collect her thoughts. She was frightened, but she could not run away from the situation. She would have to face it. She had never been at sea before, and she rather liked the gentle rising swell of the waves. It was soothing and comforted her fear, but she was still lost and alone. More importantly though, she was hungry and would have given anything for a hunk of bread. Her head span and she felt terribly tired. At long last she managed to sleep again, rocked by the gentle waves.

This time her sleep was natural and she woke in the middle of the night feeling refreshed. It had stopped raining, and she pushed back the stiff folds of her covering so she could see the stars, intensely bright in the inky blackness above. At last she found she could think.

She remembered the last few days, the way the strange storm had put out the Ring Fire, and her longing to give up being Fire Wielder, her tiredness, and her strange visitor with his seemingly kind offers of help. Suddenly she sat bolt upright, making the boat rock violently. 'That's it!' she gasped. How could she have been so stupid! That blue fire, those unnaturally blue eyes, she had seen them all in the Great Hall at Porthwain. 'Domnall *is* a wizard! He has the same knowledge that the old Chancellor had. Only this time he wants the Ring Fire itself, not just the royal ring.

'He must have sent the storm to test my strength as Fire Wielder. He must have been delighted to see how bad I was at my job. I wonder if he succeeded in taking the Ring Fire from me?' She opened her palms and stared at them. It was too dark to see much by the faint starlight, but they felt very sore where she had scratched at the skin in her dreams, trying to pluck the Ring Fire out. But there was no sign as to whether the Fire had gone or not. But it did not always burn when she thought she needed it most.

Gemma knew it had still been with her after the

strange storm: it had scorched the sleeves of her robe. The rain and the blue lightning had simply doused the flame, it hadn't killed it… but why had the blue magic defeated the Ring Fire so easily?

For the first time it occurred to her that maybe things hadn't been as they had seemed. Maybe the rain had damped the flames as any rain would do, but she had seen that the Fire still burned. So perhaps it was only a battle that had been lost, not the war. She had been too tired and worn down to see how things were. Lord Domnall could have been planting suggestions into her mind for a very long time. The Ring Fire wasn't defeated, and it mustn't be. And above all, it must not end up in the hands of a man like Domnall! It made her search for a new Fire Wielder even more urgent.

She lay back in the boat and sighed with relief. She could not have given up the Ring Fire in her dream, even though for a short time she had wanted to. She knew now that the man was Domnall, or at least his shade. He was very angry with her and had left her with threats before she had woken.

'The Ring Fire would never let itself be given,' she reminded herself. 'It is not like a necklace or a sword which can just be handed over. It is alive, after all. If the Fire Giver does not will it to be given then it cannot go.' Gemma pulled the oilskin over herself and smiled. *She* might or might not be the Fire Wielder any more, but the Ring Fire would be safe, wherever it was. It was in the hands of the Fire Giver to give or take back. It was not hers to give.

But what would Domnall do next?

At the Battle of Porthwain, the Chancellor of All

Wizards had thrown more and more magic at her and Fleabag, culminating in the blue flames that had consumed himself instead of her. If Domnall wielded blue flames, he must be the new Chancellor of All Wizards. Would he be as cunning as the old one? She lay still, watching the myriad stars above her. They were so cool and bright, with such a gentle light. Vaguely she remembered that Rowanne had tried to teach her how to find her way by the stars, using certain constellations as points of the compass. But it had meant nothing to her. And what if she *had* understood? This boat had no oars.

She was adrift, all alone on a vast ocean.

Back in his tiny room at the very top of a lonely tower, Domnall resumed his human form. He stared angrily out across the plains towards Beulothin and the sea. It had taken him almost three years to discover the secret of the blue flames that his father had used against Fleabag and the Fire Maiden. Because Domnall did not believe there *was* a Fire Giver, he saw the Ring Fire simply as a particularly potent magic to be taken and used like any other.

Now Domnall realized he had made a mistake. The girl did not have the power to surrender the Fire. He could not use his most powerful spells on her, as he did not know her real name. Moreover, she seemed protected from direct magic by the accursed Ring Fire. But he should have had her thoughts almost completely under his control. His skilled cook had prepared her food with many potent herbs, opening her mind to his hypnotic suggestion – and she had *still* disobeyed him.

Could it be that she did not know *how* to hand over the

vital flame that burned in her? She was very young and inexperienced to be a sorceress in such an eminent position. Her naïvety was partly her protection. She knew nothing, so she could divulge nothing. Perhaps she had not been taught the right ceremony before the last Fire Wielder has passed the flame on and died... Domnall caressed his leather-bound book of spells. There must be something in here to do the job. It was just a matter of time before he discovered it.

Meanwhile he must look after the Fire Wielder. He did not want her dead yet. As long as she lived, there was a hope that the right words could be found to make her give up the Ring Fire. If she died, the Fire might die with her. He could not risk that.

There was always the King's Ring, which would be relatively easy to steal. But legend had it that if the wrong person held the ring, the Fire would simply withdraw. That had been his father's mistake, to go for the Ring, not the heart of the flame itself. If the worst came to the worst, he would kill her and that so-called King, and take the land by force. If both Phelan and Gemma were dead, however, there was always the risk that the Ring Fire would be extinguished and he would have to rule by the power of the blue flames alone. They were powerful enough, to be sure: pure, distilled evil wrapped in an ice-cold all-consuming hate. But that would also eventually destroy everything in the land, including the riches and slaves he wished to control and enjoy.

Domnall gave an involuntary shudder. That would be the ultimate desolation, for above all things he feared being alone.

If he could be seen to hold the Ring and the Ring Fire,

his reign would be more easily assumed, leaving him rich and famous, with every living thing trembling at the sight of him. That was what he really wanted.

He had been rash. Now he must keep the girl alive a while longer. Domnall poured water into his silver scrying bowl and said the words that would enable him to watch over Gemma while he prepared deeper spells to fulfil his aim. Peering into the silver sheen on the surface, the Chancellor could see his captive had drinking water. She was miserable but safe.

Like a spider keeping a fly alive in a cocoon of silk for a later meal, Domnall wound her little boat in spells to keep her secure until he could see his way more clearly.

Gemma felt hot and sick. The water pooled in the oilskin tasted foul. The fabric had been sealed by boiling it in animal fat, and that left rancid rainbow oil slicks floating on the surface. There had been no fresh rain for several days, and her feeble attempts to catch fish had all failed. She had almost caught one or two small fry by tickling, as Rowanne had taught her to do with trout, but they did not seem to like that game and would not play.

She lay still and dazed in the bottom of the boat, staring up at the sky. Day after day the sky promised rain, but always lied. Her head ached.

She began to think of the Ring Fire again. She did not understand it. She had never understood it. But she wished it would help her now. If only it would either rescue her or let her die, not let her live on and on in this torment. She was so miserable. She knew she had let the Ring Fire down. Phelan and the people of the land had trusted her to be their Fire Wielder… But she was only a child who had never been allowed to be a child. She did not even have a real name. What did everyone expect?

Gemma looked over the side of the boat into the jade-green depths of the sea. It looked so cool and inviting. She longed to go for a swim, but was scared that she would be too weak to keep alongside the boat. Would being in all that water just make her thirstier? Perhaps she should just slide into the depths and go to sleep. Then it would all be over. She wanted to cry, but did not dare waste water in tears.

Just then a glistening shoal of pretty silver fish swam past. If only she could reach one... She hated the thought of eating raw fish, but she knew it would give her food and some fresh juices at the same time. It might save her life.

She leaned over the side. The fish slid below her fingers, this way, then that, darting and zigzagging, always just out of reach. How pretty they were! Gemma did not want to kill them. But she had to live. She was frightened of dying alone out there. She leaned over the gunwales of the boat and stretched out her arm. Her fingertips brushed the smooth side of a silvery fish. She opened her fingers to try to catch the next one as the shoal slipped past again, so beautifully, so silently.

Now, *now*, NOW! But as she clenched her fist around a fish's tail, the boat tipped, and Gemma fell in. She was so shocked with the sudden coldness of the water, she let go her prize and swallowed brine, which was so salty she retched. Splashing in panic she realized the boat was on a swift current and slipping away from her. Collecting her wits she began to swim, but her long white night-gown clung heavily around her legs. She tugged it up above her knees and knotted it. Now her legs were freer she kicked strongly, and soon came alongside the boat. With a weary hand she caught the gunwales and her fingers grabbed a rowlock. Lifting her head above the water she took a deep breath as she put up her other hand and tried to drag herself up out of the water.

But the boat was small and light, and the weight of her and her water-sodden robe were too much for it. Instead of heaving herself over the side, she managed only to flip the little craft over and bring it crashing down on top of herself.

The boat's plank-seat hit her very hard on the head. She gulped and swallowed more water in the darkness. She felt very cold and frightened and dizzy. She could not remember what had just happened to her. All she knew was that she must survive, at all costs.

Groping in the darkness she found the seat. She slid her arms over it so her head was held out of the water. There she clung, staring blankly at the little tiny light that flickered between her fingers.

Then she passed out.

10

Aidan

Domnall had not seen Gemma's boat capsize. At that very moment he had been searching through his scrolls and manuscripts for the solution to his problem. He had to discover the words that would release the Ring Fire to his domination. His name meant 'World Ruler', and he intended to live up to it. At any cost.

Meanwhile, there must be spells and potions strong enough to control this slip of a girl and the flame she was supposed to be carrying.

Then, suddenly, something made his heart miss a beat. He turned to his scrying bowl and peered in. There was the boat, yes, but something was wrong! He stilled the water with a gesture of his forefinger to make the vision clearer. The boat had capsized! Where was the girl? He passed his hand over the water again and commanded to be given sight of her, but there was just the naked wooden hull bobbing on the sea. Then the vision faded into nothing. Only darkness.

Was she dead? What had happened? How could his spells protecting her boat have failed? He cursed his manuscripts and kicked the table over, scattering parchments this way and that. His cup of wine tumbled too, spreading a pool of blood-red liquor across the mystic pages.

In his fury, the wizard took the scrying bowl and flung it across the room. The clear water spilled haphazardly across the floor as the silver bowl landed with a clatter, dented and misshapen.

Far out at sea, the waves stirred and rose in answer to Domnall's rage. Great clouds gathered and piled high, and the winds began to blow.

Less than two hours later Gemma's little boat came within sight of a small island, one of an archipelago scattered across the Eastern seas. A skinny lad of Gemma's own age stood on the pebbly shore and watched the storm rising, hoping that amongst the driftwood there would be something useful: something saleable, or even burnable. The sight of a small boat cheered him immensely. To own a boat was a great thing indeed! He would not have to work for his tyrannical father any more. He could be his own master and sell his own fish. If he worked hard he might even be able to rent a room and leave home entirely. No more scoldings from his mother for having eaten too much when his belly was scarcely half full.

'Indeed,' he thought as he swam strongly towards the upturned vessel, 'one day I might be able to buy a wife to mend my nets and cook for me.' Yes, a small boat was *just* what he wanted!

The boy grabbed the boat's trailing rope. Then clenching it between his teeth, he turned his face inland and soon had his prize in the shallows. But something was caught underneath, preventing him from dragging it ashore. He stood and grasped the rim of the boat then, with a great effort, he managed to flip it over.

There, under the seat, was a girl's body.

He pulled the limp form out and left her lying at the water's edge. He beached the boat first, as that was by far the more valuable find. Then he returned for the girl. She might be wearing jewellery. She looked very oddly dressed in what seemed to be a night-gown, although it was a good one with no patches or tears in it.

He grabbed her under her arms and dragged her roughly up the shingle. The stones hurt Gemma's feet and she coughed and cried out.

The boy dropped her just above the high-tide line and turned her over with his foot. So, she was still alive! He must search her quickly. She didn't look as if she could put up much of a fight, but he wanted to take no chances of being seen at his work. Quickly he unclasped a fine gold chain from her neck and slipped a heavy gold ring from her finger. It was an expensive one with a device engraved on it that might be a small flame in a circle. He would have to be careful how he sold that. It could be the arms of a noble family on the mainland. He did not want to be accused of murder or theft.

She did not seem to have anything else of value. He looked down at her. He thought she might be strong if fed a little. He did not have much to share, but now he had a boat he was his own master. He also had a gold chain to sell. For a little while at least he could afford black bread for two. He would shelter her for a day or so, and if she recovered well and seemed adept at mending nets, he would keep her. If she behaved herself and minded her tongue, he might marry her. She would be useful, and he would not have to find a bride price either.

If she was useless he would make enquiries as to what family carried the arms of a small flame, and he would collect a reward. Either way his luck was in.

But where to hide her? He scanned the shoreline. He did not want to take her home. It was too crowded there already, and he did not want his parents to think of putting her to work for them or collecting a reward for themselves. She was his prize. His alone!

He left Gemma face down on the pebbles so the water could drain from her lungs, as he stood in thought a while.

Aidan was short and scrawny. Lank, straw-coloured hair whipped into his sharp-featured face as the wild wind blew off the sea. His shirt was sailcloth, hacked rather than cut, and his breeches were of the same material, several sizes too big and caught round his waist with rough twine. The bones in his face were square, and his eyes were pale and narrowed from squinting into the wind every day.

At last he nodded to himself and dragged the boat further up the beach. He had no paint to mark it as his own, so he found a sharp stone and into the sticky tar of the boat he scored the device from the ring, a small flame set in a circle. Then he scratched a large A. He could not write his name, but he knew it began with an A. Now the boat was marked as his, he could afford to think about his other prize. He lifted the craft onto his shoulders and, looking for all the world like a tortoise, began to carry it up the beach. Once it was secured above the high-tide line, he turned and called to the wet, shivering figure on the shingle, 'Come on then. Don't just sit there!'

Gemma looked up, a little surprised. It was only beginning to register in her waterlogged brain that she was safe on land. She could not remember who she was, or even what she was doing there, but she knew she was glad, and grateful to something, or someone. She supposed it must be the boy, although she did not know who he was, or why she should be grateful.

Aching and feeling sick, she clambered shakily to her feet. Then, slipping and struggling on the loose stones, she followed her rescuer.

They scrambled up a steep cliff path, then walked for about ten minutes across dunes and marram grass. Gemma's legs were weak and her head ached and span. She could feel a lump on the back of her head where the boat had hit her. Suddenly her legs gave way beneath her and she collapsed onto the soft, dry sand.

When she woke she was lying on old sacking in a dark, smelly place. What looked like planks arched overhead, with bluish curves of light in between each one. She blinked and rubbed her eyes. She was cold and thirsty, but her headache had lessened. Next to her was a plain earthenware pot. She peered into it. Water! Greedily she drank most of it and fell asleep again.

In the late evening, a stiff breeze blew up, whistling through the planks of her sparse shelter. She roused herself, drank from the pot again and ate from a slab of dry black bread next to it. Then she got up. The only way out of the shelter was by crawling low under a curved opening to one side. When she was out, she stood up and looked around. Her new home appeared to be a half-rotted old boat, about the length of three men, but not quite high enough to stand up in. She shivered and hugged herself. Then she spotted a figure hurrying towards her.

Striding along the path between the dunes was the scrawny boy she had seen before. He was struggling with a cumbersome-looking bundle. He shouted. 'Oi you! Inside! You don't want them to find you, do you?'

Gemma did not know who 'they' were, but she obeyed. Crouched inside the boat, she helped to pull the bundles inside. It was mostly sacking, some of which was sparsely stuffed with straw. As she unrolled it a few bits of ragged clothing fell out. There was a sailcloth cape, a coarse apron, a skirt and a loose shirt. They stank, but Gemma pulled everything on, glad to be not so cold for once. The boy helped her arrange the rest of the sacking into some sort of bedding.

'I'll be back for you in the morning. Don't try and run away.' He shrugged. 'Not that there's anywhere to run to. This is a very small island, and you're mine now, anyway.'

'What do you mean, *yours*?' Gemma was very confused. She did not have the foggiest idea what was happening.

The boy looked at her. His face was almost moon-like in the pale half-light of the hulk. 'I found you, you're mine. I'll be back in the morning. Don't move from here or you'll be sorry. Goodnight.'

And with that he started to slither away under the lip of the hulk.

'Just a minute – please,' Gemma called, 'Where am I? Who are you?' Then she hesitated. 'Who am *I*, come to that?'

The boy stuck his head back inside. The wind was blowing so hard he had to keep pulling his hair out of his mouth so he could talk. 'This is called Spider Island. I don't know who you are, but as you're my servant now, I'll call you Ahanet. That means "hard work", in the old dialect of our island. My name is Aidan.' And with that he stepped back and stood up.

For a few moments Gemma could hear his bare feet walking swiftly away through the rough grass. Soon the wind covered every other sound, and she fell asleep.

11

Cleo the Smuggler

Fleabag had been most put out when Phelan forbade him to set sail with Rowanne and Captain Marcus. 'You need rest, old friend. The vet said you had to lie quietly for several days yet, and the voyage is so urgent we dare not wait an hour longer than necessary.'

Fleabag sat with his back to the King, staring out of the window towards the sea, twitching the very tip of his tail in tightly controlled fury. But he said nothing.

Phelan stood next to his friend and tried to scratch him behind the head, but Fleabag simply put his ears very flat against his skull and turned to glower at the King. Phelan tried again. 'Look, it won't be so bad. I am staying home as well. Even with Gemma gone, I still have to fulfil all my duties and rule the land. I would like to go too, but I cannot. Stay here and keep me company, for I'll need a friend. I'll be quite lost without Gemma. I need you around to keep me cheerful. More than that, Tabitha will be having her kittens any day now. I'm sure you want to get back to her.'

Fleabag grimaced. 'The last place I want to be is home. I adore my Tabitha, but she's always so cross when she's had kittens. She tells me to clear out because I'm in the way!' He stood on his three legs, arching his back into a long stretch. Then without a backward look, the cat jumped down from the window sill and stalked out of the room.

Fleabag was tired and he *did* feel unwell, but he was determined not to be left behind. Gemma needed him. He whispered to Cleo to investigate Rowanne's baggage to see where a respectable cat like himself might hide without too much discomfort. Cleo slipped past the maid with a purr and an appealing look, and jumped onto Rowanne's kitbag. She tried her claws on it. It was stuffed full. No room even for one of her elegant paws in there, let alone the whole of her large, comfort-loving father. The golden cat cast around for other possibilities. Ah, on the dressing table was a basket of the delicacies that Rowanne liked to eat: dried fruit and sweet pickles. Cleo smirked. Just what she needed!

When Rowanne left the room for a moment, and the maid had her back turned, Cleo said, very clearly, imitating Rowanne's voice almost perfectly, 'Oh, fetch another basket, and put it next to my kitbag, will you? I have a few more bits and pieces to take.'

The maid did not turn around, instead she just curtseyed, said, 'At once, Madam,' and scurried away, looking just a little surprised as she met Rowanne coming in the door. Cleo gave the princess a sweet, innocent smile, and ran to where Fleabag was catnapping.

'Dad, Dad,' she prodded the older cat with her nose.

'Avast, ye dreaded rats. Have at you!' The black cat was obviously dreaming great deeds. Cleo prodded him a little harder. 'Dad, hurry! I've got you a passage on board ship, but I think you'd better come now!'

Fleabag opened one golden eye, then the other. 'Good girl!' he grinned, and followed her down the corridor. As they turned into Rowanne's room, they could see that the heavy kitbag had already been collected, but the maid had found a large wicker basket and left it by the bed. Cleo whispered, 'In there! Quickly!' Then she trotted over to Rowanne and miaowed to be stroked. Rowanne, who realized she *almost* liked cats, obliged, saying, 'Send my regards to your father, will you? Sorry he's not well enough to travel, but tell him I'll catch him a fish.'

Fleabag took the opportunity of the distraction and slipped into the very commodious hiding place. With his teeth he grabbed a night-gown from the end of the bed and pulled it down over himself. Inadvertently he left his tail hanging over the side, so Cleo gave it a quick nip as she went past. Her teeth were needle-sharp, and Fleabag had to bite his tongue to prevent himself calling her every dreadful name under the sun. Cleo ran away chuckling, but a little jealous that she wasn't included in the jaunt.

Fleabag heard Rowanne's voice calling out to the maid not to forget to give the men her basket, and the girl picked it up and handed it over. The cat kept his ears low and his tail tightly wrapped around himself, lest a whisker betray his presence.

Cleo, being every bit as inquisitive as her father, could not resist following the man with the basket down to the quayside to see the ship off. She sat primly next to the ship, watching the loading, and made sure the Princess' belongings were all handed down the hatch to the small cabin that Rowanne had decided was hers.

Cleo grinned as Fleabag's hiding place was bumped and shaken on the way. 'Never mind,' she thought. 'It might knock some of the rudeness out of him!'

But scarcely had her father been safely stowed when a strong, brown hand caught Cleo under her belly and held her up for inspection. 'A ginger cat!' boomed Captain Marcus' deep voice. 'Just what we need! You are the young lady who gave me such useful information in the King's study. Would you like to come along and keep the rats well mannered and polite, eh, puss? Are you a ratter?'

Cleo looked into Marcus' black eyes and decided that not only would she very much like to be on the same ship as Fleabag and keep an eye on him, but it would be a fine thing to be a ship's cat and have adventures with the handsome captain. Cleo opened her delicate pink mouth and gave her new friend a wet, raspy lick, right down his cheek. 'It's a deal!' she purred. Then she draped herself around his big, comfortable shoulders and smirked.

The *Flora* had been at sea for two days before, as far as Rowanne was concerned, disaster struck.

Up until then, the water had been calm. But now the storm Domnall had created, by throwing his scrying bowl, was spreading all across the eastern seas. Captain Marcus had skilfully caught the winds, guessing the direction in which the tide would have swept Gemma's little boat. But the suddenness of the storm caught everyone unawares.

The *Flora* was far enough away from the eye of the storm to escape the worst of the winds. It was a rough ride, but not a dangerous one. But Rowanne, who had never been to sea before, was horribly sick.

Until this happened, she had been moderately pleasant to everyone, not wanting to reveal that she was very apprehensive. She was a warrior, not a sailor, and the feeling that her feet were being tugged from under her, while her head was left somewhere completely different, again and again, hour after endless hour, was more than she could stand. Her stomach protested strongly and Rowanne had to hang her head over the side in case she was sick. But worse than the discomfort was the thought that anyone should see her in this state. The embarrassment was more than she could tolerate.

When Captain Marcus ordered her below, she refused to go. But he was not used to being disobeyed. The last thing he wanted was a sick hand on deck. 'My Lady, if you don't go below then I swear, Princess or not, I will have you clapped in irons for the rest of the voyage.' Then he turned away from her and smartly began to climb the mast, to help furl the mainsail before another squall took it away.

Rowanne leaned over the rails and was sick at last. Then she did as she was told.

It was only when she lay in her hammock, which swung dizzily with the rocking of the boat, that she realized she was not alone. A small, black mop of fur slithered stealthily from behind her kitbag. Rowanne sat up as best she could in the ever-moving, ever-sagging hammock.

'Rats!' she hissed as she threw a well-aimed boot at the lithe shadow.

'Hey!' moaned Fleabag indignantly, 'Don't do that! You might ruffle my fur!'

Rowanne buried her head in her arms and tried to turn over. 'Oh, it's you! I thought you'd been told to stay home and keep well away from the sea!'

Fleabag put up a paw and tapped his right ear. 'Sorry,' he said, 'I didn't catch that. I've been a bit deaf since my wetting. I find I miss a lot of things people say.'

Rowanne groaned. 'I hope Phelan skins you for a fur collar when you get back. He's probably worried sick about you.'

Fleabag sat up and began to wash. 'My Lady, you have threatened that for years, but you will never catch me. Neither will he. Anyway, he won't be cross, he'll guess where I've gone.'

Just then a clatter at the door heralded the cabin boy with a tray of stew for Rowanne. She groaned at the smell. 'I'm going to throw up again!' she wailed and fell out of her hammock to droop her sore head over a bucket.

But Fleabag only had eyes for the dinner tray. 'Oh goody, can I eat your dinner? I've only had a couple of mangy rats since I took berth in this fair vessel, and I'm famished!'

'You'd be doing me a favour if you did,' Rowanne moaned.

The stew was excellent. It was much better than seafaring rat, which is nutritious but tough, and has a distinctly over-salted taste which Fleabag did not entirely like. Cleo had, of course smuggled him chunks of steak and chicken from the galley but, as far as he was concerned, they didn't count and he wasn't going to let on about them. The role of half starved stowaway suited him better. It evoked a more practical sympathy.

When Rowanne had righted herself again, and had washed, she sat on the edge of her kitbag and surveyed her old friend. 'So, what are you doing here? I thought you were at the palace.'

Fleabag licked a small drop of gravy from his paw and grinned. 'I've come to help you out, of course.'

Rowanne was puzzled. 'How do you mean, "help" me?'

'By eating the food which you are unable to eat because you haven't got your sea legs yet.'

Rowanne was about to swipe him for his cheek, when the ship suddenly gave a great lurch to starboard, sending the cat, the Princess, the kitbag and the dinner into a great, gravy-covered heap in the far corner of the little cabin. 'Yuck!' bewailed Rowanne, plucking at the long coils of her dark hair which were now liberally bathed in stew.

'Allow me to assist,' Fleabag offered, trying to nibble one of the bigger lumps of meat from behind her ear.

But Rowanne was in no mood to be 'assisted'. She pushed the cat aside and stumbled out of the door. Scrambling up the steps as fast as she could, she clung onto the railing at the top, unable to move for the tossing of the ship. From there she bellowed at Captain Marcus who stood on the bridge, Cleo draped adoringly across the back of his neck. Despite her encumbering presence, the Captain was standing solidly at the wheel, keeping a steady course. He ignored Rowanne as she ranted and raved at him for what she called his 'bad steering'.

However, as Fleabag approached, the Captain looked

down. 'Aha, another cat, and indeed, one that I might have mistaken for a pirate, with that great golden earring, had I not already seen you in the King's study. I hope we have enough rats on board to satisfy you both.'

Cleo stretched gently around the Captain's neck and whispered, 'Oh, throw him overboard, Marcus. He's just a flea-infested old stowaway. Hang him from the yard-arm, make him walk the plank!'

Fleabag looked up and sneered. 'Is that all the thanks I get for my bravery, coming on board despite my life-threatening illness? I had to make sure my daughter, whom you are presently wearing as a scarf, was safe, and to offer you my experience and wisdom on this adventure. The noble Fleabag, at your service, sir!' and he bowed, or tried to. But just at that moment the ship lurched, Fleabag lost his balance, toppled over and slid down the sloping deck with all his three paws stuck up in the air.

He hated losing his dignity, so immediately started to wash. But then he spotted Rowanne who had managed to let go of the railing and was staggering across the deck, glowering and red in the face, furious at being ignored. For once he decided she could have the limelight while he slipped down below to clear up some of that excellent gravy. Purely to help out, of course.

Rowanne now stood squarely in front of the Captain. He nodded curtly to her, without taking his dark eyes off the sea. 'Are you feeling better, my Lady? How can I be of service?'

Rowanne clutched the rigging and hung there like wet washing. 'I came to see what the matter was! You're driving this thing like a maniac – can't you take it any slower? You have passengers aboard, or had you forgotten?'

The Captain looked at her for a moment. He hated bossy landlubbers. He turned his attention back to his wheel. 'Madam, the wind is, as you call it, driving the ship. I merely steer it. We go as fast as the wind goes, and if the wind chooses to play games and buffet us a little, we have to go with it. I recommend you go below and try and get some rest. By the look of those bluish clouds on the horizon, we are in for a long night.'

12

On Spider Island

The storm did not abate that night. Captain Marcus took short rests, preferring to be at the helm himself. His crew of fifteen men worked almost as hard as he did. There was no thought of steering any sort of course; all they could do was to try to avert disaster. Dawn broke, but still the wind did not lessen. High above, blue clouds rose and spread, blocking out the stars and the sun, leaving everything in a dull haze, day and night.

After a few days the Princess had found her sea legs, and was actually enjoying the work of sailing. She was as strong as any man, and her sword-trained arms could haul a rope without any trouble.

The captain spent hours peering at his compass; he could not use the sextant without a clear sun. He looked worried. His tall frame stooped over the brass compass housing as he shook his head. 'I don't see how it is possible, but we seem to be going round in circles,' he told Rowanne at last.

She looked out to sea. The unnatural blue pall overhead gave the ocean a dull, thick, turquoise colour. With monotonous regularity, the waves rose and lifted the *Flora*'s bow, then slapped her down again into a deep valley between the watery mountains. Rowanne was good at orienteering on dry land, but she conceded that sea navigation was beyond her. 'How can you tell we're going in circles?' she asked.

'Look, we've been swinging through the points of the compass at an even speed for two days now. If I didn't know these seas better I would say we must be caught at the edge of an enormous whirlpool.'

Rowanne stared at the compass, then out to sea again. Marcus had gone forward to talk to one of his men. He never elaborated on anything, but he left Rowanne with a cold feeling of apprehension creeping down her back.

And she was not the only one feeling odd.

Neither Fleabag nor Cleo were quite themselves. The strange sense of 'something' had come back. All day, and long hours of the nights as well, the two cats found they could not rest. Every time they closed their eyes their whiskers twitched, and their dreams were full of blue shadowy flames that reached for them.

Fleabag was worried. He guessed that the approaching blueness meant that Domnall or some power of Porthwain was near at hand. It also probably meant that they were nearing Gemma. Whatever happened next would be important. He tried to collect his thoughts, but every time he sat in a quiet corner to think, he found he couldn't. As soon as he began to concentrate on what to do, he simply *had* to jump up and chase and leap and fling himself this way and that. He had to catch, or even better, kill whatever was pestering him. Only there *was* nothing there.

Very soon, both he and Cleo were quite worn out. Their coats were unwashed and had lost their sheen, and they were getting thin. They were both so obsessed with the 'somethings' they even left the rats in peace. Not that the rats would have been difficult to catch. They were acting very oddly themselves and almost flung themselves into the cats' paws, so blindly were they leaping.

The humans did not seem to be affected in the same way. They did not have the same sensitivities as cats. But what could the animals *do*? Fleabag wished Gemma or Phelan were with them – they understood the Ring Fire (although Gemma did not think she did). They needed that flame now to give them some wisdom and perhaps just to be a steady light as they sailed through this endless and ever-thickening blue.

Fleabag sat in a corner, with his back wedged between the luggage and the wall. 'Nothing is behind me, and nothing can *get* behind me,' he told himself, 'so I must not jump around, however much I want to. Neither the King nor the Fire Wielder are here,' he told himself firmly. 'I may be only a cat, but I am just going to have to sort this out for myself. Now I must concentrate,' and he closed his eyes and imagined the Ring Fire, small and steady, a tiny golden fire within the King's opal, then tall, majestic and glorious in Gemma's hands as Phelan was proclaimed King by the old Fire Wielder. In his mind, the Flame burned so steadily and strongly that Fleabag soon began to feel better in this terrible, dark place.

But he could not concentrate. His whiskers tickled again. He ignored them for a long time, but at last the feeling was so insistent, he opened his eyes. There was Cleo, curled up next to him, her ears flat against her head, looking very worried.

'Marcus says the circle we are in is getting tighter. Each circuit we make is taking less time to complete. We are being sucked into something.' The marmalade cat snuggled up to her father. 'I'm scared. Tell me again how Gemma burned the Ring Fire to save Phelan from the wolves.'

In his study at Porthwain, Domnall peered into his scrying bowl. It was badly dented, so the image he saw was distorted. He did not have time to make another bowl. This one would have to do.

Gemma was alive, he could tell that much. She was on a small island with two domed hills, one large, one small, so it looked like a huge spider. It even had several long outcrops of rock stretching out to sea like giant legs. The girl was sitting in a dark place. She was cold and miserable, but fed and alive. Good. She was safe. He knew the King had sent a search party to fetch her, but they stood no chance. He had all the power of the Order of Wizards at his fingertips; they did not even have a weather-maker on board.

He turned his gaze to watch the little ship tossing in the blue maelstrom. He stirred the water and laughed as the ship spun around once or twice and he heard cries of terror from the crew. He stretched his hand out and searched the minds of the sixteen men and one woman on board, finding mostly fear and dread. The Captain was strong-minded, but he did not know where he was going. This 'rescue party' was no threat.

Domnall did not bother to observe the cats. He simply threw them something to chase, and left them to their own devices. They were fun to torture, that was all.

His work now was to concentrate on making a great wall of magic around the island, blue and impenetrable. Gemma was caught in his trap. Perhaps he should make it a web, as this was Spider Island. He laughed a little as he raised his spells around the dented edge of the scrying dish, constructing a great twisting wall of blue, leaving everyone within the wall at his mercy. And those outside the wall? Well, they didn't matter. He frowned as he considered the dents in the rim of the silver bowl; they would make the wall of water weak in places. But no one in their right mind would even attempt to sail through. He would be quite safe.

His plan was to surround Gemma with the full force of the blue flames, then slowly tighten the ring until she was consumed. Then he would be waiting to capture the fleeing Ring Fire. She obviously had no control over it, so he would have to chase it out, and be ready...

Fleabag spent several hours remembering the Ring Fire, how it looked, how it felt, and how good it was to be near it. Several times he felt it was speaking to him, but heard no words. But by the end of the morning, the idea forming in his head was so strong, it was almost a shout.

Suddenly it came even more clearly than before. It made Fleabag jump, waking Cleo. 'Quick!' he ordered. 'Run to the Captain! You climb quicker than I can. Tell him to head for the centre of the storm. Do it *now*!'

Cleo sprang to her paws instantly. She wanted to ask what on earth her father was talking about, but the look in his eyes brooked no argument. Immediately she fled out of the cabin and leaped up the steps, her paws scarcely touching the rungs of the ladder.

'*NOW*! Tell him the Ring Fire says he's got to do it *NOW*!' Fleabag bellowed as he struggled behind her on his three legs.

Cleo caught the urgency and sprang with a flying leap right onto the Captain's shoulder, her claws digging into his right arm so that his hand slipped from the wheel and the ship turned sharply to port. Blood welled in hot streaks as Marcus swore and struggled with the cat. But the turn had been made. Already behind them a great wall of water was rising, pulling the ship into a whirling frenzy of white and blue waves.

'All hands on deck!' the Captain bellowed as a great rocky outcrop suddenly loomed, huge and jagged, out of the blue ahead of them.

Gemma had been put to work the morning after her rescue. Aidan had brought her twine and nets to repair. He was not a good teacher, but during her years as a Fire Wielder, Gemma had not forgotten how to use her fingers. She quickly learned how to twist the string and pull it tight to repair the holes in the huge nets he brought. At noon he gave her bread and water.

The wind was howling and the rotten hulk was scarcely any protection against the weather. Aidan let Gemma gather moss and driftwood to caulk some of the wider cracks. But he would not let her light a fire. He said it was in case the ancient hulk burned down. As he could not put to sea in the wild winds that were whipping frantically around the island, Aidan sat next to Gemma and watched her working.

He still hoped that she might be the daughter of a rich merchant and perhaps worth a reward. On the other hand, she was very good at her work and had been worth rescuing; he could not decide whether it would be better to keep her or not. What was more advantageous? A good worker around, perhaps for life, or a great deal of money?

His indecision was made worse by her inability to answer his endless questions about who she was and where she had come from. All she knew was that she had been adrift for several days, and that a man had put her in the boat. But why, she did not know. She still could not remember her name, so Aidan still called her Ahanet – the hard worker.

He fed her as well as he could in case she proved to be worth exchanging for a reward. He did not want her to say she had been mistreated. Thankfully her memory was so hazy that she did not even miss her golden chain and her heavy ring with the emblem of the Ring Fire on it.

One day she was sitting sewing, in the bluish light at the entrance to her little home, when she realized she had a white band of skin around her middle finger where the Fire Wielder's seal had been. 'I wonder why I have a pale mark there?' she asked Aidan, who was sitting with her. For a second his heart missed a beat. He shrugged and said nothing. She forgot it and went on with her work.

Another time she was standing, looking out to sea when Aidan brought her daily food. 'Another day of no work,' he said, miserably. 'I'll be ruined if this strange weather doesn't change soon.' His sparse fortune from selling the gold chain had almost gone, and the endless wind was keeping traders from the island. He could not sell the ring to another islander. It was far too precious; and besides, too many questions would be asked about it.

Gemma took her ration of bread and bit into it. 'Is everything always this blue here?' she asked.

Aidan shook his head. 'No, only since you came. What's it like where you come from?'

Gemma found she could remember that. 'Oh, blue skies. But a nice blue, not a heavy, threatening blue like this. And green hills, and I can remember a city. And I can remember a fire. I'd like a fire; I'm cold,' she added, pulling her stiff sailcloth cape more closely around her.

'No!' he snapped. 'It's too dangerous in there.'

'How about one out here then?'

Aidan was adamant. He did not want anyone from the village seeing the smoke. If they did, his parents would take his precious servant from him and set her to work for them. But something else occurred to him... they might well put her to death. For the heavy blue clouds and terrible winds *had* come when she had. Perhaps she was a sorceress who brought the evil eye with her. The villagers were malicious gossips, and would convince themselves that their imminent ruin was Ahanet's fault. There would be nothing he could do to help her... No, he had to keep her a secret.

He wasn't superstitious. And Gemma did not *look* like a sorceress. The storms would pass.

'No fire!' he ordered as he turned to go. Then he looked back at her. 'If you light one I'll whip you; then you'll be sorry.'

Gemma looked down at her hands. They were scarred

from where something had hurt her palms before Aidan had found her. Her fingers were sore from the hempen twine she used on the fishing nets and sails she was given to mend. Her skin was too soft for this sort of work, although there had been calluses on her hands once, she was sure of it.

Where, when? She knew she didn't belong here, but where did she belong? And why did she dream every night of sitting by a lovely fire? She shrugged. Probably because she was cold.

She dragged the pile of nets she was working on inside. She lay down on her sackcloth and straw bed and closed her eyes. All she could see before her eyes was fire. Not a great roaring blaze, but a steady, gold-red light.

13

Gemma Remembers

Gemma awoke colder than ever. 'Does that wind ever stop blowing?' she wondered as she left the old upturned boat, once again in search of something to try and fill the gaping spaces between the shrunken boards.

She returned with armfuls of bracken and moss, but as soon as she had pushed the wadding into the cracks, the raging wind tugged it all out again and infuriatingly tossed everything away.

After a while, Gemma gave up. She had no time for this; there were so many nets to mend. She guessed that Aidan was getting her to repair other people's as well.

Something kept making her shiver and look around. It wasn't the cold, it was a feeling… a feeling of something, some*one*, watching her. It made her uneasy, so she crawled back inside on her hands and knees, and sat cross-legged near the entrance with her nets. The light was poor, but she could just about see. As she worked, she found herself singing. It was a song about the hope each season brought and a fire that burned at the centre of all things… She stopped and thought for a moment. Who had taught her that song? She closed her eyes and put her head on one side.

Someone not like her at all, but someone nice. A friend. A man or a boy, not the one who had put her into the boat, someone with dark, golden-brown skin and thick black curly hair, and was there a beard? Someone very untidy and smiling, looking contented. Who was he, and why that image of fire again?

Fire, fire, what fire? She was so cold she would have given anything for a fire at that moment, even if Aidan did whip her for it. She was so cold! Even inside, the wind kept wrapping her hair around her face. It was a mousy brown, with a red tinge which came off on her hands. The colour must have been dyed. Why should she dye her hair red? The colour of fire…

She tried to put the thoughts out of her mind. She had work to do, and Aidan would be angry if it lay unfinished when he came. Bending her head over her task, turning the nets so they caught the mean, blue light from the entrance, Gemma tugged at the twine, twisting and knotting it, hour after hour until the morning was over. Aidan would be here with food soon. When he had gone, she *would* light a fire, just a small one. She had to have warmth and solace.

Fire seemed to be important to her; she always seemed to be thinking about it. Perhaps if she saw a flame, it might give her a clue as to who she was and where she belonged. She had to find out the truth soon, for at the back of her mind there was an urgency she could not push aside. The wind was blowing harder. Her fingers grew too cold to work. She put her needle down and began to rub her shoulders and arms to try and revive some warmth in them.

And warmth came. Suddenly she felt very warm indeed. In fact, her hands were hot. She held them out to see what had caused the change, and she screamed – for there was fire in her palms!

Hurriedly she pushed the nets away from her and tried to scramble outside. The nets caught fire from her hands, and tangled around her feet. In terror she tried to kick free as she staggered a few steps up the nearest dune where she fell face down, filling her mouth and eyes with fine, pale grains of sand.

But the flames did not go out.

Far away, Aidan's voice was calling, half scolding, half terrified. Gemma tried to answer so he could find her, but she had too much sand in her mouth. Behind her the hulk was fiercely aflame and the crackle of the wood drowned out her terrified whimper.

Unheeding, Aidan stood helpless, looking at the flames. There was no way for him to get inside and rescue Ahanet. He realized suddenly that he had quite liked her. She was quiet and did as she was told, and he enjoyed being with her. She would have made a good wife, he was sure. Now he was sad. The villagers would soon come to investigate the smoke, and when they found a skeleton in the burned-out wreckage, there would be questions asked. Questions he did not want to answer.

There was nothing for Aidan to do now but to wait for the flames to die down. He sat down heavily, at the bottom of the dune where Gemma lay. She kicked sand down on him, making him turn around.

'Help!' she spluttered, spitting sand, 'Help! I'm on fire!'

Aidan heard her this time, and scrambled up towards her. 'No you're not!' he said, pulling a small gutting knife from his pocket so he could cut the net from her feet. 'That's a good net you've ruined! Anyway,' he scolded, 'what were you thinking of? I told you no fires!'

Half of him was so angry he wanted to carry out his threat and whip her, and the other half was relieved she was unhurt.

'Why aren't I on fire?' Gemma asked, looking at her hands, 'I was a few moments ago.'

'You put it out by rolling in sand. Best thing to do.'

Gemma held open her hands. They were hot and, although it was difficult to see in the daylight, a tiny flame burned in each palm. She closed her fingers quickly. Suddenly, she knew what that burning feeling meant. Terrible danger was near. She knew what the Fire was. She knew who *she* was.

Gemma grabbed Aidan by his sleeve. 'You have got to help me find shelter! Quickly! I know who I am and what I've got to do!'

'I've *got* to do nothing of the sort. If anything, I've got to give you a thrashing for disobeying me!' Aidan replied, taken aback at Gemma's sudden boldness and change of character.

'Oh, don't be silly!' she replied urgently. 'There's no time. If you won't help me, I'll help myself, but you are in almost as much danger as I am. Will you help or not?' Gemma had pushed her hair back and stood staring up at her rescuer – or was he her captor? Her clear eyes challenged Aidan, but she wasn't bullying, like his parents. This girl who had once been timid and obedient, suddenly had dignity and presence. In her mind she had ceased to be the submissive kitchen-maid, and become once more the Fire Wielder she actually was.

Aidan did not understand any of this. He swallowed hard as he looked at her. In an odd way she seemed almost to have grown several inches since that morning. She must be from a good family, used to ordering servants around. He would play along with her; the reward could be better than he had even imagined. But she mustn't think she could boss him around just like that. He crossed his arms and shrugged his shoulders. Then with his head on one side he took a step back and looked her up and down. 'All right then, who are you?'

When she told him, he laughed and shrugged again. 'They're only in stories!'

Gemma did not have time to argue. She could sense the presence of Domnall all around her. The Fire in her hands was burning. As the flame grew in strength, the wind was whipping up, whistling around, tugging her hair every which way. Blue lightning started to crack across the skies.

Gemma threw off her stiff, cumbersome cape, leaving her arms free. She raised her burning hands to the blue clouds and called clearly, 'Lord Domnall – or should I call you Chancellor of All Wizards – I hear your challenge and I answer you. I, Gemma, Fire Wielder of this Land, servant of the Fire Giver, will meet you and do battle. I will no longer believe your lies and deceits. You have held sway long enough. Whether or not I am sufficient for my office no longer matters. The Ring Fire is here!'

Domnall stood back from the scrying bowl, watching the tongues of flame rising from Gemma's hands with full strength and authority.

He rubbed his well-shaven chin. 'Well, at least I know she still has it, but she seems to have grown in strength. I wonder where *that* came from?' he mused. 'So she will not surrender the Fire, and now she summons me to battle; then battle it is!' He leaned over the scrying bowl and breathed on the water.

At the same moment a thick blue mist covered Spider Island. 'He has heard me,' Gemma said quietly. 'Now, I need that shelter, please. I must make my preparation for what is to come.'

Confused and frightened by the blue mist and Gemma's sudden change, Aidan stammered, 'C-come this way, but stay close, you will lose me very easily in this fog.' Running this way and that through the dunes, he led her down a rocky path and onto the shifting stones of the beach. He said nothing. This girl was definitely a sorceress. She had powers. He didn't want anything to do with this sort of thing. He was a practical lad, and he kept magic and the stuff of legends firmly at arm's length. Above all, if she was really what she claimed to be, what would she do to him for the way he had treated her?

But despite that, he still liked her and hoped she won this challenge, whatever it was. Deep down he was certain that whatever she was, she was on the side of good. He must give her shelter, then leave her to her own devices as quickly as possible. The sooner she forgot about him, the better.

After a short walk across the noisy pebbles, the air

suddenly cleared, and Gemma found she was standing in a small, damp sea cave.

Aidan was standing in the cave entrance, dark against the eerily swirling mists. 'At this time of year, the tides don't reach this far up the beach. You ought to be safe,' he said. 'But given how strange things have been since you came, I won't guarantee anything. Watch the tides, and get out quickly if you see the water coming in. The path is to your right. Follow the bottom of the cliff and you'll get to it. Goodbye, Gemma or whatever your name is. Thanks for mending the nets. I...' he hesitated. 'I hope there're no hard feelings?'

Gemma smiled. 'None. Thank you for saving me.'

Aidan stepped backwards, deeper into the mists. 'You're not going to put a spell on me or anything when my back is turned, are you?'

Gemma smiled again. 'No, why should I? Anyway, I don't do spells. I am not a sorceress. I only carry the Ring Fire. I am the servant of the Fire Giver. *I* have no powers. I simply challenge evil with what is true.' And with that she held out a hand with a small clear flame burning in it.

Aidan opened his mouth in amazement at the clear calm beauty of the little light. 'You, you didn't bring the blue clouds and the strange wind then?'

'No. That's none of my doing, but I suspect that it *is* here because of me. There is an evil wizard called Domnall who wants to take this Fire from me and rule the land with magic and spells for ever.'

'You're not going to give it to him?'

'It's not mine to give. But if you can help me find my boat so I can get back to King Phelan on the mainland, I suspect the blue evil will follow me and leave your island in peace. Will you help?'

Aidan stepped further away. Even now he was too scared to turn his back on this strange girl. 'I'll bring you food, and I'll give you back your boat and ring, but I sold the necklace to feed us both…'

Gemma nodded. 'That's fair, I prefer to pay for my keep. But where is my boat?'

'It's beached just along a bit in a small cove, but you'll not get anywhere in it – the waves are too high. You would drown in minutes.' He looked at her sidelong, wondering, perhaps, if she would be able to ride the craft, skimming over the tops of the waves like the magical creatures in legends.

Gemma glanced out of the cave towards the raging sea. 'You could well be right. I know nothing about seafaring. I'll stay here for a while and listen to what the Fire says before I decide what to do. By the way, don't bother to return the ring. Sell it and buy us both food and warm clothes. You can keep the change for another boat if that's what you want.'

Aidan was about to say, 'I'll do my best,' when there was suddenly a terrible crashing sound, followed by screams and shouts.

'A ship on the rocks,' Aidan said, and ran down to the sea.

14

Abandon Ship!

Gemma's first instinct was to rush out and help rescue any survivors. She might be able to use the Ring Fire to give light to the rescuers or to guide the struggling crew to land.

Yet she knew the Ring Fire wanted her to leave that to others. Instead it was telling her to sit quietly and listen. There were other islanders to help, maybe the crew of the ship were safe. Whatever the reason, she knew what she had to do.

Silently she sat on a cool, damp rock at the back of the cave. She was hungry and thirsty and worried about the poor souls at the mercy of the sea. Gemma surrounded whoever might be in the shipwreck with the glow of the Ring Fire to keep them safe until help came, as she had done when Phelan faced the terrible monster on the scaffold at Beriot. Then she turned her attention to the Fire itself.

The sweeping of the angry waves had impaled the *Flora* on one of the rocky arms of Spider Island. The ship had been driven so hard between two huge, granite boulders that she was held quite firmly.

'Abandon ship!' Marcus bellowed. 'We're on the rocks! Over the starboard side, quickly. It's too misty to see properly, but I think you'll be able to scramble to land, or at least be safe until help comes!'

Calmly and carefully, Marcus took Cleo from his shoulders and lowered her over the side into the arms of the first mate. The ship shuddered as wave after wave battered the sides and slapped across the decks. Soon all the crew were safe, but Rowanne hesitated.

'I can't see Fleabag!' she yelled down to Cleo. 'Is he with you?'

The ginger cat winced as another breaker drenched her. 'No, he was just behind me last time I saw him.'

Rowanne spun around. The decks were awash with swirling sea water. 'I can't see him... just a minute, what's that?' She staggered across the shuddering planking, clinging to ropes and rails at every step, trying to stop herself being swept overboard by the pummelling waves.

A small, pathetic, black shape was peering out of the aft hatch. 'Fleabag!' Rowanne yelled, springing forward. But as she let go on the gunwales to grab at her friend, a huge wave broke across the ship, sweeping her off her feet and swirling Fleabag into the hold below.

Without hesitating, Marcus heaved himself back over the side. Cleo had climbed onto his shoulder again, and was yowling for her father.

Rowanne leaped blindly into the pitch-black hold, landing knee-deep in a tossing torrent of baggage and water. How could she ever find her friend in all this?

Just then, a sharp set of claws embedded themselves desperately in her thigh.

Rowanne scooped up Fleabag's sodden body and grabbed at the ladder. As she stepped on the first rung, Marcus bellowed down, 'Hurry, the ship is breaking up!' And with that a thunderous wave caught the *Flora* amidships and tugged her groaning and creaking hulk so badly that Rowanne was thrown back into the hold.

Fleabag clung onto Rowanne's neck and shoulders with all his claws. His little dagger points were agonizingly sharp as the friends tumbled together into the shuddering darkness. Rowanne gritted her teeth and, holding onto the terrified bundle of black fur with one hand, she stood and tried the ladder again. The seas pounded the ship relentlessly, each wave hitting the vessel without mercy.

'Quick!' Marcus ordered, putting his hand down to pull Rowanne up.

Cleo was standing on the gunwales howling at her father to hurry.

'Jump!' Fleabag ordered. 'Don't wait for us!'

Just then, with a terrible cracking and groaning, the stern of the ship broke away, swept off into the raging depths as if a giant hand had ripped it asunder. As it did so, the swirling sea swept into the shell of the forward section, scooping out goods and luggage and equipment like a great, hungry tongue.

Marcus grabbed Cleo, flung himself overboard, and landed on the rocks beyond. He leaned over and tried to grasp Rowanne's fingers. 'Grab my hand! I have a good foothold, I'm firm!'

But Rowanne could not hear him. The roaring of the engulfing waves filled her ears and eyes and throat. The last words she heard as they were swept away from the ship were Fleabag muttering, 'Oh no! Not again!'

Rowanne lay exhausted on a stony shore. She was not too bruised or battered, but she could not see where she was, for a thick, blue mist hung like a heavy blanket over everything.

Rowanne managed to right herself. Then, spotting Fleabag a few steps away, she picked him up, almost kindly. 'You all right?' she spluttered.

The cat coughed sea water and groaned. 'Yes. I suppose I have to say "thank you" now?'

'It's not so hard, is it?' Rowanne laughed. 'Never mind, at least I got to wear your pelt as a fur collar as I always said I would. But you're right, I didn't like it. You pricked!' Rowanne pulled her shirt back from her neck and felt the bleeding scratches gingerly with the tips of her fingers. 'Ouch!'

'Serves you right!' Fleabag grinned. 'I always said I wouldn't suit you – now you know why. It'll teach you to treat me with the respect I deserve! Flinging me over your shoulders like that, I ask you. Is that the way to treat a royal cat?'

Rowanne playfully tossed a small pebble at him. 'Ungrateful animal, I was saving your life!'

Fleabag began to wash himself to get the sticky salt out of his fur. 'OK. I'll let you off this time, but next time you attempt anything like this, I require at least two servants to fetch my best basket and carry me out properly, with a royal guard, a marching band and everything. Being rescued, like everything else I do, has to be done with style and dignity.' Then he stopped washing, and rubbed his nose against Rowanne's hand. 'But thanks anyway,' he added quietly. 'And I'm sorry I hurt you.'

Rowanne could hardly believe her ears. Suddenly she laughed and picked Fleabag up and hugged him. But when a flea jumped onto her face, trying to escape the wet fur of the bedraggled cat, Rowanne put her friend down again, very quickly. 'Let's not overdo this, eh?'

Fleabag shook himself and licked a few more hairs. 'Just what I was thinking myself. But what we really should do is to see if the others are safe.'

'I should think they'll be all right. They were on pretty solid rock. Even if they are cut off, they'll be safe until we can get a boat to them.'

'If we can find a boat, let alone get it through these waves… and the mist… where *are* we?'

'I don't know, but there's a something that could be a boat beached over there.' Rowanne slipped and climbed up the shingle until she reached a long, low shape, upside down at the foot of the cliff. 'It's a boat all right. Look, it's got something scratched in the side, "V" and a circle with a teardrop shape in it.'

Fleabag, who was a lot nearer the ground than Rowanne, twisted his head around. 'It's not a "V", it's an A upside down, and that circle pattern is… could it be? I don't believe it!'

'What?' demanded Rowanne impatiently, crouching down low. 'What are you talking about?'

'Turn the boat over quickly,' Fleabag said. 'Look, Rowanne, it's the sign of the Ring Fire! I don't know what the "A" stands for, but Gemma's been here, I'm sure of it!'

15

The Cats and the Ring Fire

The excitement of the shipwreck meant that none of the islanders noticed Gemma's burning boat. Now that Aidan knew that she was safely away from there he was not so worried. If anyone asked, he'd say the hulk had been struck by lightning.

But for now he had to take a look at what was coming ashore. It had been a well-provisioned ship, judging by the good quality of the wreckage. Shouts from Aidan's left meant that there were survivors on the rocks. They would get to land easily enough from there. He spotted some good clothes and barrels of dried fruits and started to pull them clear of the water. Then he left them in a heap while he thought.

Good-quality cargo meant wealthy people, and that

meant handsome rewards! Perhaps it would be better to leave the salvage and guide the people to safety first. But he would make it look difficult and dangerous on the way, to impress everyone with how brave and courageous he was.

But his delay made him too late. Already the dark figure of Captain Marcus was stepping down from the rocks onto the pebbly shore. He was followed by his crew and the lithe Cleo.

Marcus bowed slightly to Aidan. 'Good sir! If you can find lodging for myself and these people, you will be repaid handsomely. We are from the King's ship, the *Flora*, run aground not far from here, and His Majesty does not forget those who do good in his name.'

Aidan was impressed with this speech. His quick mind was also thinking that he could slip Gemma in amongst them and get good lodgings for her as well. Soon he would be a rich man indeed! He grinned quietly to himself. 'I will do my best for you, sir,' Aidan replied, bowing deeply in response. 'Come and rest in this small cave while I run up to the village for you. Another lady is also sheltering there. Are you all saved, or is anyone still in the sea?'

Marcus looked pleased. 'Indeed, we were missing another lady. I am relieved to find she has come ashore so quickly. Was a black, three-legged cat with her?'

Aidan led the way towards the cave. 'I don't think this is the lady you are hoping to find, sir. She came ashore a few days ago, but like you she is stranded and in need of proper lodging.' He trudged ahead of the men up the shifting shingle to the cave mouth. 'Lady Gemma,' Aidan called, 'may I bring in the people who survived the wreckage?'

Gemma was about to be cross about the interruption, but as she turned from the flame that burned steadily in her hands, Marcus and his men immediately knelt at her feet. 'My Lady,' he said, 'we have been searching the high seas for you. I thank the Fire Giver you are safe.'

Gemma allowed the Ring Fire to settle back to a tiny flame in her hand. She looked at the kneeling sailors. 'Do get up, please. Is anyone else with you?' she asked.

Marcus glanced around. 'All my men are here, my Lady, but the Princess Rowanne was swept out to sea, along with the three-legged cat.'

Gemma went pale. 'Is the King with you?'

'He had to remain in Beriot, my Lady.'

Gemma stepped decisively towards the cave entrance, and stood there contemplating the swirling mists. 'Aidan?' she called over her shoulder.

The boy ran to her side and tried to kneel as well. 'Oh do stand up,' she chided. 'I hate all that nonsense. When the Ring Fire is burning, that is one thing, but now I am just like you. Tell me, is there a chance that anyone else could have been washed ashore?'

Aidan was nervous. Gemma was obviously a greater personage than he had imagined, maybe even a Fire Wielder as she claimed. But he had to keep calm and concentrate. His future comfort was at stake. 'Ordinarily, anything would come to shore away to the east,' he waved his hand to the right. 'But the tides are strange at the moment…' he added lamely as Gemma went crunching down the shingle as fast as she could run in her bare feet. After a moment the others followed.

It was not long before Gemma spotted the dark figure of the Princess treading the stones as she made her way inland. Behind her trotted an ungainly three-legged black cat. Gemma called out, running and stumbling across the noisy pebbles, flinging herself at her old friend with a bear hug. 'Rowanne! You're alive, and Fleabag! I'm so pleased to see you! There is so much I have discovered. There is a terrible danger hovering above this island, greater than anything we have ever met before!'

Marcus' voice boomed through the heavy mists, 'This lad has promised to find us lodging. When we are snug in a hostelry with a meal inside us, we can all swap tales. But let us get out of this mist first.'

Aidan guided the party up the cliff path towards the village, looking nervously over his shoulder every few minutes. He half expected Gemma to be putting spells on him. He had heard tell of the Fire Wielders, of course, but they were always strange, mystical figures from stories. They were never real, let alone someone almost his own age, skipping along, carrying a flame-red cat in her arms with a tatty black three-legged one at her heels, talking nineteen to the dozen to a Lady Knight.

It was all odd. Very odd.

The little port lay on the south side of the island, where the two dome-shaped hills met. It was a ramshackle place built of ship timbers, which were added to every time there was a wreck in the area. The only inn was similarly built of huge, curved beams and roughly dressed stone, but it was warm and welcoming enough, especially when Marcus presented the landlady with gold. She was pleased to have the custom. Sailors and merchants usually stayed there, but it had been empty since the coming of the strange winds which had kept the usual trading ships well away.

Seated around a roaring fire with plenty of good stew inside them, the travellers told their tale to Gemma. She sat quiet and still. She had bathed and dressed herself in a gown she had bought from the landlady, a long green dress with a wide skirt and huge white buttons down the front. It was big enough for two Gemmas and swamped her in copious folds of material. But she did not mind. She was grateful to be warm at long last.

Marcus and Rowanne both had cat scratches on their shoulders and necks. The Captain's were worse by far. 'Why did you leap at the Captain's shoulder so viciously?' Rowanne asked Cleo as she gently pulled the blood-soaked shirt away from his wounds.

The red-gold cat stretched luxuriously in front of the flames and purred. 'Fleabag told me to. I always do as *he* says.'

Fleabag got up and cuffed his daughter's golden ears playfully. '*Cleocatra*! How dare you! I told you no such thing, I simply asked you to request the Captain politely to change course very quickly indeed.'

'But why so *violently*, Cleo? Why didn't you just *ask*?' Marcus asked, wincing as Rowanne began to dab an ointment onto the wounds.

But before Cleo could answer, Fleabag jumped up onto the Captain's knee and peered at the ten little lacerations on his upper arm. 'Um. Nasty. Well, I had been thinking about the Ring Fire to cheer myself up, you know like Gemma does, then suddenly I just knew what we had to do. The Ring Fire wanted us to go right into the eye of the storm, and we had to do it immediately.'

'But could Cleo not simply have discussed the matter with me?' Marcus shrugged his shirt on again.

'No time.' Fleabag jumped down. 'The Ring Fire told me. We had to do it *then*.'

Gemma nodded. 'It must have been about then that I challenged Domnall and he tightened his spells very suddenly. If Cleo had stopped to ask Marcus nicely, the wall of sea would have risen to such a height you would have been crushed beyond all help. By turning at that instant, you were probably saved.'

'Does this mean that even a *cat* can hear the Ring Fire?' Rowanne was genuinely shocked, and rather put out. However much she longed to serve the Ring Fire, it always seemed to speak to others, never to her. She could only ever comprehend battles and stratagems, sword thrusts and armour. At times like this, she felt hurt and excluded. To make matters worse, this time it wasn't just another human who had heard the Ring Fire speak, but a *cat*, and the mangiest, scraggiest, worst-mannered one at that! The Princess folded her arms and glowered menacingly at Fleabag as he stretched himself on the hearth.

Gemma could tell Rowanne was upset. 'Why shouldn't Fleabag hear the Ring Fire speak? *You* might hear it if you listened and watched and tried to put warfare out of your head sometimes! In fact, one day the Ring Fire will be there for everyone, and you won't need a Fire Wielder.' There was an uncomfortable rustling in the room, as Gemma's listeners shifted and murmured apprehensively. They were shocked and confused. What *was* she talking about? But Gemma ignored them. She didn't know where that idea had come from, but she knew it was true.

At the back of her mind she felt the familiar urging to surrender the Ring Fire. But that was something different. That was what Domnall wanted her to think. Today she was still the Fire Wielder, and she was still needed. For better or for worse, she had to carry the Ring Fire as best she could until people learned to listen for themselves, or until someone took her place. Everyone was relying on her, and she mustn't let them down.

Gemma stood as tall as she could and started to speak again. 'You will all see what I mean in time. But for now I must explain what is happening. I suspect that Lord Domnall is the successor to the old Chancellor of All Wizards that Fleabag and I saw die in Porthwain, and he is attempting to take the Ring Fire from me. In past months, I have not been listening to the Ring Fire as I should, and Domnall would have won his battle to steal the flame if it had been mine to give it up. But the Fire Giver chooses who holds the Ring Fire, and,' here she smiled and opened her hand towards the disreputable black furry lump on the hearthrug, 'the Fire Giver also chooses who hears its wisdom. It is not for us to make rules that contain the Fire and where it may or may not burn.'

Everyone in the room was silent, looking at Gemma in her too big green dress, standing next to the fire, hands behind her back, almost like a school-girl reciting her lessons.

Gemma looked out of the little window. The mist had blown away, but night was falling, leaving the little island deep in the deadly blue of Domnall's spells. Everything in the firelit parlour at the inn seemed cosy and safe, but the small party of sailors led by Marcus and Rowanne was as tense as a new bowstring as they listened to the Fire Wielder's words.

16

Fire Cat

'The Ring Fire has challenged Domnall to meet him and do battle,' Gemma said. 'It will not be a battle with swords and spears, but one between the Fire Giver and the forces of magic and sorcery that Domnall has at his disposal. Soon I will meet him. I am only human, and can be killed, but even if I die, the Ring Fire will go on.

'I had hoped to be able to leave the island and join the Ring Fire with the King's Ring. By doing that I would draw this terrible blue magic away from the islanders. But it cannot be done. The winds and sea around the island are too strong for any boat. The battle will be fought here, and soon.

'While I am fighting Domnall, you must all do as Fleabag did, and look to the Ring Fire to protect yourselves and to help me. I cannot tell you what you must do, but I need you all, whether you are a cat, a princess, a sailor or a fisherman. Meanwhile, we must all get some sleep, for I do not know when Domnall will call me – or any of us – to the battle. Goodnight.'

And she turned to go to her room.

She left a shocked and silent group of friends behind, but Rowanne rushed after Gemma and caught her arm. 'Look, we can find weapons here; there must be knives I can sharpen. If we beg and buy all the pots and pans we can, I can reforge them into armour. There's a lot we can do with very little, you'll see! You aren't alone. We'll go into battle together. Give me a few days and I will be ready for any army...'

Gemma reached her bedroom door and turned towards her friend with a smile. 'No, Rowanne. Thanks, but – I don't know how to explain this to you – it's just not going to be like that...' Then she shut the door, but not before the two cats had slipped through as well.

In the dark of her room, Gemma sat on her bed and let the Ring Fire glow within the pink goblet of her fingers. Fleabag jumped up beside her and sat, tail neatly turned around his paws, as he contemplated the soft, strong light. At their feet, Cleo, who felt a little shy, sat and looked up. The neat, white triangle on her face stood out clearly in the gentle light.

Gemma looked a long while. Then her shoulders shook a little, and tears began to flow down her cheeks.

'Don't cry, we're with you,' Fleabag assured her, licking the back of one of her hands.

Gemma sighed and placed the Fire on the table next to her bed, like a comforting nightlight. Then she turned and hugged her old friend. 'Oh, Fleabag, I know you are, you dear, faithful thing. And I owe you an apology, I think...?'

'An apology?' Fleabag scratched a wandering flea under his chin. 'What for?'

Gemma picked the offending creature from the cat's fur. 'You've been trying to tell me something for weeks, and I didn't want to listen… And I didn't want to listen because I knew what you were going to say, and I didn't want to hear it because I knew it was true!'

'Do Fire Wielders always talk like this, Dad?' Cleo whispered to her father. 'I can't understand a word she's saying.'

Fleabag glowered. 'Cheeky kitten! Be quiet or I'll send you to bed with no mice on toast!' Then he hesitated and raised his whiskers questioningly. 'All right, Gemma,' he said, 'we both give up. *I* don't understand a word of what you said either!'

Despite her sad mood, Gemma couldn't help but laugh as she scratched the cat behind his ears. 'In the garden, that day of the blue storm, you must have seen me reach for the window to shut it against the rain…'

'Yes…'

'And you saw the Ring Fire was burning in my hands?'

'Yes.'

'Then you saw how the rain put it out… At that moment, Lord Domnall's rain was more powerful than the Ring Fire… probably because I had been ignoring it, not listening, not watching the flames. It was pretty scary. That was when I realized I would have to find a new Fire Wielder. I came on this so-called "holiday" in the hopes of thinking of someone else I could appoint, then go off on my own somewhere. I knew I had let the Ring Fire down – I'm not the right sort of person to carry it.

'I realize now it will always be burning somewhere; its

strength does not depend on me... But I still want to find a replacement as soon as this is all over. Perhaps the time of everyone carrying the Fire for themselves is close. Who knows? But I was wrong not to discuss it with you and Phelan at the time. I should have faced the truth and not run away from it.'

The deep velvet brown and black shadows shifted as the Ring Fire danced. The light gleamed on Fleabag's earring like a tiny flicker of flame in his black fur.

There was a long silence. At last Fleabag said: 'But that wasn't what I wanted to say at all.'

It was Gemma's turn to look bemused. 'What *did* you want to say, then?'

Fleabag climbed onto Gemma's lap and rolled upside down so she could rub his barrel-like tummy. 'I wanted to warn you that I had seen the blue forks of lightning searching for you in the storm. When you reached out to shut the window, and the Ring Fire was burning in your hand, the flame went out. But it wasn't because of the blue magic or the storm or anything else proving stronger than the Ring Fire...' The cat paused and stretched a front paw up. 'Just scratch there, please...'

'But what *did* put it out then?' Gemma was so on edge she stopped scratching completely.

'If you stop, I can't think!' he moaned.

Gemma resumed the thorough rubbing and ruffling of Fleabag's tummy fur. 'Sorry.'

'I should think so too!' Fleabag closed his eyes, as if he were watching the whole scene happen again. Then he said very slowly, 'The Ring Fire put *itself* out. Whatever was searching for you through the blue lightning came very, very close. Too close. The Ring Fire ceased to show itself in order to protect you. Burning as it was, it was like a beacon in the storm, saying "here she is!" By ceasing to burn at that second, it probably saved your life!'

Gemma lay back on the bed and closed her eyes. 'You're right, of course, you irritating old ratter. I'd have seen it too if I'd let myself. I suspect I wanted an excuse to give up. I was so weary. I let Domnall convince me that I was damaging to the Ring Fire, that I wasn't good enough to carry it. I'd forgotten how simple and beautiful the Ring Fire is. It's not a matter of being good enough or not, it's just a matter of allowing it to burn.'

She opened her eyes again and watched the steady golden flame for a few seconds. 'I have been so stupid!'

Fleabag put his forepaws onto Gemma's shoulder and licked her face. 'Well, we're all together with the Ring Fire again, and that's what matters. Now, what can we do to help?'

Gemma leaned over and reached out to stroke Cleo on the floor. 'Sleep up here with me tonight, then I won't feel so lonely. I'd like that.' The ginger cat sprang up onto the bed and stretched. Gemma smiled as the light from the Ring Fire caught the soft, luxuriously shiny golden fur of her back. 'Your daughter is beautiful, Fleabag. She looks like a Fire Cat!'

Fleabag stiffened. 'Hush!' he snapped. 'Who told you? You must never repeat that! Come, Cleo,' he snapped. 'Curl up and go to sleep as you've been told.'

Cleo began to knead the covers and purr before turning around several times and settling down.

For a little while, Gemma lay still, worrying. Why had Fleabag snapped like that? Of course: 'Fire Cat' must be Cleo's real name. Cats were especially careful about not using their real names in case spells were put on them by evil-minded people like Domnall. 'Sorry,' she murmured, reaching out to touch the cat's ginger fur as she went to sleep.

17

The Dreams

Far away, in Porthwain, Domnall was preparing his spells to take to Spider Island. He would have to go in person to take the Ring Fire from this stupid girl, who not only frustrated his plans, but then had the gall to challenge him. *Him*! The Chancellor of All Wizards, the destined King and Fire Wielder! How dare she!

His preparations were intricate. His shade would not be powerful enough to make the spells hold, or to grasp the prize as it slipped away from the child at the end of the battle. He would have to face her himself.

But first he needed dreams for the islanders… dreams telling everyone for certain that a tall, freckle-faced girl with mouse-coloured hair was to blame for the terrible blue clouds and strange winds. The dreams promised riches and glory for those who helped to defeat her. The images were powerful enough to last for several nights and even to linger during the days.

At last, Domnall spread his arms and shivered in delight as his silk gown shimmered, darkened and became the smooth blue-black feathers of a crow. He turned his head and preened the soft down around his neck. Even when he shape-shifted he liked to look immaculate.

The night was getting dark as he rose up towards the stars. He would scatter the dreams over the islanders' dwellings as he flew past. By dawn he would be on Spider Island, and by sunset the Ring Fire would be his.

Gemma did not need a scrying bowl to know what Domnall was up to. The Ring Fire told her all she needed to know. She slept badly, knowing that all the time the evil wizard was on his way.

As another unnatural blue dawn broke, Gemma rubbed sleep from her eyes and sat up. What was that dreadful clanging noise outside?

She stood by the window and looked out. Walking towards her down the street, was the familiar figure of Rowanne, her dark hair tied back severely, and her arms full of pots and pans. Behind her, Aidan struggled with more of the same. Rowanne grinned up at Gemma's window and tried to wave, but succeeded only in dropping a large stewpot that clanged like a dull bell as it hit the cobbles. 'Look what we found on the town's rubbish heap!' she called, delightedly. 'We'll have good armour made in no time. We're off to the forge now!'

Gemma stepped back and shut the curtains. 'Oh no!' She shook her head. 'How can I make Rowanne understand?'

Aidan had insisted on arranging accommodation at the inn. When everyone was settled, he slept in the stables all night as a self-appointed servant to the newcomers. At first he did it to ingratiate himself and be certain of a reward, but he found he actually liked the strangers and wanted to help them. He was fascinated by all this talk of the Ring Fire, which had never meant anything to him before. He had, after all, actually *seen* it, which was more than anyone else he knew.

Rowanne had summoned his help at dawn. Now he was struggling down the road behind her, carrying scrap iron, thrilled at being asked to help yet again. They dropped their clattering burden outside the forge, and Aidan hammered at the door.

The smith was still in bed, but flung the windows wide and peered down into the street below.

'This is the Princess…' Aidan began.

But the smith did not let the lad finish. 'I know who they are – troublemakers from the mainland. I'll not have any of them in my forge!'

Rowanne stood firmly, her muscular hands gripping a large ladle, and briefly considered bashing the man's brains out for his insolence. She put her head back and bunched the muscles in her jaw. But when she saw his face, she changed her mind. He was not just being difficult; there was real fear in his eyes. *Something* had terrified him.

She decided to try a gentler approach. 'There is a great evil threatening your island. I am a soldier of the King's Guard, and a warrior of many years' experience. If you let me use your forge to make swords and armour, we can help you defend your home… Furthermore, we can pay you well.'

But the smith did not wait to hear. He slammed his window shut and would not answer Rowanne's persistent thumping at the door.

Just then, another door opened across the street, and Gemma and the cats stepped out from the inn and crossed the cobbles to greet their friends.

'You're up early,' Rowanne remarked.

'We've been thrown out like last week's rotten fish,' Fleabag replied indignantly.

'What did you do? Criticize the landlady's breakfast?' Rowanne laughed.

'Didn't even get to taste it,' Fleabag replied. 'She said she had a dream last night that we were the cause of the evil weather and were come here to bring destruction on the island.'

Gemma looked around worriedly. All the doors were shut, except for the inn, where fifteen bleary-eyed sailors were also being evicted. Marcus shook his head. 'Even the baker won't serve me. It seems the whole village has had the same dream.'

'Domnall!' Gemma whispered. 'He's here at last, I know it.'

Marcus looked across at Aidan. 'You, lad, will you help us, or will you go to your people? No one will blame you if you want to stay with your friends and family. It would be understandable. You and the islanders will be in no danger from us. Our quarrel is with Lord Domnall and his magic. We will leave your island as soon as we can.'

Aidan blushed and stepped forward. He glanced around at the tightly shuttered windows and barred doors. He guessed they were being watched through every crack and keyhole. If he went back to the villagers he would be treated with suspicion and what was there to go back to? He had not had a particularly happy life. These people from the mainland were different from anyone he had ever known. He liked them: they seemed to be fair-minded, and they might offer him a way out of his narrow, miserable existence. But would they want a lad who had made the great Fire Wielder mend rotting nets?

Aidan decided he had nothing to lose. 'I too had a dream last night. I dreamed you were the cause of all this evil, and I would gain great riches and power if I betrayed you. But it didn't make sense. I knew it wasn't true. I may be a bit of a thief and out to make my life easier, but I hope I know what is wrong and what is right... or at least...' he hesitated, giving Gemma a sideways look, 'at least, I think I'm learning. I am with you, if you'll have someone like me.'

Gemma smiled and went to shake his hand. 'I'm glad, Aidan. Without you I'd have been lost. But what about your parents, won't they be upset?'

Aidan blushed at Gemma's thanks. He felt he didn't really deserve it. 'I'm sick of being beaten and half starved. My parents don't need me. They don't even like me.' Then a thought struck him and his face brightened. 'The Captain promised I'd be rewarded if I helped you...'

'Yes, indeed you will. In the King's name I give my word that if we get home, you will be rewarded.'

Aidan plucked up his courage. 'Well, can my reward be to go with you... if we win this battle?' he asked doubtfully.

At this Rowanne clapped an iron pot on the boy's head to look like a lopsided helmet. 'You work hard, Aidan. I need a good squire – I haven't had one for quite a while.' She grinned at Gemma, remembering what a useless squire the girl had been on their quest for the Ring. 'If you'll work hard – and *honestly* –' she added with emphasis, 'I'll take you with me.'

Aidan grinned under his improvised armour. 'I will, ma'am. I will!'

'Then that's settled,' Marcus said. 'Now we have to think what we are going to do next. We will get no more help here.'

'I know how to get bread for us all... *honestly*,' Aidan volunteered. 'May I borrow the black cat?'

'Ask him yourself. He has a very good tongue in his own head!' Rowanne laughed, handing the boy a fistful of coins.

Aidan led Fleabag towards the baker's shop. The two whispered a little before going in. Then Fleabag sprang up onto the counter.

'Let us hope they've never heard a talking cat before,' Aidan muttered.

18

Preparing for Battle

The baker was astounded when Fleabag walked sedately along the top of his counter, looked him up and down and pronounced very clearly, 'Nineteen of your best loaves, please. Now!' he added when the fat little man hesitated.

Sweat dripping as he shook and trembled, the baker stuffed the loaves into a canvas kitbag that Aidan handed him. At last he stood back, staring in horror at the pile of money Aidan pushed across the counter. 'Take it, there's more than enough there!' the boy said.

'You... you won't put a spell on me, will you?' The little man shook his flab and his eyes bulged. 'You won't turn me blue? The dreams... the dreams said...'

'What do you think, cat?' Aidan raised an eyebrow at Fleabag as he slid from the counter, landing awkwardly on his three legs.

'No,' Fleabag replied, yawning widely. 'We won't do anything if the bread's good.'

The little man hastily filled a large bag with cakes and pushed them across the counter. 'With my compliments, no need to pay,' he squeaked, his voice rising with his panic.

Rowanne, standing in the doorway of the shop, pushed a large silver piece across the counter. 'Thank you, but we would rather pay for the cakes. And remember, if anyone turns blue around here, it will be none of our doing!' She took the heavy kitbag and slung it over her wide shoulders, leaving the poor little man staring at the silver coin as if it was about to bite him.

Rowanne ordered the sailors to carry the pots and pans, and the company walked out of the little port and across the dunes to where Aidan's burned-out hulk lay in ashes. The boy led past the blackened ruin and pointed to a small patch of scrubby bushes and bent trees just a little further on. 'There is a stream nearby, and we will be in a dip there, sheltered from this awful wind.'

Aidan dropped his share of the ironmongery on the marram grass. 'Can you really make armour out of this rubbish, your Highness?'

'Of course!' Rowanne answered as she turned some of the pieces over with her foot. 'Every squire learns how to make and repair armour for their Lord or Lady. If you are ever knighted, you must teach your squire the same. Now, to work. Without a proper forge this will be very makeshift, but we must do our best. Gemma has a great battle to fight. We must be prepared. She thinks I don't understand what she needs, but I do. She knows about the Ring Fire, but I understand about battles. I know what I am doing.'

The Captain sent his men down to the beach to salvage all they could from the wreck. Soon torn sails were being patched and spread over broken spars and planks to form three large tents. Bread, cakes and dried fruit were handed round, and everyone began to feel better.

In the ashes of the old boat, Rowanne had built a small hearth of flat stones. Then, selecting charcoal from the remains of the burned-out hulk, she built up a furnace, walling it in with stones and mud. Aidan worked with improvised sailcloth bellows to blow the fire to a good heat, then the work began.

For hour after tedious hour, the bellows wheezed and Rowanne clattered away with a small, bent hammer that she had found amongst the scrap iron. The white-hot metal was folded and shaped, dipped in the stream and then heated again before it was layered with mud to slow the cooling and strengthen it. The princess was determined that however odd their weapons might look, nothing would shatter. After a while everyone, especially Gemma, began to develop a headache from the noise.

In the blue afternoon, Gemma slipped away, followed by the two cats. She wandered over the dunes until she found another small, wooded hollow, almost out of earshot of the camp. There she sat and dabbled her feet in a pool between the trees. The cats sat like guards on either side. Marcus, watching from a distance, made sure she was safe, then left her alone.

Gemma was cold and tired. Indoors, the dress the innkeeper's wife had sold her was warm enough, but the strange, biting wind still pervaded everything. She shivered, and hugged the cats, one under each arm.

No one spoke for a long time, but when the light began to fade, Gemma brought the Ring Fire to life, and put it gently on the ground where they could all look into its glow.

'It doesn't look like something that would defeat an evil wizard, does it?' Cleo asked timidly.

'You'd better believe it!' Fleabag said quietly. 'The Ring Fire burns in so many strange ways, you're never quite sure what it is going to do next.'

'Ssh!' Gemma put her finger to her lips and looked anxiously up into the darkening sky. There was a new noise, a booming. It wasn't Rowanne's perpetual hammer strokes, but a deeper, more threatening sound, like the depths of the earth cracking. Gemma looked up as a flicker of black crossed the dull blue sky. High above, a crow circled and landed on the tree behind her.

Then came silence. There was no sound or movement. The whole world seemed to be holding its breath.

'It's beginning!' Gemma shuddered. Then of its own accord, the Ring Fire flickered and rose higher and stronger, spreading the golden glow into something that resembled a camp fire, warming and heartening, yet without burning anything.

'Would you mind if I asked you to stay with me?' Gemma asked the cats. 'I'd be frightened on my own.'

Cleo crept into Gemma's lap and curled up small. 'I'm too frightened to go away,' she mewed, and hid her head under a ginger paw.

All night the lightning cracked and sparked. The thunder rolled and shook the ground with its noise. At the main camp, Marcus, Rowanne and the men sat silently, watching the terrifying storm. They felt helpless and small against the terrible blue powers swelling and throbbing around them. It was as if they were being swallowed into a deep and terrible throat, with only the steady golden light of the Ring Fire to cheer them.

Peering down from between the leaves of the tree, Domnall in crow form watched his adversary. It was almost dawn, and they would do battle when the sun rose. He had to learn what spells and incantations she used to control the Ring Fire so, when he pulled the ring of blue magic tight, the elusive flame would not escape him.

But soon Domnall began to find the light of the Ring Fire intolerable. He flew a little further away where he could watch but not have to look into that terrible light. It burned him. It occurred to him for the first time that he might not be able to carry the Ring Fire. If that happened, he would have to extinguish it and rule by the destruction of the blue flames. He was disappointed. That meant he would not have the adoration of the whole world for ever: for in the end the blueness only killed. Without the Ring Fire he would be the monarch of everything that existed, but eventually there would be nothing left for him to rule. He would be alone... and that was his only, terrible, dread.

But it might never come to that. He might be able to control the Ring Fire – it was probably a matter of time and finding the right spells to subdue it to his will. He could not see or hear what gestures and incantations the girl was using. The terrible flame seemed to burn without the slightest command from her. She must be more powerful than he had guessed.

Still, all was not lost. He had time on his side. Ultimate

destruction was a long way off. Anyway, the Ring Fire was destructive too. Look how it pained him to be near it! Surely *that* was the real threat to the world! He would do humanity a favour by destroying it and smothering it into oblivion.

He considered the approaching morning with pleasure. He would be the saviour of the world, the destroyer of the Ring Fire! With smug satisfaction, Domnall preened his crow-feathers. This would be the day of his coronation as King and Fire Quencher!

Meanwhile Gemma and the cats sat by the Fire in the little wooded dip. The Fire Wielder remembered how she had surrounded Phelan with the Ring Fire as he went out to face the monster of Beulothin. Now she did the same for her friends just a little way off, then for Phelan waiting anxiously at Beriot. If she were killed in this fight, he would have to rule as King *and* Fire Wielder until someone else could be found.

Gemma did not know whether Phelan enjoyed being King. She knew he disliked having people asking him what to do all the time, and bowing and scraping to him. What would he think about being Fire Wielder as well? Perhaps it would not happen. But while Phelan was surrounded with the Ring Fire, he would be safe. If he had to take on the role, things would sort themselves out if he just watched and listened for the Fire's guidance. One by one she thought of all her friends, and the people she served in the land, then of the people of Spider Island. It was not their fault they had been deceived by Domnall. She held them safe in the Fire as well. She hoped they would not be hurt by the storms or by any of Domnall's doings.

As dawn broke, the thunder and lightning subsided. The winds and the heavily oppressive blueness still buffeted and smothered everything. Gemma was glad the battle was coming. None of them could take much more of this.

Flying away, Domnall came to land on the crown of the larger of the two domed hills that made up the island. Then, reaching out to Gemma's mind, he called out to her:

'Come, *child*, I accept your challenge. Are you still willing to face me?'

19

Battle Commences

Gemma found she had slept. Had she dreamed the trumpeting call of Domnall's challenge resounding across the island? What had really woken her was a clattering noise coming down into the dip behind her. She sat up quickly. Above her the sun was struggling to peer through the heavy blue clouds. It was a warm day, but the dry, endless wind still battered from all directions at once.

There, coming triumphantly towards her, were Rowanne and Aidan with a large wheelbarrow loaded with all sorts of strange objects. 'Look what we've got you!' Aidan shouted. 'Didn't we do well?'

Fleabag was perched on top of the pile, grinning widely under his whiskers. 'You're going to *love* this, Gemma!' Then he sprang down and trotted over to his friend. He clambered up into her lap and whispered, 'Be nice to Rowanne; she and Aidan have been up all night making this stuff. Personally, I think it's going to make you look like an unopened tin of dog food, but never mind, she meant well!'

Gemma's heart sank at Fleabag's warning. What *had* the Princess been up to? She got to her feet and brushed twigs and grass out of her dress and hair. Gemma could accept that Rowanne and the men would want armour, but they had not *really* made some for her as well, had they? Holding her windswept hair back, Gemma stepped forward to see what Rowanne was so proud of.

As she approached, the Princess grinned as she held up a pot-like iron helmet, a breastplate that looked suspiciously like a roasting tray, and a sword which might have been several carving knives beaten together. Rowanne was smiling broadly. 'It looks a little odd, I know, but it'll hold, I'll stake my life on it!'

'Why, Rowanne, it's...' Gemma could not think of the right words, but Fleabag purred and rubbed against her legs, whispering, 'magnificent!'

'Why, it's magnificent!' Gemma declared, grasping the breastplate. As she took it, the bluish light caught a device hammered into the centre. It was the emblem of the Ring Fire, a circle with a small flame in its centre. Standing a little behind the Princess was Aidan, blushing slightly. Gemma guessed it had been his handiwork.

'Why, Aidan, what a lovely idea to put the sign of the Ring Fire in the centre! How skilfully it's been done!'

'You will wear it, won't you?' he blushed again. 'We've made ourselves some too; not as good as yours, of course, but we're going with you.'

Gemma felt a lump rising in her throat. How was she

going to tell him she couldn't possibly wear this sort of thing? They must have worked until they dropped. Aidan and the Princess looked quite exhausted; they were black with soot, and stank of sweat and iron.

'Help me strap it on!' she smiled. After all, she thought, the battle might be between powers and forces which could neither be seen, nor attacked with a weapon, but what harm would it do to please her friends by wearing their gifts? It might well raise their spirits.

Soon Rowanne had Gemma strapped and buckled in every conceivable place, as piece after piece of bent, black iron was tied around her body. She knew she looked stupid and vulnerable. The skirt of her long green dress billowed and flapped around her legs, and she felt as if she was struggling to keep afloat, just as when she had fallen into the sea.

But she did not have any time even to think about such things. She kissed her friends and thanked them for their gifts, then turned towards the higher of the two hills. Something told her that was where she had to go. She felt terribly alone. Although she knew her friends were going with her, Gemma sensed the battle would be between herself and Domnall.

Around the crown of the hill flapped a huge, blue-black crow, calling hoarsely in the wind. No words were spoken, but Gemma could hear the challenge ringing out again, clear as a bell.

'Time to go,' she said quietly, and slowly clanked away, the others following just a little behind.

Fleabag was by her side in an instant, with Cleo not far behind. 'Want a tin opener Gemma?' he asked cheekily.

'I may well,' Gemma muttered from behind the heavy

visor which looked as if it had been cut from a colander. 'Do you think I'll taste good?'

High up on the hill the crow landed. With a shimmer of blue light the wizard resumed his human form. Domnall could hardly contain his laughter. What did the girl think she was up to? She would take all morning to reach him at this rate, and he had planned to be at Harflorum for his coronation feast by evening. With a long-suffering sigh, he waved a hand and sent a small whirlwind to scoop the party up. But apart from a blustering and battering, nothing happened.

Irritated, Domnall drew back his hand and threw the spell again, this time harder. For a few seconds Rowanne was taken off her feet and dropped a little way off.

Fleabag threw back his head and shouted through the wind to his companions, 'He can't put a spell on us! He doesn't know our real names. The old Chancellor knew Rowanne's, so she might be at risk. When magic is involved, it's anyone's guess what secrets are known! Clear your minds, everyone, don't think of who you really are!'

Cleo stood still and sank her ginger head between her paws. 'I keep being asked my name; he keeps demanding I tell him! What do I do, Dad?'

'Fight it!' Fleabag growled, teeth bared and fur blown flat by the wind.

'Think of a brick wall!' Aidan suggested. 'Keep imagining it, count the bricks... There's ivy on the wall...'

'And spiders!' squealed Gemma. 'Huge grey and purple ones with... Oh, I can't keep this up. I don't *know* my real name, but he's demanding, so loudly I can't think of anything else. I remember, I remember my mother. I could never think of her face before. She died when I was very young. I can see her leaning over my cradle and talking to me. What's she saying? She's calling my name...'

Suddenly Fleabag started singing, a painful experience for everyone listening. The raucous caterwauling distracted Gemma for a few seconds. 'But my mother was beautiful,' she pleaded. 'I want to see her again...'

But Cleo sprang into Gemma's arms and started singing too, so loudly that Gemma could not but listen. She sang better than her father, and the words of the riddle-song were heart-warming:

'First came a burning bright:
the peerless one in darkest night
And then into a golden ring,
The second in a tiny thing.'

The tune was so strong and insistent that Gemma soon found she had joined in and was singing the song again and again; they all were. Flat and noisy the chorus rose into the blue wind as the five friends bent their heads into the blast and began to walk towards the hill.

After a little while, Fleabag added another verse, and the others picked up the words. Gemma wondered what the song meant. The words seemed familiar and strange, all at once.

'From milky stone came clearest sight
a wisdom that was crystal bright.
The third in stone and fire and gold,
the strongest story ever told.'

But as she sang, she found she could hold the thought of the brightly burning Ring Fire before her eyes, and she felt more courageous. She would have liked to remember her mother's face. But was it really her mother, or just an image Domnall was using to mislead her? It didn't matter.

What *did* matter was remembering that Domnall had no power over her while he did not know her real name. More importantly, he could not cast spells on her while she remained within the Ring Fire.

As she struggled up the hill in her clanking armour, Gemma vaguely wondered how he had managed to get her so deeply asleep and into the boat the night she had been kidnapped. Probably the servants had drugged the food. She had been so far from the Ring Fire that night, Domnall could easily have influenced her. Perhaps he had hypnotized her. She had a vague idea that she might even have been quite willing to get into the boat: she remembered thinking that if she was gone, the others would *have* to find a new Fire Wielder.

Who knew? But she must not let it happen again. She was who she was, until the time came for things to change. The Ring Fire was not unkind; there would be a way through all this. She would have a long talk with Phelan and Fleabag when she got back.

Head down she trudged on, hot and out of breath as she climbed the hill. As best she could, she tried to walk in time to the rhythm of the strange song. But the makeshift armour was making her very sweaty and uncomfortable. Blisters were rubbing under her arms where the straps of the breastplate chafed. She felt she could hardly breathe under the heavy helmet. She longed to take it all off, but it occurred to her that it might be wiser to keep it on, at least for a while. If Domnall could not defeat her by magic, perhaps he might try using a sword?

She kept singing.

Far behind her, Gemma could hear shouts and jeers from the islanders who were gathering at the bottom of the hill. They were gathering to cheer Domnall on.

Whether they won or lost this battle, any of Gemma's friends who survived would be torn to shreds by vengeful islanders. Fighting for the Ring Fire there were nineteen humans and two cats. Fearsome battle cats it was true, but still no bigger than ordinary mousers.

Suddenly Gemma tripped and sprawled in a most ungainly, clattering way on the ground. Rowanne sprang to her side and helped her up. From below the sound of derisive laughter echoed around. Gemma was glad for a few seconds that she wore a helmet to cover the blushes in her cheeks.

'Get up,' Rowanne said kindly but firmly. 'We're almost there.'

'I'm going on alone,' Gemma said. 'If I fail, you'll still be alive to fight. There's no point in us all dying at once.'

Rowanne knew better than to argue, but the cats followed Gemma closely, pretending they hadn't heard.

On the crown of the hill, Domnall stood staring down at his adversary as she approached. Dressed in a badly fitting woman's dress, with bits of home-made armour strapped all over her, the girl looked derisively funny.

With a few more steps she stood before him. She was hot, sweaty, out of breath and had the lower ground with no flat place for her to stand comfortably, leaving her off balance. Good. Domnall stroked his clean-shaven chin as he looked the Fire Wielder up and down. She was young, and even under the makeshift helmet was visibly scared. She looked neither strong nor awe-inspiring. It had been the same when they had met at Harflorum. Gemma had been heavily made-up and swamped in trappings.

He jerked a thumb at her. 'Why do you always hide behind so much *stuff*, my dear girl? Are you afraid to meet me properly, face to face?' He spread his hands wide. 'Look, I don't have as much as a pocket knife on me. You come so... dauntingly arrayed to challenge an unarmed man. It is hardly fair, is it?'

Suddenly, Gemma made a decision. She lifted the helmet from her head and threw it to the ground. Then she dropped her sword and unbuckled her breastplate. Kicking them aside, she turned to face Domnall.

'No,' she said. 'I wore them out of loyalty and love for the people who made them for me. I had no real intention of wearing them for the battle.'

Domnall was surprised. He had expected her to clutch her armour more tightly around her, like a timid tortoise in its shell. But she was obviously stronger than he had guessed. The way his spells had bounced off her worried him too. But he would find a way. Victory was his destiny, after all. 'Look,' he said, pointing down the hill. 'We have company.'

Gemma's heart missed a beat, for not only were her friends valiantly trudging up the slopes towards them, armed and arrayed in their own makeshift gear, but the islanders had decided to move in for a closer look as well. They were in an ugly mood, shouting and waving their fists, carrying swords, knives, billhooks – anything that might inflict damage.

'They think you brought the blue clouds and the endless wind. They think you are a sorceress who has angered the seas. Perhaps I should give you and your friends to them. Then they can pull you all apart, limb from limb. It would save me the trouble of fighting you... Not that it'll be a *fight*, really...' he paused and inspected his fingernails in a leisurely way. 'More like a cat playing with a mouse before he eats it!'

Fleabag tutted. 'Tsk! I never play with my food before eating it. Do you, Cleo?'

'No, Dad,' she replied primly. 'Mother would be deeply shocked if I did that.'

Both cats turned to glower at Domnall with their gold-lamp eyes. The wizard was discomfited by their stares, but pretended they were beneath his notice.

Gemma unstrapped the rest of her armour piece by piece, and tossed it down towards Aidan and Rowanne. 'They might need it; I don't,' she said simply.

'Oh no?' Domnall jeered, his pale face looking almost moon-like in the eerie light. 'So what are you going to use for armour?'

'The Ring Fire is all the armour I need,' Gemma replied curtly. She felt small and stupid, looking up at the grey willowy figure sneering down at her from his advantageous position. She folded her arms and put her head back, meeting him with a cool, freckle-faced stare, straight in the eye.

Deep inside she was still the timid, uncertain girl she had always been. But more importantly, she knew that this was the Ring Fire's battle, not hers. She could believe in that, even when she had no faith in herself.

Domnall shrugged. 'The Ring Fire your armour? But you don't even *like* carrying the Ring Fire! You told me yourself how wearied you were by it.'

'I was carrying it badly.'

Domnall laughed. 'I'm astounded they even made you Fire Wielder. Why, if you had been any good at all, you would have known months ago how strong my powers were growing… Ever since you murdered my father in the Great Hall of Light at the University, I have been planning this day. But I cannot imagine why the Fire Giver (if there is one, which I doubt), chose *you* to carry the flame. It shows how few *real* sorcerers there are in the land. A mere child who doesn't even know how to handle the simplest little fire trick!'

Domnall had stepped closer to Gemma during this speech and was holding out his right hand to her. Although he was speaking out loud, he was silently putting words into her mind:

'Give me the Ring Fire. Give it to me! I will quench it and you will be free from your terrible burden for ever!'

Through gritted teeth she muttered, 'I am not a sorceress. I do no magic. I cannot give what is not mine to give.'

But this time Domnall's demand came from even deeper inside her mind. 'Give me the Ring Fire! Where is it?' he demanded. 'Give it to me!'

20

Death to the Blue Sorceress!

'I don't think much of your Ring Fire armour!' Domnall jeered. 'I'm right inside your head! I suppose it works like the rest of the Ring Fire… it is only any good when you carry it properly? Well, you're a lost cause then, aren't you? You never *did* do it right. You're hopeless. You forgot the Ring Fire, you didn't bother to look into it, you allowed these poor islanders to be put in danger because you didn't see me coming. Oh my, what a brilliant choice *you* were for Fire Wielder!'

Gemma felt her heart sinking. All her old fears and feelings began to flood back to her. He was right. It *was* all her fault. But she must not let him get to her. She clenched her jaw.

Domnall came closer and put his wide, pale face next

to hers. 'Oh dear, did I upset you...? Well, it's true, isn't it? You are useless. The so-called Fire Giver chose a failure in you! Remember...' He passed his right hand in front of her eyes and Gemma saw the times she had ignored the Ring Fire – the times when she had not just been too busy, but simply couldn't be bothered to go and watch and listen. Then she had been officious, and had ordered servants around unnecessarily, becoming like the sort of arrogant courtier she had always despised...

Gemma turned her head away and ground her teeth. Deliberately she bit her tongue. The pain jerked her back to reality. She was *not* going to be sucked once more into Domnall's trap of being overwhelmed with worthlessness and shame. He had almost defeated her that way once... Not again! The Ring Fire loved her, and that was what mattered.

But before she could answer him, he reached out and passed his hand in front of her eyes again and her vision blurred. 'Why do you fight me? Everything you see is all true. I'm only showing you what is inside your own head. I'm not putting anything in there which didn't happen.'

Then he laid one finger on her right temple. 'Show me how you became Fire Wielder,' he commanded.

Gemma closed her eyes and smiled. This time she felt happy. This was something she *did* want to see again. Domnall wanted her to experience shame and failure. But Gemma knew that she could use this moment as she chose. He wanted her to feel bad and guilty. She could use it to remember how glorious it had been and be heartened by it. So she welcomed the images that came flooding back into her mind...

Soon she was remembering that evening when she had

stood with Phelan and the old Fire Wielder in the Hall of Light at Harflorum. The old man had grown so weary and thin when they had come to him at last with the royal ring. Phelan was made King, and Gemma swore to carry the Ring Fire well. She remembered that the Fire had suddenly flamed up in her hands to fill the evening-darkened room with a glorious light. 'All homage to the Ring Fire,' the King had said, 'in which we live and move and have our being!'

As she recalled that moment with delight, Domnall reeled back, calling out as if in pain. He had failed.

Gemma opened her eyes in surprise. The wizard was crimson in the face. 'Don't you ever do that again, or I will slay you on the spot!' he threatened, coming close to her again, then beginning to pace around her in an anticlockwise direction.

'Do what?' Gemma asked, wishing she knew what she had done to make Domnall stagger so.

'You know, you impudent child!' Suddenly Domnall stopped behind her and whispered in her ear: 'Give me the Ring Fire, as the old Fire Wielder gave it to you!'

'But he didn't give it to me!' Gemma replied. 'I've just shown you that. You saw the pictures in my mind as clearly as I did! No one gave it to me – it just appeared of its own free will.'

'Give the Ring Fire to me now!' Domnall demanded. 'I am tired of asking you. The time has come. Give it to me!'

'I cannot.'

Domnall came to face Gemma again and seized her. 'You may have some magic that prevents me from casting spells on you, but I can still hurt you!' he jeered, giving her arm a painful twist. Gemma knew the Ring Fire rarely came when bidden, so she was just as amazed as Domnall when the Flame momentarily roared out at him, burning his silk robe and scorching his face.

In fury he slapped her. Gemma fell sprawling on the rough grass at his feet. Domnall cradled his burns. 'You think you are so clever, don't you?' he scoffed. 'That was a child's trick. My patience has run out.' Shaking with fury the wizard pointed downhill at the awe-struck spectators. 'They will put you to the death you deserve. As soon as I raise my little finger they will come up the hill and destroy you and your so-called friends for bringing this terrible weather to their island.'

Gemma breathed deeply. Instinctively she knew the truth was more important than anything. She plucked up all her courage and struggled to her feet. 'It is true – I *am* a failure, and I have let many good people down. But the Ring Fire has never let anyone down. Getting the islanders to kill me won't mean you escape the torment of the Ring Fire's brightness for one second of your life. Now you have seen it and touched it, it will never let you go. It will burn you for ever. There will be no escape.'

Standing tall, Domnall raised his arms and bellowed as loudly as he could. 'Hear this, good people of Spider Island. This sorceress accuses me, Lord Domnall, your future King and Fire Wielder! She says that *I* brought this terrible torment on your island. What do you say?'

The islanders bellowed in reply: 'Death to the blue sorceress! Let us deal with her!' and the braver amongst them took a few steps up the hill, waving their billhooks and scythes menacingly.

But Domnall was not finished yet. He stretched out a calming hand towards the crowd. 'You will have her soon,

I promise you. But of course,' he faced Gemma again, 'it *was* you who brought this evil. If you had paid attention to the Ring Fire, I would never have been able to come this close. Your negligence summoned me here!'

Gemma looked around at the anxious faces peering up from below. She felt sorry for them. They were only ordinary people who understood nothing about the strange battle on their hilltop. They did not deserve this. Between her and death were Captain Marcus and his fifteen men. They stood facing the islanders, defending her.

The Ring Fire did not need to be protected. The sailors had come across dangerous seas to help *her*. Even though she could not see their faces, she could feel their fear and their longing to be home. She did not deserve their faithfulness. She hardly knew them, yet they were steadfastly risking their lives for her.

'In a way, this *is* all my fault,' she said to herself. 'The things I am facing are my own responsibility. I certainly shouldn't be asking this of them.' She felt herself sagging at the knees. Why were so many lives threatened because she had failed? Men, women, children – people who worked hard against severe odds, trying to earn a living.

Once again she felt the great longing to pass the Ring Fire on. The blue magic was Domnall's, but *she* had allowed it to grow and to come here endangering so many others…

She sank back to the ground and buried her head in her arms. Fleabag and Cleo rushed over to her and began to lick her face with their rough, warm tongues. 'Don't listen to him, Gemma. It's not like that!' Fleabag urged. 'We're all here to help in the battle; it's *everybody's* battle, not just yours. If Domnall hadn't fought us here, he'd have done it somewhere else. And if you weren't the Fire Wielder, someone else would be feeling just as awful as you!'

Gemma said nothing. Suddenly she felt so tired. If only there *was* someone else to bear the Ring Fire... This battle had wearied her beyond belief.

But Domnall had not finished. He stood over the little group of friends and crossed his arms, a look of pure contempt on his face. '... And that so-called king of yours, he is a common thief, and deserves to be hanged, not crowned. Born at the back of a junk shop, the son of criminals, and a criminal himself. What sort of a society has a convict as a king? No sensible, civilized community would give such a man the crown!'

Then he turned his attention to Fleabag. 'And what sort of land allows black, mangy cripples like this to advise their kings and princes? Eh?' And he hooked his foot under Fleabag's belly and tried to toss him in the air.

That was his first mistake.

21

Spells and Promises

Fleabag twisted as he was tossed in the air and landed on his attacker's leg, all claws firmly caught in the man's flesh.

Domnall howled and buckled in searing pain, but before he could throw a spell at the cat, Cleo had clambered onto his back and perched herself on his head. There she sat, her claws firmly caught in her victim's scalp, purring deafeningly in his left ear.

Slowly and steadily, Fleabag crawled up Domnall's front, taking each step deliberately and carefully, sinking in each claw as far as possible before putting his weight on the next paw. When he reached Domnall's neck, he smiled sweetly, twitching his whiskers in the man's eyes. 'I suggest you sit quietly while we explain a few home truths to you. If, on the other hand, you so much as twitch one eyelid, Cleo and I may momentarily mistake you for a large grey rat… purely accidentally, of course.'

Cleo stretched out a glistening talon and inspected it. 'That *would* be a shame – especially as I've just sharpened my claws.'

Fleabag looked up to grin encouragement at his daughter perched in Domnall's ruffled hair. The cat-warrior's golden earring reflected the glow of the Ring Fire that hovered above Gemma's slumped form. As the gleam of light caught the wizard's eye, he winced and shrank away, causing the cats to dig their claws even more deeply into his flesh.

'Get off!' he howled as he shrank to his knees. 'I can't negotiate if you are causing me such agony… I'll come to an agreement. What if you become Prime Minister when I'm King? What do you say?' The dishevelled young man looked cunningly into the fish-breath face of the cat, only a finger's breadth from his own nose.

Fleabag pretended to consider the option. 'What do you say, dear? And you'd be a princess, of course.'

'Oh, at least,' Cleo purred, curling up on Domnall's head like a huge ginger hat, pinned carefully in place with needle-like talons.

Domnall turned his eyes from Fleabag's insistent stare as he desperately tried to unhook Fleabag, claw by claw, but as he pulled each talon away, the last one was replaced more firmly than before. All the time the infuriating cat purred.

This made Domnall so furious he flung a spell at Fleabag. But the cat heard the muttered incantation and saw the wizard's fingers flicking. In the blink of an eye he scrambled over the man's chest and onto his shoulder. Consequently the spell missed completely, slipped past the cat and caught Domnall in the face, turning him into an enormous toad. There he sat on the top of the hill, swallowing air and looking quite confused. He was a very ugly toad indeed – fat and lumpy with slimy green-grey skin, covered in brown warts. His eyes bulged round and pus-yellow with fury. Domnall blinked, narrowed his gaze and looked down at his green, pad-tipped fingers, then at his huge webbed back feet. He tried to move and found he could only hop. The suddenly jerky movement meant that Cleo and Fleabag had to dig their claws into the toad's smelly, mucous-covered skin even harder.

Domnall gulped air again. Then, hissing with pain and sheer malevolence, he let out a loud 'ribbit' as he changed himself back into human form.

'You missed!' Fleabag announced gleefully as he clambered further up the wizard, to where he could drape himself comfortably around Domnall's neck. There he hung languorously, closely resembling the black fur collar Rowanne had always coveted.

Domnall smiled sarcastically, showing firmly clenched teeth. 'Maybe. We'll see,' he growled. This time, he spun a spell by his waist, flicking his fingers in time to his incantation. With the final flourish a great snake appeared, wound several times around the wizard's middle. It was a heavy, smooth boa constrictor, with millions of minute rainbow-oiled scales. At Domnall's command it writhed and heaved its weight upwards, and opened its jaws to devour Fleabag. But the cat hissed and scratched the snake on the nose so hard that it twisted away and slithered to the ground, allowing its heavy body to flow away like a muscular river towards a large rock behind which it hid.

Domnall swore roundly at his failure. Once again, he tried to tug and pull at the entwined cats, but they were there to stay. He would have to try a different approach. 'What more could you *want*, dear creatures?' he wheedled.

Fleabag and Cleo exchanged glances. 'What about you making my Dad handsome and four-legged again?'

'Anything, anything, just let me go!'

Fleabag stuck his nose in Domnall's ear and whispered, 'What about you making my daughter obedient and good?'

'I'll try, but that might be difficult.'

'Difficult! It's impossible!' jeered Fleabag. 'That proves you're an impostor.'

'In fact it proves you're lying on every point!' Cleo added gleefully, kneading her claws in and out of Domnall's head. 'I will never be a good little cat, and Fleabag will *never* be handsome and four-legged. We are what we are, and we're proud of it!'

'And Gemma is what she is!' Fleabag added. 'And she may not always have got things right, but it isn't whether we think she's a good Fire Wielder or not, but whether the Fire Giver wants her to be one that matters. You may be telling the truth about her past, but what is gone is only half the story and it doesn't count any more.'

The wizard looked as if he wanted to interrupt, but Fleabag didn't give him the chance. He pushed his smelly face in front of Domnall's mouth so he couldn't speak. 'And most important of all,' he went on, 'none of us were dragged into this; we're all here because we want to prove you're a liar and a bully. And we're not making any deal with you!'

And with that, he sprang from the wizard's neck and

landed awkwardly on the ground, followed closely by Cleo, who stalked away, her tail erect and proud.

Domnall, clutching his neck, flicked his left hand towards the cats, who just turned and stared at him in a supercilious way, then sat down to wash. The wizard looked in horror at his fingers, then made the gesture again, but this time he recoiled as the spell flew back in his face, turning him into a rather moth-eaten tiger rug, with glaring eyes.

Fleabag walked across him, kneading his claws into the back of the rug-animal's head and smirked, 'Now *you* should know you can't put a spell on a cat unless you know its real name, and you certainly could not *begin* to guess mine!'

Domnall was so furious he shrugged himself free of the tiger shape, picked up a small rock and threw it with all his strength at the sniggering felines. 'Take that!' he roared.

They both leaped out of the way. 'Temper, temper!' chided Fleabag. 'That will get you nowhere. Now what was that you were saying about striking a bargain with us?'

'I'll not make a bargain with you two,' he muttered between clenched teeth. 'But I will crush you if it's the last thing I do!' With that, Domnall picked up another rock and threw it at Fleabag, catching him on his one remaining back leg. Howling, the cat sank to the ground and began to lick furiously at his wound. Domnall picked up another rock.

Cleo did not hesitate. She leaped in front of her father and stared wide and golden-eyed at her attacker. 'If you throw that at my father I swear the Ring Fire will burn you.'

Domnall just laughed as he pulled back his arm, but he never threw the rock, for from behind him, he heard a noise. He looked round and saw the Fire Wielder getting to her feet. In her right hand the tongue of Ring Fire was rising.

Domnall dropped the rock and threw up an arm to protect himself from the pain of the sight. He swore again, for Fleabag and his daughter had succeeded in distracting him from his real purpose – that of either taking the Ring Fire from this stupid girl, or crushing her and quenching the Fire.

He glared at the cats. 'I'll see to you two later,' he promised. 'But first, I must complete what I came to do!' Then he raised his right hand, and for the first time, Gemma realized he carried the same ring his father had worn at the Battle of Porthwain. It closely resembled the royal ring of the land, but at the heart of it, there was no glowing Ring Fire, but an ice-blue flame. The living fire of evil – the source of all his power.

22

The Fire Cat Runs!

Gemma ducked as blue flames flashed across her vision, leaving her feeling icy cold. She stood again and met Domnall's glare with a steady gaze. The wizard seemed to have shrunk and aged in the last few hours. The constant shape-changing was sapping his strength deeply. He was hunched thin, grey and fearsomely angry.

Domnall twisted his lips into a devastating sneer. 'Well, my dear, have you had a nice little rest while I played with these charming little puss-cats? Have you thought about things? Are you ready to see reason now? It is surely time to stop endangering your friends and give me the Ring Fire.' His eyes were wild and unfocused. 'He's quite mad,' Gemma thought. 'But he's dangerous too. I must be careful.'

Out loud she said: 'I've let the Ring Fire down in lots of ways, but I still love it, and it still loves me. I will not and cannot give it to you. Anyway, it would destroy you: look!' And she thrust out her hand which held the clear, steady flame in the palm.

Domnall recoiled, shielding his eyes from the unbearable glare. 'Kill her!' he bellowed to the silent islanders, waiting at the bottom of the hill.

But none of them dared to move. From where they stood, they could see nothing for the thick blue cloud hanging heavily above their heads. From time to time they heard shouting, as gold or turquoise lightning flashed from the cloud, and terrible thunder rolled.

Not so far away, Rowanne and Aidan waited with the faithful sailors. The princess and her squire were still clad in their cooking pot armour, makeshift swords in their hands, and deadly looks in their eyes. At the call for Gemma's death, they ran uphill, yelling and screaming battle cries, determined to plunge their swords into the wizard. But he was too quick for them.

With a flick of his long fingers he threw a spell in their direction, but the glow from the Ring Fire that Gemma had given them before the battle caused Domnall's curse to slither harmlessly to the ground and dissolve into millions of slimy white maggots.

Gemma did not hesitate. She was furious that Domnall dared to attack her friends! She stooped down and called Cleo. Gently she laid the living flame on the back of the golden cat, making her the Fire Cat she really was. 'Run!' Gemma ordered. 'Give a little to all our friends.'

Swiftly Cleo darted hither and thither like a lithe sun flare, bringing each of the company a small portion of the light to hold, until the Ring Fire made a great circle of renewed, steady brightness that wrapped everyone in its golden light. The sailors all moved into a circle around Gemma and Domnall, then one by one, they began to sing the song the cats had taught them.

But Rowanne did not join in the song, nor did she try to find her sword. Instead, she stood and stared, open-mouthed at what she held in her hands. She had always felt so far from the Ring Fire; now she was actually *holding* it, and it was not slipping away from her like mercury between her fingers.

In the middle of the circle of Ring Fire, the blue cloud darkened, thickened, and recoiled. Domnall howled in rage and flung back his head, uttering terrible words that Gemma did not understand, although in her bones she could feel the hate and malice. She stood still, and watched, and waited, as Domnall brought his hands down to wrap his opponent in the dreadful spell of final desolation.

23

The Spell of Desolation

Gemma put her head on one side for a moment and listened to the cruel, cracking syllables of Domnall's spell. Then she stepped forward and tapped him on the arm.

'Excuse me,' she said. 'Excuse me...'

He slapped her aside, and glowered at her, but the interruption made him stumble over his words. He raised his arms again and repeated the complicated gestures and syllables.

Gemma shook her head. 'I've got to get his attention, Fleabag; there's something very important I've got to say to him.'

Fleabag grinned and nodded to Cleo. The two cats opened their mouths and began to sing. Not a special, tuneful song this time, but they howled as gleefully, loudly and badly as possible, making Domnall put his hands over his ears. As soon as they saw the spell was interrupted a second time, the cats stopped their noise. Fleabag then put on a prim face and coughed politely, 'Lord Domnall, sir, the lady wishes to speak with you. Please be quiet and listen to what she has to say...'

Domnall rolled his eyes and spat at the cats, then he started his incantation again, so again the cats began their racket. This time, to make it special, Cleo sang a rather splendidly out-of-key descant she had composed only a moment before to honour the occasion.

At last Domnall stopped the spell for a third time. 'Well, what *is* it? It's very dangerous to interrupt mid-spell. Anything could happen,' he snapped.

Gemma shrugged. 'That's what I'm trying to tell you, Lord Domnall. I suspect that what you are saying is a very dangerous spell indeed. If you finish what you are doing, then everything will be destroyed... You will be alone.'

Then she turned on her heel and began to walk away from him.

Domnall made a noise in his throat that sounded as if he were choking. He pounced on Gemma and grabbed her by the shoulder. 'And *you* will be the first to die!' he snarled, shaking her hard.

Gemma shrugged. 'So? What does that matter? Everything will be dead... except you. You will be completely alone. There will be nothing for you to have sway over, it will just be you floating through the nothingness for ever!' And she continued her walk down the hillside.

Domnall stamped with rage and exasperation. 'The aloneness won't come for many years,' he bellowed after her. 'I will have time to create a race of slaves to entertain me.'

Gemma had a hunch. She turned back, just as Domnall was trying to complete the spell again. 'By the way,' she shouted, 'I suspect you *won't* have time on your side. If you finish that spell, everything may be destroyed very quickly; it may be that everything will happen faster than you think.'

Domnall was incensed. He shook his fist. 'How dare you presume to advise me? What do *you* know about magic? Come back here and fight me properly! Don't just walk away from me! You're a coward running away. You're scared the Ring Fire won't win, aren't you? Well, it won't. I can tell you that now…'

Gemma looked back over her shoulder. 'No. I'm not a coward, but you are just a bully, and there is no reason for me to stay here and take what you are doing. If you want to destroy everything, go on, do it. But I think you will not enjoy your eternity of aloneness.' And she stooped to pick up the helmet Rowanne had lovingly made for her, and walked down the hill.

Domnall climbed back to the top of the hill and breathed deeply, but as he tried yet again to utter the spell of desolation, he faltered and hesitated. He had forgotten the words, and mismatched the intricate gestures. He knew the spell was going wrong… it was not what he had intended it to be at all. Domnall went pale and cold, and looked around for help, but he was alone within the seething, dull blue evil, as it tightened around him, closer and closer.

Sweating with fear, he tried again, but his eyes were staring wildly as he cast around for something to give him comfort or confidence. At last, shaking and breathless, the terrified wizard finished the final words – but were they the right ones? Had he forgotten a phrase, or missed a vital movement?

Domnall lost his balance and began to sway. He felt as though he was slipping down a slope. He glanced at his feet; they were still planted firmly on the rocky hillside... but the feeling was getting faster and faster, and it was not a controlled slide. Blue winds rushed past his face and caught at his clothes as he spun downwards into the nothingness. In terror he called out, but there was no one to hear him.

Suddenly the blue that had lain everywhere became indigo, then as blue-black as ink. Slowly, malevolently, it heaved and swelled, smothering, swamping, intense and so heavy it suffocated itself everywhere it lay.

The blueness was collapsing in on itself like a dying star. Suddenly there was a brilliant burst of blue light, then it was gone.

Far below at the foot of the hill, the islanders screamed and fled. Gemma, who was still quite high up the slope, was caught and lifted by the spell, suspended in nothingness: no earth below, no sky above.

But in the all-consuming silence that seemed to quench all life, the Ring Fire burned on, golden and life-giving, dissolving the blue as finally as ice melting on a glorious spring day.

24

The Way Home

Only a small, infinitely lonely sigh of wind disturbed the grassy hilltop, sending a last puff of blueness out across the sea.

At last, a soft, westerly breeze blew the final strands of the blue mist away. Far below, the sea fell back into its own tides again with a soft roar.

Gemma did not waken for several days. The tidal wave from Domnall's spell had knocked her unconscious. She lay oblivious to everything for two whole days. When she awoke, she and her friends were far out at sea in a fishing boat.

High above, Cleo was in the crow's nest – or as she preferred to call it, the cat's nest – keeping a look out for a shoal of fresh fish for supper, or maybe a few pirates to bring to justice. As she scanned the horizon, the ginger cat was singing 'North-west Passage' with a good pair of lungs, while her father snored loudly on a bed of folded sails below.

Gemma sat up and rubbed her eyes. 'Where am I? What happened?'

Rowanne brought a cup of water. 'The battle is over. Domnall is gone and we are on our way home.'

'But how did we get here?' Gemma tried to sit up, but felt very weak and sank back onto her mattress again.

Rowanne loved to tell of great battles, and this was surely the greatest ever fought! All the more so because the Ring Fire had rested in her own hands. She would never forget that moment!

Gemma smiled as Rowanne embroidered the tale as only a warrior can do. But at the description of Domnall's end, she shook her head. She found Rowanne's words distressing. She didn't wish a terrible death even on someone as evil as the wizard had been.

'What happened next?' she urged, eager to get past that bit.

Rowanne hugged her knees and her eyes glowed. 'Well, then the blue clouds parted, the strange winds dropped and the sea returned to normal. Of course, once the blue mist had lifted, the islanders realized that it was Domnall who had caused things to go wrong, but they still thought you were a terrible sorceress, one greater even than Domnall! I think they were ashamed of the way they had treated you – well, all of us, really – and they begged us to leave the island. They gave us this boat, food and water, and couldn't get rid of us fast enough. Perhaps they thought you would punish them for backing Domnall; I don't know. Still, we're well on our way now. Marcus reckons if this wind holds we'll be back by noon tomorrow. Talking of which, I had better go and do some work.'

Gemma heaved herself upright and leaned over the side. She stared into the reassuringly green waters, breathed deeply and looked around. The boat was an open craft, with no separate deck. Above, a huge, wide-footed single sail had a full belly of wind, making the vessel slip along at a great rate of knots. The boat was cramped, but adequate. The weather was fair, and everyone seemed in a good mood.

Fleabag sprang up onto the gunwales and walked carefully along the narrow edge to greet his friend. Gemma smiled and reached out to stroke him. 'Hello, you disreputable doormat!' He put his untidy black head up to be scratched. He roared a delighted purr.

Despite the way things had worked out, Gemma felt worried by something. 'Is everyone all right? Did anyone get hurt?' she asked.

Fleabag thought for a moment. 'Rowanne got a speck of something in her eye that went a bit nasty, but we washed it well and it cleared up. No one got *hurt* as such, not anything Rowanne would consider a proper injury worth a song or tale. As you so kindly noticed, *my* fur is intact, and that is all that matters really.'

Gemma laughed, then looked serious. 'Have I been intolerable lately?'

'Oh, totally!' chided the cat.

'You deserved it!' Gemma grinned.

Fleabag sat upright and looked offended. 'How now?' he demanded.

'For being right most of the time, I expect,' she laughed. Then she looked around. 'Is Aidan on board?'

'Indeed he is. Rowanne is already teaching him bad manners to cats. He actually refused to give me his supper last night when I said I was still hungry after I had eaten my own.'

'Shocking!' Gemma laughed. Then she looked serious again. 'I suppose this was all my fault. I should have known it was coming. If I had been doing my job, Domnall would never have got as close to me as he did.'

'But it was his choice to try to take the Ring Fire. You didn't ask him to, did you?'

'I almost did.'

'But if he had not found this means of attack, he'd had found another... Someone else, somewhere else. He would have endangered people whatever he had done. He was like that.'

'Rowanne said Domnall was just a pile of blue dust now...'

'That's right. Not a very pretty blue either, a sort of thick, sickly colour, if you know what I mean.'

Gemma leaned on her hand and stared out to sea, watching the gulls diving and swooping in their wake, hoping to catch leftovers of food thrown overboard, or small fish churned up by the boat's passage. 'What happened to that dust?' she asked, suddenly realizing what had been bothering her.

Fleabag frowned under his long whiskers. 'It blew away in the last of the blue wind. It was so fine there was nothing we could do to sweep it up. I am sure it could still be dangerous, but with any luck it's all blown away over the sea by now.'

'I hope so,' Gemma said thoughtfully. 'I really hope so.'

At the quayside Fleabag leaped ashore first. 'I'm not a sea-cat like my daughter,' he announced. 'I am now returning to life as a confirmed landlubber.'

Cleo sprang gently onto Marcus' shoulder, and held herself there by twisting her tail around the Captain's neck, and gently pushing her claws just a little way into his thick leather waistcoat. 'If you're going back on land, may I have your pirate's earring?' she begged.

Fleabag was shocked. 'Indeed you may not! When you are knighted for some great deed, King Phelan may see fit to give you your own, but I doubt it. You are far too wilful a cat to get an honour as great as mine!'

Cleo looked crestfallen. 'Oh *please*! Marcus is going to take me to sea on every voyage for ever!' she announced gleefully as she was gently but firmly disentangled and put down.

'Only as long as you continue to catch rats!' Marcus said firmly. 'This last voyage had rather too many nibbles purloined from the galley and too many rodents left loose for my liking!'

Cleo flashed a row of pointed white teeth at her father. 'He loves me really,' she grinned. 'It was he who did the "purloining" of the titbits for me.'

'I should hope so!' Fleabag rejoined. 'The thought of a daughter of mine left to feed on sea rat for the rest of her life is more than I can stand.'

'I will do my best to feed your daughter like a queen,' Marcus laughed. 'But for now, please excuse me; I must be about my business.'

Just then Phelan ran across the quay, arms wide to hug his friends. His dark eyes twinkled as he laughed out loud to see them all back safe and well.

He took Gemma and Fleabag to the nearest inn, and ordered a meal. While they waited for the food, Gemma told him all that had happened, and everything she had felt. Then she tried to explain why she had not told him the truth about her fears. 'It wasn't that I didn't trust you; it was just that I wanted to protect everyone from suspecting that their Fire Wielder no longer knew how to carry the Flame. I had hoped to find a replacement quietly, without anyone knowing they had ever been in danger.'

Phelan nodded and rubbed his hands through his black, curly hair as he thought. 'I can see your point, but wasn't it more dangerous *not* to tell Fleabag and me, at least?'

'Yes, it was silly of me. I'm sorry. But I still feel as if I don't want to go back to Harflorum.'

Phelan looked dismayed. 'But everything has turned out so well, why ever not?'

Gemma shrugged. 'Perhaps not everything I have been thinking lately has been wrong. I still have a hankering to go the cottage in the rocks. I don't know if it's just for a holiday, or to live. But if I'm not so tied up in ceremonies and duties, then perhaps I can learn to listen to the Ring Fire without distraction. I know the old Fire Wielder used to live somewhere quiet with his wife and a few friends. He would only come to Harflorum when he was needed... when he really felt he had something to say.'

'Then I think that's a good idea, if that's what you want to do, Gemma. Who will you take with you? I will make sure the cottage is rebuilt and waterproof, and well stocked of course. But it's not safe for you to be all alone up there.'

'If there have to be guards, can I at least have the

cottage all to myself? Really I'd just like a couple of goats... and Fleabag, I wonder if any of your talking offspring would like to join me?'

Fleabag was about to open his mouth and indignantly protest that *he* hadn't been invited, when a fat, brown tabby ran across to them. 'Excuse me for butting in, old man!' he miaowed in cat language. 'I've been looking all over for you... You'll never guess!'

Fleabag eyed the other cat suspiciously. It was Prince Tomas' butler's cat, a nice enough fellow but a bit slow in the rafters. He was waddling as fast as his fat legs could carry him, obviously bursting with some vital news.

'I give up,' Fleabag chuckled. 'Tell me what I'll never guess, then I'll know whether I could have guessed it or not.'

The fat cat blinked at him, looking rather lost and bemused. 'Um. Yes. Quite. Well, the day after you left, a rider came from the royal palace at Harflorum. Your lady wife has produced six kittens. Three daughters and three sons. Congratulations, sir! You're a father!'

Fleabag, who was fairly experienced at being a father, just nodded and said, 'Thank you' politely, and translated the news for the humans in the room.

At that moment Rowanne came across the room with flagons of mead and just caught the end of the conversation. 'Do I take it you'll be needing a lift home post-haste, old friend? You can travel in my saddlebag tonight if you like.'

'I suppose so,' Fleabag replied reluctantly, sad at the thought of missing out on a few weeks in the mountains with Gemma. He knew she would not hear of him staying when his wife Tabitha might need his help. 'But I'm not looking forward to going back,' he grumbled. 'I adore my wife, but she's so grumpy when she's just had kittens. It'll be "hold this one, lick that one, take this one for a walk and box that one's ears." There'll be no sleep for months and then when peace starts to reign again, last year's kittens will be bringing *their* kittens home for Granny and Grandpa to look after. No, I'm not looking forward to this at *all*.'

Suddenly his eyes lit up at the sight of Captain Marcus crossing the quay with Cleo swaying like a huge, golden parrot on his shoulder. He climbed onto the back of a chair and called out of the window: 'Hey, Marcus, I've changed my mind about going to sea. Might you have a berth for one more on board your next ship?'

'No,' Marcus shook his head. 'One cat is quite enough, especially when that one cat is as much trouble as your Cleo!'

'Nothing for it,' Rowanne teased. 'You'll have to hop onto my shoulder and pretend you're my fur collar.' The Princess stretched out a strong hand to grab Fleabag by the scruff of the neck.

'No, thank you,' he laughed as he sprang out of reach. 'I miss my Tabitha too much, and apparently one of the boys is just like me – with four legs of course! Much as I'm honoured to be asked to be your fur collar Rowanne, I think I'd rather go home and face the mews-ic!'

Fleabag and the Ring's End

Contents

1

The Fiddle Player

The boy bent his head over the fiddle and lifted the bow across the strings. Then, with a small jerk of his right shoulder, the music began.

The notes ran so fast and furious everyone in the marketplace stopped to listen.

Stallholders let onions fall back into boxes, and old women stopped their gossiping. Children who had been about to steal apples forgot what they were doing and squatted on the stone cobbles to listen.

Time seemed to have stopped as the thin-faced boy played on and on. The crowd grew silently bigger and bigger as the spinning notes filled the air.

At first he played jigs and reels and merry dance tunes, then almost imperceptibly the melodies became slower and sadder, until at last he dropped his arms and let the bow and fiddle dangle between his thin fingers. After a moment he put his head back, closed his eyes, and sang a sweet, yearning air.

When he stopped there was a long, long silence.

Then just as suddenly as the seeming spell had been cast, it was broken. With one voice, the whole crowd roared its approval and burst into thunderous applause. The boy was showered with coins and fruit and small gifts as, one by one, the listeners went about their business.

The little musician bent to pack up his things and to gather his earnings into a basket. When he straightened again he was alone – except, that is, for a mangy, black, long-haired cat, who was staring at him with golden eyes.

'What do you want, cat?' the boy sneered.

'Nothing,' the cat replied, as he scratched at a passing flea. 'I just wondered...'

'Yes?'

'I just wondered what your fiddle strings were made of.'

'Catgut,' the boy said, snapping the locks of the violin case shut.

'Hmmm,' the cat grunted disapprovingly, as he pulled himself up stiffly onto three legs. 'Do you want a job playing for the evening? You'd be paid and given somewhere to sleep.'

The boy slung his basket over his shoulder and tucked his fiddle under his arm. It was a bitterly cold day, and the night would be worse. He was tempted. But he had his orders, and the sooner it was all over the better. 'No. I don't play for performing animals,' he sniffed. 'I'm after real work.'

'Suit yourself!' The cat twitched his whiskers as he turned to go. But just as he did so, the pale winter sunlight caught the glint of a large golden earring in his right ear.

The boy almost dropped everything. Could he have found his enemy so easily? He mustn't let him slip away. A three-legged rough-looking street cat with a golden earring? No, it must be some strange coincidence. But he had to find out.

'Just a moment,' he called, grabbing at the basket that swung from his shoulders as he ran. 'I'm sorry, I didn't mean to sound rude. My name is Kern. Where did you say you wanted me to play tonight?'

An hour later, the boy was eating bread and cheese in the servants' kitchen of the royal palace, seated by the warm fire. Fleabag and Kern watched each other intensely. The boy's fair straight hair was cut in an old-fashioned way, all the same length, framing a long, thin, pale face with large, grey-green eyes. Outwardly, there was nothing unusual about him, a wandering musician, probably from the West. He had extraordinary skill, it was true. The cat had an odd feeling in the tip of his tail about this lad.

But was it good or bad... or maybe both? Whatever it was, he wanted to keep him well within sight until he had put two and two together. The Battle of Spider Island had taught him to pay strict attention to funny feelings about strange visitors... at least until things were a bit clearer.

When Domnall the evil wizard had come, pretending to be nothing more than the Chancellor of the University of Porthwain, Fleabag had let him slip through his paws, and what terrible things had happened in consequence! Domnall had kidnapped Gemma the Fire Wielder and the Blue Magic had almost swamped everything. Now, this lad had more of a... well, of a *green* feeling to him than a blue one, but he still needed watching.

As he ate, the boy forgot his suspicions and concentrated on his food. At last, he pushed his wooden trencher aside and leaned back in his chair contentedly.

'Finished?' Fleabag enquired kindly. 'Would you like a tankard of nettle beer?'

The boy looked around. 'I would. Where is it?'

'I'll get it for you,' came a voice from behind the kitchen door. Just then a tall, thin, freckle-faced teenage girl walked in, surrounded by a sea of kittens, all mewing for their tea.

As soon as they saw their grandfather Fleabag, they all swarmed around him until the cat was drowned under a pile of soft balls of multicoloured fur.

The girl drew two draughts of nettle beer and sat down opposite the boy at the kitchen table. 'Hello, I'm Gemma,' she introduced herself, smiling. 'Are you a friend of Fleabag's?'

'Not really,' he blushed, already ashamed of his deceit. 'I'm a musician. I met the cat while I was busking in the market this afternoon. He asked me to play at the Fire Festival tonight and I agreed.'

Gemma clapped her hands with delight. 'Excellent! Are you playing for the procession or for the dancing afterwards?'

The boy blushed even more deeply. 'For the dancing, I suppose. I... I don't know any of the Ring Fire tunes. We don't play them where I come from,' he added hastily.

'That's a shame. There're some great songs, and my friend Phelan has a wonderful singing voice. I'll introduce you to him later; perhaps you can work out one or two melodies?'

He forced a smile. 'Thanks, I'd like that.' He had no intention of learning his enemy's music, but if this girl and her friend could keep him in favour at the palace, he might be able to hang around long enough to work out a way of getting close to the King, and maybe even that terrible harridan, the Fire Wielder. If it meant he had to play a tune or two, what did that matter?

'Do you work here?' he asked as he wiped the nettle beer away from his mouth.

'Yes,' the girl laughed. 'I have my own home in the mountains near Beulothin, but I work here when I'm needed.'

'Rubbish!' scoffed Fleabag as he jumped up onto the table, having led his grandkittens away to the scullery where the day's scraps had already been put down for them. 'Getting you to lift a finger to de-flea me takes far more effort than it should. I really will have to have words with the King about you!'

'Well, you shouldn't encourage the fleas. If you used flea powder and let the maids comb you every day, you'd have no trouble at all!'

Fleabag pounced suddenly on a wandering black speck and licked his whiskers. 'But fleas are so nice and *crunchy*, with that *hint* of sweetness in the middle... they're just... Ummm!'

Kern smiled. Despite himself, he couldn't help liking this creature. 'So are you in charge of the cat?'

Gemma threw back her head and laughed loudly. 'Ha!'

Fleabag jumped off the table and flicked his whiskers in mock annoyance. 'I'd like to see her try to be in charge of me. I'm in charge of *her*, more like! See you later. Nap time!' And with that he strode out of the kitchen, tail erect, followed, inevitably, by a few of the kittens, chasing and pouncing and clambering all around their granddad.

Gemma picked up the boy's dishes, washed them in the huge stone sink and left them to dry. 'I'll show you where you can have a bath and a chance to tune up before the Festival starts. Then I'll have to leave you to your own devices, I'm afraid. I've got to put an uncomfortable costume on and take part in the parade. But afterwards I'll make a special point of listening to you in the dance hall.'

Gemma led him up to the servants' quarters. No one was around. 'Everyone is over in the King's palace getting ready for tonight, but that cupboard over there has spare clothes for anyone who needs them, and the bathroom is here...' she pushed open a door to her left. 'Hal is the chief kitchen boy. Tell him Gemma asked for him to look after you. I may not get a chance to speak to you later, but I hope all goes well.' And with that she smiled and ran back down the stairs and into the gardens that surrounded each of the palace buildings.

Just as she stepped outside onto the frosted gravel path, a husky voice behind her whispered 'Psst!' urgently.

'What's the matter, Fleabag?' She bent down and picked him up so she could scratch him under his chin.

'I don't trust him,' the cat growled.

'He seems a nice enough lad,' Gemma smiled. 'You're getting suspicious in your old age!'

'No. Seriously,' Fleabag answered, 'he uses *catgut* strings!'

2

The Blue Crystal

Kern pulled the clean shirt over his head and combed his hair. He did feel better for a bath, but he hated himself for liking Fleabag and his friend. She must be one of the higher servants at the palace, to be able to give Hal orders, but her plain linen dress and brown embroidered waistcoat looked like something a parlourmaid might wear on her day off. Perhaps she was just Fleabag's friend. Kern decided to be nice to her. She might be able to get him into all sorts of places and she might know some of the Fire Wielder's servants...

When Kern was dressed he sat at a small table at the end of the attic room. He placed the chair so he would have his back to anyone who came in. He had tried to shut the door, but it wouldn't catch properly. He daren't put something against it; that might look suspicious.

He opened his basket and from the end of his violin

case pulled a small blue velvet bag. Carefully he pulled the laces apart and let a smooth blue crystal ball roll out onto his open hand. Then, placing it in front of him, he peered into it.

The clear blue stone shone with a chilly light that came from its heart; as he looked, he felt its cold pervading everywhere. He shivered, but did not dare look away. M'Kinnik, the chief wizard at Porthwain, would know if his mind wandered, and he would be punished with cramps all night.

Soon he felt the wizard's mind touching his own. 'I'm here, M'Kinnik. I'm in the palace, and I have been hired to play at the Festival tonight. I have already made the acquaintance of the cat, Fleabag, and a maid who seems friendly enough.

'I'm certain they are not suspicious. I will speak to you again as soon as I have more information for you.'

A chill crept between the boy's shoulderblades as he felt the cruel mind of the wizard threatening, 'And you know what will happen if you fail?'

'I know, Master.' The boy shivered, and put his hand over the ball to shield himself from its cruel blueness. How he longed to throw it as far out of the window as he could and walk away for ever. But too much was at stake.

Kern did not understand why the wizards of Porthwain wanted so badly to take over the Ring Fire and the Kingdom. They had already been defeated by the treacherous Fire Maiden at the Battle of Porthwain, and at the Battle of Spider Island. What was the point of trying again? All the wizards seemed to care about was making everyone do as they said. They were bullies, that was all.

True, Kern had his own reasons for agreeing to be the wizards' emissary. He longed to get his own back on the Fire Maiden. After the Battle of Porthwain she had become the Fire Wielder, which probably made her the Ring Fire's own all-powerful chief wizard. It was said she had more authority than the King, and if you looked her in the eye, you would shrivel up in an instant. She had been responsible for the death of his father, the Chancellor of All Wizards, and his two older brothers, Sethan and Domnall.

He wasn't worried by the death of his father or Sethan. They had never had any time for him, but he missed Domnall.

If Kern had been a girl, things would have been different. She would have been his third daughter, and in wizard families, the third girl was usually the most powerful magician of all. But he already had the six sons he needed for his spells, so Kern was of no use to him.

Besides, his father had been horrid to Claire, his mother. She was one of the Hill People, and had grown up on a farm owned by the University. When her father became too poor to pay the rent, Claire was taken instead. A fortune-teller had foreseen that this girl would give birth to an extraordinarily powerful daughter. The Chancellor already had several wives, and he hated Claire on sight, but he tolerated her until the baby was born. When he heard it was a boy, Claire was sent to work in the kitchens. Neither Sethan nor their father had looked at Kern since.

Domnall, on the other hand, had always been at least a little kind to Kern. When he was younger Domnall had given him sweets and outgrown clothes, and had taught him to read and to say a few simple spells. Kern was good at the reading, although he didn't like the spells. He only learned them to please his older brother.

And it had been Domnall who had given him his first violin…

Then Domnall too became Chancellor of All Wizards, and in his turn was killed by the Fire Wielder. Kern hated her for that. When his work for the wizards was done, he would avenge himself on the woman. She had killed the only person in all the world who meant anything to him, apart from his mother, and it was his mother who would suffer most if Kern failed.

He didn't dare think about it. He must concentrate on playing well at the Festival tonight. That would ensure that he would be allowed to hang around the palace until he found who he was looking for…

As he put the crystal ball back in his basket and pulled out his violin, Kern thought he saw a flicker of a dark shadow by the door. He looked again, but it was nothing. He rested the fiddle under his chin and began to tune up.

Meanwhile Fleabag sat outside in the corridor and thought hard. Had the boy seen him slipping out through the doorway? Well, what if he had? He was only a cat, and cats wandered everywhere. But what had Kern been doing with that crystal ball? Maybe nothing. It was probably only a glass bauble he had picked up on a market stall.

But the cat was beginning to feel increasingly uneasy…

Just then Hal came thumping up the stairs, followed by a gaggle of other lads his own age. He stopped to stroke Fleabag and pushed the door wide open.

'Hello,' he called out cheerfully. 'Are you Kern?

Gemma said I'd find you here. She said we had to take you with us to the Festival. We're just going to bathe and change. It's been a long day, we've been up since before dawn, but everything's ready now. Cook's pleased, and she jolly well should be. The roast swans look wonderful and the jellies are made into the most incredible shapes. You can't imagine!'

Fleabag slipped away, as Hal and the other kitchen boys swept Kern along in their excitement.

The cat trotted out of the servants' quarters and across the gardens towards the side entrance of the King's palace. The gravel pathways were already bitterly cold under his paws. There would be a hard frost tonight, and the daylight was fading fast.

He found Phelan and Gemma sitting in the library, which smelled of lavender and beeswax polish. The scent made Fleabag long for summer days. The cold weather was annoying him; he must be getting old.

The cat jumped up onto Gemma's lap and turned this way and that, purring as he trod his paws up and down on her knees and considered how he was going to make himself comfortable with the maximum inconvenience to Gemma.

Phelan laughed and scratched the cat's ears. 'How are you, my rat-chasing friend? Gemma says you are worried about our young visitor.'

Fleabag decided that the King's lap was bigger than Gemma's, and so probably more commodious. He jumped across the gap and began to claw gently at Phelan's richly embroidered robes. The cat frowned as he looked up into Phelan's dark, golden-brown face. 'Indeed I am, and with good reason. I saw him with a blue crystal ball in the servants' quarters. He seemed to be peering into it very intently.'

Gemma leaned forward so she could speak quietly. She trusted all the palace servants, but if this lad was an enemy spy, then walls might have ears. 'Did he say anything into it?'

Fleabag shook his head. 'Not that I heard, but I think he was communicating somehow. He didn't look at all happy – in fact he looked quite miserable, and he was shivering the whole time he had it in his hand.'

Phelan stroked his black, curly beard and frowned. 'Hmmm. What does the Ring Fire tell you, Gemma? Is he a danger or just a stray musician acting oddly?'

Gemma opened her hands and peered into the cup of her pink palms. Nothing glimmered. That didn't surprise her. The Ring Fire only burned when it was ready to. She was the Fire's servant, she never controlled it. But her skin *did* tingle.

'I don't think there's any immediate danger, but I will keep my hands open. Last time the wizards made a move I was completely taken in by Domnall and his smooth words! I was too wound up in my own miseries to see what was really happening. The Battle of Spider Island was all my fault and I won't let it happen again!'

Fleabag wrinkled his nose. 'I certainly hope not. I *told* you something was wrong at the time!' he smirked.

Phelan picked the cat up by the scruff of the neck and peered at him. 'Listen, *Sir* Scrag-Belly, if you speak to the Lady Fire Wielder in that tone of voice I'll have you skinned, boiled and fed to the field shrews for their Festival banquet!'

'Point taken, my Lord,' the cat replied meekly. Phelan

was the only human he treated with the slightest glimmer of respect, for the King had once bested him in a fair fight – daggers to claws. 'But all the same,' the cat added, 'I feel in my whiskers that something is wrong.'

Gemma looked at her hands again with her head on one side as if she was listening. 'You know, I get the feeling that, for the moment at least, he isn't here for *us*... he's got some other purpose in mind.'

'Hmmm,' Fleabag screwed up his furry face. 'I'll keep an eye on him tonight. I'm *still* suspicious of anyone who could even contemplate using catgut for fiddle strings.'

3

The Fire Festival

As the sun went down, a trumpeter stood on the western balcony outside the Hall of Light. He raised a great brass horn to his lips and played a sad lament for the passing of the sun and the coming of the longest night.

The mournful sound was picked up and repeated by trumpeters across the city of Harflorum. Then there was silence. All the people were indoors. Everything was dark and still. No one ventured out into the marketplace, no one lit a candle or a lantern, fires and cooking stoves were extinguished, and everyone huddled under thick woollen blankets.

Kern tried to stop his teeth chattering as he stood amongst the kitchen staff and other servants at the back of the Hall of Light, waiting for total darkness. Then the great ceremony would begin. No one moved, no one breathed a word.

The Fire Wielder, dressed in a heavy cloak, did not move as she stood framed in the deepening dark of the eastern window, thrown open to the night winds.

Beside her, the King stood tall and equally still. They did not flinch as an icy blast swept hail into their faces.

'What are they doing?' whispered Kern to Hal.

'Hush!' the older boy replied. 'You'll see.'

After about half an hour of seeming torture, when the last vestiges of light had long gone, the King threw back the hood of his cloak and sang in a rich, deep voice:

'There is no hope.
The great night has come,
the light has gone away.
There is no dawn.'

Then the Fire Wielder lifted up her arms and replied, singing:

'Fire Giver,
In our darkest hour,
give us light.
Breathe amongst us,
banish night.
Give us once more
the flame by which
we live and move,
and have our being.'

Then Kern could hardly believe his eyes, for a minute star appeared in the darkness. Everyone in the room gasped as the light swelled and deepened into a rich, warm, red glow of living flame. They had all seen the full glory of the burning Fire many times before, but it never ceased to thrill them. Then the one light became two and Kern could see that each flame was born in the upraised palms of the Fire Wielder.

Kern bit his lip, for he knew enough magic to be able to tell that this was no trick, but real fire. Indeed, it was more than ordinary fire; it was *alive*.

His brother Domnall had taught him how to make fire. It was a beginner's trick, but that was nothing to the breathtaking beauty of this light. Despite himself, Kern was impressed. He would have to be very careful; this woman would be a formidable opponent.

The wizards had been wrong when they had told him the Fire Wielder knew no magic and was naive and inept. It seemed that she could *create*, and that was more than even his father or Sethan could do. They had only been good at destroying.

Suddenly he felt a sharp nudge in the ribs. 'The Light has come – pass it on.'

'What?'

Hal pushed a small lighted candle into Kern's fingers. 'The Light has come, pass it on!'

Kern suddenly realized he was expected to do something. A small boy on his left was looking up at him expectantly, holding a candle up to be lit.

'Oh, er – the Light has come, pass it on!' The boy grinned and turned to his neighbour, leaving Kern to stare in amazement at the little golden flame in his hands. This was just an ordinary candle flame, yet there was something about it...

But he didn't have time to think for long. The windows in the Hall of Light had been shut against the winter gales, and everything was beginning to warm up, as candles were lit in every hand. High above, heavy crystal candelabras were hoisted into the huge glass lantern of the ceiling, making great mountains of swaying, glistening lights. Everywhere seemed suddenly to be awash with warmth and glowing colour and a heady scent of waxy sweetness.

Then the singing began. At first a few people began humming, and slowly others joined in, followed by fiddle and bodhran players near the front, swelling together into a joyful swaying tune. Then came the words. The people on the far side of the room seemed to be singing one line, with the people on Kern's side carolling an answer. Despite himself, Kern found that he too was humming, and even working out harmonies to the lilting melody.

Suddenly a blast of cold air made his flame flicker, as the main door to the hall was thrown open and the Fire Wielder moved through and down the stairs to the palace's main door below. Outside, the crowds that had gathered shouted, as the Fire Wielder and the King stepped outside and repeated their songs. The crowd cheered again as the Ring Fire flared up from the hands of the cloaked figure, spreading a golden glow across the city.

'Come on,' Hal urged. 'It's time for the feasting and dancing now. Aren't you playing music for us?'

Kern hesitated. 'I've never been to the Fire Festival before. I'd like to stay a bit longer and find out what happens next,' he said hopefully, craning his neck to see beyond the crowds gathered at the bottom of the stairs.

'Oh, I can tell you that,' Hal grinned. 'It's the same as you've just seen, but it happens over and over again. The

Fire Wielder's bodyguard, the Princess Rowanne de Montiland, draws her sword and leads the Fire Wielder and the King through all the streets so they can hand the flame of the Ring Fire to anyone who comes with a candle. People take that flame home and light their fires and cooking stoves from it. Then everyone goes to their nearest hall or barn, then they dance and eat until they drop, sometime about dawn usually!'

'But why do they do it at all?' Kern asked. 'What's it for?'

'Well, there's a lot more to it than getting the kitchen fire going!' Hal laughed. 'But I'd have thought they'd have taught you that at least, where you come from! Look, I haven't got time to explain now, Cook needs us all to help carry food into the Throne Room. If you're not playing yet, can you lend us a hand?'

Late into the night, Kern sat propped against a pillar in the Throne Room, chewing on a chicken leg and swigging at a bottle of ginger cordial, watching the merrymaking. He felt full and happy. His music had been well received, he'd played jigs and reels until the dancers could dance no more. He'd been well paid and now he was eating the best food he had ever tasted in all his life.

Suddenly servants came into the room and extinguished all the lights. Everyone fell silent in the darkness. Kern sat bolt upright. Was there going to be more magic? But there were no icy winds this time, just a soft drumbeat that slowly became louder and louder. Soon Kern glimpsed a flickering light that seemed to move in time to the music. Then up on the stage, where he himself had been playing earlier, four figures dressed in black appeared, faintly outlined by the flaming torches they carried. The drumbeat quickened and the two men and two women began to sway and move in time to the beat, swinging burning torches as they moved, reflecting warm gleams from heavy golden bangles around their wrists and arms. Kern was sure that the flowing black garments worn by the women would catch fire as they quickened their pace, swaying and dipping, swinging their arms this way and that. As the dancers moved, their flames left strange turquoise-coloured patterns that seemed to hang in the air like echoes of light.

Kern was mesmerized. He could not move; the ginger cordial spilled on the floor, but he did not notice, for the dancers were now throwing firebrands to each other, catching them as deftly as if they were ordinary juggler's clubs.

Then the drummers were joined by three more who played slightly different rhythms from each other, allowing the beats to twine and twist around each other. At the same time, all four of the fire dancers made their own pattern of flames, yet, with the music, they joined up with each other, tossing the firebrands into blazing patterns in the air.

With an abruptness that made Kern jump, the dancers stopped, with their burning torches held in a glowing star shape. After a few moments, the star pattern broke as one of the men moved into the middle and, collecting four of the torches, began to juggle, sending the brands high into the rafters.

The beat went on, faster and faster, and the juggling became more and more complex, yet the movements were as solemn and relentless as a heartbeat.

Then, with a final crash of the drums, the torches went out and there was silence in the pitch blackness.

Suddenly there was thunderous applause and candles were relit all around the room. The fire dancers were rewarded with gold and silver coins, and Kern even found himself throwing some of his hard-earned pence into the dancers' baskets as they came through the crowd.

'When it's dark like that, it makes you appreciate light and warmth, don't you think?'

Kern glanced around. Who had spoken?

'I'm down here, shrew-brain, unless you decide to be helpful and pick me up, so I can see better!'

Kern looked down and saw Fleabag getting his paws trodden on as people milled here and there to fetch food from the supper tables.

He picked the cat up. 'I suppose that's what the Festival is about, then? Is the Fire Wielder the wizard who makes light-magic in the darkness? Is that why it's held on the shortest day?'

'Sort of,' replied the cat. 'But it's nothing to do with magic or wizards. It re-enacts the Fire Giver giving us the Ring Fire, so we needn't be without help or afraid of evil any more. The Fire Wielder is just the servant who carries it for us. Grab me some fish from that plate, will you? Humans seem to get upset when I help myself.'

'Since when has that ever stopped you?' demanded a woman's deep voice from just behind them.

'I only need to help myself when you don't look after me properly!' sniffed the cat. 'But while someone fills up my plate for me, may I introduce my young friend Kern? Kern, this is the Princess Rowanne de Montiland, ruler of the royal city of Erbwenneth, and protector of the Fire Wielder's person.'

The Princess Rowanne de Montiland bowed her head briefly as she forked a large chunk of sea bass in aspic onto a plate. She handed it to Kern. 'Make sure you put it right under the table for him to eat, push it well back. He is *disgusting* when he eats. He slobbers, and the way he crunches bones makes my stomach turn!'

'But it's good for my teeth to chew!' protested Fleabag.

'Yes, my Lady,' Kern mumbled, and felt himself blushing as he bent down and pushed the food well out of sight.

'You played well earlier,' the Princess said kindly to Kern. 'You will be welcome in Erbwenneth.'

'Thank you, my Lady,' Kern muttered as the Princess strode away, her hand on the hilt of her gold sword as it flashed against her ceremonial flame-coloured silk tabard. Kern had been half blinded by her gold-plated breastplate, glittering with topaz and rubies set into the sign of the Ring Fire.

But, worse than that, the boy had felt a familiar and unwelcome blast of cold as he glimpsed the Princess' too-blue eyes. He bit his lip nervously.

'Oi!' said Fleabag, 'put me down. I'm famished, and if you grip me any harder, I'll snap!'

4

Kern's Message

So this was it! The moment he'd been dreading. He had found the person he was looking for.

When the Battle of Spider Island had been lost, Domnall had been sucked into his own spell and the Blue Magic had been reduced to ashes. The winds that had followed had scattered the ashes across the seas, where they could never be gathered again. But the wizards had looked into their scrying bowls and had seen that just one speck had been caught in the eye of a human, where it had stayed. The wizards could sense the speck was still alive, but who was the carrier? They knew that the right spells would rekindle the Blue Magic to its former power and strength, but the carrier had to be willing!

Kern had been sent to Harflorum to find someone whose eyes were 'too blue', the colour of Blue Magic, and to deliver him or her to Porthwain to be trained as a wizard. In no one else in the entire land would the Blue Magic be as potent or as pure as in the carrier of that one blue speck! The old Chancellor had failed to grasp the Kingdom, as had his sons Sethan and Domnall. The auguries had showed that if *this* chance failed, then the wizards' power would dwindle and fade for ever.

Kern did not care about prophecies. All that mattered to him was that the wizards had promised that if he succeeded, he and his mother would be free to leave the University, to go wherever they wished. But if not, then they would both remain as slaves of the wizards for ever. The wizards had not dared to go on this errand themselves, for the Ring Fire was strong in the hands of the Fire Wielder. She would know if any of them came near.

Even Kern could see he was the perfect choice for this errand. He nursed resentment against the Fire Wielder, but he was not a wizard so he would not be detected. Kern sensed he was a weak and easily expendable pawn in their deadly game. Blackmail and fear bound the boy to their slightest whim.

For his own part, Kern dared not contemplate failure. He could only think of the hope that success would bring. Yet he was very frightened. He hated working for the wizards, especially M'Kinnik. He knew their plans were evil, but what could he do against them? He would get this one job over, exact his own vengeance on the Fire Wielder, and then leave, never to think about the Blue Magic or the Ring Fire ever again. He would take his mother and together they would roam the world. He would play his music, and she would sing, and they would be free.

Suddenly a cheerful voice jerked him from his thoughts. 'Hello there, I enjoyed your playing.' It was Gemma, the maid who had been kind to him earlier. He rubbed his eyes sleepily. She was dressed in a formal court dress, made from red and gold silk. She must have had something very important to do in the Festival, although Kern hadn't noticed her in the Hall of Light.

'Thank you,' he yawned. 'Did you join the dancing?'

'No, I couldn't in this get-up,' Gemma smiled. 'But I was listening. If you'd like to stay around for a few weeks and play, you'd be welcome, and I'll bring Phelan along for a dance.'

'Thank you, I'd like that,' Kern nodded. Suddenly he remembered that he had work to do, and his quarry, the Princess Rowanne de Montiland, was already out of sight.

'Please don't think me rude, but I have to go; there is someone I must give an important message to.' Gingerly he began to move towards where he had last seen the Princess, talking with courtiers.

'Well, I'll see you around,' Gemma smiled. 'Goodnight.'

Kern turned and slipped amongst the crowds, but he could see no sign of the Princess. Terrified in case he had let her slip through his fingers, he darted along the grand corridors, peering this way and that, until he saw a few soldiers disappearing around a corner. They would know where the Princess' quarters were...

'Stop, please stop!' he called out, running as fast as he could behind them. Suddenly he tripped and tumbled onto the tiled walkway, rolling over. His violin twanged and cracked with a stomach-sickening noise, but Kern found himself crumpled in a heap at the feet of none other than the Princess Rowanne de Montiland herself.

Once more the boy shivered as he looked up at the Princess' too-blue eyes. The Lady Knight bent over and helped the boy up. 'I know why you're here,' she said quietly. 'You have a message for me.'

Kern sat miserably in a corner of the Princess' room, nursing the broken fragments of the violin across his knee. His eyes were stinging, but he told himself he was too old to cry – in public at least. He would scream and rage to his heart's content once he was alone.

Meanwhile, he was reciting the message of the wizards, word for word. He had learned it by heart. In fact he had been made to repeat it, before he was allowed to eat, every day for a month before he left Porthwain. It was engraved into his brain.

'My Lady, the Wizards of Porthwain greet you most humbly with the honour your most noble rank deserves. They have known and seen how, despite your noble personage's faithful service, the so-called Ring Fire has never recognized your true worth and great skill in the realms of magical power.

'It is the Wizards' intention, therefore, to rectify this great wrong to your noble self, and to invite you to the University at Porthwain as the guest of the most noble Chancellor and his wisest men and women for as long as it may please you. Here you may learn, at your leisure, the noble art of magic, for which the Wizards have not the slightest doubt that you were chosen and marked from the very moment of your conception.'

Kern sighed, but did not look up. The speech was over.

He felt cold and drained, but he was almost free. Or he would be, if the Princess agreed to accompany him. That would be the difficult part.

Rowanne said nothing. She simply finished unstrapping her Ring Fire breastplate and laid it on the chair. Divested of her trappings, she was merely a dark-haired woman with a square face and determined eyes, for she was a Lady Knight by training as well as in title. Would she agree to go? Kern stole a sideways look. The candlelight reflected on the Ring Fire regalia, but through the window in the far wall daylight was beginning to stain the night sky with pale grey-blue streaks. Suddenly he felt an overwhelming sense of urgency. If only she would run out of the door with him now… this very second!

'Do you have proof?' she said at last, in a deep, slightly husky voice.

Kern put down the pieces of his violin and rummaged in his pocket until he drew out the blue velvet bag. Pulling the strings apart, he said: 'Would my Lady be so good as to open her hand?' And into her outstretched palm he gently tipped the blue crystal ball.

The Princess looked at the glassy depths and her eyes widened, although she said nothing. Kern knew she was meeting with M'Kinnik in thought.

Suddenly a firm knock sounded at the door. Kern jumped, but the Princess scarcely moved a muscle, except to close her hand around the ball. 'Come!' she called curtly.

The door opened and Fleabag entered, tail erect, golden earring gleaming. He was followed by a tall man with golden-brown skin and a thick black curly beard and hair. Behind him came a thin, freckle-faced girl: Gemma, the maid.

Kern reddened and felt embarrassed, although there was no reason why he shouldn't be there. He had a legitimate message, which was only between him and the Princess. He stepped back behind the door and tried to slip away, but the man shot out a strong arm and caught the boy around the wrist, firmly, but without hurting him. 'Wait there!' he ordered.

The Princess said nothing, but raised her chin defiantly.

'What's happening, Rowanne?' Gemma asked urgently. 'There is danger around. The Blue Magic is in the palace. I can see it plainly, I can feel my hands burning like they did on Spider Island. Something is happening, or is about to.'

Kern was amazed that the girl should speak to the Princess like an equal, but he said nothing.

'I suppose you know the boy's message? I expect the Ring Fire has told you already?' Rowanne raised a dark eyebrow and stared coldly at the visitors.

Gemma shook her head. 'Only that there is danger. And it is hovering around *you*, Rowanne. Ever since Spider Island, there has been something not quite right. But now it is coming alive. I'm sure the Ring Fire can help you...' and with that Gemma stepped forward and held out her hand, which cupped a warm, golden flame.

Kern gasped and jerked back. The tall man put his other hand reassuringly on the boy's shoulder. 'Don't worry, lad, Gemma is the Fire Wielder. Everything will be all right, she isn't really on fire, and she won't hurt the Princess. They are old friends.'

Kern stared wide-eyed at the man. How could this friendly girl, only a little older than himself, be the evil woman he had sworn to kill? And how could he get the Princess away from her now? He slumped in the man's grip. All was lost. He was bound to be accused of wizardry. The only question now was, in which prison would he rot? Harflorum or Porthwain?

5

The Wizards' Challenge

But Kern did not have time to worry about his future.

An urgent hammering on the door made everyone jump. A breathless equerry entered and bowed to Gemma and Phelan. 'My Lady, your Highness... Forgive my intrusion, Princess, but news has come from the gates. A delegation has arrived from the University at Porthwain, and they are... forgive me for mentioning it,' he gasped, '... they are openly wearing insignia of the Brotherhood of Wizards!'

'Oh, I wish I'd had some sleep last night!' groaned Phelan, clutching his head.

'Your Highness,' the equerry bowed, 'may I suggest you get some sleep now, and we will receive the delegation at noon? I am sure they will want to rest as well.'

'Don't count on it,' Phelan sighed. 'They probably slept nearby last night and have only just woken up. They chose this moment because they knew we would be tired and not at our best. There is definitely something afoot.'

Kern looked up at his captor, open-mouthed. *This* was the King? Of course, the King's name was Phelan, and he had sung beautifully last night. Gemma had said her friend Phelan was a wonderful singer. Why hadn't he been more careful when making friends at the palace? He should have been more aware that things had been too easy. They probably had been warned of his presence by this Ring Fire of theirs and he had walked straight into a trap. Kern hated himself for being so stupid.

Gemma scooped up Fleabag and turned to the equerry. 'Give the Princess a guard; she may be in danger. And take the boy Kern to a room where he can be comfortable, but carefully watched. We will receive the delegation at noon, as you suggest. Feed our guests from Porthwain and provide them with hot baths and comfortable guest suites. With any luck they will be tired, and they might be tempted to sleep rather than to get up to mischief.'

'I wouldn't bet on it,' muttered Fleabag.

When they were outside the door, the cat whispered, 'Put me down, Gemma. I want to keep an eye on things here.'

Gemma scratched her furry friend behind his ear as she wished him happy hunting. As she straightened, she noticed that Kern looked very dejected as he was led away by a guard.

She ran down the corridor to catch him up. 'Don't worry. You aren't in trouble, we're just a bit concerned at the moment. I'm certain you aren't the real danger. You can go for a walk in the grounds or play your violin if you like. You aren't in prison. I will come and see you later; I think we need to talk.'

Kern glowered at her. He despised himself for liking her earlier, so now he hated her. She must be trying to lull him into a false sense of security, so he'd betray the wizards without realizing it. He scowled and hung his head, saying nothing.

Gemma tried again. 'I'll have your violin sent to you, if you like. Where did you leave it?'

'Smashed, in the Princess' room. Doesn't matter though,' he grunted.

Gemma turned to the guard. 'Make sure a very good violin is provided for this boy. He is my personal guest.'

And with that she turned and followed Phelan out into the garden that separated the royal private chambers from the main body of the palace.

The icy chill of the night was beginning to lift as the early morning air warmed a little in the dawn.

'I am going to my room to consult the Ring Fire. You get some sleep, and call me before you meet the delegation. We can talk then.'

At half-past eleven, the King knocked on the Fire Wielder's door and waited. There was no reply. He knocked again, and at last a sleepy voice called, 'Come in.'

Gemma looked as if she had slept in a heap. Her clothes were dishevelled and her hair was tousled. She groaned as she glanced at the clock. 'Oh no! I came and sat down, meaning to look into the Ring Fire, and I must have fallen asleep straight away. This is terrible.'

'Never mind,' the King answered. 'Straighten yourself up a bit, and come with me to meet the wizards. When we know what they are here for, you can make time to do things properly.'

'We had better ask Rowanne to be there.' Gemma looked worried. 'If she is in some kind of danger from the wizards, we might be able to see what it is. If we hide her from them, the danger may remain hidden too.'

'I'd be glad of her presence for other reasons, I must admit,' Phelan added. 'If the wizards' visit has any military implications, I want Rowanne to be the first to know. We are going to need all the help we can get.'

'Shall we ask the boy, Kern, to be there?'

'No.' Phelan shook his head. 'Did you see his face? He was terrified when he heard the wizards were coming. He's involved, but not willingly, I'd wager. He knows something, but showing him to the wizards now won't help anyone.'

Meanwhile, the Princess Rowanne de Montiland had not slept. The few hours she had been alone she had peered unceasingly into the blue crystal ball that Kern had put into her hand. During that whole time, she had not uttered a word, nor had she moved a muscle. But when she got up to answer the summons to audience, her eyes were even bluer than before.

The wizards were already seated in the Throne Room when the King and the Royal Fire Wielder entered. The Princess followed behind, with Fleabag hiding beneath the copious sweeping folds of her long woollen cloak. He knew the wizards would be angered by his presence – they hated cats, especially black ones – and he did not feel like being fried by Blue Magic this early in the morning. Anyway, he wanted to keep within a claw's scratch of his old arch-enemy, Rowanne, just in case…

Chancellor M'Kinnik was a fat, sour-faced man in his early sixties. On his right and left were his two Vice Chancellors, one a tall, beautiful woman of about middle age, very black-skinned and obviously from the far south of the Kingdom, and the other, an elderly, almost skeletal old man with a bald head. All were dressed in richly embroidered blue silk robes, and heavy indigo-dyed fur cloaks.

None of them rose as the royal party entered; they just stared rudely at Gemma as she took her place, making her feel decidedly uncomfortable. The King bowed formally to his guests and started to greet them cordially with a speech of welcome.

M'Kinnik was obviously not listening, and after a sentence or two, he suddenly stood and interrupted the King.

'Look, I'm not interested in pleasantries.' He slapped the table with the flat of his hand. 'We're here to issue the Great Challenge. Three trials, and whoever wins takes the crown *and* the Ring Fire. Once and for all. No more silly petty battles, no more arguments. A fair fight according to the rules. Tests of strength, wisdom and magic.'

Phelan stood amazed with his mouth open, staring in disbelief, not only at the Chancellor's rudeness, but at the Challenge itself.

The Chancellor then nodded to the beautiful woman, who stood and unrolled a scroll. 'According to the law of the land, laid down by the Fire Giver himself, if a ruler or Fire Wielder is suspected unfit to rule, then three trials may be set in the Great Challenge. Whoever performs the trials without defeat is then undisputed monarch for ever.'

Phelan and Gemma looked at each other. It was by this Law of Challenge that Rowanne had become the Princess of Erbwenneth. There was no disputing the fact that the wizards had every right to do this. The King was sweating as he clenched and unclenched his hands. Gemma turned deathly pale and shivered.

Suddenly Rowanne leaned forward. Her face was flushed, and her eyes sparkled with excitement. 'Good!' she whispered hoarsely. 'Now's our chance! Accept, Gemma, and we can be rid of the wizards for ever!'

Phelan stared at the Princess in disbelief. 'You're serious, aren't you?'

Rowanne sat absolutely straight in her chair. 'Perfectly. And why not? We have the Ring Fire, and surely that is more powerful than the Blue Magic. What have we to fear?'

M'Kinnik gave a small signal to his companions. 'We did not come here to listen to you squabbling amongst yourselves. You have until sunset tonight. If the Challenge isn't accepted, then we have no choice but to declare war on Harflorum. Then any deaths will be on your heads. It will not be our fault; you will have had the choice to take the peaceful and honourable way out! Good day.' And with that he swept his great fur cloak around him and walked out of the room, without even waiting to be dismissed or bowing to the King and the Fire Wielder. Fleabag hissed as the Throne Room doors were shut behind the backs of the retreating wizards.

'Well!' declared Fleabag, crawling out from under Rowanne's cloak and jumping onto the table. 'By my whiskers, I declare that of all the blackmailing rats I have ever seen, they take the prize!' The cat jumped up onto the polished oak table and began to pace up and down. ‘How disgusting, how dishonourable, how, how…’

‘How much are your claws scratching the wood?’ Gemma chided, lifting the cat onto her lap. His hackles were raised and his great lantern eyes glowed as if they were live coals in his scraggy face. ‘Let me go after them, Gemma! I’ll show them, I’ll scratch their nasty blue eyes and pee on their spell books, I’ll…’

‘You’ll do nothing of the sort,’ Gemma said firmly. ‘In all seriousness, what do you think, Phelan?’

The King leaned back in his chair and sighed. ‘Well, legally, they have every right to do this. The fact that they *believe* we are bad rulers is enough for them to issue the Challenge. They don’t need permission or a provable case. The proof will be in their success.’

‘Or failure,’ Fleabag added sourly.

Gemma looked at her old friend Rowanne. ‘Why do you think it’s such a good idea?’

‘Well, as I said, it’s obvious. The Ring Fire is so much stronger than the Blue Magic and it cannot be won or taken anyway. It is the gift of the Fire Giver, so I don’t see that a Challenge can be a problem. Let us accept, prove our point, then settle down to peaceful lives, knowing the question of who should be King and Fire Wielder is settled for ever. I, for one, have a great deal to do at Erbwenneth, and I would like to get on with it.’

‘Why are you convinced it will be so easy, Rowanne? We almost failed twice before.’ Gemma wished she could have Rowanne’s courage when danger threatened. Her friend was a trained warrior, but, for her part, Gemma still felt more at home in the kitchen than handling affairs of State or working with the Ring Fire in a real crisis.

Rowanne leaned across the table. 'Think about it. What happened to the Blue Magic when Domnall fell into his own spell?'

'Everything turned to blue ash,' Phelan replied, looking perplexed.

'Exactly!' Rowanne replied enthusiastically. 'And the ash?'

'It blew away across the sea,' Gemma replied.

'So the Blue Magic must be very weak. Even a wizard could not collect up all the specks of dust from everywhere, unless their powers were very great, and they can't be...'

'Because the Blue Magic blew away, so their power is weakened. I see,' Phelan said thoughtfully.

Gemma said nothing, but stared hard at the palms of her hands. 'The Ring Fire looks rather odd today, but maybe it's because I'm tired. I wish they would give us more time. How real would their threat of war be?' She looked across at Rowanne.

The Princess was trying hard to contain her excitement at the possibility of getting to Porthwain so easily. Secretly, she could not wait to take up the wizards' offer of going to the University. 'Give me leave to go, Gemma, and I will assess the situation. We could visit Porthwain and talk with their advisers about the Challenge, without saying yes or no. Then, once there, I could find out all sorts of things about their strategic strength.'

Phelan and Gemma exchanged glances. 'I'm not happy about you going, Rowanne,' Gemma said. 'I still feel there is a great danger very close to you.'

The Princess looked offended. She pursed her lips and scowled. 'I am a knight of many years' experience. I think

I know how to look after myself. I am certain I can stall the decision for a few weeks at least. It's time we're buying, and knowledge. If we rush a decision we'll make a mistake that we'll regret deeply for a very long time to come.' She squeezed the little crystal ball as she spoke, and wondered why the stone remained so cold in her hand. But she did not look; she did not want the others to see it.

Gemma nodded and rose to her feet. 'I will consult the Ring Fire.'

The King beckoned to his equerry. 'Summon my ministers. I need an urgent meeting in half an hour.'

Fleabag jumped down from the table onto the floor. 'And I will nose around the stables and see whether the wizards have any intelligent horses with them. Horses tend to know everything that's worth knowing. I'll see what I can find out.'

'We will meet here just before sunset then,' Phelan said.

In an upstairs room, Kern cowered well away from the window. He knew M'Kinnik was mind-searching for him, but the Princess had the crystal ball. Kern did not strictly need the stone. He had only to open his mind. The ball simply helped him to focus. But now he did not want to be found.

He had not even looked at the new violin he had been given. Miserably he fingered the fragments of his old one that a servant had salvaged for him. He dabbled a brush into a pot of wood glue and plotted revenge.

6

The 'Sending'

'The wizards conduct a fair fight? By my paws and whiskers, that'll be the day!' Fleabag grumbled as he sat on the window sill of Gemma's room. 'Anyway, I don't know how we can answer their Challenge by sunset. There are thick clouds everywhere, and it's beginning to snow. No one can see the sun setting at all.' He twitched his tail irritably.

'It'd be about as fair a fight as I would expect from *you*,' Gemma retorted.

Fleabag sniffed. 'My dear wife Tabitha says I am the most honourable mouser she knows. I *always* wait until the dear creatures have eaten before I pounce. Even a condemned rodent is entitled to its last meal, I always say!'

'Rubbish!' Gemma snorted. 'What you mean is you wait until the poor things are nice and fat before you gobble them up!'

'Well, if the kitchen staff fed me properly, I wouldn't need to hunt to keep a fur coat over my poor old bones!' he sighed. 'I really am wearing away to nothing; Tabitha says so.'

Gemma stretched out an arm and scooped her old friend onto her lap. 'You're fed well enough, you old rascal. You should be living in luxurious retirement and leaving your kittens and grandkittens to keep the mouse population down.'

Fleabag growled his deep, rolling purr and turned his barrel-like tummy upwards, demanding to be stroked. 'But the long and the short of it is, I don't trust those wizards further than the length of a shrew's tail. That fiddle player Kern is involved, but he doesn't *smell* bad. Rowanne is in danger, and something in her pocket *does* smell decidedly bad!'

'What do you mean, "in her pocket"?'

'Dunno.' The cat gave a wild squirm and jumped up to the window sill again. 'It just does.'

Phelan looked at the darkening skies. 'It must be nearly sunset. What is our decision?'

Gemma opened her hands and looked at the tiny glow of Ring Fire that nestled in her palms. 'Something *is* wrong. Fleabag got no sense out of the wizards' horses whatsoever. It could be that they are all under a spell of stupidity, or they are particularly "dumb beasts". Either way, he found out nothing from them.'

'They were really strange!' Fleabag added. 'They just looked straight through me as if I didn't exist. They really gave me the shivers, I can tell you!'

'Anyway,' Gemma continued, 'I get the feeling that it would be a good idea to go to Porthwain. I'm certain that this Challenge idea is a trap, but I do feel that the Ring Fire wants us to go. Perhaps to put paid to the wizards once and for all.'

'I think the same,' Phelan nodded. 'But my ministers have come up with an interesting twist to the Challenge. Apparently, by law, if we accept, we also have the right to set three trials of our own. This means that even if we fail the wizards' trials, if they fail ours as well, they cannot claim the crown or any position or title anywhere. The whole thing will be thrown completely open, for they will be deemed to be unfit challengers.'

Gemma smiled. 'That's good. So we accept Rowanne's plan that we should send an emissary to Porthwain. We will say we wish to discuss the Challenge, but without accepting or rejecting it. This will give us time to try to understand what is happening and how the Ring Fire wants us to handle it.'

'Agreed,' Phelan said. 'What do you say, Fleabag?'

The cat looked down from his perch. 'I agree too. But whom should we send?'

'Rowanne wants to go, but I'm sure it's too dangerous for her,' Gemma said thoughtfully. 'She has never really understood why the Blue Magic can't be fought with swords and shields.'

Phelan stroked his beard and wrinkled his forehead. 'Neither you nor I can go until the twelve days of the Fire Festival are over. There's so much to do...'

'Forget the Fire Festival,' Fleabag interrupted urgently, peering out of the window. 'Look down there in the distance, beyond the gates... It's Rowanne, I'd recognize the way she sits on a horse anywhere. And who's on that second horse, behind her?'

Gemma gasped. 'By the shape of that peculiar basket across his back, I'd say it must be Kern, the fiddle player!'

Gemma and Phelan dashed from the room, followed hotly by Fleabag, running as fast as his three legs allowed.

Phelan called to a guard to send out soldiers to stop the travellers. But as they reached the great doors, the Captain of the Guard met them, quite out of breath. 'We cannot stop them, your Highness; all the horses have been lamed and the palace gates have been jammed shut, though we cannot work out how.'

Phelan and Gemma exchanged glances. 'The wizards! Where are they?'

The Captain shook his head and shrugged. 'They have gone too, Sire. In fact, it's very odd. They left so suddenly, no one saw them go. There weren't even tracks in the snow. In fact, no one saw them arrive either. They were just here, then they were gone!'

Gemma felt herself go white. 'It was all a "sending".'

'A what?' asked Phelan, bemused.

'It was a sending – an illusion. The wizards weren't really here at all. They sent images of themselves. That was how they managed to turn up just at the most awkward time possible. They must have smuggled something into the palace by which they could watch us, and scry our movements.'

'That's probably what stank in Rowanne's pocket!' Fleabag added. 'I thought it was rather worse than dog-breath. Humph!'

'But it would also explain why you could get no sense from their horses. They weren't really there either. They just sent us illusions of horses, so we wouldn't suspect anything until it was all too late! I wonder if that *was*

Kern riding with Rowanne?' Gemma beckoned to a maid standing nearby. 'Go up to the guest quarters where the boy musician was staying, and bring him to me.'

'Oh, I can tell you now, your Ladyship,' the girl curtseyed. 'He's gone. The Princess Rowanne came and demanded he went with her, urgent-like, about half an hour ago. I had to fetch food and wine for the journey. They seemed in a terrible hurry, and the boy was kicking up a fuss. But the Princess showed him something, and he quietened down, all of a sudden. After that, he went meek as a lamb.'

'Did you see what she showed the boy? Quick, it's important,' Phelan demanded.

'No, your Highness. I was packing saddlebags on the other side of the room. But whatever it was, it was definitely a nasty blue colour. I glimpsed that for sure.'

Gemma bit her lip and frowned. 'Is there anything else you can remember, anything at all?'

'No, your Ladyship,' the girl replied, 'except… except one thing. I think what he was screaming about was his fiddle. The Princess wouldn't let him take it. There was a really posh violin in there, but that wasn't what he was fussing about. He wanted the old broken one. He left it behind when the Princess calmed him down, though.'

'What happened to it? Can you remember?' Gemma asked urgently.

The girl blushed. 'Begging your pardon, ma'am, and I hope I didn't do nothing wrong, but I took it upstairs for my little brother. It's only a bit broke, and my brother's always wanted a fiddle.'

Gemma sighed with relief. 'Good. Fetch it, and you will be given the other violin for your brother.'

The girl ran, and Phelan looked puzzled. 'Why is an old broken fiddle so important?'

'It's just that Kern loved it. It was probably the only thing he had in the world. Perhaps someone he cared about gave it to him. Who knows? It obviously meant more to him than just something to play to earn money. He's a very sad boy. If we can give him back a bit of happiness then that's what we must do.

'But first things first: we must get these gates open.'

And with that, she strode to the main entrance. Without hesitating she circled the locks on the huge iron gate-catches with the sign of the Ring Fire, and one by one they snapped apart. Similarly, the horses responded to her touch. 'There was nothing wrong with them,' she told the amazed stable hand. 'They were spellbound, that's all.'

'What do we do now?' asked Phelan. 'It's too dark and cold to go after them tonight.'

Gemma looked up at the swirling snow falling against the bitter blackness. 'But they won't get far either, even with the Blue Magic to help them. The boy has none, and we don't know how much Rowanne carries. I suspect not much. Tonight, we get some sleep, and at first light we set off after them.'

7

In Pursuit

Kern said nothing as he rode, day after miserable day, next to the Princess. The snow had soon turned to rain, and the countryside was grey and muddy. High above in the cold, dark skies crows circled endlessly, calling their lonely cries into the wind.

The boy hung his head, pulled his thick cloak tightly around him and kept pace. He felt a deep sense of foreboding and loneliness. He tried to think about how delighted he had been when the Princess had told him he was to accompany her to Porthwain. He told himself he would surely get his freedom when he delivered her to the Chancellor. He had been frightened that the Fire Wielder and the King would dissuade her from going, but it had all been so easy!

But these thoughts did little to lift his mood. Kern was angry. The Princess had not allowed him to stop even for a few seconds to pick up his violin. And he had almost had it mended, too! He would never forgive her for that. He would return to get his vengeance on Gemma and the King some other time. He ground his teeth and clenched the horse's reins in his icy hands. At least he would see his mother soon, and they would both be free from the wizards' service for ever. Moreover, things could be worse. He had arrived at Harflorum hungry and on foot. Now he was returning on a horse, well fed, and with good clothes on his back.

For her part, the Princess wanted Kern alive and well when they reached Porthwain. The boy's message had been a strange one. If the invitation to spend time at the University was genuine, then it was important that the wizards' emissary must appear to have been honoured and well cared for. If, on the other hand, she was being made a fool of, she would slit Kern's throat. She had no qualms about that.

Rowanne had so many reasons for making this journey, even she was not sure which one was most important to her.

On the one hand, she was fairly sure that the boy was some sort of bait, and if anyone was going to walk into a trap it must be herself and not Gemma or Phelan, for in her heart she was still loyal to the King and the Fire Wielder. She cared very much about them both. Gemma wasn't much more than a child, and she had been through enough terrible battles. Phelan was needed to concentrate on being the King and attending to matters of State. There was much to be done to maintain justice in the land. Rowanne felt it was *her* turn to fight a battle to protect the Ring Fire – by whatever means possible. If she could learn some of the secrets of the Blue Magic, she could tell Gemma and use her knowledge to help the Ring Fire win this Challenge and settle matters in the land, once and for all.

She could not understand why Phelan and Gemma were so scared of the Challenge anyway. If the Ring Fire was on their side, who could be against them? She had left Harflorum suddenly, because she was convinced that the time had come to be decisive. She wasn't going to wait to be mocked by the wizards or told to be patient by Gemma. *She* would accept the Challenge on everyone's behalf, and the more of the Blue Magic's secrets she knew to help her win, the better it would be for the Ring Fire!

And, as the wizards' message had said, it was also true that she had always felt passed over by the Ring Fire. Whenever she had tried to use her sword and her battle skills to defend what she knew to be true, she was always told 'this isn't that sort of battle'. What did Gemma know? This was Rowanne's big chance to prove her own worth.

The journey took ten days, for the roads were slushy and difficult. Kern was exhausted and often dozed in the saddle. But Rowanne never seemed to sleep. At night, when they stopped at an inn or a lodging house, she would eat her meal and find a quiet corner. There she would unwrap the blue crystal and stare into it until dawn, unspeaking and unmoving as the pale blue glow bathed her face and hands. Kern closed his mind tightly and turned away, with bed covers over his head. He did not want to know… He did *not* want to know…!

Rowanne had been to Porthwain before, and had been drugged and charmed into a deep sleep by the old Chancellor. He had used ruthless spells to take her mind from her body so she would betray the Ring Fire. She had almost died. Rowanne's ambition to be taken seriously as a Champion of the Ring Fire was so great she pushed all those terrible memories aside. She did not realize that her education in the Blue Magic was already well under way, and that, as she stared into the crystal ball, the tiny speck of blue that had caught in her eye on Spider Island had begun to grow and spread within her like fine tendrils of mould. Rowanne's skin was already taking on a strange blue tinge, and her eyes glowed with an unearthly ice-blue stare. By the time she had arrived, the Princess Rowanne de Montiland was already nearly an arch wizard.

The delegation of soldiers, dressed in ceremonial dark- and light-blue uniforms, that greeted her at the gates of the town and escorted her to the university did not surprise her. She had foreseen it.

Back at Harflorum, delay after delay prevented Gemma, Fleabag and Phelan from pursuing Rowanne. Each problem was petty and annoying and had the mark of the wizards' work. But the delays cost three days.

Phelan and Gemma delegated their Fire Festival duties, and Fleabag spent extra time with Tabitha and the kittens. Phelan would only accept a bodyguard of three men and his sergeant at arms. The more travellers there were, the more equipment and food would be needed. Speed was of the essence. The Prime Minister complained bitterly, and Rowanne's faithful squire Aidan begged to come along, but he was refused as well. Even Fleabag did not try to smuggle any of his kittens into a saddlebag this time.

At dawn on the fourth day, six swift horses were saddled and four more were loaded with essentials for the journey. Gemma let the Ring Fire burn for a few moments in her hands to cheer them all up, then she swung into the saddle and dug her heels into her horse's flanks. The great gates of Harflorum swung wide, and the travellers set off.

Persistent rain kept their roads clear, but made everyone feel miserable. Day after day, they rode as hard as they could without exhausting the horses. They stopped at farms and inns, and often heard that Rowanne and Kern had been that way only a few days earlier.

Every evening, when they had found lodging, Gemma watched the Ring Fire in her hands, with Fleabag and Phelan either side, caught in the beauty of its glow for an hour or more. It gave them the heart to keep going.

'Can you tell what Rowanne is doing?' Phelan asked one night as they neared Porthwain. 'Are we too late?'

Gemma shook her head and folded her hands so the fire was enclosed. 'No, the Ring Fire's not like the Blue Magic. I can't see what *I* think I need to see. Only what it wants to show me. Most of the time I don't see anything, but I can usually tell whether something is right or wrong. I have been trying to surround Rowanne with the glow of the Fire, but it keeps slipping away for some reason. It won't stick. It works for Kern, though. He's safe, I'm sure, but I'm very worried about Rowanne.'

Phelan tugged at his beard and frowned. 'Do you remember when she was in that terrible trance-like sleep after she went to Porthwain the first time? When you tried to put the Ring Fire on her to waken her, it kept slipping away then as well?'

'Yes I do,' Gemma sighed. 'And that is what is worrying me. It's all too similar. But this time I don't think they want to take her mind from her. The wizards have a different plan. She seemed awfully keen to go when she heard about the Challenge. I think the best thing we can do is to get to Porthwain as quickly as possible, before too much damage is done.'

Fleabag jumped up onto Gemma's lap and began to scratch himself hard, spraying a few fleas onto his friend's clothes.

'Ugh, you're *disgusting*!' she groaned, and tried to put him down.

'Well, if you don't want to hear what I've got to say, I shall go and tell it to the mice behind the skirting board.' Fleabag bristled his fur and began to stalk away on his three legs, head held high and whiskers splayed.

Phelan scooped the cat up and peered into his eyes. 'Well, you *are* disgusting... But you do have your uses. What is it that you remember?'

'Rowanne said something about a message...'

'I remember that too. Did you find out what it was?' Phelan asked.

The cat shook his head. 'No, but she did say that Kern had delivered it.'

'So he *was* a spy from the wizards?' Phelan gasped.

'Not a willing one,' Gemma replied. 'He was terrified when he heard that the wizards had arrived. But after the Fire Festival, in the Throne Room, I was talking to Kern and he scurried off, saying he had to deliver a message.'

'There was the awful smell that hung around Rowanne's pocket. I think Kern must have given her something from the wizards,' Fleabag added.

'Something that they could then use to create their sending with!' Gemma opened her hand and looked into the tiny speck of Ring Fire that burned there. 'I am certain it *is* right for us to go to Porthwain, but we will have to be very careful.'

Fleabag leaped from Phelan's lap onto the hearthrug and curled up. 'And to be prepared for this great adventure, I am going to get some beauty sleep. I feel in my whiskers that this is going to be a bit like swimming in a bowl of goldfish who are all twenty times my size, and all bent on revenge.'

'But,' Gemma added thoughtfully, 'who knows? Just as there are probably little bits of Blue Magic in our own palace at Harflorum, we might find the Ring Fire burning somewhere in the University. I can't imagine that there can be anywhere within this world that is entirely without hope.'

Fleabag grunted through his thick tangled fur, 'I'm not sure about that. I've munched a fair few goldfish in my time.' And he went to sleep.

8

Rowanne the Wizard

Kern wasn't particularly surprised to find himself being ignored in Porthwain. He didn't exactly expect the blue carpet rolled out for *his* arrival.

But what upset him deeply, was that his mother was missing. The kitchen staff she usually worked with said that she had disappeared soon after he had left. He went to the attic room they used to share, and found all their things were gone. The room was occupied by two foul-mouthed and extremely smelly stable hands who neither knew nor cared about Kern or his mother.

Kern tried to see M'Kinnik to ask if he knew anything, for his mother *was* a wife of the old Chancellor even though she had always been badly treated. He also wanted to claim his long-promised freedom.

But however often he called on the Chancellor's secretary's office door, he was always told that his

Holiness was out or busy, or to come back next week, or month, or year.

Finally, he was given a huge pile of papers to fill in (in triplicate) about his mother and himself. He was told that once that information was on file, procedures for tracing his mother's whereabouts and considering his application for release from the University's service could be put into motion.

Kern didn't believe any of it, but he took the papers up to the loft above the barn where he now slept.

But, as he crossed the stableyard, he saw a strange sight – one he had never quite expected to see in Porthwain. Ten horses were being led across the cobbles. They were fine animals, though very tired and sweaty. There was nothing unusual in that, but what did catch his eye was the Ring Fire symbol, embroidered in gold and red silk on the saddlecloths.

Letting go of his papers – which landed in the nearest horse-trough – Kern ran back inside and crept along a top corridor until he came to the servants' entrance to the Great Hall.

There, in full view, were Gemma the Fire Wielder and King Phelan, being received most politely by M'Kinnik, the Chancellor of All Wizards. And sitting smugly at their feet was Fleabag, the irrepressible three-legged talking cat!

Fleabag spotted Kern as well. Knowing that he created a stir everywhere he went in Porthwain, he got up on his three legs and calmly strolled across the hall to where Kern peered around the doorway. 'Excuse me,' the cat called back to his friends. 'I've found a rather fascinating mouse.'

The Chancellor blanched at the sound of the cat's

voice, for all the wizards had a particular terror of Fleabag. An old prophecy had warned that Porthwain's downfall would be caused by a Fire Maiden and a black cat. Even after the Battle of Porthwain when Gemma and Fleabag had defeated the old Chancellor, everyone still held a deep-seated conviction that all black cats were evil, though the city was still standing and the Blue Magic was still alive.

Fleabag didn't care. He slunk around the door-jamb. 'Hello,' he mewed. Before Kern could move, Fleabag had leaped into the boy's arms and was licking his face like a long lost friend.

'Ugh!' Kern tried to push him away. But the cat was not going to allow himself to be put down just yet.

'Come to our room after dinner,' he whispered, 'and I guarantee you will have a very pleasant surprise.' Then he jumped down and stalked back into the reception room where polite speeches of welcome were being made. There he sat down in the very middle of the room, burped extremely loudly, and began to wash.

The wizards glanced nervously at one another, but the Chancellor just smirked and complimented his visitors on having such an entertaining pet.

Phelan bowed and requested leave for them all to go to their rooms, as they, and their *friend* the cat, were very tired.

Upstairs Phelan and Gemma unpacked and then met in the small circular study that had been assigned to them. Fleabag had already taken command of the hearthrug in front of the fire. He did not look happy. 'Isn't it strange how a suite of rooms was ready for us? This fire has been lit all morning, I'd say.'

'They were expecting us,' Gemma agreed.

'I'm certain of it,' Phelan replied. 'But they were talking as if the Challenge had been accepted and was due to start in a few days' time. How can that be?'

'It must be Rowanne. What on earth has she done?' Gemma groaned.

'I expect we will find out soon,' Fleabag replied. 'But the good news is that I've found Kern. I've told him to come up and see us after dinner.'

'And did he say he'd come?' Phelan asked.

'Well,' the cat replied, 'he looked sort of worried, but I think he will.'

Just then, a servant knocked on the door. 'I have a humble request from the Princess Rowanne de Montiland, wizard of this University, if it please you, to meet her in the library when you have refreshed yourselves.'

Phelan thanked the girl and shut the door carefully behind her. '*Wizard of this University*?'

Gemma had her right hand resting on the table in front of her and was staring at the Ring Fire burning there. 'Yes. Things are getting very dangerous indeed.'

An hour later, Phelan, Fleabag and Gemma crossed the piazza where they had once rescued Rowanne from the burning hall after defeating the old Chancellor. Everything was rebuilt now, and there was no sign of fire on the milky white stone of the wide columned entryway.

On the other side of the square was an equally grand building housing the library. Servants ushered the visitors into the main room, a long cool gallery, lit by many windows all along the walls. The books were arranged in wide bays, with ancient gold script describing the contents of each section. Every bay was three or four metres high, and filled floor to ceiling with books, all leather-bound and very old. Strange sliding ladders hung from rails at the top of each bookcase, so the volumes on the uppermost shelves could be reached.

As the visitors stared up at the ceiling they saw that above the ground floor there were two more galleried floors, similarly filled with books, all the way up to a finely vaulted ceiling high above them.

Just then Rowanne's familiar voice called down cheerfully from above the balustrade around the top floor. 'Oh good, you're here at last! I knew you couldn't be far away. Just a moment, I'll be down!' And with that she disappeared.

Gemma and the others felt a moment's relief to be greeted so warmly, but their hearts sank, and their skin went quite cold when they saw their friend *floating* down the ornate spiral staircase, one hand resting lightly on the gently curving banister. Her feet hovered just above the steps as the uncanny silence of her motion was broken only by the light swishing of her clothing brushing the wrought ironwork at the side.

Rowanne was dressed in fine robes of dark- and light-blue, with her long black hair brushed loosely over her shoulders. She looked very beautiful, although her skin and eyes were quite blue, and even her lips were purple.

Fleabag surveyed her for a moment and put his head on one side. 'You couldn't possibly want me for a fur collar now, Rowanne. I'm entirely the wrong colour – I wouldn't match your skin!'

The Princess stooped down to pick him up and laughed as she rubbed him under the chin. '*Dear* Fleabag, you are always so amusing. What a pleasure to see you all here. Now, we have some talking to do.' And she put the cat down.

He immediately began to wash and scratch all over, as if he had been touched by something disgusting. 'Ugh, I smell of poodles now!' he muttered.

But Rowanne ignored him, and gestured to a small reading table in a corner by a window.

'I am so pleased you could come. The Challenge is fixed for three days hence. But I expect you are all prepared and raring to go, aren't you?'

Gemma suddenly stood and leaned across the table. 'Rowanne. Snap out of it! What *are* you blabbering on about? You know we agreed not to accept the Challenge. The plan was to stall and play for time. You aren't even supposed to *be* here! It was quite wrong of you to accept the Challenge on our behalf. It can't hold as an acceptance. You had no authority.'

Rowanne shook her head and smiled. 'But we're committed. What's the harm? The Ring Fire cannot possibly fail, especially with me on its side.'

Phelan and Gemma exchanged glances. There was a moment's silence, then, 'What do you mean, exactly?' Gemma ventured.

Rowanne grinned and winked. 'I've learned loads of their secrets. They've been teaching me to become a wizard.'

'We did notice,' Fleabag muttered. 'It sort of shows, you know.'

'Well,' Rowanne grinned. 'The joke is, that although I've been here working for the Ring Fire, *they* think I'm working for them, and that I'm going to be a good wizard, and a true member of the University. I've been working really hard during the last few days, and I've qualified already.'

'But it must take years, surely!' Phelan protested.

'Normally, yes,' Rowanne replied. 'But you remember that speck I caught in my eye after the Battle of Spider Island? Apparently it was a tiny bit of Blue Magic ash, and because it's *inside* me it works really fast. So I've read the whole library and done all the practical work in less than a week!'

Gemma went pale. So that speck of dust had been Blue Magic. She stared at her old friend in horror. 'The *whole* library?'

'Yes, it's dead easy, look.' Ignoring the ladders, she floated up to the top of one of the bays, and picked out a book at random. 'All I have to do is hold the book to my head for a few seconds, and I can read and memorize the lot. Look,' she passed the book over to Phelan, 'test me.'

Phelan looked at the book. '*The Logik of Transformation Described and Discussed*, by Professor Cum-thidymus.'

'Go on,' Rowanne urged. 'Open it, any page, any line...'

Phelan opened the book. It crackled as the dry leather moved. 'Er, tell me what's on page 276, third line up from the bottom.'

Rowanne laughed, 'Oh yes, that's the very witty part where he proposes that transformation of one object into another is perfectly possible, because in essence, nothing really exists anyway. The line you are referring to says: "I would therefore argue that the way towards total transformation lies less in the perception of the object, and more in the question of existence versus non-existence." '

Gemma raised an eyebrow in Phelan's direction. 'She's quite right,' he said quietly.

Rowanne clapped her hands in almost girlish glee. 'Test me on another, oh, do try me again!'

'No, no, that's fine, we believe you,' Gemma replied.

'I insist.' Rowanne floated across to another bookcase. Show me a book, and I'll get it down for you,' and she started to drift upwards towards one of the upper galleries.

'Oh do stop bobbing up and down like that, you're making me quite seasick,' Fleabag begged.

'I'll choose a book I can reach in the normal way,' Phelan replied, and he pulled a volume from just behind where he was sitting.

'If I tell you the title, you should be able to know what's in it already. Or do you have to hold it first?'

'I've read them all. Just tell me the title.'

'*Obscure Parameters of Astrology*...' Then he pushed the book back, brushing musty red leather dust from his fingers. 'Look, Rowanne. This is wasting time. We believe you. What did you mean by saying "the Ring Fire cannot fail with me on its side"? That can't be right. The Ring Fire is good and the Blue Magic is evil. The Ring Fire would never want or need help from a wizard.'

Rowanne grinned. 'Look, it's so obvious. You three are so cautious, but the Ring Fire always wins, and now I know all the wizards' secrets, I can let you in on how they are planning to do things, so we cannot possibly fail. I really am going to make a difference for once. I'm going to be *doing* something, instead of standing on the sidelines while you two do all the clever stuff. This time, *I'm* going to be the Champion!'

9

The Three Trials

Later that night, Phelan and Gemma were poring over a parchment scroll containing the three trials of the wizards' Challenge and Fleabag was busy running from bedchamber to bedchamber, testing the respective beds, to see whom he was going to grace with his presence for the night. At last he gave up, sat on the middle of the scroll and began to wash. Just as Phelan was about to put him firmly onto the floor, Kern knocked timidly on the door.

Gemma opened the door and smiled. 'Good to see you, Kern. How are you?'

The boy grunted and shrugged. He wasn't going to start telling *her* how he had spent the afternoon drying out the thick pile of forms he had fished out of the horse trough. He had tried to fill them in but the paper was all stuck together, and the ink had run. He had added to the wetness with a few tears of anger. He was utterly miserable. He had almost not come to the study, but somehow he knew that, enemies or not, they might be kinder to him than anyone else around.

'Come in!' smiled Phelan. 'We have a surprise for you!' He went to his saddlebag, brought out an oddly shaped bundle wrapped in green velvet and handed it to Kern.

The velvet fell away to reveal his fiddle. His *own* fiddle! But it was expertly mended. The boy looked from Phelan to Gemma and then to the cat in delighted amazement. 'How… Why?' he stuttered.

Gemma laughed. 'We knew how much it meant to you. We were badly delayed setting off for Porthwain, so while we were waiting I asked the palace luthier to look at it for you. He wanted to put another coat of varnish on it, but we didn't have time to wait. If you come our way again, it'll be done.'

'And it's been restrung,' Fleabag added, 'with spun silk from the giant gaudy moth. No catgut!' he added triumphantly as he jumped onto the table.

Kern's eyes opened as wide as they could possibly go. 'But those are the best strings possible!' He gulped. 'That will cost a fortune, I haven't got that sort of money!' And he put the violin on the table and pushed it reluctantly away from him. 'I can't take it.'

Phelan smiled. 'It's a gift. But if you're really worried about paying, come and play for us one evening.'

Suddenly Kern snatched up the violin and bolted for the door muttering, 'Thanks,' as he ran.

'What's the hurry? Stay and have supper with us,' Gemma urged. 'Play a little now if you'd like. We haven't heard how it sounds with its new strings.'

Kern narrowed his eyes and stared at her suspiciously. 'Why?'

'Why what?' asked Phelan.

'Why should you do this for me? You must want something. Perhaps you think I'm going to betray the wizards to you. Well, I'm not. Not as long as they've got my mother!' and he ran out of the room crying.

'There's an awful lot more to that boy than meets the eye,' Phelan remarked as the door slammed. 'And I would very much like to know what.'

'But meanwhile, we mustn't be distracted from the matter of the Challenge,' Gemma replied. 'We have serious problems ahead.'

'But I'm not sure that Kern *is* a distraction,' Fleabag added. 'Something in my whiskers tells me that he is very important to whatever is going on. In the morning I will ask around and see what I can find out. Obviously, there are no kitchen-cats to chat to, and I refuse to sink to the level of asking the butler's dog. But I might allow a few local rats to live if they provide me with information...'

Gemma shook her head. 'You are incorrigible, cat. I am not sure whether I should commend you or berate you for your murderous tactics!'

'Oh, commend, of course!' Fleabag exclaimed with a delighted grin. 'I expect at least a second knighthood by the time this adventure is over, and another golden earring, of course... But I think it should have a diamond-studded field mouse hanging from it this time, don't you?'

Phelan laughed as he tried to push Fleabag off the parchment scroll that spelled out the Challenge. 'I'm not so sure that the local rodent population would agree with you. Now move, please. We must concentrate. We have only three days to try to work out what the wizards may be up to and to sort out our tactics. Gemma and I have discussed the possibility of refusing to accept the Challenge, but it seems that Rowanne's acceptance is considered binding, as she is the legal ruler of one of the Kingdom's provinces in her own right. Withdrawing at this stage is apparently the same as conceding defeat. But the good news is that the wizards have agreed to us challenging them as well – although they could hardly have refused.'

'I know the Ring Fire will see us through,' Gemma sighed, 'but I do find it daunting facing hundreds of wizards with nothing more than a shred of trust and a glimmer of light between my fingers.'

'Nothing wrong with that,' Fleabag retorted. 'Anyway, what does the parchment say? Let's know the worst before we start worrying.'

'Well, if you move your fur, I can read it,' Phelan replied.

Fleabag sniffed and moved.

'Day one,' Phelan read, running his finger along the line of ornate, illuminated script: *'The trial of strength. Each contestant may challenge the opponent to a trial of physical skill and stamina.'*

'Have you any idea what that will be?' Gemma asked.

'Yes, they've told me: it's broadsword fighting.'

Gemma shook her head and Fleabag turned as pale as a black cat can. 'Do you think we dare ask Rowanne to take that trial for us? She's the greatest sword fighter in the Kingdom, without a doubt.'

Phelan sat back in his chair and bit his lip. 'I know, but

I'm not sure I want Rowanne doing anything for us at the moment. Do you? It's not that I don't trust her, it's just that... well, she doesn't *feel* like Rowanne any more.'

Gemma opened her hands where the small glimmer of golden Ring Fire burned in each palm. 'I just can't believe she's turned evil – not *wholly*. She's just infatuated with the idea of power and is being very silly...'

'But what induced her to accept the Challenge on our behalf anyway? Do you think it was really so the Ring Fire could win once and for all as she says, or was there some other motive? Where are her loyalties? Would she be fighting for us or...' Phelan hesitated. 'I've just had an awful thought. Do you think she might, willingly or unwillingly, be the *wizards'* champion? She's so famous they must know that no knight or soldier in the Kingdom could beat her.'

Gemma and Phelan exchanged worried glances, but Fleabag just began to scratch, sending fleas all over the place. 'Speak for yourself. I'd match my claws against a rusty old broadsword any day of the week! In fact, give me leave, Phelan, and *I'll* be your champion.'

Phelan's face broke into a broad grin. From where he was seated he swept a bow from the waist. 'Sir Scrag-Belly, what king could expect a more noble offer? My only reason for refusing you is that it might be argued that the match would be unequal.'

Fleabag grinned back. 'You mean she might be daunted by having me as a foe? Spoken like a true and honourable King, Sire. However, I have always wanted to repay a few personal debts owed to the Princess, and the opportunity would give me great pleasure...'

'But what if it *isn't* Rowanne?' Gemma asked earnestly. 'What if it is some other knight? He or she might complain that your multitude of claws was unfair against one mere iron sword?'

'True,' conceded Fleabag. 'It will have to be you then, Phelan.'

The King nodded. 'I suppose so. I have worked hard at learning sword skills but I don't know if I will be good enough. Anyway, if I live through that round, I'll challenge them to running. I was always pretty good at that. And if their champion *is* Rowanne, I'll win. She can never get her breathing right in a full-length race.'

'But we still don't know for certain that she'll be working against us,' Gemma added sadly.

'We must be practical,' the King added. 'We don't know she is working entirely *for* us either, despite all the things she was saying about finding out the wizards' secrets to use against them.'

Gemma looked sadly down into her hands where two tiny points of the Ring Fire burned. 'I wish I could understand what the Fire is saying. It looks so very calm at the moment. I wish it would *tell* me something!'

'It will, in good time,' Phelan smiled, turning to the parchment again. 'Ah, now, Fleabag, here *is* something you can do – *the trial of wisdom*!'

Fleabag raised a whiskery eyebrow. For all his pomposity, he had never thought of himself as being particularly wise. 'You're kidding, of course!' he muttered, slightly apprehensively. 'Gemma or you ought to do that one.'

'No. I'm absolutely serious,' Phelan replied, looking straight at the cat with a very determined expression. 'In any argument, you are the one with all the clever answers. Your tongue is even sharper than your claws. You're quite a wise old hearthrug, you know!'

Fleabag still looked worried. He was not quite certain whether the King was mocking him or not, but ever since the day when they had first met, and Phelan had swung Fleabag by the tail, the cat had always treated his friend with genuine respect.

'What will I have to do? I'm not a great reader, and if someone like Rowanne starts spouting quotations at us like she did earlier, I'm lost!'

'No, I think it will probably be riddles, although they can choose book learning if they want... Just a minute, it says here... blah, blah, blah... yes, riddles it is. *The most noble and ancient art of word cunning*. That's a posh name for riddles, isn't it? Do you know any?'

'One or two,' the cat replied dubiously. 'I'll do it, because you've done me the honour of asking, as my King and all that... but I'll have you know, I'm not happy, not happy at all.' And he jumped down from the table and began to walk towards Gemma's bedroom with drooping head and loosely hanging tail.

Gemma ran after him and picked him up to scratch behind his ears. 'Cheer up, old friend. I'll keep you surrounded by the Ring Fire the whole time. I'm sure the Fire Giver will give you all the wisdom you could ever need. What will your Challenge to them be?'

Fleabag momentarily lost his anxious look and smirked. 'I will set them a puzzle – how to get out of a locked room filled with the fleas of a hundred camels. Beyond that there will be a locked room with the lice of a thousand camel-drivers, then beyond that there will be a locked room with the mange of a hundred thousand mongrel dogs. They have to escape it all with one movement. How?'

Gemma looked amazed and laughed. 'I've no idea, how?'

Fleabag sniffed contemptuously, jumped down and slunk away. 'You'll have to wait to find out. I'm not telling *you*. If you can't work that one out, I can see why the King realized that I am obviously the best choice for this task!' and he disappeared under the hanging folds of the tablecloth.

'You get out by jumping out of the window, that's an old one!' laughed Phelan. Then, as Gemma sat down, he looked serious. 'Day three, of course, is the trial of magical powers. It will be you, or more rightly the Ring Fire against the Blue Magic. Once and for all.'

Gemma leaned her elbows on the table in front of her and hunched her shoulders. Despite three years of working with the Ring Fire, and slowly beginning to understand its ways, the thought of situations like this still terrified her and made her feel small and inadequate. 'This is the one Rowanne really wants to fight for us, isn't it?' she asked miserably. 'She thinks that by learning the secrets of the Blue Magic she can help us... Do you think she really believes it?'

Phelan leaned back and looked at the ceiling. 'Yes, I do. But I also think she's wrong. She can't possibly fight for the Ring Fire with the Blue Magic inside her. It can't be done. She'll have to choose.'

Gemma opened her right hand and stared long and hard at the Ring Fire. 'I don't know what we are going to do, but I know *I* shouldn't fight that battle. I'm certain the Ring Fire has other ideas about how that trial will be met. *My* job is to wait, and watch the Fire burn. Oh, that's the most difficult thing of all – to do nothing!'

And she buried her tired head in her arms. From somewhere outside, the strains of a violin playing a familiar melody seeped in through the shutters.

10

An Offer of Help

For the next two days, Fleabag read every book of riddles he could find, although in the ends of his whiskers and in the tip of his tail he felt that swotting up on witty lines wasn't going to save the day. He was very nervous.

Rowanne often met him in the library, floating up and down in her spooky way, offering him this book and that. But her presence only made him feel uncomfortable, so on the third day he slunk off to the roof tiles where even she did not follow him. There he sat in the wintry sun, peering down at the practice yards below.

There Phelan was working himself into an uncomfortable sweat training with his sergeant at arms.

Just watching all that exercise made Fleabag tired, so he curled up and snuggled his nose under his matted tail. He decided that a well-rested head was probably better than one full of words from wizard's books. Tomorrow would come when it was time to for it to do so. He would let the Ring Fire do the worrying.

Far below Phelan rested on the pommel of his sword and panted. He wiped sweat from his face with his handkerchief and winced. The muscles on the back of his neck were knotted and swollen. Every sinew in his arms and legs screamed for rest. He had worked left- and right-handed, with broadsword in one hand and dagger in the other, then changing, left to right, right to left. He'd tried every sword that he and his sergeant had with him. Nothing felt quite right somehow: the balance was wrong, the hilt was too long or short or the haft was out of true. In the end he felt irritable and tired.

His favourite blade was in the armoury at home. If he had guessed what Rowanne was up to he'd have brought it with him. But he had thought this was going to be a diplomatic mission.

Just as he was about to give up, Rowanne stepped out into the bright winter sunshine of the courtyard. For once, she was dressed in knightly gear of steel armour strapped over a red woollen doublet rather than the long flowing dark- and light-blue robes that made her look so eerily unlike herself.

Without saying a word, she unsheathed her own sword, knelt and handed it to the King, hilt first. 'My sword is yours, my Lord,' she said at last. 'Really,' she added, looking him directly in the eye. 'Take it, it's better than any of the others here. It's your only chance.'

Phelan hesitated. For once, the blue seemed to be fading from the Princess' skin, and almost the flush of her old brown tan seemed to appear across her cheeks. The King took the sword.

'It's all right,' the Princess assured him as she stood. 'It won't bite and it's not enchanted or anything. It's just a very good sword, probably a little light for you, but that's a good thing because you're over-tired.' Then she took one of the other swords that Phelan had been working with and raised it between her eyes in salute. 'Can I help you practice? I can see exactly what you are doing wrong...'

Phelan looked at her. This wasn't magic. This was friendship and loyalty. 'Thank you, I'd be grateful.' He bowed slightly.

Then for the next hour he worked as he had never worked before, sweeping this way and that as the Princess showed her true skill as a warrior – the skill that had once made her a member of the old Queen's bodyguard and one of the most valued knights in Phelan's Kingdom.

As the sun began to lose height and the air began to chill, Rowanne flopped down on a bale of hay and smiled.

It was the old, true Rowanne who was there, with normal blue eyes and deep-tanned skin from her outdoor life. Her grasp was honest and firm as she shook Phelan's hand. 'You will fight well tomorrow. I've managed to discover who they are putting against you in the fight. It's a knight called Grimbold, and he's not a wizard! But watch his left foot. He uses it when you least expect it.'

Then she dropped her gaze and stared at the point of her sword, which she used to scratch the emblem of the Ring Fire on one of the cobbles at her feet.

'I do know what I'm doing,' she said, looking at Phelan again. 'Although I don't know whether I'll live through this. But whatever you see me do, or hear me say, please remember I'm doing it all for the Ring Fire. Someone's got to stand up and face the Blue Magic once and for all, and I'm proud it's me.'

'But not like this,' Phelan began. 'Come and see Gemma and let us help you get rid of the Blue Magic that's taking you over. We can all get through this together, but joining the ranks of the enemy isn't the way. It never has been...'

Suddenly Rowanne turned her head, although Phelan heard no one calling. 'I must go now. Remember what I said about Grimbold.'

Then she saluted the King formally with her sword and turned away. As she did so, she lifted her helmet from her head and pulled off her woollen under-cap, letting her hair tumble over her shoulders. All the blue had gone; it was dark brown again.

Then she turned back and smiled. 'You will use the sword, won't you? Promise!' And she ran inside.

Phelan could not find Gemma in their suite of rooms. He didn't go and look for her because he ached so much all he wanted was a hot bath. Anyway, perhaps it was best to have a quiet think about the changes in Rowanne before he told Gemma his suspicions. If only there was some way of distracting the Princess from the Blue Magic before the Challenge began.

Phelan stayed in his bath for a full hour, trying to remember what Rowanne had taught him about swordsmanship. He would never be a master, he knew that, but he would do his best, and hope that Rowanne was right about Grimbold not being a wizard. He was grateful for the Princess' sword. It was a good one. Although it was a little light and short, it felt as though it belonged in his hand.

As he soaked, he decided that he would save some of his strength from the sword fight for the trial he had set for the wizards – a long sprint. He knew he had a chance to win that. If he exhausted himself in the fight, then lost the race because he was over-tired, he would throw everything away. The best he could hope for was a draw.

The ultimate fate of the Kingdom rested on the trial of magic – the Ring Fire against the wizards' blue power – and although the Ring Fire was indisputably the stronger, would they carry it well, allowing it to flow as it should? Had the whole way the Challenges had come about forced the Ring Fire into a bad position? If this battle was lost, would it mean more Challenges and maybe even wars in the future?

Gemma had steadfastly refused to accept the magical trial, and Rowanne equally steadfastly kept offering to fight the contest on Gemma's behalf. As soon as she left Phelan in the practice yard, Rowanne had changed into her wizard's robes again and cornered Gemma in the library. Her skin had regained its blue tinge almost as soon as she had taken off her armour and turned her thoughts back to magical things. It was as if the real Rowanne was hung in the armoury lockers along with the steel plate greaves and cuirasses, the leather straps and the burnished shields. But the blue-haired woman with purple fingernails was oblivious to her own changes.

Gemma gulped as Rowanne floated along the great room, arms wide, as if to enfold her old friend in an affectionate hug.

'I do wish you wouldn't *do* that,' Gemma muttered, ducking the outstretched blue arms.

'Do what?' Rowanne asked in amazement, not a little hurt at Gemma's evasion.

'*Float* like that. It's disconcerting. What happened to the old Rowanne who liked solid floors, a sturdy horse and a cold iron sword in her hand?'

'But I've changed, Gemma dear. Only for the better, I assure you. I've seen how futile the old ways of fighting for fighting's sake really are. Life is so much more *subtle* than that. Swords are playthings for children.'

'Tell that to the wizards,' Gemma retorted.

'What do you mean?'

'We have been challenged to a sword fight tomorrow, in case you've forgotten – or didn't they tell you what the specific trials were?'

Rowanne tossed her indigo-black hair and laughed lightly. 'Oh that – that's just a formality. I've been helping Phelan train this afternoon, but that's not the serious trial.'

'So we don't have to do it?' Gemma sounded hopeful. There was no point Phelan risking life and limb at the hands of some bloodthirsty knight, probably with an enchanted sword, if it wasn't strictly necessary.

'On the contrary. Three trials are the rule, and three trials must be fought. It's the law.'

'But we didn't accept the Challenge – you did, on our behalf. Why should we fight at all?' Gemma was angry. She felt tricked into the whole situation.

'But you know that I did it for the glory of the Ring Fire so that these silly disputes should be ended, once and for all.' Rowanne smiled condescendingly, 'Anyway, if you don't fight, you'll be deemed to have conceded. Come, be sensible, let me fight the magical trial on your behalf. In fact, if I take on your likeness, no one need even know it's me. I know this terrific transformation spell that makes me look just like you. Even old M'Kinnik doesn't know the difference. I tried it on him for almost half an hour this morning, and he kept talking to me as if I were you. I had to excuse myself in the end, it was getting awkward.'

'You did *what*?' Gemma was furious. 'How dare you impersonate me? You had no right...'

'Calm down,' Rowanne laughed. 'I know what I'm doing. I managed to discover who they're putting against you in the sword fight. I've told Phelan all about him already. It's a knight called Grimbold who's as human as you or I...'

At this Gemma glanced across at her old friend and winced. Rowanne's blueness was getting disconcerting, although she seemed unaware of it. The Fire Wielder shook her head. 'Please stop all this nonsense, Rowanne. Come home and we will see what wisdom the Ring Fire has to fight the wizards on its own terms. The more involved you get in this magic nonsense, the more blue you become, and the more oblivious you are to the truth!'

Rowanne looked at Gemma with total incomprehension. 'What *are* you talking about? *Me, blue*? Look...' and she stretched her arm next to Gemma's own. Gemma winced and wanted to pull her arm away, for a wave of icy blueness blushed across the Princess' skin as they compared arms.

'I'm every bit as pink as you – perhaps a little browner, but that's because of the outdoor life I used to lead.'

'You can't see it, can you?' Gemma gasped, jumping up. Now she was certain she wanted Rowanne to be no part of the Ring Fire's response to the Challenge. 'You really are totally unaware of what's happening to you!' and she started to run out of the library.

'Wait! If you won't let me fight for you, at least let me advise you. I know what spell they are intending to use on the third day...'

But Gemma had gone. She ran along corridor after corridor, heading towards the study and trying very hard not to cry. Her friend was rapidly being taken over by the Blue Magic, for which there was probably no cure. She was certain they were fighting senseless battles in which they would probably all die.

The Ring Fire *would* win, she was still certain of that, but she had no idea how – or when. It all seemed so senseless and such a waste. Suddenly, she had an urge to go outside and breathe some air. She pushed at the nearest door that looked as if it might lead outside.

But although sunlight streamed into the narrow passageway as the door creaked on its hinges, what she saw made her stop in her tracks.

11

Within the Flames

The door did not lead outside, but to a small circular room with a dozen lancet windows, allowing a stream of yellow sunshine to spill across the floor. On the far side of the room was a wide-spanning carved stone fireplace, cut to look like a forest of intertwining trees. In the grate burned a warm, welcoming blaze of golden flames. But in the middle of the fire lay the figure of a shabby young woman.

Kern was kneeling in the grate, trying to stretch his hands through the flames to take hold of the woman. He was talking rapidly, and although he could not touch her it was clear he was trying to get her out.

Gemma ran forwards and tried to grasp the woman's wrist, but the fire was too hot. She jumped back and rubbed her arms, brushing her skirt in case the flames had caught the cloth. It was then she realized that the woman seemed to be quite contentedly asleep. The flames did not appear to burn her, nor even to make her hot or scorched. Her fair skin looked quite cool and comfortable. She looked so peaceful she could easily have been lying in the middle of a grassy field with her long brown hair spread out amongst wild flowers instead of white and black ashes.

Kern looked up at Gemma, tears streaming down his ashy face. 'Do some of your fire magic, *please*! It's my mother! It's Claire!' Then he pulled his shirt sleeves down over his wrists and tried to tug again; 'Come *on*, Mother, get out of that fire! You'll get burned! Wake up and we'll both escape. They'll not keep either of us here any longer. Tell her, Gemma, tell her I've done all the wizards said, and we're both free!' And with that he collapsed in an exhausted heap on an old tapestry rug that covered the floor and started to sob.

Gemma knelt next to Kern and peered at the figure. Suddenly it struck Gemma that Kern's mother was not at all like him. He was a wide-cheekboned westerner like one of the old wizards... but this was no time to think of such matters. Once again she put her hands out towards the sleeping figure, but drew them back very quickly. As she stared into the flames, a warm feeling spread through her own arms and face and she realized how cold she had become during the afternoon.

Claire did not stir, except to breathe gently. She was still unharmed by the fire. 'I wonder if this is real, or another sending?' Gemma murmured to herself, looking hard for any clues. 'How long has she been like this?' she asked, sitting back on her heels.

'I don't know,' the boy replied, choked by a voice that

was trying not to cry. 'I found her an hour or so ago, I suppose. She seems to be stuck somehow. I'm sure it's magic, and I will kill the next wizard I see, I swear! They have lied to me at every turn and I *will* be avenged. I will kill them all!' he bellowed, rising to his feet and clenching his fists in fury.

'Hush!' warned Gemma. 'Not so loud. I will do what I can, but I'm going to need help. Run quickly and fetch Phelan. He will either be in the practice yard, or in our rooms. I'll try to find Fleabag. Meet me here as soon as you can. Oh, and ask Phelan to bring my cloak.'

With that Gemma slipped back inside the long corridor. Kern ran past her, as soft and silent as a shadow. Gemma soon found a small understairs broom cupboard where she could open her hands and let the Ring Fire burn safely. She had to think, and she needed help against this spell – whatever it was. As she looked into the tiny flame within her palm, the Ring Fire's golden glow seemed to be burning very brightly.

She felt calm, and almost happy. But she could not think of a way to help Kern's mother. It seemed that the Ring Fire wasn't interested. That made her angry.

'Oh, where is Fleabag?' she found herself asking out loud. 'Why is he always under my feet when I don't want him, and never here when he's needed the most? He could be anywhere in this rabbit-warren of halls and passageways, and there are so many buildings here. Oh, where do I start?'

Suddenly a warm, purring rub of fur against her leg made her jump.

'Did somebody call?' Fleabag whispered as he jumped into his friend's arms.

The sudden weight of the cat made Gemma stumble back against the brooms and brushes. 'What are you doing here?' she gasped as the cat rubbed his nose hard under her chin.

'I thought you wanted me,' Fleabag replied. 'I'll go away again if I'm *not* wanted. I was just about to pounce on a nice bit of supper when I heard you take my name in vain. I bet I've lost it now – as juicy a bit of fresh house mouse as you could wish for!' And he wriggled to get down.

But Gemma had him firmly by the scruff of the neck. 'Oh no you don't. I was just wondering out loud where you were, that's all. But now I've got you, you aren't going to escape. Someone needs your help more than you need your supper!'

'I can't imagine anything could be as important as that!' the cat replied. 'Anyway, what are you doing skulking in a dark cupboard like a field shrew caught indoors? I thought you were the great Fire Wielder, scared of no one?'

'This is no time for jokes,' Gemma said urgently. 'Although I must admit, dreadful company that you are, I am more than pleased to see you.' She told him briefly about the strange figure in the fireplace who wasn't burned by the fire. 'The flames are real enough, and I can't get near her. I wondered if she's another sending, but she *seems* very real. I've sent Kern to find Phelan and to bring my cloak. Perhaps we can wrap our arms in it to try to rescue the poor woman. The next problem will be getting her back to our rooms without being noticed. Come and see what you think.'

Gemma led her friend back along the shadowy corridor until they reached the door. Gemma opened it cautiously and a blast of icy air blew in, carrying flurries of wet snow with it. Dark night had fallen. There was no sunlit little room with a roaring fire under a wide stone mantelpiece.

'Brrr!' moaned Fleabag. 'I've only just come in from the roof tiles. Now I've got to go out again!'

'This is strange,' Gemma murmured, stepping outside into a cobbled yard. 'I'm certain there was a room here, only a few moments ago.' The door slammed behind her as the wind whipped her hair against her face and the snow caught in her eyes so she could barely see.

Just then, the sound of the door handle being turned behind them made Gemma and the cat flatten themselves against the wall and hold their breath. Suddenly the wind caught the door and flung it open, almost knocking Gemma flying, but she bit her tongue and tried to stay out of sight.

To her relief it was Kern and Phelan, with Gemma's cloak.

Kern looked around the courtyard, and it seemed to Gemma as if he was trying not to cry. 'Where is she?' he begged, 'Please tell me where she is! What have you done with my mother?' he demanded. 'You're as tricky as those wizards, you've magicked her away! I knew I shouldn't trust you. You killed my father and my brothers, now you've burned her to death too. I'll kill you, I'll...' and he ran across to Gemma and began to kick and thump her.

Phelan grabbed at the lad. 'Steady, can't you see? Gemma doesn't know what's going on any more than you or I do. But I have an idea, and if I'm right, your mother's quite safe – safer than we are at the moment! Come inside and let's talk.'

The friends led the frightened boy back into the

hallway. 'Do you think we just went to the wrong doorway?' Gemma asked.

'No,' Phelan replied, peering cautiously around. 'You *and* Kern wouldn't have both taken the wrong door. From what Kern tells me, there's more to it than that. Fleabag, run ahead and warn us if you see any wizards coming. Kern, trust us. At least long enough to talk this over. Now, which is the quickest way back to our rooms?'

Kern pointed along the corridor and shuddered. It was empty but it looked terribly long and dark. The servants had not yet lit the torches in the sconces. How would they ever get to the end of it, let alone reach safety? The cat slid around a bend and disappeared. Kern led Gemma and Phelan swiftly to the left, then they sank into a gloomy niche where Fleabag was already waiting for them. Kern flattened himself against the wall to peer around the next corner.

'Back!' hissed the cat. 'I smell a wizard!' He slipped into the farthest corner of the recess and curled up very small so he looked like an even blacker part of the black shadows.

Phelan opened the wide folds of the cloak, pushed Kern and Gemma underneath and thrust them to the back of the recess. 'Don't move!' he warned. Then stepping out into the corridor he stooped down and turned his back to the approaching figure.

The wizard marched on with a heavy tread then, as she drew close to the friends, her steps hesitated and slowed.

'What are you doing here at this hour, boy?' she demanded in a deep voice. 'It is almost time for the Great Convocation. This area should have been cleaned hours ago.'

Phelan half rose, then bowed, keeping his head well down as he tugged at his forelock and replied in a gruff voice. 'Beggin' your pardon, your Holiness, 'twas a spillage an' all.'

'A spillage?' the woman demanded. 'What do you mean?'

' 'Twas a spillage of beans an' lentils, ma'am.'

'Beans and lentils? What are you talking about, boy?'

'I don' know how they came to be here, ma'am. I jus' knows they was 'ere an' I bin sent to pick 'em up, so please your Holiness.' And he bowed again.

The wizard stepped forward and grabbed at Phelan's chin and tugged his beard forward so she could look at his face. At the same time she lit a magical blue flame between her fingers.

But before she could register who she was looking at, Phelan drew back his fist and punched the wizard in the nose. 'Run!' he hissed to the others. 'That was not well done. They will all be after us now.'

With that he tugged the cloak over his shoulder as he fled, leading the group up the next staircase and onto the landing above. Gemma suddenly stopped dead. 'Oh no! My hands! Why does the Ring Fire *do* this to me?' and she held out her hands as tongues of Ring Fire flashed out in the shadowy corridor. Just at that second, a group of giggling servant girls brushed past them, and Phelan spread the cloak over Gemma, covering her from top to toe.

The girls threw odd looks as they squeezed to one side. But as they moved, one of them caught the cloak against her arm. The heavy cloth fell back, revealing Gemma's fiery hands. All the girls fell silent and made the sign against the evil eye as they turned their faces to the wall, holding their breath until the company was past.

Suddenly a terrible screeching noise and a flap of wings made everyone look up. The servants screamed and ran, disappearing up an iron staircase and through a heavy wooden door which they slammed behind them.

Gemma, Phelan and Kern were left facing a huge bird, black as night with a wingspan that swept the stone walls either side of the narrow passage. Its beak was icy blue and its eyes were piercing azure sapphires that made the watchers shiver with dread.

'How did *that* get inside?' Gemma gasped, eyes wide. Wherever the crows flew, the wizards were never far behind.

'I don't know, but I think we ought to run!' Phelan urged.

Fleabag yowled and hissed and slashed upwards with his front claws, balancing precariously on his one remaining back leg as he tried to rake the belly of the mage-creature with his dagger-points.

Kern ducked as the creature swung around in the width of the stairwell to take another swoop. This time its talons were extended towards the cowering figures. It did not seem to be after any particular one of them, but it struck terror as it flew.

As the creature passed, Phelan was able to straighten himself enough to draw Rowanne's sword and get a good balance. As the huge crow turned again, Phelan knew he had only a few seconds to plan his defence. He carefully watched the way the bird moved, and anticipated how it would attack. He breathed deeply, waiting as the great bird loomed towards them.

It was almost on them again, screeching with its

deadly, razor sharp beak wide open, and talons ready to gouge and rip.

Gemma raised her hands, but the Ring Fire had faded. Her hands were quite empty. 'Where *has* it gone?' she exclaimed in horror, cowering behind Phelan. 'Why is it never there when I need it most?'

'Quick!' hissed Fleabag. 'Our quarters are just along there, first corridor to the right, then left at the end. Go!' Gemma dared not look back, but she ducked as another terrible screech signalled the arrival of the creature's mate from above the stairwell.

The first bird swooped down and scraped Fleabag's back with its deadly talons, just as Phelan leaped up, plunging Rowanne's sword hilt deep in the night-blue feathers until hot blood drenched his arm.

The King fell under the weight of the dying creature, and it took all of Kern's strength to heave the corpse aside before Phelan could wrest his sword from the tangle of blood and feathers.

Gemma swept the bleeding Fleabag into her arms as she turned to flee. She glanced back for one second, and saw Phelan and Kern staring in horror as the second bird landed and began to devour her own mate, tugging strips of flesh from the still-warm corpse.

Phelan moved quietly to where Kern crouched. 'Do everything very slowly. Don't frighten the bird,' Phelan warned, as he edged along the wall.

Fighting a dreadful feeling that she was going to be sick, Gemma ran.

12

Kern's Story

As Gemma flung open the door to their darkened rooms, her heart was pounding and she could hardly breathe. Sweat dripped down her face and into her eyes.

The study was quite dark, except for a faint bluish glow from the bookshelves and a dull red glimmer from a dying fire in the grate. Gemma laid Fleabag gently down on a towel and went to look at the eerie light. 'Of course,' she muttered. 'They're *wizards*' books! Ugh,' she shuddered, 'that blue colour gives me the creeps.'

Just then, the sound of Phelan and Kern clattering through the door made Gemma spring into action.

Without thinking about finding the tinder box, Gemma touched each of the lamps with her fingers, so they burned with the glow from the Ring Fire. Then she stirred up the dying fire in the grate. The warmth of the clear light made everyone feel better.

Gemma fetched warm water to bathe Fleabag's wounds. 'You're lucky, they're only light scratches. How do you feel, old friend?' she asked kindly.

'Sore,' the cat replied. 'It isn't bad enough to give me a decent hero's death, but I'll need pampering and a great deal of fish and sympathy for a few weeks if I'm to make a full recovery.'

Gemma laughed as she carried him into her bedroom to sleep.

Back in the study, supper had been left out for them. Phelan pulled out a chair and made Kern sit. 'I will tell you what I think is happening to your mother, but I must eat first,' he said. 'I need to revive my wits before I do anything.'

Kern was fidgety, and kept throwing suspicious sidelong glances at Phelan and Gemma, but he too ate and said nothing. It was not long before only crumbs were left, and a rather stiff and bedraggled Fleabag decided that he needed nourishment too.

'Hello, Fleabag. Nice to see you. How are you feeling?' Phelan laughed, and put a plate loaded with fish on the floor for him to eat.

'Miserable!' the cat replied. 'They've *only* got fresh cream and smoked salmon for my tea.' Then the incorrigible animal picked up the fish from his plate and jumped behind the settee to eat it.

'Oh, you'll live!' Phelan laughed.

Fleabag stopped eating, licked his whiskers and peered around the edge of the settee, looking serious for once. 'I don't know how that thing caught me, but his talons were *sharp*, then I just went all cold. The next thing I knew, I was in here feeling warm as toast with a nice comforting circle of friends all around me, and supper laid out, just as it should be for a cat of my rank. Pity it wasn't the lightly grilled field mouse on toast I ordered. Then my bliss would have been complete.'

Gemma scratched her old friend behind the ear, enjoying the way the firelight caught on his earring. 'Nothing to be ashamed of. Still, the warmth of the Ring Fire seems to have done you some good, even if it hasn't mended your table manners. You've spilled cream all over that cushion.'

Suddenly Kern could contain himself no longer. 'Look, I've been patient with you all,' he snapped, 'and now I want to know what's going on. Why didn't you help me get my mother away from that horrid fire, and why did you magic that room away when my back was turned? I should never have left you. You tricked me out of the room... you...'

'Calm down,' Phelan said gently. 'Listen to what I *think* happened. Although I wasn't there, I do have an idea. You know you said the room was bright and warm, even though it was dark, cold and already snowing outside?'

'Yes,' Kern replied, hesitantly. 'What of it? Things are rarely as they seem around here. That's nothing.'

'Yes, but you know some magic, Kern; was it real or a spell?'

Kern hesitated before answering. 'It was... real... I think.'

Phelan nodded. 'Yet the courtyard was real, too, wasn't it? Not an illusion?'

The boy nodded again.

'And Gemma, when you put your hands into the fire, what happened?'

'It burned me,' she replied, looking at her hands. Then she hesitated. 'No, it didn't. It just hurt a bit, but I've got no blisters or anything... How strange!'

'And how did Kern's mother look?' the King persisted.

'Well, content, and comfortable too!' she added, as light began to dawn.

'What *are* you talking about?' Kern demanded, thumping the table with his fist. 'You're all talking in riddles, worse than any wizard! I saw my mother being burned alive in a huge fire and you did nothing to help her, Gemma. Then she was magicked away. This is all too much. What *is* happening?' he demanded.

From behind the settee Fleabag chuckled. 'Oh Kern, you should have a cat's brain in your head, as well as catguts for strings. Then you might see what's at the very end of your nose.'

Kern looked put out, and his foot twitched as if he longed to boot Fleabag. 'What *are* you talking about?' he muttered.

Fleabag purred, tried to roll over, and remembered he couldn't because of the great bird's scratches on his back. 'The Ring Fire has her. She's safe. Safer than she has ever been in all her life.'

'But where was the room? Wasn't that a wizards' trick?'

'Oh that's real, all right,' Phelan assured the boy. 'But it's no *place* in particular. It's everywhere and anywhere, wherever the Fire Giver wants to put it. You were just being shown that she is safe, and being told not to worry.'

Kern frowned. 'But if it *was* the Ring Fire, why did it hurt Gemma's hands?' he asked.

'To warn her not to interfere,' Phelan replied. 'To tell Gemma she had to leave your mother where she was.'

This did not comfort Kern at all. He jumped to his feet and stood glaring in front of Phelan. 'But how are we going to get her back? What are you going to do to rescue her from this Ring Fire of yours?'

'We don't need to,' the King said quietly. 'Your mother is asleep somewhere, safe, and well cared for. When the Fire Giver knows the time is right, your mother will waken, and you will find her. You just have to trust!'

Kern went bright red in the face and thumped the table again. 'Trust! Trust! Why should I trust you, when you're all talking such nonsense. I don't care if *you're* a King and *you're* a Fire Wielder and *you're* a cat of ninety-nine lives...'

'One hundred and ninety-nine,' Fleabag put in with a grin.

Kern didn't even stop to scowl at the cat. 'This is ridiculous. I want my mother back. What's the difference between your magic and the wizards'? Only the colour, as far as I can see. And that means nothing!'

Gemma held open her hand and let the Ring Fire burn gently. 'Look into it,' she said quietly. 'How does it make you feel?'

Kern said nothing, but stared open-mouthed at the gentle, gold flame. Then Gemma got up and picked up one of the books that had been glowing blue before she had lit the lamps. 'And now look at something that carries the wizards' magic...'

Kern took the book, and dropped it immediately, kicking it across the room. 'I don't want to look at it – it's horrid!' he muttered, hanging his head. 'Well, perhaps the Ring Fire isn't so bad... You think it's taken her to look after her while things are too dangerous here?'

'Exactly,' said Phelan.

'I suppose it could make sense.' Kern sat down again and looked thoughtful. 'If M'Kinnik thought I was about to claim my freedom, he might have tried to hide my mother to keep us here. He knows I would never dream of leaving without her.'

Phelan leaned back in his chair and sipped at his wine. 'If your mother was taken by the Ring Fire to a safe place, the wizards aren't about to admit that, so they let you think they've hidden her. But talking of trust, isn't it about time we knew a little about you? Who *are* you? Why are you and your mother so important to the University? The Ring Fire went to great lengths to protect your mother.'

Kern reddened and shrugged as he began to kick at the table leg. 'How should I know? I'd never heard of your Ring Fire before I came to Harflorum.'

Phelan noticed the evaded question and leaned forward as he tried to look Kern in the eye. 'But why did you come to Harflorum in the first place? And what was all that about "doing everything the wizards said"?'

The boy sighed, and stared into the golden firelight in the grate. It was soft and gentle, like the Fire that was caring for his mother. 'I was told that my mother and I would be free to leave here for ever if I did an errand for the wizards... I had to go to Harflorum and find the last carrier of the pure Blue Magic and bring him or her back here... But when I got back, Mother had disappeared. Until today I thought the wizards had taken her.'

'They may have done,' Gemma replied. 'But whatever happened, the Ring Fire has her now, and that is the important thing.'

'How could I have been so *stupid* as to have believed the wizards?' Kern went on. 'Especially M'Kinnik! He was my father's friend. I thought he meant me well.'

'But who was your father?' Gemma asked, hoping not to hear the answer she dreaded.

Kern sighed. 'The Chancellor of All Wizards, whom you killed in the Hall of Light three years ago,' he replied, looking Gemma directly in the face.

Gemma hung her head. 'Oh, I'm – I'm sorry...'

'Don't be!' Kern smiled ruefully. 'Mother was forced to marry. She was given to the University in lieu of rent on my grandfather's farm. She was not wanted by my father. Neither was I. Let's face it, what wizard of the Blue Magic wants a *seventh* son? They are supposed to be omens for good. The main reason my father married my mother was some weird idea that she was going to give him a daughter. There were already two older girls in the family, but third daughters for wizards are considered something rather special.

'So when I was born a boy, my father never spoke to either of us again. I was always considered to be a nuisance and in the way. My older brothers and sisters had no time for me, except Domnall. He was always very kind,' Kern said. 'He gave me my violin and treated me like a brother... That meant a lot to me.'

Gemma stared at the floor and bit her lip. 'I didn't exactly kill either of them, you know. They both got caught up in their own spells. I didn't mean anyone any harm. I just wanted both your father and your brothers to stop using magic for evil ends. In fact we tried to ban the use of magic altogether after the Battle of Porthwain, but it didn't work. I suppose that was too much to expect.'

'I thought you were the evil one,' Kern said quietly. 'I had sworn that once I had delivered the carrier of the Blue Magic to the wizards and Mother and I were free, I would have my vengeance on you. But I was wrong. You were only fighting for what was right and, as you say, my father, Sethan and Domnall all became entangled in evil of their own making. I can see that now. I'm sorry...' and he held out his hand in friendship.

But just as he did so, the flames in the torches around the room flickered and sank to mere pinpricks of light and the room went very cold.

Gemma sprang to her feet and looked around wildly. 'What's happening?' she gulped.

'We're under attack!' Phelan said, jumping to his feet. 'But how, and where?'

Gemma turned to Kern. 'Phelan and I must go and see what we can find out. Please, fetch your violin and play the air I heard you trying out the other evening... the Ring Fire song from the Fire Festival. It will help us think. Songs and music are very important to help keep the Ring Fire bright in our minds.'

Kern nodded. 'I'll get it straight away,' and he left the room, with Fleabag close behind him.

Silently he slipped along the dark corridors, looking carefully this way and that, darting from shadow to shadow as the wan blue light from the torches along the way guttered and flared in the uncertain draughts.

'How brave are you, Fleabag?' Kern asked the cat. 'There is a short cut if we turn left here, but it involves going along the gallery at the top of the Great Hall.'

Fleabag puffed himself up so his tail turned to a bottlebrush and his whiskers splayed as wide as they would go. 'I am the *epitome* of courage, my dear boy. After all, I am the cat who took on your father single-pawed – well, almost,' he muttered quietly under his breath. 'I suppose Gemma and Phelan did help a bit at times...' And he followed the boy through the small door that led out onto the balcony, his eyes glowing like coach lamps in the dark.

Kern stooped low, so as not to be seen from below, and he moved swiftly and stealthily, reaching the far door within only one or two heartbeats.

Fleabag, however, jumped up onto the balustrade and surveyed the scene below.

Kern was white with terror. 'Get *down*!' he hissed, flapping urgently with his hands. 'They'll turn you into a mouse as soon as look at you!'

But Fleabag sat quite calmly where he was. 'I don't think they will,' he said. 'They've got other things on their minds. Come and look at this...'

13

The Return of the Fire Maiden

The vast round hall was filled with light from a thousand blue-burning torches held high by servants in bright cerulean livery. Seated all around were the wizards, mostly dressed in indigo robes, but some in ultramarine and cobalt blue, depending on their rank. Each wore a small, turquoise cap with a navy tassle in the middle.

In their midst, seated alone, was a tall figure dressed in white. Her long blue-black hair was brushed out around her shoulders. Her arms and head were bare, and her skin was a glowing aquamarine colour.

As Fleabag looked down, the figure looked up and smiled, but said nothing.

Trembling, Kern peered over the edge of the balustrade. His knuckles and his face were quite white and he was sweating with fear. He stared wide-eyed at the cat.

'Umm,' Fleabag commented as he jumped down to sit beside the boy. 'We've found out what's happening. It looks like trouble for the Ring Fire. Go and find your violin; we will need the strength of your music to give us courage. I'll fetch the others. Run as fast as you can; you needn't hide. They won't be after you. As I said, they've got other things to think about.'

Kern, still stooping low, slipped through the door at the far end of the balcony. Fleabag could hear his nervous steps running along the warren of hallways beyond.

The cat shivered as the gathered wizards began a slow chant. The sound made him feel cold. He sprang through the gap of the open door and ran back towards their rooms. As he rounded the last corner, he ran right into Gemma and Phelan, almost knocking them both over.

Fleabag did not waste time on apologies. 'Quick, come with me! Kern and I have found what is wrong. By the looks of it, the wizards are doing something to Rowanne!'

Gemma and Phelan followed Fleabag until the cat signalled a warning. The door creaked open, making the friends wince, but the noise was swallowed by the wizards' chanting, which had swollen from a soft sound in the choir to a full-throated anthem taken up by all present.

Everywhere was bitterly cold. Gemma and Phelan huddled together with Fleabag for warmth. The chill seemed to be sweeping through the air like a winter's gale. Yet this was a more sinister cold than a mere drop in temperature. It soaked into the skin of the listeners, beckoning them deeper and deeper into the blue, magical world, until there seemed no hope of ever again coming up to light and warmth...

The words of the wizards' cantor were clear and sharp as an icicle piercing the heart...

'There is no hope,
the great night has come,
the light has gone away.
There is no dawn...'

Gemma shuddered. The words were from the opening part of the Fire Festival ceremony! She nudged Phelan. How often they had sung that together. But surely the wizards wouldn't sing the next part, the proclamation of hope? What were *wizards* doing singing this, of all songs?

But the next verse *was* different:

'The night is ours
as surely as the day
has died for ever.
The night is ours
to work in as we will.
The night has come
when ice and fear will reign,
with Fire's death
at our command.'

Fleabag began to scratch at a wandering flea. 'What do you two think?'

Phelan shook his head. 'I don't believe it! She's gone over to the wizards! Goodness knows what secrets she'll tell them!'

'Not Rowanne!' Gemma went pale at the thought. 'She's no traitor!'

'But she *is*!' Phelan insisted. 'Use your eyes! She's about to be invested down there, and she's turned her back on the Ring Fire and everything.'

'But she told us that whatever we saw or heard, she would be doing it for the Ring Fire's sake!' Gemma replied. 'She may be unutterably stupid, but she would never betray us!'

Fleabag stretched his head over the balustrade. 'I think you'd better *see* what's happening down there,' he whispered.

The friends peered cautiously over the carved stone balcony, and watched Rowanne being dressed in a brilliant robe of shimmering blue light. It hurt their eyes to look at the scene. Rowanne did not look happy.

'See,' Gemma whispered again. 'She's not doing it for herself – she's suffering!'

Gemma's heart missed a beat as Rowanne looked up at them. She opened her mouth as if to say something... then shut it again.

Phelan and Gemma ducked and hid, hearts pounding in their mouths. Everyone would know they were there. As Fleabag would have said, if they were caught they would be dog meat!

Just then the anthem came to an end, and a clear voice rang out: 'Do you, Princess Rowanne de Montiland, Arch Wizard of our order, accept the honour of the High Chancellorship of the Holy Order of All Wizards for as long as you live?'

There was a split second's hesitation, then Rowanne's deep, clear voice echoed around the hall, 'I do.'

'And do you swear to give your life's blood to promote and maintain the principles of the Holy Order of All

Wizards, to keep the Blue Flame burning in the hearts of all who follow you?'

This time there was a definite uncomfortable pause. Rowanne stared around the hall filled with expectant faces, then up at her friends in the balcony. Her eyes were wide in what seemed to be panic. 'Help!' she mouthed.

Her friends looked down in horror. They could see she was terrified, but they could do nothing to help her.

'She wasn't expecting that one,' Fleabag commented. 'I'll bet my last three paws that whatever is happening down there is more than she ever bargained for.'

'Sssh!' Phelan warned, 'they're not finished with her yet!'

The clear voice of the questioner rang out again and repeated the question. Rowanne swayed a little and whispered, 'I do.'

'And do you swear on your life's blood to destroy utterly the enemies of the Blue Flame?' The questioner's voice spoke with a gloating thickness in it.

This time Rowanne looked terrified and said nothing. There was a long, deadly silence.

Gemma glanced at Phelan again. 'I don't honestly think she expected any of this. She just thought that the Blue Magic had to be stood up to, and being on the *inside* to do it put her in a stronger position than being on the outside. But they've trapped her. The wizards will never let her renege on these vows. She's either very brave or very foolish.'

'Perhaps she's both,' Phelan replied sadly. 'I also fear there's nothing we can do for her. We now know the truth. She has been very cynically and very carefully manoeuvred into position to become our enemy. She wanted to be our friend from within their camp, but it's all miserably backfired.'

The unbearable silence stretched on and on, until from below came a small strangled cry as a silver sword was pressed to Rowanne's throat.

Suddenly, from somewhere not far away, came the strains of a violin playing the anthem of the Ring Fire.

Fleabag bristled his fur and tail until he looked twice his size, then launched himself over the balcony. With a bloodcurdling caterwaul, he landed on the back of the neck of Rowanne's assailant, who fell to the floor, gore streaming from several long cuts that ran down his back. Though they were no deeper than a cat's claw, they made the man writhe and scream as his blood stained his blue robes a deep warm red.

Gemma knew what she must do. She did not have the courage to jump like Fleabag, but she held her arms open wide, letting the Ring Fire burn as she called out loud: 'Behold, the Fire Maiden and the Black Cat have returned!'

At the same moment, Phelan threw back his head and sang, in his rich, warm voice:

'Fire Giver,
In our darkest hour,
give us light.'

14

Rescuing Rowanne

Confusion broke out in the hall below. No one seemed interested in trying to capture Phelan and Gemma. The wizards didn't really know what had happened.

Fleabag's victim was rolling around on the floor, complaining that a whole army with knives had attacked him, and others were telling tales of blinding lights in the skies and terrible voices from the depths that had filled the hall at the moment of the new Chancellor's initiation. Some said this meant she would be the greatest Chancellor ever, and others that she would be the worst.

No one even knew for sure whether or not she had taken the final vow.

No one could think of what they were supposed to be doing. Wizards and servants were rushing this way and that, hopelessly blocking every passageway. For some reason, everyone was elbowing and pushing to be in the thickest part of the crowd where the pandemonium was greatest.

A hundred different arguments raged in every part of the hall. One or two of the senior wizards were arguing about whether the right spells had been used during the ceremony. 'Old M'Kinnik is past it!' exclaimed the tall, beautiful Vice Chancellor. 'I clearly heard him say *Dominus*, not *Domina*. That's bound to mess up the ceremony if you have a female Chancellor! M'Kinnik is losing his marbles, if you ask me. He was just not concentrating... Now, if only they had let *me* do the initiation, I'd have...'

And a freckled young man with a mop of ginger hair was wildly gesticulating with his wand while he tried to explain how a wrong movement at the vital moment could have sent sparks across the ceiling and set some drapery alight somewhere, giving the appearance of lights in the air. But his listeners didn't care, for his wild wand-waving had turned them all into pale blue frogs. He ducked in alarm as the wizards' giant crow swooped down from her perch, high in the rafters, and began to pick the frogs up, one by one, for her supper.

At one end of the hall, the air was crackling with strange glowing patterns as wizards swooped their wands this way and that, analysing whether M'Kinnik had done a withyshins double extraloop with the left hand, as he should have done, or a dipped double sweep. The difference was slight, but vital. They didn't seem to care that they had burned their robes, and scorched the fine polished woodwork of the floor.

In another corner, a group of more academic wizards had summoned whole libraries of books which arrived unescorted, floating through the air like a flight of disorderly hornets, bashing and battering their way through the crowds. Anyone in the way of a stray volume was clouted around the ears by heavy tomes of disruptive spells and discourses on bad omens at inductions.

The resultant dizzy heads and concussed brains only added to the confusion; wizards sat or lay where they fell, nursing their heads and shoulders, and yelling for servants to fetch bowls of warm water to bathe the wounds, poultices for bruises and bandages for bleeding faces.

As the menials scurried away to do as they had been bidden, a whole detachment of the University guard, in their dark- and light-blue costume, came marching at double time down the long corridor, knocking the servants aside, and tangling their spears and swords in each other's legs. The more they became entangled, the faster they tried to march onwards, ploughing into an ever-increasing heap of angry comrades as they did so.

Soon everywhere was a mass of squirming, screaming and complaining bodies, lit by the pale-blue torch lights. No one could see clearly enough to work out how to get untangled, and no one was willing to give way to anyone else, so determined were they that their mission or errand was more important than anyone else's.

Within moments fighting broke out. Fists and swords and silver serving trays, even torches from the brackets on the walls, were pressed into service as impromptu weapons.

Phelan and Gemma did not wait to see the fun. They fled the balcony and managed to get back to their rooms without being challenged, without even a spell or a crow or a booby trap to stop them. The people of the

University were so turned in on themselves, they seemed to have forgotten about the cat, the Fire Maiden and the singer: if they had ever really seen them in the first place!

Gemma did not feel like reminding them.

Down in the hall, Fleabag and Rowanne slipped through the angry crowd of shouting wizards. In their midst were a group of philosophical mages who were so busy arguing about whether Rowanne had or had not been inducted as Chancellor of All Wizards, that they did not notice her slipping between them, an indigo cloak pulled low over her face. Fleabag nudged her feet this way and that until he had manoeuvred her through a doorway which led to a deserted passageway beyond.

'Quick, in here!' he hissed. In the blink of an eye, Fleabag sped forwards, with Rowanne hard on his paws. The Princess opened her hand, and a small flame of blue light cast eerie shadows along the black shadowed corridors.

'Put that out!' Fleabag snapped crossly. 'I will *not* be led by the Blue Magic, and I can see perfectly well without it, anyway.'

'But *I* can't see a thing,' Rowanne whined as she closed her hand, extinguishing the baleful glow.

'Well, I can!' Fleabag retorted. 'You'll just have to trust me for the first time in your silly life!' he snapped.

'What do you mean, "silly"? You don't appreciate the dangers I have put myself through for you!' she replied angrily. 'I am a hero for the Ring Fire! I have risked everything to become a spy in the wizards' midst!'

'Rubbish!' Fleabag replied. 'I don't know what you thought you were doing, but it was far from heroic, and now you have got us all into terrible trouble!'

'Ouch!' Rowanne gasped as she stumbled into a wall.

'Sssh!' the cat ordered. 'Bend down and keep your hand on the tip of my tail. That's it. Don't grip it, it's very sensitive, you know!'

And within a few minutes, as they turned a corner, the soft strains of Kern's violin could be heard.

'Thank goodness, it's not far now,' Fleabag whispered. 'I was beginning to wonder if I had taken a wrong turning a little way back. Follow that sound!'

'I can't...' Rowanne gasped, letting go of Fleabag's tail and clapping her hands to her ears. 'It hurts! I can't bear to hear it! It makes me want to run away! Oh Fleabag, what's happened?'

'You've been extremely stupid! That's what!' the cat replied, as he pushed at a door with his front paws.

The door swung open, and a bright splash of golden light flooded the corridor with its glow.

Rowanne jumped back, yelping as if she had been burned. 'Help! I can't stand it!' she cried, shielding her eyes, yet still trying to block her ears at the same time.

Gemma stood in the doorway and held out her hands to her old friend. 'Come in. Have some food, and we'll talk about what is to be done.'

'But I can't...' Rowanne protested. 'It's the Ring Fire – it's burning me, I can't take it... and that music... it's like nails scratching down a chalk board... I'm frightened, Gemma. I wanted to help you, but now I find I can't stand you!'

'Well, come in, at least. No one's going to hurt you...'

'But I can't... I physically can't...' Rowanne wailed.

15

Banishing the Blue

Gemma and Phelan exchanged glances. They knew what this meant: Rowanne had too much of the Blue Magic in her to be able to stand the sight or the sound of the Ring Fire!

Rowanne was no longer the tall, powerful woman she had once been, but smaller and almost frail-looking. She seemed to have aged at least twenty years in the last few days.

'She can't have gone over to the Blue Magic altogether,' Gemma whispered to her friends. 'She's still standing there, despite the fact that it's causing her terrible pain to do so.'

'We can't leave her here all night,' Phelan whispered. 'The wizards will be after her blood. She didn't make the final vow; they'll kill her if they find her.'

'I don't think so,' Fleabag answered. 'No one knows

what *really* happened. From what the wizards were saying down there, it seems I acted so heroically – at precisely the right moment (as usual) – that they are totally confused. They believe the man who was initiating Rowanne was attacked by an army of knifemen. Gemma, holding the Ring Fire, was a flash of lightning or something, and Phelan's singing was a voice from the deep. All good stuff, but at this precise moment, none of us is in danger – we're just not in the equation.'

At that moment, Kern came into the study, holding his violin. He saw Rowanne standing outside the door, and tried to run. Phelan grabbed his arm. 'Don't go, no one blames you for what you did. You were being bullied by M'Kinnik, and you didn't know any better.'

Kern stuttered something, and tried to hide.

'I won't betray you, boy,' Rowanne assured him. 'I may be the Chancellor, but believe it or not, I'm still on your side!' And with that she burst into tears and ran away. Gemma tried to follow her to bring her back.

'Please leave me alone!' Rowanne called out. 'The Ring Fire hurts too much!' Then, as she rounded a corner that took her out of sight, she called back, 'Get rid of everything that glows blue, Gemma. Anything a wizard has touched will betray you in the end!' And she was gone.

Sadly, Gemma returned to their study. 'Put the lights out. Rowanne says that anything that glows blue will betray us. I noticed that some of these books glowed blue in the dark; we'll put them outside first.'

'How can they betray us?' Kern asked.

'Who knows?' Phelan replied. 'Perhaps anything with even a smear of blue magic might carry a spell or may become the wizards' ears? Whatever it is, if it's that awful sickly blue colour, it's out as far as I'm concerned!'

When the candles were out, Gemma and Phelan pulled the books that glowed blue off the shelves and stacked them neatly outside the door. They took down a painting with strange symbols drawn around the frame. The rest of the room seemed to be quite ordinarily dark and peaceful. Phelan checked his bedroom and threw out a silver candlestick that had an eerie glow, and after that, Gemma could only see blueness around Kern's violin.

'That's the only thing that means anything to him in the whole world,' Gemma thought to herself. 'And he *is* playing the Ring Fire music on it. Perhaps that will make the blue go away.'

Gemma was torn. She knew Rowanne was right. But would the trouble it would cause Kern to take the fiddle from him prove worse than having a little Blue Magic in their midst? Perhaps a violin that the Chancellor of All Wizards had once touched might not be totally soaked with magic, just – well, smudged with it. Ordinary people left fingerprints wherever they touched, so perhaps it was the same with wizards – and equally harmless.

She relit the candles with Ring Fire to give the room extra protection, then she went outside the study door and did a strange thing: she ran her fingers all around the doorposts, step and jamb, until the whole entryway was aglow with a thin thread of Ring Fire. Then she did the same at each window. The fire in the grate already glowed with the Ring Fire's ancient golden flames.

'We are safe now,' she said, as she sat down at the table with her friends. 'Play for us again, Kern, and then we must get some sleep. Tomorrow is the first trial.'

Kern bent over the King and shook him gently. 'Sire, the wizards have sent for you. It is almost time for the fight. Your breakfast has been brought up. I've checked it, and there is neither spell nor poison in it. Come, eat and wash or you'll never be ready in time.'

Phelan groaned as he stood. He was stiff all over from the strenuous hours in the practice yard the day before. In the study he sat on the settee and stroked Fleabag, who had already claimed most of the cushions as his own. 'How are the scratches on your back?' he asked.

The cat stretched gingerly and turned his neck to inspect the wounds. 'They look clean enough.' He licked at the scars. 'Hmm, they taste all right as well. Time will tell. Where is my breakfast?' and he jumped carefully onto the floor where Phelan had placed a fresh, chopped trout. 'Why *do* they insist on cutting my food up in this place?' he moaned. 'I'm not a kitten and when it's all in pieces I can't drag it around the floor and make the carpet smell all fishy!'

Phelan laughed. 'Perhaps that's precisely why they do it!'

Fleabag sniffed in disgust, picked up the fish head and took it behind the coal scuttle to crunch in peace.

After breakfast, the sergeant at arms arrived to help Phelan put his armour on. Each part had been polished and oiled to perfection. When he was dressed, Phelan looked every inch a King, with his black curly beard poking out from under his visor, and the emblem of the Ring Fire resplendent on his breastplate.

Kern, who was to act as the King's squire, picked up Rowanne's sword and led the way to the tournament field where the trial was to take place.

A herald of the University escorted the royal party towards their own gold-coloured pavilion at the far end of the field. It was a cold, blustery day, and here and there, the snow from the day before had settled in powdery patches. The ground was hard as iron.

The refuge of the pavilion was most welcome. The King's men had lit a fire in a brazier and set out several camp chairs covered with thick fleeces. Apples were already roasting and ginger tea was brewing, giving off a heart-warming smell.

Fleabag jumped onto one of the chairs, and immediately curled up for a snooze. Gemma sat quietly in a corner to look into the Ring Fire, whilst Kern strapped the King's scabbard on for him. The boy seemed sullen and moody. Phelan tried to cheer him up. 'I know we will reach your mother soon,' he smiled. 'As soon as the trials are over and the wizards are defeated, there will be no more danger, and the Ring Fire will return her to us, I am sure.'

Kern said nothing, but shrugged.

Phelan rested his heavy, gauntleted hands on Kern's shoulders. 'We *will* win, somehow. Even if I'm killed today, all will be well in the end. The Ring Fire is stronger than the Blue Magic. I can promise you that.'

Kern turned his head away. He didn't want Phelan to sense the worry he felt. When he had gone to his attic to sleep, the stable lads were laughing at Phelan's sword skills. It was not that he was a bad fighter, but they all knew of Grimbold's reputation. He blushed and bit his lip. 'Can I make a suggestion, sire?' he asked at last.

Phelan smiled. 'Thank you. We need all the ideas we can get at the moment.'

The boy kicked his shoes nervously against a table leg. 'I really don't like magic, but I do know a few simple spells. Would you like me to use them? Just to protect you, of course.'

Phelan shook his head. 'It's kind of you, but we will not have anything to do with magic. The Ring Fire works with quietness and confidence in what is right. But if you really want to help, I should be grateful if you would hold my spare sword and give me water when I need it. Then you will have done me a great service. Now, the heralds are calling. It is time to go.'

16

The Trial of Strength

Grimbold stood a full head taller than Phelan. His armour was a light, fine chain mail covered with huge plates of blue iron. His helmet was topped with a nodding plume of azure feathers that swayed in the icy wind. The crowd that huddled under furs in the stands either side of the lists were obviously great fans of his. He lifted his massive fists to their cheers as he strode into the centre of the arena.

Phelan stepped out of the golden tent and walked forward, trying hard to remember everything Rowanne had taught him. A few cheers came from his men at arms, and Gemma and Fleabag, of course. But his walk was a lonely one. He tried not to be daunted by the sight of Grimbold. He stood a chance if he kept his head…

He shivered as he surveyed his opponent. It might have been fear, but it seemed to him that the bitter cold seeped everywhere under his woollen shirt. Steel plate is not the best thing to wear on a freezing day. The icy cold hurt his hands as he tried to grip the pommel of Rowanne's sword firmly. He hoped desperately that he would warm up as the fight got under way.

Phelan didn't have long to think about his discomfort, for scarcely had he entered the arena before Grimbold lifted his sword high above his head and slammed the blade down. Phelan swayed to one side and the sharp edge narrowly missed his shoulder.

'Don't you salute your opponent?' Phelan shouted. 'Whatever happened to the rules of combat?'

'What rules?' came the gruff reply, accompanied by a long sideways slicing cut that caught Phelan on the greaves that covered his leg. The shock almost toppled him, but he managed to straighten himself. At least he had the measure of his opponent now. Long, wide sweeps and no manners.

Phelan used his smaller size and greater agility to dodge and duck Grimbold's moves. He hoped the giant would tire before he did. But his tactics seemed to make the stranger angry. Quite suddenly the giant abandoned the long, wide manoeuvres and returned to the heavy, downward cuts aimed at Phelan's arms. Grimbold's sword was impossibly long – it was almost as long as himself, and as wide as a man's forearm. Phelan stared in wonder at the great iron blade as time after time it came thundering against him. He could not take his eyes from it; he was amazed that anyone could even *lift* such a weapon. It took all his concentration, and although he defended himself well, he could not plan an attack.

As the end of the bout was called, Kern came running to him with a drink. Fleabag came out onto the field and clambered onto Phelan's slippery metal lap. 'Each blow he is giving you is a point – you realize that, don't you? He's scored eleven so far, and you have only two. Try to at least touch him, score points, do some attacking! Stop dancing around like a jelly!'

Phelan shook his head. 'But have you seen the length of his sword? I can't get near the man. He handles it like it's a threshing machine. Anything within range would be totally demolished within seconds!'

'Well, at least try to score some points, so if you're going to lose, you won't do it so miserably!' Fleabag cajoled. Just then the trumpet sounded for the combatants to come together again.

Phelan groaned and got to his feet. But scarcely had he moved forward, when Grimbold pushed his left foot forward and swung his sword in low under Phelan's guard, unbalancing him in a single movement. The crowd went wild with joy as the young King fell hard onto the icy ground.

'I *knew* there was something Rowanne told me I had to remember,' he muttered to himself, as the marshal of the lists proclaimed Grimbold the winner.

Back in the tent, Kern played music softly on his violin as Phelan tugged the armour off. He accepted his sergeant at arms' offer of help, and drank from a horn of hot, spiced mead that Gemma gave him. He was bruised and his pride was injured, but no further damage had been sustained. Gemma put ointment on the bruises and made him lie down and rest.

'The race doesn't begin for an hour,' she told him. 'At

least try to relax. Do you want Kern to keep playing?'

'Oh yes, please,' he murmured as he drifted off to sleep. 'It makes it seem as if everything's going to be all right.'

Just before noon, Phelan roused himself and washed. This time he felt more confident as he splashed his face with water, and pulled on a light linen shirt and shorts.

'I've walked the track,' Fleabag told him. 'I can't see or smell any sign of booby traps. That doesn't mean there aren't any, of course. The ground is still as hard as stone, but the wind will be at your back for the home stretch. Your opponent is a lad from the south, like yourself. He looks rather like a human greyhound.'

'Thanks,' Phelan replied. 'I really needed to know that.' And he began his warm-up exercises.

The noon-day trumpet sounded and Phelan walked out onto the track that had been marked around the perimeter of the lists: three times around and one last home sprint up the middle. It was enough to get his teeth into, but not enough to tire him. He grinned. This time he felt much more confident, and he did not mind the lack of cheers. *This* was something he could do.

As he crouched over the starting line, he glanced at his opponent. He was a lean dark-skinned man, about his own age. As Fleabag had said, he was the nearest thing to a human greyhound. What would be his weakness? The bends or the straights?

At last a bugle sounded the start, and Phelan felt the cold air fill his lungs with an exhilaration he hadn't felt in a long time. He was running, and that to him was like flying. It gave him such a wonderful sense of freedom and joy, it always made him want to sing. But he daren't let himself; he had to keep every last breath for the race. Instead he sang in his head.

As his feet hit the cold earth rhythmically, he found he was making up words that celebrated the wonderful feeling of being alive. The sky was blue – but a healthy natural blue, not a sickly magical colour. And the freshness of the air made him feel buoyant. At the edge of the field, the town of Porthwain, with its crumbling, elegant buildings, looked very beautiful. But Phelan did not let himself become distracted. He had to think about running.

Thud, thud, thud, his feet hit the hard ground. Where was his opponent? Phelan glanced around. They were about neck and neck. The other runner had the advantage of the bend, but Phelan let him take it. The wind was against them for this short stretch and he wanted to slide into the other man's wake. It would give him a rest, ready for the much-needed push ahead.

To his surprise, Phelan noticed the marshall's flag was up for the last lap. Had they really been around twice already? He must really concentrate; he would not have been so relaxed had he realized the race was almost over. There was virtually no time left to pull forward, and the other man was already surging ahead. He would just give himself a few more strides of taking it easy, then, as they came around the next bend into the straight, he would push ahead... But he had to time it just right.

At that second, Phelan caught the edge of his foot against a stone and stumbled. He cried out as pain shot through his ankle. His opponent turned at the sound, but did not slacken. Instead he lowered his head and grinned as he sensed that the race could be his. Phelan tried to get his stride going again, but his ankle hurt too much. The other runner was a long way in front, and Phelan's heart sank. He was at least the equal of the wizard's champion. He should at least have managed a tie, but he had lost it all now. But he would keep going. There was no honour in just giving up.

Then suddenly Phelan heard something – the strains of Kern's violin, playing a stirring melody from the Fire Festival. It revived his spirit and made him sprint, forgetting his twisted ankle. He had to run with the music.

The tempo quickened, and Phelan quickened too.

Soon he was level with the greyhound-man, then, just as the blue ribbon was pulled tightly across their path, Phelan found the pain in his ankle didn't matter. He was singing and running all at the same time. His lungs felt as if they could hold all the air in the world. He had enough breath for everything! He sang and ran and ran and sang.

The other runner stared in horror and disbelief as Phelan snapped the ribbon only a few hand-spans ahead of him! Phelan shouted in triumph, and Gemma and Fleabag danced with joy around their victorious friend. Inside the tent, Kern put down his violin and sat exhausted on a chair. He had never played like that in his life. He really didn't know how he had found it in himself, or why he had chosen that tune. It had just seemed important at the time.

In her place in the seat of honour, the Chancellor of All Wizards, the Princess Rowanne de Montiland smiled as she lifted a hand to silence the angry crowd.

'The first trial is a draw. One all!' she announced. 'We

will resume with the next trial tomorrow at noon, when the cat Fleabag will meet with our noble sister Heithra in a battle of wit and wisdom.'

And with that she bowed to the crowds and left.

17

Good Enough

Phelan fell asleep as soon as he reached his room. His body ached, and he was heavy-hearted as well. Although he had won the race, he was unhappy that he had lost the sword fight. He had known he stood little chance of beating Grimbold, but secretly he had hoped that maybe the Ring Fire would help him win.

He slept heavily, hoping to blot out all thought of the next day – the trial of wit and wisdom. Fleabag was surely the sharpest wit amongst them all, but against learned academics who were capable of reading and learning a book just by holding it… redoubtable cat that he was, did even Sir Fleabag Scrag-Belly stand a chance?

Fleabag and Gemma spent the afternoon trying to remember riddles and work out cunning word plays. They wanted to find something that might just catch out an over-confident wizard. But they weren't optimistic.

Everything depended on understanding the way the wizards thought – and neither of them stood a chance of fathoming *that*! 'If only we knew a friendly wizard!' Gemma sighed as she screwed up yet another sheet of paper and threw it across the room, missing the bin entirely.

Just then someone knocked timidly on the door.

Gemma opened it and sighed. Rowanne was standing outside smiling coyly. 'I wasn't eavesdropping, honestly, but I couldn't help overhearing what you were saying. I'd love to help, and I really can!'

Gemma stepped back. 'Would you like to come in?' she asked as cordially as she could, although she didn't really want any interruptions.

Rowanne shook her head. 'No, thank you – your rooms are a little full of the Ring Fire for my comfort. It's not that I don't love it any more, I do. It just... hurts. But I do need to talk to you. I can be that friendly wizard you need. That's what I went through all this *for*, after all! If only you'd let me, there's so much I could help you with.'

As she spoke, Rowanne looked so much like the faithful friend they knew and loved – yet so changed at the same time.

Gemma swallowed hard. 'I don't want to hurt your feelings, but we cannot accept your help. Surely you can see that?'

Rowanne looked deeply disappointed. 'I wish I hadn't bothered to go to all this trouble for the Ring Fire. I always used to feel that nothing I did was good enough for it. Now I've tried extra hard to do something special, and it's only made things worse.'

Gemma wanted to throw her arms around Rowanne

and hug her, but the sight of her old friend's eerily glowing skin held her back. Instead she just spread her hands wide and looked Rowanne in the eye. 'Perhaps you've been trying *too* hard? Why don't you dump all this silly Blue Magic nonsense? You don't have to be "good enough" for the Ring Fire, you just have to be *you*! You're still loved and wanted, and there's always enough forgiveness for whatever anyone has done.'

'You don't understand, do you?' Rowanne said bitterly as she turned to go.

Gemma caught hold of the wizard's cloak, which burned her hand with its icy coldness. 'Listen, I'd love to talk with you, but only as Rowanne, not as the Chancellor of All Wizards. If you can't come into our rooms, we'll go somewhere neutral. Is there somewhere in town we could meet?'

Rowanne turned back with obvious relief in her face. 'I daren't go far,' she whispered. 'If *they* think we're going away from the wizards' part of the University, they'll suspect me of being up to something. I've got to be careful. I'll make it known that I'm going to try to muddle your minds with spells of confusion under a pretence of chatting to you. Come to the library, it's very public there, so everyone can see we're meeting, but we'll sit where we can't be overheard easily. Be there in an hour.'

And with that she turned and walked away. Gemma was relieved Rowanne didn't float this time. She shut the door with a sigh and looked at her friends.

'Well?' Fleabag asked, 'are we going?'

Gemma nodded sadly. 'I am, certainly. I miss Rowanne, and if I can do anything to help her, I will.'

'It might be a trap,' suggested Phelan. 'I trust the real Rowanne, but is that really her?'

'Let's go and find out,' Fleabag proposed.

At the appointed time, the friends walked down to the library. They had not invited Kern to join them. It seemed best that he spent as much time as possible about his old duties as kitchen boy and stable hand so as not to arouse suspicion about too many dealings with the party from Harflorum. If people did not suspect him, he was safe. The wizards might not be able to hurt Claire, but Kern's life could be in great danger.

The late afternoon sun streamed through the library windows, sending golden shafts of light across the leather-bound books, gleaming on the azure silk ribbons that held the ancient, crumbling volumes together.

Seated in a small study area at the far end of the long room was Rowanne, dressed in the simple blue robes of an ordinary wizard. Her dark indigo hair was tied back and, apart from the strange glow from her skin, she looked almost her old self. The friends pulled up chairs near to her and she began to speak very quickly and quietly. She handed Gemma a plain white envelope. 'Here are the riddles and questions that Fleabag will be asked tomorrow. Take it, and burn it when you have read it.'

Fleabag and Gemma exchanged glances. The cat shook his head, and Gemma pushed the envelope away. 'We can't. That would be cheating. And anyway, it may be a trap.'

Rowanne looked offended. 'Honestly, Gemma! *Would* I?'

Phelan smiled. 'I don't think Gemma means that *you* would trap us, but the wizards may be testing *your* loyalty.

If Fleabag miraculously knows the answers tomorrow, they will have a pretty good idea who told us. Then it would be curtains for you. Who knows whether these books, even these chairs and desks, have listening spells cast by the wizards? They could know exactly what we are saying, every second. You said yourself that anything that is wizard-blue will ultimately betray us.'

Rowanne glowered. 'But don't you think that *I* would know? I *am* the Chancellor after all!'

'We had noticed!' Fleabag sniffed disapprovingly. 'Thanks, but no thanks. We have decided on the questions we are going to ask, and we will have to take what comes from the wizards.'

Rowanne did not look pleased as she pushed the long envelope back into a pocket in her robes. 'As you wish,' she sniffed. 'But what about the day after? The trial of magic. I had, as you know, planned to take this trial for you. But, well, due to unforeseen circumstances, I won't be able to. I knew I was being inducted as an arch wizard the other night, but not that I would become the Chancellor. This means I cannot be seen to act on your behalf.'

Fleabag bristled his whiskers and frowned.

'Honestly!' Rowanne went on. 'I really *didn't* know.'

'Leave it, Fleabag,' Phelan frowned. 'Whether she knew or not is immaterial. The question is, Gemma, do you feel that *you* should be taking the trial on behalf of the Ring Fire?'

Gemma closed her hands under the table, and felt the warming, soothing trickle of golden light between her fingers. It was safe, it was calm, and it told her very clearly to do nothing.

'No,' she said definitely. 'I will not be taking the trial.'

Rowanne blanched. 'Will you let me summon a wraith to appear in your likeness and take your place?'

Fleabag leaped onto the table and hissed angrily at Rowanne. Phelan thumped the table with his fist. '*NO*!' he shouted loudly, so everyone in the library turned to listen. 'The Ring Fire will fight its own battles its own way. It does not need the help of wraiths and wizards!'

By now, Phelan was leaning across the table and quite red in the face. A small crowd of shocked wizards had gathered nearby, eager to catch the fun of the row. But Fleabag bristled his fur and yowled at them in a way that made them all turn and run. Their fear of him had not evaporated, and Fleabag hoped it never would.

Gemma stood, and said in a gentler tone of voice: 'Listen, Rowanne, whatever reasons you had for becoming a wizard, they were wrong. Whatever reasons you had for accepting the trials on our behalf, they were wrong too. Now, either renounce the Blue Magic and help us as a friend of the Ring Fire, or leave us alone.'

And with that, Gemma turned and walked from the library, followed closely by Phelan and Fleabag, who was stepping as proudly as a three-legged cat can, hissing and flashing his fire-golden eyes this way and that.

As the cat walked by, the wizards glowered, but did not dare cast a single spell.

18

Wit and Wisdom

At noon precisely Fleabag sat on a golden-red velvet cushion on an ornate chair in the middle of the Great Hall, the very room where he, Gemma and Phelan had defeated the old Chancellor. The memory of that day gave the cat confidence, despite the sea of threatening faces and gowns of various hues of blue that washed around him.

Fleabag faced his opponent, a thin, sour-faced woman in an indigo gown. She leaned on the highly polished table between them, put her skeletal fingertips together, and peered over them at Fleabag. She did not seem to be the least bit daunted by the feline nature of her opponent.

On the contrary, she looked more as if she was contemplating a rather succulent-sounding menu, and about to order the lot!

So this was Rowanne's 'noble sister' Heithra.

Fleabag looked a great deal calmer than he felt. He had

spent all morning with Gemma, peering into the flame of the Ring Fire in the Fire Wielder's hands. The comforting warmth had spread though his three legs, right out to his ear-tips and his whiskers. But even though Gemma had promised to keep him surrounded by the safety of the Fire while he went through his ordeal, he was now shivering inside. He hoped it did not show, but he could not help the tip of his tail twitching as he caught sight of Rowanne, coming to sit on one of the judges' seats on the dais at the top end of the hall.

M'Kinnik rose to his feet and read from a scroll. 'Each contestant will challenge the other with feats of wisdom and wit, strictly taking turns, until one contestant fails to answer. The trial will then have been won by whoever has answered the greatest number of questions correctly.'

At the sound of a small silver gong being struck, both Heithra and Fleabag stood and bowed formally to each other, although neither contestant took their eyes from each other's faces for a split second.

'Pray, go first,' Heithra said, in a voice that sounded like dry paper being screwed up.

Fleabag coughed slightly and stroked his whiskers with his paw. Here went nothing!

'My first is nobility, my second jumps high,
my third carries all, whatever I buy.
My fourth belies my expensive taste,
and my fifth and my last lies under my waist.
Who am I?'

Fleabag swallowed hard. It was an easy one, obvious even, but he had to test the water somehow. So much depended on *how* this woman thought.

Heithra scarcely paused to take breath. '*Sir* is a title of nobility, but I'm sure I can't see why you should be so honoured, just because you wear a golden earring. *Fleas* jump high, *bags* carry everything in them, *scrag* is the cheap cut of the meat – and more than a cat deserves – and your disgustingly fat *belly* lies under your waist, or it would if you had one. You are Sir Fleabag Scrag-Belly, although I strongly suspect that is not your real name.'

'You bet!' Fleabag muttered under his breath. Phelan was the only other living person who knew what his real name was. The cat had always kept it a closely guarded secret; it was his protection against the Blue Magic because no major spells could be cast without the victim's real name being used.

'*Please* try to stretch my brain at least a little, or I shall become bored very quickly,' Heithra went on. 'At least I can see this so-called challenge will be very short, if that is the best you can do.'

Fleabag blushed under his black fur and bristled his eyebrow whiskers angrily. But he could not deny she had got the answer correct. Now it was her turn. He listened intently.

'I'd better make it easy for you, poor puss,' Heithra sneered. 'I went out, and stood on a road with another road under me, a road above me, and a road on either side of me. Where was I?' Heithra put her head on one side and smiled, a chilling smile, showing neat, over-white teeth.

Fleabag took a deep breath. This was a different sort of riddle from the ones he had been rehearsing with Gemma. He had to stay calm and use his imagination. She was standing outside on a road, that was a good start.

With another road under her, she could be on a bridge over a stream, for that would be a road to a fish... then what could be the roads above and on either side? Fleabag closed his eyes and imagined standing on a road going over a bridge with something passing by on either side... That was it – *birds*! The air was their road, and that was all around! Joyfully he blurted out the answer.

He could see Heithra was annoyed, but he grinned gleefully under his whiskers. Perhaps he stood a chance after all! In his mind he threw away all the rhyming riddles he had learned. These were easier. All he had to do was think of something and find a difficult or obscure way of saying something – and he was good at being difficult!

'Who is armour-plated in silver mail, jumps higher than an athlete and goes away to come home?' he asked.

Again Heithra did not pause. 'A salmon,' she replied. 'They have silver scales and leap up waterfalls. They also leave their home rivers to grow up in far-off waters before recrossing wide oceans to come home to spawn. Now it's your turn. What was the drink I had yesterday? It was neither wine nor water, milk nor ale. It came in neither a stream nor a cup, yet only a humble person could drink it.'

'Well, that counts you out!' retorted Fleabag as his mind raced. How could anyone drink using neither a cup nor a stream? Only a humble person would drink whilst on his knees, so it was something to do with licking or lapping from something down low near the ground. That was easy – being a cat, he did that all the time. Puddles? No. That would count as water and they always tasted unspeakable. *Dogs* drank from puddles. What would he drink from that was low down? 'Dew!' he shouted out loud.

It was a bit of a stretch of the imagination. Dew was a sort of water really... He glanced at Heithra's face. He needn't have worried. Two red spots of angry colour on her cheeks told him he was right!

'What has eight feet, four eyes and carries its knees above its head?' Fleabag asked quickly. He felt as if he was beginning to enjoy this!

'A spider,' Heithra replied, just as quickly. Then she cracked her knuckles before putting her fingertips together and peering over them again. 'What flies higher than an eagle, whistles like the wind, stings like a hornet and is hard to catch until it catches you?'

Fleabag closed his eyes and tried to imagine watching something flying very high, whistling, stinging, and so swift even Rowanne could not grasp it as it passed, yet out to catch *him*? The thought of Rowanne gave him the clue he needed. For he pictured her as she used to be, with the other knights in the practice yards, swinging their swords at dummies and shooting their long yew bows at the butts... 'An arrow!' he said triumphantly.

He was ready with the next one, for it followed on easily from the last: 'Who is the great protectress dressed in bright colours who goes out for the day on a man's arm, yet comes home with blood on her bent back?' (Or it could go out on a woman's arm he thought, glancing across to Rowanne, who he could see had caught his drift easily.)

Heithra hesitated a second on this one. The idea of a great protectress who was gaily dressed on a man's arm had thrown her for a moment or two. 'A shield!' she replied at last. 'It goes out on a man's arm, painted with bright heraldry, but by the end of the day's battle, its curved surface is covered with blood. Now,' she said, 'what is the great devourer who consumes the sea and hills, yet has no teeth? It fears the sun but scorns the power of men and women.'

Fleabag grinned. Gemma had taught him a rhyming version of this one! He had planned to use it himself. 'Fog!' he answered.

But then he panicked. All the riddles he had stored seemed suddenly to have fled his fish-filled brain. He had to think quickly – something – anything just to keep going... 'Four went out walking together, four hung around, staring at the ground. Two found the way ahead, two shooed off the dogs and a long, thin dirty one swung behind them all.'

Heithra shrugged contemptuously. 'A cow. Four legs to walk with, four teats on her udder, two eyes, two horns and a dirty tail.' Then with a glance at the judges she added, 'unless you are going to make at least *some* attempt to tax my brain, I am going to ask one of the kitchen staff to take my place. This really is becoming very tedious.'

Fleabag stared very hard back. 'Well, you can't be so very clever yourself! I'm only a mere cat and you haven't caught me out yet, have you?'

Heithra flushed very red at the insult and rose to her feet. From her thin heights she stared down at Fleabag and hissed: 'Who is the traitor in your midst, and how should she be punished?'

Fleabag almost fell backwards off his cushion. He felt himself go pale under his matted, black fur. He glanced quickly over his shoulder at Gemma, who looked equally stunned. Then from the corner of his eye he saw Phelan lean forward and shake his head.

Fleabag could sense Rowanne's fear from where she sat, although he did not risk looking at her. The cat knew what Phelan was trying to say: one betrayal never deserves another.

Fleabag had to risk losing the entire Challenge. He would have to trust the Ring Fire to think of something. He could only answer this one honestly. Even though he knew the answers to both questions, there was only one possible reply, and he gave it. 'It is not for me to say.'

The wizards cheered and clapped loudly and long. Heithra was lifted out of her seat and carried shoulder high around the hall. Fleabag turned to slink out of the room as quietly and inconspicuously as possible, but as he jumped down from the cushion, a loud, stentorian voice rang across the jubilant hubbub.

'*SILENCE*!'

Everyone stopped and turned to the figure of the High Chancellor, standing on her dais, her arms flung wide, and her too-blue eyes blazing in fury. Heithra was gently allowed to stand again.

'The cat has one more question!' Rowanne commanded. 'The trial is won by the person – or cat – who answers the most questions. Is that not right, M'Kinnik?'

The elderly wizard nodded, but looked confused. 'It is, my Lady, but what is your point?'

'My point is, that Heithra asked *two* questions last turn, which means that she has asked six, and the cat, although he opened the trial, has only asked five.'

M'Kinnik shrugged. 'So what? Those were two questions he couldn't answer, so he has doubly lost!' The crowd laughed at this, but Fleabag jumped back onto his cushion. If Rowanne was trying to get him a second chance, he would have to think very quickly. If the riddles they had begun with were wit, and Heithra's last two questions were wisdom, then he was also entitled to ask a question of wisdom. What should it be? He had no time to confer with the others. He would have to have something ready in case Rowanne won him a chance... Fleabag looked across at Gemma who was holding the Ring Fire in her open palm. The question he needed was in there somewhere...

Rowanne wasn't going to be put off by M'Kinnik. 'My point, my Lord,' she persisted, 'is that the cat should not have been asked two questions *together*. Heithra broke the rules that you yourself read out. You stipulated that the contestants were to take strict turns! She cheated, and therefore for that reason alone, the cat deserves one last question.'

Heithra shrugged as she strode back to her place. 'It makes absolutely no difference to me, my Lord M'Kinnik. I did not intentionally cheat. I was, I freely admit, a little carried away. I am quite happy to let the cat have another question if this makes my Lady, the High Chancellor of All Wizards, happy. The cat's questions are so inferior, that there will really not be a problem. Let him ask whatever he likes.' And she smiled magnanimously at Fleabag as she settled herself down, and once again peered disconcertingly over her thin fingertips.

Fleabag managed to focus beyond her, at the small

glow of Ring Fire between Gemma's fingers.

And without thinking, he opened his mouth and asked, 'Where is the Ring's End?'

19

Another Riddle

Heithra went very pale and dropped her pointed fingers to the table. 'No one knows that! That is not a fair question!' She looked pleadingly towards the dais.

Rowanne spoke briefly with M'Kinnik and the third judge, an elderly man on her left. Then she waved her hand dismissively. 'You have trapped yourself out of your own mouth, Heithra. You said before all witnesses that the cat could ask any question he liked.'

Then M'Kinnik turned to Rowanne and hissed angrily, 'I told you she'd foul it up. *I'd* have done a far better job, if only you had listened to me!'

Rowanne said nothing, but rose from her seat. 'I declare this trial a draw,' she said, and turned and walked out.

No one moved or spoke. At last M'Kinnik stood and very slowly followed Rowanne. As he reached the door, he spoke quietly to a guard, and walked out.

The crowd broke into a noisy hubbub of dispute.

But as Gemma, Phelan and Fleabag tried to slip away, the guards barred their way with business-like spears and swords. 'You ain't goin' anywhere,' a mean-looking man informed them. 'You're all under arrest. M'Kinnik's orders.'

'Arrest', thankfully, meant house arrest, in their rooms rather than in a dungeon. Fleabag was irritated not to be allowed out onto the tiles to think, but he soon found the wide window ledge reasonably comfortable. Only Gemma was cross, because it meant opening the window every time he wanted to come in or out – which was frequently – and the winter air was very cold.

Phelan asked if Kern would be allowed to come and play his violin to them, and a generous bribe to the guard on duty ensured that the lad was not long in coming.

The boy played softly all afternoon, folk tunes, ballads, and wistful airs. Phelan, Gemma and Fleabag (when he eventually came inside to settle) sat quietly around the log fire, listening to the soothing tones of the boy's playing. No one spoke for a long time.

At last Fleabag broke the silence. 'Well, Gemma, where *is* the Ring's End, and what is it?'

'That's two questions! You're only allowed one!' Gemma laughed. Then she looked serious again. 'I don't know. In fact, I don't have the foggiest.' She looked questioningly at Phelan. His parents had once been servants of the Ring Fire in Rowanne's city of Erbwenneth. When they had been wrongfully put to death, he had lived with a wise man called Aelforth. All of these good people had told him stories and wisdom of the Ring Fire, long before he could understand what any of it meant.

Phelan looked at the heavy grey sky outside. 'I think it's something to do with where the Fire Giver is to be found:

"If the Fire Giver you truly seek
follow no track, green or bleak.
Listen to the words I say:
To the Ring's End make your way."'

'But what does that mean?' Gemma asked. 'It's like one of those riddles Fleabag and I were working on; a ring doesn't have an end!'

'It must mean something,' Fleabag argued. 'I'd not heard that rhyme before, yet I knew the question I had to ask just by looking into the Ring Fire in Gemma's hands. I don't know,' he sighed. 'I'm going to sleep. My head hurts, and not being able to run over the tiles for a snack to keep me going before teatime is really sapping my will to live.'

And with that he stretched out on the hearthrug and began to purr.

'How can he be so contented at a time like this!' Gemma grumbled affectionately. And she stroked his black, barrel-like tummy with the toe of her slipper. A few fleas jumped off, but Gemma brushed them away before they could nibble at her ankles.

Suddenly Kern stopped playing his violin. 'Do you mind if I make a suggestion? I know I'm not one of your Ring Fire people, but I've got an idea that might help.'

Phelan smiled and moved over so Kern could sit by the fire. 'It's not a matter of being "one of us" or not. I don't even know what that means. But you're our friend, and that's what matters. So give it a whirl, what's your idea?'

Kern twiddled his violin between his fingers and watched the firelight reflecting on its varnish. 'It's just that... Oh no, it sounds silly, and I don't know anything of your stuff. Sorry,' and he got up to play again.

'No, go on,' urged Gemma. 'Please. Even if it isn't the answer, it might give us a clue.'

Kern took a deep breath. 'Do you remember when I found my mother asleep in the strange fire, and you told me it wasn't magic, but it was real, and the Ring Fire had her, and she was safe?'

'Yes? Go on,' Phelan urged.

'And you said that the room could be wherever the Fire Giver wanted it to be?'

'Yes...?' Even Fleabag had woken up again.

'Well, it's just that, well, it seems to me that if that is so, then perhaps this Ring's End is somewhere near there. Because if that's the Fire Giver's room, then he or she might be there.' And Kern slumped back against the settee's cushions and waited for the laughter.

But none came. Instead Phelan slapped him on the back. 'Well done. You're quite right. It's obvious!'

'I've always felt that the Ring Fire could exist anywhere, even here,' Gemma added. 'And when you think about it, that would explain why you can't follow a "track" to get to it.'

Fleabag opened one golden eye. 'Of *course* he's right. *I* knew it all along, I just didn't want to embarrass you pathetic humans by my wit and wisdom. I knew you'd get there by and by. I was just testing to see how long it would take you to get the answer!' And with that, the incorrigible cat rolled over to toast his other side by the fire. In the wink of an eye he seemed to be asleep once more.

'It's all very well,' Gemma said thoughtfully, 'but *how* are we going to find that room again? We're under arrest, after all. We can't leave here without an escort.'

Kern bit his lip. 'I know you don't like magic and stuff, but I might be able to help there. I've known for a long time that I can do all sorts of things with my violin...'

'Well now you've got rid of that dreadful catgut you might be able to,' said Fleabag, although he was supposed to be asleep.

'Yes, well, sorry about that. But I can do things like put people to sleep, and wake them up, and I can make them feel happy or sad or anything really. But it's not magic, or at least I don't think it is. It's just something I can do, and I use it to help people, when they're tired or upset or sad. Never to harm them.'

'So what's your suggestion?' Phelan asked. 'If you're not using spells or potions, but it's just a natural talent you have, then I'm happy to hear what you have to say.'

'I agree,' said Gemma. 'I can't see anything wrong in soothing people's worries or making people want to dance.'

'Well,' Kern went on, plucking up courage, 'I know this building like the back of my hand. If you come with me, I might be able to lead you past guards, either with stealth, or with a little musical help to put the soldiers to sleep. And between us, we can spend the night searching for this secret room. I must admit, I want to find my mother again. I do believe what you say about her being safe and well, but I would like to see her for myself.'

'Of course you do. I'd feel the same – if I had a mother.'

Gemma felt sad for a moment. She could not remember anything about her parents, and often wished she could. 'What do you think, Phelan? Are you happy with Kern's plan?'

Phelan nodded. 'Yes, I think we ought to try. If we can find the Ring's End, then we will be able to ask the Fire Giver what to do tomorrow. That is...' he hesitated, 'if you still don't think it's right to take the magical trial yourself, Gemma?'

'Certainly not!' she replied emphatically. 'I'm more certain than ever that the Fire Giver will sort this out in a way we haven't even thought of. But we do need help, and that room was a very special place. I'm certain I would feel stronger and more confident just by sitting there. Do you think that would be all right, Phelan?'

'Definitely!' he grinned. 'But Kern, if you can put people to sleep just by playing to them, how are *we* going to stay awake?'

Kern laughed and reached over to a candle softened by the heat of the fire. He pulled off a thick chunk of creamy-white wax. 'It's easy. Ear-plugs! I don't need them. I can play without affecting myself – unless I want to, that is. I'll lead you by touch and hand signals.'

20

Secret Ways

No amount of persuasion would entice Fleabag to wear ear-plugs. So, in the end, Gemma told him that if he fell asleep on the job she would leave him next to the nearest door and pretend he was a draught excluder. She was *not* going to carry him around for the whole evening.

Fleabag sniffily replied that he *never* fell asleep at inappropriate moments, least of all on the job, but his comments were only met with derisive laughter. So to test whether he could withstand Kern's music (and to be sure the ear-plugs worked), Kern played one of his best melodies for producing sleep.

Fleabag sternly sat to attention the whole time, and stared straight ahead, with his eyes as wide and golden as carriage-lamps. His eyelids did not flicker once. 'You see?' he said when Kern had finished, and the others had unblocked their ears. 'I'm perfectly in control of myself. I succumb to nothing!'

'Except to mouldy fish heads!' Gemma laughed, producing one from behind a cushion. 'How long has *that* been there, you miserable creature?'

'Ah!' Fleabag purred contentedly. 'I've been looking for that. Give it here!' and he jumped up, snatched it from between Gemma's fingers, and took it off into a corner to give it his full and undivided attention.

That evening, when supper had been served and cleared away, Gemma contrived to open the study door a crack, without the guard challenging her. Once the wax earplugs were all in place, Kern lifted his violin and began to play. This time Fleabag's head nodded, and even Gemma and Phelan found their minds drifting as soft strains seeped though the candlewax plugs.

After a little while, Kern eased the door a little wider with his foot. There was still no challenge. Kern nodded to Fleabag who slipped outside to the dark, shadowy corridor. He disappeared with a whisk of his bottlebrush tail. Gemma followed, and Phelan came last, carrying Rowanne's sword strapped around his waist. He didn't want to use it, but took it along, just in case.

Phelan closed the door, in case anyone should be suspicious. With any luck, the sleeping guards, who were leaning against the wall, snoring nicely, would waken in a few moments and think they had just dozed off and no harm had been done.

Kern led them swiftly to the right, then up a steep spiral staircase. Up and up they went, seemingly for ever. At first the treads and banisters were made of ornately wrought patterns but, as it twisted nearer and nearer to the servants' quarters, the treads became narrow wooden boards with a plain iron rail.

At last, the friends found themselves breathless in a hexagonal room at the top of a tall tower, with views far across the plains beyond the town.

The moon was full. In its light, Gemma could see in the distance the mountains where she lived. How she wished she could be back there at her tiny cottage in the rocks with her two cats (talking grandkittens of Fleabag's) and her garden. There was peace and quiet, time to listen to the Ring Fire and, best of all, no magic – blue or otherwise.

She sighed. But this had to be dealt with first. In the soft moonlight, Gemma could see that Kern looked disappointed. 'I had hoped that as this room is so nearly round, we might find the stone fireplace and my mother here. But I can see that it is not going to be as easy as that. At least here we can talk and think without being overheard.'

'Just a moment,' Fleabag warned. 'I had what I thought was a private chat in a place like this once, and I found one of Chancellor Domnall's crows was sitting on the roof, listening to every word.' The cat jumped up on the window sill and craned his neck to look out. 'There's too much of an overhang; I can't really see.'

'I know,' Kern volunteered. 'I'll play one of my sleeping melodies.'

'At least if anyone is up there they can be sure of dropping off that way!' laughed Fleabag.

Phelan, Gemma and Kern looked most disapprovingly at the cat, but none of them could resist laughing at his awful joke. They all needed to laugh to ease the fear they were all feeling. Then they put their ear-plugs in, and Kern played.

After the tune was finished, Kern nodded, and the two other humans cleared their ears. Fleabag, however, had to be woken up. He protested he had his eyes closed because he was trying to hear what he thought was a spying mouse. But no one believed him because he had been snoring so loudly.

'Now,' Phelan began, 'we are here to try to find the circular room with the stone fireplace. Perhaps it is a special room, that is always here so people who love the Ring Fire can always find a safe place to be. But it could also be somewhere that the Fire Giver has created to keep Kern's mother, Claire, safe. We've no way of knowing but, if we can find it, we may discover some clue as to where or what the Ring's End may be. That should lead us to the Fire Giver himself, then we can ask him what to do about the trial of magic in the morning.'

'I wish we could just refuse to take part,' Gemma said sadly. 'But that would be the same as conceding. I do feel that Rowanne was right about one thing, though.'

'What was that?' Phelan asked.

'That, somehow, the Ring Fire will win in the end. If we make a mess of things tomorrow, it may take a little longer and someone else to make things turn out as they ought, but everything *will* be all right in the end.'

'The trouble is,' Fleabag added ruefully, 'that one story's end is the beginning of another. Once one situation is sorted out, it inevitably becomes the gateway to the next lot of problems. There won't ever be a "happily ever after" until we reach the Fire Giver's own world, the Land Beyond.'

'Oh my, you do sound doleful this evening.' Gemma gave her friend a playful rub behind his ears that made him purr warmly. 'Now, how do we start looking? Kern, you know this place well. Have you any ideas?'

'No. This turret room was my only bet, and that was wrong. But what I *do* know is that although this building looks square and ordinary from the outside, it's constructed very cunningly. Instead of being a simple four-sided design, like the others in the University, it's actually a star shape on the inside, and in some places it can fold and tuck in on itself, so when you think you are walking in one direction, you're actually going somewhere completely different. It causes chaos amongst new servants; some have been known to go missing for weeks at a time! Domnall showed me how to get around when I was quite little.

'There is a knack to it: you must not be afraid of how odd things may *seem* and you have to think clearly at all costs. It has nothing to do with magic, and a lot to do with courage. It was built that way to confuse intruders, and as a test of determination for people who came here wanting to study. That was in the days when a wizard was simply a wise man or woman, not a practitioner of evil arts.'

'So we must all stay close to you, Kern,' Phelan said. 'Do we have to go all the way down to the ground floor again?'

Kern laughed. 'No, it's easier than that.' And he opened a door in the wall that no one had noticed before. Beyond was a long attic room filled with servants sleeping in their truckle beds. Bewildered, Gemma, Phelan and Fleabag looked back into the turret room behind them. There it was, with windows on every wall, looking out high over the roofs. They were way above anywhere that could possibly join to another part of the building.

Kern put his finger to his lips and whispered, 'As I said, don't be afraid, and stay together. We won't lose each other as long as we stay in the same room as each other. Hold onto someone else as you step through the door. If one of us steps over a threshold without the others, it could take for ever to catch up again.' And with that he quietly walked from the turret room into the attic ahead.

He nodded. 'We can let go now.' Then he set about very softly opening the two doors at the far end of the attic. 'No, no sign of the room here. Follow me.'

Kern bent down and pushed a rug aside. There in the floor was a trapdoor. He pulled on the iron ring and softly lowered the cover back until it rested on the floor. 'Come quickly, and hold on!'

Phelan put his hand on the boy's shoulder and Gemma grabbed Phelan's shirt. Fleabag jumped onto Gemma's shoulder as she bent down to slide through the opening.

The next room was a long, stone-arched gallery, lit by blue flaming torches in wall brackets. Kern led the way down the wooden stair from the trapdoor. As Gemma let the wooden cover fall back into place, it closed with a click. She looked back up at it, but there was no sign that there had even been a way through the ceiling.

'Ugh!' she exclaimed as she jumped down from the ladder. 'This is beginning to give me the creeps!' And then the ladder disappeared.

The gallery had doorways between each stone arch on the left, and on the right, a long row of lancet windows, tall, plain and with thick rounded pillars between each one. The friends spread out along the length of the gallery, opening doorways and peering through the windows. The first few looked out over a moonlight garden, but then the scenes began to change.

Sometimes the explorers found themselves watching a feast in what appeared to be a private dining room, yet the next window which was scarcely a man's hand-span away, showed a practice yard with knights fencing or wrestling in broad daylight in summer.

'How much of this is real?' Gemma asked.

Kern just shrugged. 'As real as anything the wizards do,' he replied. 'If we go to the end of here, we should get to the centre of the star, and from there it might be easier to find our way onwards. But whatever you do, stay in contact with each other as you go through doorways, and if a path looks impossible keep going. Remember, things are not as they seem!'

Gemma threw a worried glance at Phelan. For the first time, she was wondering whether Kern was to be trusted, and if his story about his mother and him being the unwanted relations of the old Chancellor had been a complicated lie to lead them all into a trap.

Gemma opened her hand and looked at the Ring Fire while she thought of Kern. It was burning small and clear. She closed her hand again. Kern was not a traitor, but was this the way to find the small room with the stone fireplace? She was about to look into the Ring Fire again, when suddenly guards rushed in, yelling challenges.

Kern put his fiddle to his shoulder and drew the bow across the strings. Gemma did not wait to put the plugs in her ears; she grabbed Fleabag, put her hand on

Phelan's shoulder and ran through the nearest doorway with Kern hot on her heels…

The Great Hall was the last place Gemma wanted to be. It was the room where Rowanne's initiation had taken place, as well as Fleabag's trial of wisdom and wit. It was also the room that was built to imitate the Hall of Light back at Harflorum, the very room where she, Phelan and Fleabag had defeated the old Chancellor. It had been rebuilt since the fire, of course, but every time they came there since, visions of the coloured magics he had thrown at them always flashed through her memory.

Thankfully the hall was empty.

Kern walked straight to the central point, which was more or less where Fleabag's red-gold cushion had been placed the day before. Then he put his violin to his shoulder and began to play a different sort of music, one that cleared the mind. 'Think!' he said urgently. 'Think of the room, and we will find our way to it.'

But as the image of the room and its strange fireplace began to drift through their minds, M'Kinnik ran into the hall with his arms raised, already chanting a spell.

Kern turned and played his music for all he was worth, subtly changing the tune from one that cleared the head to a different melody, that was so complex and intertwining that no one could think at all.

Gemma had been clenching her fists, trying to concentrate on the image of the Ring Fire burning around the friends, protecting them from M'Kinnik's malice, when she saw him hesitate and falter, stumbling and stroking his chin as he tried to remember what it was he had been trying to say or do.

'Quick!' hissed Kern, 'this way,' and he slipped

through a tiny wooden door set into a thick, carved pillar.

Kern did not miss a note as he pushed the door wider with his knee, and Gemma, Phelan and Fleabag slid behind him into a long, vaulted hall.

'Phew!' sighed Kern as he leaned against the wall, eyes closed, and the fiddle hanging loosely at his side. 'That was close!'

Gemma, Fleabag and Phelan did not reply, for M'Kinnik and his wizards were straight ahead – less than a wand's length away.

21

Descending into Darkness

Kern played frantically as he ran straight through the crowd of blue-clad men and women. Heads nodded and knees sank as his music swept across them like a soporific wind.

Phelan and Gemma kept as close as they could behind Kern, but Fleabag could not keep up on his three legs. Gemma turned and grabbed him, just as Kern was stepping through a doorway that had suddenly appeared only a few steps ahead of them. She took hold of Phelan's coat again just as he crossed the threshold.

They found themselves standing inside the top of a dizzy-looking tower with a narrow stone stair twisting away below. Gemma gulped. She did not like heights, and on their left was just a black space. There was no handrail, just cold, dark nothingness.

'Kern... Kern, I think there's something you ought to know...' Her voice sounded shaky as she tried to take a few steps downwards.

'Yes?' The sound of their feet echoed up from out of the gloom. Gemma groped her hand down the cold stone wall on the right and tried not to think of the slippery steps under her feet.

'What is it?' Kern's voice drifted up out of the depths. It sounded so far away, muffled by the echoing tread of their feet.

'It's just that...' Gemma tried hard not to look down. She gulped. Her head was swimming, she was certain she was going to fall... or even worse, to fling herself down into the void. She was feeling sick, so she stopped and turned to face the cold wall. She clutched Fleabag so tightly he mewed. She couldn't walk and talk at the same time.

'Stop, please!' she called urgently. 'I've got to tell you that every time we think we have put our pursuers to sleep, we haven't. When I turned to pick Fleabag up just then, M'Kinnik and all his followers were fading away. They are just *sendings*. They aren't real. Somewhere in this place, the real wizards are watching us, and we are running round and round, exhausting ourselves, like mice on a wheel. They are playing with us, Kern!'

The boy stopped. Gemma could hear him breathing hard. Although they were standing in almost pitch black, the violin glowed an eerie blue.

Fleabag pushed his furry face into Gemma's ear. 'Light the Ring Fire, Gemma. I'm certain Kern doesn't mean to, but I think he's leading us the wrong way.'

Gemma passed Fleabag onto Phelan's shoulder. 'You take him, I need both hands free,' she said. Then, standing with her back to the wall, she held out her right hand so the Ring Fire gave a strong, golden light. But what they saw made them gasp, for instead of standing on a stair spiralling down into terrifying empty space, they now found a floor on their left, with a stone wall and a wide, oak door slightly ajar.

Without thinking, Gemma stepped down from the stair and pushed the door wider. It creaked on its hinges. It was solid. The floor was solid.

'Hey,' she whispered. 'This way. The Ring Fire wants us to go in here.'

'Careful,' Kern warned. 'I've never found a doorway at that point before. It could be a trick, maybe even another sending. You'll be killed if you take a wrong turn here; that empty space below us is real – I promise.'

But Gemma was already halfway through the doorway, with Phelan and Fleabag close behind her. Kern did not hesitate, but ran back up the last steps and jumped in through the entrance, just as it disappeared.

Inside, the glow from the Ring Fire in Gemma's hands was bathing everything with a warm golden light.

For one second, Gemma was hopeful that they had found their strange little room for by the light of the Ring Fire they could see it was very similarly built. This room was quite bare, and circular, constructed from close-fitting blocks of plain, white stone. All around were tall, lancet windows, shuttered against the bleak, black night outside. The wind howled, rattling at the shutter catches. Gemma instinctively stepped towards the grate, to see if there were coals that could be stirred to some sort of life.

But the fire had long died. A few ashes and lumps of black charcoal were all that was left. Gemma stared at the stone mantelpiece, and shook her head. Something was very familiar about it, but also very wrong, all at the same time.

This was not the place they were looking for.

Just then, the wind blew even harder, lashing the outer walls and wailing. The door creaked open, then slammed shut. The Ring Fire flickered in Gemma's hands and, for a split second, everything was dark. Then the golden light sprang back, revealing a tall, dark-swathed figure, standing in the very centre of the room.

Kern raised his left hand and lifted his violin towards his shoulder.

But the figure stepped forward and put a dark gloved hand across the strings. 'Don't touch it, whatever you do,' a familiar voice warned.

'Rowanne!' Gemma gasped. 'Are you all right? What are you doing here?'

The Princess, draped in blue-black from head to toe, pulled her hood forward and shielded her eyes from the sight of the Ring Fire. 'I hoped I would catch up with you. Kern uses these secret ways very skilfully. But he kept playing the violin so I couldn't get close.'

'Was that because it reminded you of the Ring Fire? Does it hurt when Kern plays it?' Phelan asked kindly.

'No, on the contrary,' Rowanne replied. 'It is infused with Blue Magic. It summoned me, but it also summoned every other wizard for miles around. I didn't want them to find me trying to help you.'

'Thank you for all the help you've tried to give us so far, especially for the sword…' Phelan began.

But the dark figure put a finger to her lips. 'Hush, there is no time to talk now. Kern, or whatever your name is, give me the fiddle. Every time you play it, you might as well wave a flag, blow a trumpet and shout, "Kern is here!" '

'Oh I don't know; it's not so bad now it has decent strings on it,' Fleabag said. 'I'd have agreed with you when it had Great-Aunt Bertha's guts strung on it. I never liked Bertha particularly, but I didn't think it was right for Kern to play jigs on her intestines.'

Phelan glowered at the cat, then glanced at Kern. The boy looked deeply hurt as he clutched his most treasured – and probably only – possession in the whole world to his chest, and scowled.

Rowanne spread her hands and looked appealingly at Phelan. 'Surely you know that Domnall gave it to him. Even if the person who plays it is playing the Ring Fire's own music, the instrument itself is made with magic. Did I not warn you that everything that was wizard-blue would ultimately betray you? Why do you think I wouldn't let Kern bring that thing from Harflorum when we left? Even though I had no training at that stage, I could sense that it was dangerous, and that the wizards wanted Kern to have it. I did not know why at the time, but I do now.

'They can't use it to *do* magic, only to be aware of where you are and what you're playing. They've been following you all evening. And what's more, you've been giving away who you really are with every note you play. You've got to give it to me, or at least stop playing it!'

Rowanne stretched out her hand, but Kern cowered back, clutching his fiddle so tightly he almost snapped it again.

‘No!’ he shouted, ‘No! It’s not true! You’re lying!’

Phelan, Fleabag and Gemma stared at Kern. When Kern saw they believed Rowanne, he tried to slide towards the door.

‘How *dare* you say such things?’ he howled. ‘Domnall was my brother. He was the only person who ever cared about me.’

Rowanne shook her head. ‘Domnall didn’t give it to you to be kind. He gave it to you to trap you. Isn’t that so?’

Kern turned red and stamped. ‘No! He gave it to me because he knew I loved music. I’ll never part with it, never!’ And with that he turned and ran through the door by which they had entered.

Phelan, Gemma and Fleabag weren’t quick enough to catch hold of him as he went through. Without him they had no idea of how to get back. There was no point trying to retrace their steps.

‘Bother!’ Fleabag moaned. ‘Now we’ll have to get back a different way, and I’d just spotted a nice juicy rat before the door slammed.’

‘How could you think of your stomach at a time like this?’ Gemma chided.

‘Quite easily,’ the cat replied. ‘It never stops thinking about me, so why should I forget *it*?’

Rowanne laughed, but it was not a merry sound. It was as lost and lonely as the wind outside the walls. ‘Dear Fleabag,’ she said with genuine affection, ‘I expect when you get back to your study, you will find supper laid out just as you ordered it.’

‘But where *is* our study?’ Fleabag scratched himself behind an ear. ‘Even with my super feline sense of direction, all this folded space and the twisted dimensions we've been through have thrown me entirely. Where are we, and how do we get back?'

'This way,' Rowanne moved a stone in the wall to one side with a light touch and, as she did so, another stone moved on the other side, making an opening wide enough even for Phelan's broad shoulders.

Fleabag jumped through first, followed by Gemma and Phelan. Ahead was the warm glow of the study fire, and an evening meal laid out, just as Rowanne had promised.

'Thank you, Rowanne,' Gemma said, 'I know you really are trying to help, it just seems to have all gone terribly wrong.'

The Chancellor nodded. 'I know,' she replied, but her voice sounded choked.

Just then Phelan had a thought and put his head back through the opening. 'Rowanne, what did you mean by the violin being a trap for Kern?'

Rowanne was just a dark smudge in a darker darkness now the Ring Fire had left the room with Gemma. She raised her arms. 'Ask Kern. She knows the truth.'

At that moment, the door behind them opened, and Kern slipped in, looking pale and frightened. Phelan turned back to speak to Rowanne again, but she was not there. They were staring at a bookcase with a small gap where a few volumes had fallen down.

22

The Woman of Flowers

Kern sank miserably into a deep leather armchair – and got up again very quickly, apologizing profusely. Fleabag disliked being used as a cushion by any human – even Phelan.

The boy paced the room swinging his fiddle between his fingers as he walked. Once or twice he raised it to his shoulder, but lowered it again as he caught Phelan's warning look.

The boy glowered back at the King. 'But I *need* to play it or I'll explode. You don't understand!' he sulked. 'I just can't stand *not* playing it.'

Gemma put a small flicker of Ring Fire onto the candle on the table. 'Watch the glow, it will help to calm you,' she said kindly. 'We're not unsympathetic – it's just too dangerous. For you as well as for us.'

Kern pushed his violin behind a chair and turned his back on them all, staring out of the window into the wintry blackness beyond. Snow flung itself at the window panes like millions of white bees endlessly swarming around and around, until Kern began to feel dizzy. He rested his head on the glass and fought the sting of tears in his eyes.

Just as he had decided to go to bed and try to forget everything until the morning, Gemma suddenly gave a shout. 'How *could* we have been so stupid?'

'Speak for yourself,' Fleabag groaned as he rolled over on the chair to stretch and grin up at his friend.

'Well, you've been daft too!' she teased. 'Look!' then she jumped up and pranced around the room, swinging her arms this way and that. 'Well?' she shouted triumphantly, 'what do you notice?'

'That you've gone nuttier than a fruit cake and battier than a belfry!' Fleabag replied. 'Either that, or you've decided to launch a new career as a pigeon, and can't wait to start.'

'No, *look*!' she demanded, beginning her tour of the room one more time. '*Look*! *This* is a circular room! It is just that there are so many bookcases and bits of cluttery furniture in here, we never noticed before! It even has lancet windows too, as well as a huge old stone fireplace...'

She ran across the room and traced the worn edges of an ancient carved pattern springing up from the floor, and intertwining across the front of the fireplace, under the mantelpiece. 'Look!' Gemma explained, 'this is a very faint version of the tree design we saw in the circular room where Claire lay.

'Now I know what was wrong with the room where we met Rowanne just now; everything was inside out. The carving was there too, but it was all done backwards – parts that should have stuck out were indented. It was all negative – the opposite of what it should have been.'

'I see...' Phelan said, running his fingers over the carved stonework. 'And the windows were dark and shuttered, instead of light and open. It felt cold and lonely, instead of contented and peaceful!'

'But this isn't *quite* the room, either,' Gemma went on.

'But *that* is,' said Fleabag, peering through the flames of the fire.

Gemma and Phelan both knelt down on the faded old hearthrug to look through the grate from a cat's-eye point of view.

'Well I never!' whistled Phelan. 'It was here all the time!'

'The answers usually are,' Gemma added quietly. 'That's why it's so difficult to find them – because they are under our noses.'

'Well, *I* knew all along, of course,' Fleabag added in a superior voice.

'Then why didn't you tell us?' Phelan demanded, picking the cat up by the scruff of the neck and glaring into his big golden eyes.

'Just testing,' he replied, cheekily. 'But I told you in the end because it became tedious watching you all running around this place like kittens chasing their tails.'

Phelan threw back his head and laughed heartily.

'Well, at least thanks to your leadership, redoubtable mog, we might be somewhere near finding the Fire Giver now. I will definitely have to knight you all over again and get you that second golden earring!

'Now, if only we could get through to that other room, we might find a clue as to where the Ring's End is,' and Phelan leaned low under the mantelpiece and peered through the flames once again.

'Can you see my mother there?' Kern asked quietly.

'Hold on a moment,' Phelan replied, leaning further in. 'I'm trying to see.'

Gemma tugged at her friend's shirt and pulled him back. 'Careful, you'll catch fire. Your beard and hair were right in the flames just now...' Then she looked at the King's face and clothes. 'But you're not even singed,' she said quietly. Then she stretched out her own hand into the flames. Instead of snatching it back quickly, she held it in the heart of the fire, quite calmly.

'Phelan,' she said, after a few moments. 'How could I have been so stupid? I lit this fire myself. It is no ordinary flame, it is Ring Fire, and it's letting us through. We are free to go to the other side if we wish – and if we have the courage.'

Within seconds, Phelan had crawled under the mantelpiece with the golden flames licking his breeches and shoes. But the fire did not even scorch the cloth. Fleabag followed quickly, with Kern and Gemma close behind.

As Gemma straightened, she rubbed her eyes, for the sunlight streaming in through the tall lancet windows all around the little room was very bright. She dusted the grimy streaks from her dress and pushed her hair back out of her eyes.

The first thing she noticed was that there were more people in the room than had come through the fireplace. Under one window was an elegant chaise longue, and on it, dressed in a green brocade gown, was a beautiful young woman, fast asleep. Kern noticed her too, and went over and touched the sleeper's cheek. 'Mother?' he asked. 'Where have all your rags gone? You look like a lady now! Mother, wake up! It's me, I've come to get you.'

'Not yet,' came a creaky voice from near the fire. Kern and Gemma turned to see an old, old, dark-skinned woman with fine, white, wispy hair, dressed in a gown covered in blossoms, so exquisitely sewn that they looked quite real.

She was seated by the fire in front of a tambour frame, sewing a half-finished tapestry of a field of tangled wild flowers.

'Your mother is still sleeping,' the strange flower-woman said, nodding towards Kern. 'She'll come to you when the time is right, and when the truth is told.' Then she smiled, folding the ancient skin on her face into a million wrinkles. 'And who knows? Perhaps it is almost time for both things to happen, eh?' and she cackled a merry laugh that seemed to make the sun shine even more brightly into the little room.

Then she turned her dark, wrinkled face towards Phelan and Gemma, her sloe-black eyes twinkling. She pointed a long, bony finger in their direction. 'And what do you two want, eh?'

Phelan found himself lost for words, but Gemma knelt

down on the hearthrug and looked up at the old woman. 'I can't think where, but I've seen you before...'

'Of course you have and of course you haven't, my dear. Now, it's getting late. Tell me why you're here. This thread is getting very short.' And then she began to sew so fast that no one could even see her hand, it was a complete blur. But the fine scarlet thread between her fingers stayed clear and bright, although visibly shrinking every second.

'I can't keep the gateway open any longer than this thread,' the old woman said, 'so tell me quickly what it is you want.'

Gemma stared at the fine silk, and then at the brightness in the black eyes. Now she knew where she had seen it before: in so many places and times, but most of all four years ago, in the Hall of Light at Harflorum. She had to find the courage to be honest and ask for what she needed, just as she had that night when she had first spoken to the Ring Fire.

'We need to find a champion for the trial of magic tomorrow, and we need to find the Ring's End,' she blurted out, all in one breath.

The old woman peered at Gemma over her tapestry, then suddenly she stopped sewing. Quite kindly, but very firmly, she said, 'Go back. You have everything you need, although all is not what it seems. As I said before, all will be revealed when the truth is told, and your poor friend Rowanne has already told it to you once. But, as to the other, your King friend has *that* under his nose. It has often been under yours as well, my dear, but at the moment, it is all around you.

'Now goodnight. Go and get some sleep. You will

need it.' And the old woman bent over and kissed Gemma on the head. Gemma twisted herself around to go through the fire again, for she could see the scarlet thread was getting impossibly short, although somehow the old woman kept on sewing with it. But as she glanced at the mantelpiece, she gasped, for the carving on it was the same as on the other side of the fire, but sharp and freshly cut as if the mason had only finished his work that day. It was an intricately cut woodland, with intertwining branches and every individual leaf shaped with such precision and love it seemed almost alive.

She hesitated. She didn't want to leave. Phelan knelt on the rug beside her and gently pushed Gemma onwards.

'Time to go, time to go!' the old woman chided. 'It is midnight,' and she picked up her scissors to cut the thread.

But as the friends passed through the flames, they heard Fleabag asking, 'Mistress, when I see you again, may I sleep on your lap?'

'Of course,' the reply came. 'For ever, if you like.'

Gemma reached the hearthrug in the study and glanced backwards, but all she saw was the back of the fireplace. There *was* no other room. Scared in case the fire should burn her, she kicked hard, and stubbed her toe on the stonework. Phelan grabbed her by her arm and pulled her up.

Fleabag was already curled up on the hearthrug, snoring gently, and Kern was nowhere to be seen.

'Well, what was that all about?' Gemma sat down and stared into the fire in amazement.

'I think,' Phelan said slowly. 'I think, though I'm not sure, that we just met the Fire Giver herself.'

'Himself,' Gemma corrected absently. Then she sat up straight, wide-eyed. 'But if that's true, and *she* was the Fire Giver, then where is the Ring's End?'

23

Rowanne's Visit

In the morning, a maid knocked on the door with breakfast.

Phelan opened the door, bleary-eyed, and Fleabag shot past into the corridor. The guard challenged him, but he yelled out, 'I need the garden quick!' and slipped through their legs.

Gemma woke and stared out of the window at the leaden skies above. A few minutes later, Fleabag bounced in with cold wet paws and snow-covered fur. He jumped on Gemma's bed and rubbed his grubbiness all over her face and hands.

'Go away, you horrid animal!' she groaned, trying to roll over.

Fleabag ignored her protests. 'Time to get up. We only have four hours to go.'

Gemma did not feel like getting up. She reached out

and scratched Fleabag absently behind one ear and smiled rather ruefully. 'I'm scared, old friend. What happens if we don't make it?'

'Then we don't. There's a whole world of cats and humans out there, who all have their part to play. We will do our best for them. If we win we win, and if we don't, it'll be their turn next. No reason to be all morose and not get up.' The cat started to knead his claws in and out of Gemma's chest.

'Ouch!' she squealed, pushing him away. 'Get off me, you assassin. I'll call the guard!'

But Fleabag jumped back and settled under Gemma's chin, where he began to lick her with his hot rough tongue. 'Come on, if you shift now, I'll share my mackerel with you, and that's a promise. Though it is a bit old. I suspect we don't get the best service in this place. I'm glad my poor, dear wife Tabitha isn't here. All this second-rate food would upset her digestion terribly.'

'I bet you do wish Tabitha was here,' Gemma smiled. She could not remember anything about her own family, and she rather envied Fleabag's endless tumbles of kittens that were always getting under everyone's feet at the palace in Harflorum. She had Fleabag's talking sons Hereward and Rufus to keep her company in her cottage in the rocks, but sometimes she did feel very alone. Especially this morning. So much rested on *her*.

Fleabag jumped down and ran towards the study. But, just as he was about to disappear around the door, he turned back. 'Actually, I'm *very* glad Tabitha isn't here,' he admitted. 'Even I am finding all this a little scary.'

Gemma made herself get out from under the warm covers and pull on a dressing gown. She could hear voices in the next room and wondered who their visitor could be. The University servants never spoke when they brought coal or food.

She pushed the door wider and looked in. A tall, dark-cloaked figure stood hunched by the door, with a deep hood pulled down low over its face. Could it really be Rowanne? How could she bear to come into the study? Perhaps she wore the hood to hide the sight of the Ring Fire from her eyes.

'Good morning, Rowanne, how are you?' Gemma smiled, and held a hand out in greeting.

Rowanne ignored the hand, and seemed, if possible, to shrink even more into her hood. 'Fleabag came and fetched me this morning. He said you wanted to see me,' she said simply.

'It was all his idea,' Phelan replied, getting up from the breakfast table. 'But it was a good one. We just wanted to say that, whatever happens, Rowanne, we thank you for all your help and your faithful friendship over the years. And if you want to come back with us, we would love to have you with us again...'

Gemma hung her head. Rowanne was so drenched in the blue magic, there was barely a shred of her real self left. Could their old friend ever be happy with them again? 'Yes, of course,' she managed to say, because she really did wish it were possible.

There was a long uncomfortable silence. 'My offer is still open,' Rowanne said at last.

'What offer is that?' Gemma asked.

'To help you with the trial of magic. I can't fight it for you, as you know, but I can help you... That's why I went through all this in the first place... to help the Ring Fire.'

Suddenly Gemma saw red. She was *not* going to let Rowanne get away with this self-righteousness any longer. That could not have been the reason – at least, not the whole reason – for her becoming a wizard. She stood squarely in front of her old friend, hands on hips, and head held high. 'What else was behind all this, Rowanne? If helping the Ring Fire was your only motive, however misguided, you just could not have become as – well – as *blue* as you are! Loving the Ring Fire and becoming a cauldron-stirring, spell-throwing wizard, don't mix. It just can't happen! The Blue Magic only works for evil and for controlling people, but the Ring Fire always helps good things to happen.'

Rowanne hung her head and muttered, 'Witches stir cauldrons, not wizards!'

'Oh, so *what*!' Gemma stamped her foot. 'You know perfectly well what I mean. Why did you do it? Knowing the real Rowanne, I can quite believe that wanting to help the Ring Fire by doing something very practical was at least part of your becoming a wizard – but what else is going on inside you, Rowanne? If you can face whatever it is, you might be able to find a way out of this. For sure as eggs are eggs, I can't see us taking you back with us the way you are. As you yourself have told us several times, whatever is wizard-blue will ultimately betray us.'

At the end of this speech, Gemma was pink in the face and quite breathless, but she stood her ground, waiting for a reply, undaunted by the sinister shape of her old friend.

But Rowanne said nothing. She did not stir or even lift her head. She just stayed quite still and began to crackle and fizz with minute blue sparks like a tiny electrical storm. Then she began to fade, slowly at first, but after a few seconds the process speeded up, as if an unseen hand was angrily rubbing her out. Quite suddenly what was left of her disappeared with a small 'pop' of blue sparks – and she was gone.

Phelan came and quietly took Gemma's elbow and drew her away to sit on the settee.

Fleabag jumped up and looked Phelan in the eye. 'I know Rowanne and I have had our differences, but I do love her. She's been a first rate cat-hater all her life. I wish there was something I could do.' And a tear rolled down his untidy furry face.

Phelan shook his head and stroked Fleabag, pushing away moisture at the corners of his own eyes. 'You were a bit harsh, don't you think?' He frowned. 'Even the Fire Giver called Rowanne our "poor friend". If *she* can have sympathy for her, *we* should give Rowanne another chance too. Somehow we've got to trust the old Rowanne is still deep inside the blue wizard. She's been incredibly brave coming to see us at all. I'm certain she only wants to help, even if her motives are muddled. There must be a corner of her that isn't completely absorbed by the wizards' magic.'

Gemma felt her cheeks go hot. 'You're right. I'm sorry. Perhaps her longing to help the Ring Fire will still win out in the end.'

'But we haven't got time to worry about it this morning,' Fleabag reminded them. 'Breakfast is getting cold and we have the most important trial of all at noon.'

Gemma sat at the table. She felt miserable and lonely. She toyed with her food and stared into the fire. What had happened last night? Had they dreamed going through the fire into the small room with the strange old woman?

Phelan followed her gaze and answered her thoughts. 'We did go through, we did see Claire, and we did see the Fire Giver.'

'Are you certain?'

'Certain we went through or that it was the Fire Giver?'

'Certain of any of it?' Gemma had never really had any image of what the Fire Giver might or might not be like – except perhaps fiery in some way. 'Certain that we "have everything we need, but that all is not what it seems"? And what is that truth that must be told that Rowanne has already told us?'

Gemma looked across at Fleabag who had his nose in a dish of cream on the hearthrug. The cat looked back at Gemma, eyes wide. He shrugged. 'Don't look at me. I'm no good at riddles. I thought you knew that!' and he returned his face to the bowl where he made awful slurping noises with his tongue.

Suddenly, Gemma looked up. 'Has anyone seen Kern this morning? What did that old woman mean by "the truth being told" when she was talking to him? None of it makes any sense!' And she began to stir her tea so hard that the cup began to rock.

Phelan got up and put his arms around her shoulders. 'It will be all right, I promise. What matters is that we have been promised that we will have all we need to meet the trial. I don't know where the Ring's End is, but I'm certain we were there last night and we met the Fire Giver. But perhaps he – or she – isn't quite what any of us imagines or expects; she may not look like an old woman next time we see her.'

Gemma rubbed her nose on the sleeve of her dressing gown. 'That's all very well as fine words and stuff. And I'm sure you're right: when you lived with wise old Aelforth you learned more about the Ring Fire than I shall ever know. But what do I do now… today… this morning?

'I can't help feeling that I am expected to take the trial of magic because I'm the Fire Wielder. But I know in my bones that I mustn't do it… So what do I do? Just sit up here and watch the clock tick by, one minute to twelve, twelve o'clock, one minute past…? Tell me, Phelan, Fleabag… What do I *do*?' And she burst into tears and ran into her bedroom, slamming the door behind her.

Phelan and Fleabag looked at each other. 'I know how she feels,' admitted the King.

'So do I,' replied the cat. 'Will you open the door so I can go and curl up next to her? Humans sometimes like a cuddle when they're feeling bad.'

Phelan let Fleabag into Gemma's room, then he sat in the study all alone, and drank tea.

24

Battle Lines

Gemma stood up and tried to breathe calmly. The knock on the door told her it was time for her armed escort to take her down to the Great Hall to face this last and most frightening trial.

All morning, Phelan had tried to get messages to his men in the barracks to have the horses ready for a sudden flight. But no communication was allowed. They tried to find the secret bookcase passageway out of their study that they had used the night before. But without Kern or Rowanne, they were stuck. They could not discern any opening, or any way of making one appear. They were truly imprisoned.

Their windows were too high for even the redoubtable Fleabag to jump down and so he had pleaded to be allowed to use the garden. But he was pushed back into the room and given a dirt box, which did them no good at all. 'I'm not using that anyway,' he sniffed contemptuously. 'Dirt boxes are for kittens and invalids. I'll go on M'Kinnik's lap if I get caught short!'

Gemma had tried to calm her thoughts. She had to at least turn up for this trial, even though she still felt very strongly that she should take no part in it. 'Perhaps the Fire Giver will provide her own Champion,' Phelan suggested. 'She did say we had everything we needed. So perhaps something we haven't thought of yet will happen, right under our noses.'

'Like the Ring's End is under *your* nose!' Gemma managed a smile.

'Exactly!' Phelan laughed. 'It's almost time to go. Are you ready? The worst that can happen is that we will have a draw. Then the fight will go on another day, in another way.'

'No,' Gemma said quietly. 'That's not the worst that can happen.' And she walked out of the door, with a blue-clad guard on either side.

Gemma had decided to dress as she had done for the time she had played the Fire Maiden with Fleabag as her 'terrifying' black cat. She wore a flame-red silk dress, and a plain woollen cloak. 'Perhaps,' she had explained to Fleabag, 'the memories of how we defeated the old Chancellor will still be fresh in some people's minds. It wasn't that long ago. It might give us a slight advantage.'

'We'll see,' grunted Fleabag, slipping between the guards' legs to lead the procession with his strange, lopsided three-legged walk. He held his tail high like a scruffy black banner, and spread his whiskers wide. The wizards did not like cats, particularly black ones. Perhaps

Gemma's idea might do some good, especially if he was there as well...

Phelan came behind, walking tall and dressed like a king in his full regalia. He had not been allowed to come armed, and had reluctantly left Rowanne's sword behind. He was worried that the wizards might somehow force or trick Fleabag's true name from him, allowing them to put a spell on his best friend. Gemma was safe; she had no knowledge of her real name, and although he could remember the name his parents had given him at birth – well, he didn't matter. If the wizards put a spell on him, as long as Gemma and Fleabag were safe, that was all that was important.

The King lifted his head and followed the procession along the winding corridors to the Great Hall, built to imitate the wonderful Hall of Light at home in Harflorum. Whatever was about to happen would be over very soon now. But he couldn't help wondering whether Kern was all right, and where he was. He would have liked to help him find his mother and to escape. He would have offered him a home at Harflorum. But he put the boy out of his mind. He had to concentrate. He had to give Gemma all his attention. He glanced down at the Great Ring of office, the huge opal that all the kings and queens of the land wore.

It glowed richly with the deep golden-red of the Ring Fire, and comforted him. If only the answer to the Fire Giver's riddle was as plainly under his nose as the Ring. He might be able to help Gemma, if only he could work out what was meant by the old lady's riddles. For Phelan was in no doubt that even if she *wasn't* the Fire Giver then she was at least one of his (or her) friends.

They reached the Great Hall. Gemma was led to a seat in the exact centre, with wizards, in rustling blue gowns of every shade, thronging in all around.

'It's a good job we're not relying on magic,' Fleabag muttered. 'You'd need a powerful lot of it to defeat this crowd!'

A trumpet blast announced the arrival of her Holiness, the High Chancellor of All Wizards, her Ladyship, Princess Rowanne de Montiland. Rowanne swept in between the crowds to sit in a lapis-studded throne opposite Gemma. Guards tried to force Gemma to bow to Rowanne, but she would not, despite their kicks and prods.

'Leave her!' the Chancellor ordered. 'It will soon be over. Obeisance does not matter.'

Gemma looked hard at Rowanne. Was this a sending or the real thing? Was it Rowanne at all or just some blue creature who looked like her? The features looked the same, and the blue-black hair was tightly drawn back as if their old friend was about to pull on a woollen snood and put her helmet on. How much stronger and more beautiful she looked when she was being herself in battle gear as a Lady Knight, than in all these silks and satins with blue embroidery and encrusting gems. Gemma was very sad, but what Rowanne felt she could not guess.

The Chancellor rose to her feet and signalled to Gemma to do the same. Then she spoke, clearly and loudly. 'Be it known that the outcome of this trial will decide the fate of the sovereignty of the land and the ownership of the Ring Fire for ever.

'If I win, then all is ours, for ever. If the Lady Gemma Streetchild or her Champion wins, then everything belongs to the Fire Wielders and their chosen monarchs for ever, and the Noble Order of Wizards will unravel their magic so it can never be rewoven again.'

'So be it,' responded the wizards, roaring so loudly that the foundations of the hall shook.

'So be it,' Gemma, Phelan and Fleabag said as clearly as they could, although they could hardly speak. Then Gemma swallowed hard and added: 'But, my Lady Chancellor, you must know that even if we lose, we cannot *give* you the Fire. It owns itself. It goes where it will. It can never be owned or used like magic.' Gemma comforted herself with the thought that whatever deals the wizards tried to make were irrelevant. The wizards would never even be able to look at it, let alone 'have' it.

Rowanne's face did not change its set expression, but M'Kinnik scowled as he settled himself next to her.

Fleabag jumped up onto Gemma's arm-rest and pawed at her elbow. 'Have courage. Whatever happens today, all will be well.'

'Thanks, Sir Scrag-Belly,' Gemma tried to smile as she sat. Then she thought of something, and stood again to speak. 'Just one more thing, my Lady – what if there is a draw, as on the other two days?' she asked.

Rowanne leaned forward, and lifted her right hand so all the spectators could see the huge, dead opal on her own finger, the one that Chancellors always wore, longing to contain the Ring Fire at its depths. 'There will be no draw,' she said simply. 'Not this time.' Then the Chancellor sat back and folded her hands. 'I understand, my Lady Fire Wielder, that you do not wish to take this trial yourself. Where is your Champion?'

Gemma took a deep breath. This was it. The time to

admit they had no Champion, and she knew now more clearly than anything she had ever known in her life that she must not fight Rowanne. As soon as she spoke the words, the trial would be lost. By the laws of Challenge combat, they would have conceded total defeat.

Gemma's heart was pounding fast as she opened her mouth. She fixed her gaze on Rowanne and took a deep breath.

Suddenly, from the back of the hall, a small voice called out: 'I am their Champion. I will take this trial for the Ring Fire!'

25

The Champion

Every head in the room turned this way and that to see who had spoken. Gemma and Phelan exchanged astounded looks. Fleabag simply slipped into Gemma's empty chair, which had a very comfortable, although rather blue-coloured cushion. 'Good,' he purred. 'I thought she'd do it. Time for forty winks while the fuss dies down.' And he went to sleep.

Guards soon cleared a path in the thronging hall for a girl in a long white dress, with a green veil over her head and a green silk bundle under her arm. She came and stood before Gemma and bowed. 'My Lady Fire Wielder, I ask your permission to fight the Blue Magic on your behalf.'

Gemma did not know what to say. She opened her right hand very quickly, and saw a small flame of Ring Fire burning with a brilliance and intensity that she had never seen before, except maybe the day she was proclaimed Fire Wielder in the Hall of Light. Whoever this girl was didn't matter. The Ring Fire accepted her. As Fleabag had promised, all was very well indeed. 'I agree,' she answered clearly.

Then the stranger turned to Rowanne and bowed again. 'My Lady Chancellor, I ask your leave to be your opponent in this trial.'

Rowanne nodded. 'I accept.'

Gemma glanced around. Who was this girl? Why was she veiled? What did the colour green betoken? If she was of the Ring Fire's party, she would have been dressed in red or gold. If she was a wizard, then in blue of some hue. But why *green*? She glanced around at M'Kinnik, who was seated at Rowanne's right hand. The man was smirking, as if he was Fleabag with a particularly delicately flavoured dish of fish. So *he* knew who the stranger was, and he was delighted! How could this stranger please both the Ring Fire *and* the wizards?

In fact, the Ring Fire was burning in Gemma's hand so brightly, she had to hide the light under the sleeves of her robe, in case she was accused of making a move before the trial had formally begun. She moved aside for the stranger to take her place.

From under the veil an almost-familiar voice spoke: 'My Lady Chancellor, as I am not versed in the ways of this trial, please take the first turn.'

M'Kinnik leaned over to Rowanne and whispered. Rowanne nodded and raised her arms. At that second, although it had been midday when they had entered the hall, everything went as dark as midnight. But there was no panic, just silence. All that broke it was an occasional shuffle of a foot or a sniff or a cough. No one spoke or moved. The waiting grew intense; it was obvious that the wizards were waiting for a magical reply from the Ring Fire's Champion. Gemma was getting nervous. At last, after what can only have been a few moments, but felt like at least an hour, Gemma stepped forward to touch the stranger on the shoulder. 'Are you all right?'

'Yes,' came the reply. 'I need the King's Ring. Will he give it to me?'

'I would,' came the reply, out of the dark, 'but it never comes off, even if I want it to.'

'Try it,' Gemma whispered urgently, hoping that this wasn't a trick of M'Kinnik's to get the Ring.

Phelan tugged, and with a gasp of amazement, he found the Ring came loose with ease. 'Where are you, Champion?' he asked.

'Here,' came a familiar voice out of the blackness.

In the dark, without the deception of appearances, Gemma realized who the stranger was. '*Kern*?' she whispered in amazement.

'Hush!' the Champion warned. 'I'll explain later.'

Then, with a few shufflings, the Ring changed hands. The girl held it high, and the warm glow at the heart of the great opal rose into the air to about the height of Phelan. Then suddenly she dashed it to the floor. There was a flash of blinding light from the Fire at the Ring's heart, leaving a shimmering circle at their feet.

The wizards gasped and hid their eyes as the blaze slowly grew to be brighter than several torches.

Rowanne stood and faced the Flame, eyes wide open. For a second, Gemma thought her old friend was about to run towards it, seeking refuge. But she did not. Instead she also raised an arm and hid her face. With the other hand, she made a fist, and pointed at the floor with her index finger. All at once, the floor was seething with what seemed to be snakes slithering towards them from all sides. With a short word of command from Rowanne, the creatures began twisting and twining themselves around Gemma and Phelan's legs, then they caught onto Kern's robe and found Fleabag last of all.

The cat hissed and spat as fiercely as any serpent, as he bit and scratched at their hard, shiny scales. But it did no good. The creatures had other plans. As each one came close to one of the friends, instead of spitting venom, their eyes swelled bigger and bigger, shining with images and memories of evil things half forgotten.

'Close your eyes, don't look!' Phelan warned.

'What *are* they?' Gemma panted, as one snake began to tighten itself around her left arm, reminding her all the while of an evil palace cook with a raised rolling pin.

'They are our worst nightmares!' Phelan gulped. 'They have no power over you unless you let them. Don't let them take hold, and you'll be all right! They can't hurt you unless you let them.'

A mocking sneer came from M'Kinnik as he pointed at Kern with his wand. 'Go on, *girl*, play your fiddle. Charm the snakes as you tried to do to us. You might even find it works this time!' and he laughed a hard, sharp sound.

Stepping free of the snakes into the light of the Ring Fire which glowed warmly from Phelan's Ring on the floor, the Champion shook off her green veil and pulled the silk from her bundle, revealing her violin. She put the instrument on her shoulder and lifted the bow.

'Kern! No!' Gemma shouted. 'Don't do it!'

'Silence!' roared M'Kinnik, as he flung another nightmare in Gemma's direction. It caught her around the neck and wrapped itself around her mouth so she couldn't speak for dread that the Ring Fire might go out.

The girl turned and looked at Gemma with a steady gaze, then she lifted the bow over the strings and held it there for a long moment. Then with a sudden flick of her left wrist, she swung the violin around, smashed it over M'Kinnik's head, and rammed the bow into his chest.

'Whatever is wizard-blue will ultimately betray you,' she said, quite calmly. 'Or so your Chancellor told me once.'

M'Kinnik sank to the ground groaning, and was immediately surrounded by three or four nightmare-creatures. Once they had caught his gaze he was helpless, drowning in a sea of memories and terrors.

The surrounding wizards dived forward to grab the Champion, but she took a deep breath and began to sing. The sound made her enemies stagger back, with their fingers in their ears. At first it was a sound without words that seemed to float in the air, conjuring images of the sea and wind, making the listener float like a gull under a golden-red sunset. Then the voice fell and became dark and green as the depth of the sea, with purples and fresh, wholesome blues swirling around in the listeners' minds.

The wizards' evil was weakened by these thoughts of good things, crumbling the power of the spell and making the nightmare creatures slither away from the Ring Fire's friends. The wizards muttered and cursed, complaining that their ears and eyes hurt, but the singer did not stop for a second. Instead she swung her voice up again to sound like green grass and wild, tangled flowers, a song made from the old woman's tapestry. Needing something to devour, the creatures began to spread amongst their masters instead, staring into their too-blue eyes and feeding on their terror.

But, with strengthened resolve, a few wizards managed to turn the snake-like creatures back towards the Champion and her friends again. And this time the dream-serpents were bigger and angrier than before.

Gemma found herself facing a snake with a wide-open mouth and dagger-like fangs. It told her her parents had never loved her. Phelan faced a beast with a sickly blue-forked tongue that licked and flickered over his face, telling him he would end up betraying Gemma. Kern's singing began to hesitate as a thick pair of pythons began to twine about her, dragging her arms down, telling her her hands were useless and she would never play a violin again.

But then Phelan's rich voice suddenly joined in with Kern's, taking up the song, making up new words, developing the melody as he went along. And Gemma managed to pull the pythons away from Kern, so she could strengthen her voice, weaving in and out of Phelan's themes.

Although the song kept the nightmare creatures at bay, it was not enough to win the trial. Gemma tried to think, but she could not. They could not keep this up for ever. They seemed to be in a sort of stalemate with nightmare evenly matched against singing. There seemed to be no way to break free from what was happening. If only they could find the Ring's End, whatever it was, she had a feeling that everything would be all right. The Fire Giver, if that was who the old lady was, had promised that they already had everything they needed to win the Challenge, and the answer was under Phelan's nose. But the semi-darkness and the hissing snakes and the impossibility of her situation crowded in on her until she felt claustrophobic and hopeless.

Suddenly Gemma realized a nightmare-snake had softly wound its way around her head. She tugged it off and threw it to the ground. And as she did so, something caught her eye.

Phelan's Ring, glowing and alive on the floor, was *not* a complete circle. How could she have been so stupid! The Ring had a beginning *and* an end – at the Great Opal! It *had* been under Phelan's nose the whole time!

She nudged Kern, who looked down in the direction of Gemma's pointing and nodded. She stopped singing and whispered, 'Of course! I know what to do now. If everything goes wrong, jump into the Ring Fire at the Ring's End!'

'But how can we? It's only tiny!' Gemma looked confused.

Kern grabbed Gemma's hand and looked her straight in the eyes. 'You asked me to trust you once, now it's your turn. Trust me!'

26

The Ring's End

Gemma looked at the King's Ring lying at her feet. It was the only part of the floor they could see; the rest was filled with writhing snake-like creatures. But how could they all step into such a tiny thing? She opened her mouth to object, then shut it again. For she remembered how Kern had led them through stranger places than this as they wandered the halls and corridors of the University, folding space and even time, then expanding it again as they slipped between dimensions.

But she had little time to wonder, for Kern had stepped forward to stand amongst the snakes and face Rowanne, face to face in the eerie mixture of Ring Fire and baleful blue light. Kern pulled herself up to her full height and spoke so everyone could hear. 'My Lady Rowanne, Chancellor of All Wizards. Do you know why I of all people was sent to fetch you from Harflorum?'

The Chancellor shrugged. 'Because no one would know you were from Porthwain, I suppose.'

'No, M'Kinnik sent me because he suspected that I was the old Chancellor's third daughter, not his seventh son. This meant that I harboured the greatest powers possible in a wizard. You and this so-called Challenge were just the bait to draw me out.'

'How dare you!' Rowanne slammed her hand on the table at her side. 'Your father may have been fooled into thinking you were a boy, but you didn't deceive everybody. It is true we tested your magical powers today, but you failed! You may be the Chancellor's third daughter, but the blood of the Hill People has made you weak. You aren't a powerful enough wizard to defeat me! You're nothing but a guttersnipe and guttersnipes belong in the gutter!' Rowanne was brilliant blue with rage, and looked as if she was about to explode.

Gemma winced, remembering her own days of begging in the street markets. She was about to say something in Kern's defence, but Rowanne had only paused for a moment's breath. There was no interrupting her.

'Tell them, M'Kinnik!' Rowanne went on. 'Tell them the truth, that I am the greatest wizard ever, and I was chosen from ages past, and as the Ring Fire ignored me and would not acknowledge my greatness, the Blue Magic made me its own to be the great lady I was destined to be.'

'Ah!' whispered Phelan, 'So *that* was at the bottom of it all, wounded pride. That figures!'

But M'Kinnik, slumped in his chair, nursing his sore head and chest, just laughed as loudly as he dared without causing himself pain. 'No, Lady Rowanne, I'm afraid our little girl there is quite right. Here she is, our real future, the greatest of all wizards. She's masqueraded as a boy these thirteen years. I always suspected, but her father forbade me to have anything to do with her. He proclaimed the baby outcast and untouchable when the midwife showed him a boy child.

'Domnall guessed, though. He put that fiddle in her hands and we all knew. No ordinary mortal could play like that. But Domnall had his own plans to be great, so he taught his little 'brother' very carefully, using spells disguised as music. He was training her to be great. Under him, of course. But no one can be greater than a Chancellor's third daughter. And look what happened to him! Defeated by that so-called Fire Wielder on Spider Island!

'But I kept believing in you, child…' The fat, sour-faced wizard stepped forward to pat Kern on her cheek. 'Uncle M'Kinnik's always been *very* fond of you…'

Kern recoiled at his touch, and plucked another serpent from her skirt. 'That's not true. You've always hated me!' she glowered. 'You were just using me for your own ends! You thought if I was the third daughter you could keep me out of sight in the kitchens, and use me secretly to enhance your own powers. You didn't even want *me* to know who I was!'

M'Kinnik grinned, although he was obviously still in pain. 'That's right, my dear,' he said. 'You *are* clever, aren't you?'

Then he turned to Rowanne. 'But the beauty of my plan was that if the "boy" Kern did not turn out to be the great wizard we had all hoped for, we still had you, our pretty blue puppet who has absorbed far more of the blue magic than any human can stand. You will grow old and physically weak, but magically very powerful, and live in our nice warm University for many a thousand years, doing our bidding and being adored by us all.'

Rowanne had indeed of late been feeling a little stiff and drained, and was no longer the fine-featured young woman she once had been. But she was still stronger than most men.

She grasped the wounded M'Kinnik by his robes and dragged him to stand in front of her. 'How dare you? How dare you treat me like this? *I* am the Chancellor! You obey me and you do not mock me! Do you understand?'

But her shouts fell on deaf ears, for not only M'Kinnik, but the whole company of wizards were all laughing until their sides hurt.

'You've been offered a wooden bone, Rowanne,' Fleabag smirked. 'You were the bait and the catch, all at the same time. Pity. You really didn't deserve it!'

In a flash, Rowanne tugged off her wizard's cloak and drew out a small sword she still carried secretly. With a swift slash, M'Kinnik lay dead at her feet, and a few more of the senior wizards followed.

With one hand, she warded off spells that were flung at her; with the other, she slashed and cut, killing and maiming more and more with every move. The crowd pressed in around her. Phelan stood guard over the Ring, which was still glowing on the floor, and Gemma held the Ring Fire high in her hands. Fleabag moved to take his stand next to Rowanne, his old enemy, and much-loved friend.

'Quick, everyone,' Rowanne called over her shoulder, 'go to the Ring's End. It's your only chance! It may be too late for me, but it's not for you. Flee to the Fire Giver!'

Phelan took Gemma by the shoulders and, before she could object, pushed her through the opal gateway in the narrow band of gold on the floor. Once again, Gemma felt a twinge of uncertainty about how on earth she could step into such a tiny space. But as they moved towards it, the Ring's stone grew huge and opened wide. She could not let her mind question it. She just had to move! Phelan was right behind her and Kern tumbled after them.

The little room on the other side was circular, with tall lancet windows all around. It was the right room, but it was empty and grey.

'Light the Ring Fire in the grate!' Kern ordered. 'Do it now, to prevent the wizards from following us through.'

'But what about Rowanne and Fleabag?' Gemma gasped, as she held out her hands in the empty grate, watching the rise of the golden flames which burned nothing.

'They'll come when they can,' Phelan assured her.

Outside, in the hall, Rowanne was growing tired as she fought off the Blue Magic and tried to swing her sword at the same time. Beside her, the noble Fleabag cut and clawed at the legs and ankles of everyone who came within reach. He ignored the spells and curses that brought illusions of huge black rats with yellow eyes and infected teeth charging across the floor at him. He concentrated and used his sixth sense that told him they were not real. The wizards did not know his real name, so they could not put spells on him, but that was not their only weapon.

For suddenly, Fleabag found himself face to face with a terrible sight – one he had thought he would never have to face again; the sight of the axe swung at his beloved Queen Sophia, so many years ago, when he was a kitten and she was not much older than Gemma.

The assassin was blue-robed and evil-eyed, with breath that smelled of dog sweat on a hot day. Once again, Fleabag relived jumping to try to fend off the blow, and watched his own back leg spin away from him as it caught the blade.

The pain was as real as it had been on that day. It seared and burned him to the bone, and he felt faint with the agony of it, throbbing and tearing into his fur, unyielding, causing him to vomit.

Then suddenly, as he tried to tell himself it was just another nightmare, he realized it wasn't. Before him stood that same ancient wizard with a blue cloak and evil eyes, leaning over him with raised hands. But, as before, he was not wielding a spell. He carried another, and a very real axe!

'*No*!' yelled Rowanne, as she flung herself across Fleabag, catching the second blow on the side of her own head. 'You'll be all right. I'll take you to the Ring's End,' she gasped as she fell. But the wizard took another swipe. 'We'll have no black cats or Fire Maidens in here!' he sneered, and kicked Fleabag out of Rowanne's arms and across the floor.

Rowanne rolled back and grabbed Fleabag's warm, limp body. Then, twisting to her knees, she turned and sprang through the Opal into the firegrate of the circular room beyond.

'Oh thank goodness, you're all right!' Gemma laughed, catching up a live and purring Fleabag and hugging him.

Then Rowanne got to her feet and pushed her dark brown hair out of her eyes. She laughed as she looked around her. Everyone was safe. 'Oh, thank goodness you're all right. I'm so sorry for all the trouble I've caused you!' she cried, as she hugged them all in turn.

'Are you all here now?' asked a voice behind them. And there, sitting next to the fire, was the old woman in her dress of flowers, once again doing her tapestry. 'My sewing is done for today,' she said, placing her needle and silks into a small box by her side.

'Fleabag, jump up onto my lap, and Rowanne, open the windows will you? All of them.'

27

Night Wanderer

As Rowanne opened the windows a warm, summer breeze filled the room.

'Now you must all choose,' said the old woman. 'Whichever window you go through will be your future. There will be no way back, for the place you knew as Porthwain is now gone. Since you left, which in your time was hours ago, the wizards have destroyed each other and everything that went with the town. Your men escaped, Phelan. They are well on their way home. But there truly is nothing left of the University or of the Blue Magic.'

Gemma picked up Fleabag and carried him to where Phelan was leaning out of the first window and saw Harflorum, with all its bright colours and happy streets. The King was smiling. 'I've missed it,' he said. 'Harflorum really is home, even with the Prime Minister and all his fussiness.'

Then Gemma moved to the next window and saw her beloved cottage in the rocks with Fleabag's sons, Hereward and Rufus, and the lonely hills that she loved so much.

At the next window Rowanne was looking out at Erbwenneth and a party of soldiers going out to patrol the forest roads around the city. At their head was her younger brother, Alawn, with Aidan acting as his squire. The young prince sat very straight on his horse, and looked a good and honest man.

'They don't really need me there any more, do they?' Rowanne asked sadly, as she leaned against the stone mullions.

The old woman shook her head and smiled. 'No, my dear, they don't. But you did a good job of making Erbwenneth safe and quiet. Your people will remember you with love.'

Rowanne blushed a deep pink. 'I don't really deserve that,' she muttered, and hung her head.

'No one ever gets what they really deserve, thank goodness,' Fleabag commented as he jumped down from Gemma's arms and walked along each window ledge in turn, peering and sniffing the breezes that came in from each direction, and making rude insinuations about the quality of mouse and shrew to be had at each place.

Then he jumped onto the old woman's flower-covered lap and purred as she stroked him until his long fur gleamed, soft and smooth, under her fine fingers.

Kern alone did not go to any of the windows. Instead, she sat on the hearthrug, clasping her knees and looking glum. 'What's the matter?' asked Gemma, sitting beside her and giving her a hug. 'You can go anywhere you like from here. You're free at last.'

'But where's my mother?' Kern muttered miserably. 'I thought she'd be here!'

The old woman laughed gently. 'Well, you haven't looked very hard, have you?'

Kern glanced up and gasped, for leaning into the room from the last window was Claire, looking well and happy, and dressed in a gown so green it might have been woven from spring fields.

Kern jumped up and ran across the room, intending to jump out to her mother, but Claire had already swung her legs into the room. The two laughed and cried and hugged until they were quite exhausted. At last Claire sat down, with her daughter cuddled very close to her side. She looked around at Kern's friends. 'I have dreamed of you people, I am sure of it,' she smiled and held out a hand to them. 'But it was a strange dream. It was as if I could see you through a great milky white stone with a warm fire making your faces glow. I feel as if I have been asleep for ever. I think I must have dreamed a whole world.'

'In a way, you have,' Kern smiled. 'I will tell you all about it later. But what happened to you? When I came back from Harflorum, you were gone.'

Claire shrugged. 'I really don't know how I got here. M'Kinnik told me you had run away and wouldn't come back. I didn't believe him, and I wanted to go looking for you. I remember trying to flee the city one night, with guards trying to catch me. I thought I was hopelessly cornered and I slipped inside a tiny doorway. I remember finding myself in a room much like this one, small and round, but bare and cold. I hid at the back of a great stone fireplace and held my breath. I remember the door opening, but nothing else.'

'The Ring Fire kept you and protected you,' Phelan smiled. 'But although I know the Fire Giver cares about all her people, why were you so important to M'Kinnik? Why was the old Chancellor so keen for you to have his baby daughter?'

Claire smiled. 'I am one of the Hill People. We have farmed the lower slopes of the mountains for many years, though we have been driven into poverty and near hopelessness by the wizards for a very long time. My people were wise and gentle. Above all we were singers, and our music was strong against the Blue Magic. But, one by one, we were killed or trapped or ruined in one way or another. We have forgotten our ancient arts; now we keep the few songs we do know a closely guarded secret. But even this prevented the wizards' power from spreading any further north.

'The old Chancellor had been told that the only way to defeat us was to have a powerful third daughter by a Hill woman, and raise her to the ways of the Blue Magic. He had foreseen that such a wizard could bring about the defeat of her own people if she was taught magic from an early age.

'My family was so poor, I was taken by the University bailiff instead of farm rent, but I did not know the old Chancellor's designs. When my daughter was born, the midwife, who was one of the Hill People as well, hid the child, and replaced it with a new-born baby boy she had smuggled into my room in a basket of linen. Even I did not know my child was a girl until I was well enough to wash and care for her myself. By that time, the

Chancellor had disowned me, and I was left to scrub and work in the kitchens like any other slave.

'But this is my daughter, Saoirse, which means "Freedom" in the old tongue. You'd probably pronounce it "Sorsha". I called her "Kern" and dressed her as a boy, until she was old enough to understand the truth.'

'But,' Gemma butted in, 'If you are a third daughter, Saoirse, you have great magical powers?'

Saoirse laughed. 'Supposedly. But I despise the wizards' magic and all it stands for. I chose not to take my father's inheritance, but to follow my mother's ways instead. I soon realized I had power in my music, but I always tried to use it for good. I want people to be free like the wind, and the wild flowers of the green hills. As you might say, the way the Fire Giver intended us to be. I learned how to listen to all sorts of living creatures, and to sing their songs. I found I often knew things: where someone is hurting, and how to heal it, or what is causing a grief and why. Many people call that magic, but I'm sure it is simply listening and watching. It is how we are all meant to be.'

Phelan and Gemma exchanged glances. 'I can understand that,' Gemma admitted. 'But what had you planned to do next? You couldn't pretend to be a boy for ever.'

'That was the difficult bit. I knew I had to leave the University by the time I was about thirteen. But I would not – in fact I could not – leave without my mother. She is all I have. Where could I go without her? I couldn't leave her to be kicked around for the rest of her life; she is a wonderful person! We planned to travel the world and sing to earn a living. But she was kept a virtual slave here. Now we know that M'Kinnik suspected us, it all makes sense. He knew if she was here I would never leave. He was just waiting to see what happened to me as time passed.'

Fleabag sniffed at Saoirse's hand. 'You never smelled like a boy – I assumed you just didn't like dressing in girls' clothes. Why didn't the wizards just smell you?'

'Humans can't smell things like you can,' Phelan explained. 'Go on, Saoirse.'

The girl shrugged. 'I can see now that the Challenge to you was all an elaborate trap to catch me out. M'Kinnik sent me to find the carrier of the Blue Magic. He promised me that if I did it, my mother and I would both be free. It was too good an opportunity to miss – we could leave together – but we should have suspected something. It was all too easy.'

'But how was the Challenge a trap?' Gemma asked.

'The wizards knew that as I became a teenager my powers would grow. They hoped that if I were faced with the Blue Magic at its strongest, I would try using it and allow myself to become one of them. They knew I didn't want to, but they hoped to force my hand. When I came to Harflorum, I never wanted to have anything to do with wizards or Kings or Fire Wielders *or* black cats: I hated you all. I wanted to find Rowanne and then run away. I *wanted* her to be Chancellor. Anyone but me!

'But I met you and your Ring Fire and realized that hating and running away wouldn't help anyone. I knew I was the only one strong enough to be your Champion. I had enough magical power at my disposal today to defeat the wizards – all of them at once, if I chose. But I didn't choose. To fight them with their sort of magic would have been to become like them. There was a much simpler and stronger way. All I had to do was to face the wizards with the truth about themselves – to show them their own worst nightmare; that I did *not* want them! Truth is always stronger than any spells.'

Rowanne shuddered at this. 'And it worked,' she put in. 'I'm sorry and I'm very grateful. I just couldn't see what I was doing!'

Gemma squeezed Rowanne's hand. 'And I'm sorry for not being kinder to you. I'm glad it's all over now,' she said.

'And it's time for you all to go home!' put in the old woman. 'Make your choices, for when the sun goes down, it will be another day for other heroes and other dreams.'

Gemma hugged Phelan and Saoirse. Then she stood by the window that overlooked the cottage in the rocks. 'I want to go home. Thanks for everything. Come and see me if you are ever on my road.'

The girl smiled. 'Thank you, too. Your home is not far from my grandfather's. I may well come and visit one day.'

Phelan shook Saoirse's hand. He smiled. 'I still owe you a violin, and you still owe me an evening's playing. You are always welcome in Harflorum.'

She nodded. 'Thanks. Musicians are treated well in your palace. Mother and I will take you up on your offer, especially if the winter gets cold!'

'Make sure you do.'

Then she turned to Fleabag who just purred and rolled over for his tummy to be tickled. 'Remember, no more catgut!' he growled.

'I promise,' she laughed, as she took her mother's hand, and disappeared through the window that looked south.

Gemma put her feet over the ledge that took her to the mountains. 'I presume you're staying here by the fire?' she asked Fleabag.

'Of course. I know where I'm well off,' he grinned.

Gemma picked the cat up and rubbed her face in his smooth, soft fur, wiping a tear away as she did so. 'Bye, you disreputable old ratter. Be good!'

Fleabag sniffed derisively. 'Am I ever anything else?' But the sniff sounded a little odd, and he hid behind the old woman's skirts.

Gemma tried to sound cheerful. 'Are *you* coming, Rowanne?' she asked.

The Princess shook her head. 'I'm not going back. I think I must stay here now. Maybe the Lady Fire Giver has work for me to do.'

'Indeed, I do,' the old woman smiled, as she rose from her chair by the fire, and stretched out her arms to pull the dark blue silk of the night across the skies. 'We all have much to do now. Even Fleabag. But I do hope he will be happy with me.'

The cat reappeared, having found his composure. He spread his whiskers wide and stalked over to the fireside where he sat on the rug with the warmth on his back. 'Why ever shouldn't I be happy here? This is heaven!'

The old lady laughed as she lit the moon. 'I don't have any fleas here. You will have nothing to scratch and moan about, and you will have to use your real name again.'

'What *is* your real name, Fleabag?' Gemma asked. 'Surely it's safe to tell it here?'

'Night-Wanderer Moon-Eyes,' the cat replied, as he jumped onto the window ledge. Then he sat down and began washing his fourth leg in the cool of the evening breeze. 'Send Tabitha and the kittens my love, won't you?' he called as Gemma and Phelan climbed through the windows into their own places, and disappeared into the shadows.

Only the gleam of Fleabag's golden eyes was left, glowing in the sable night.

Also available from Lion Children's Books:

The Witch of Wookey Hole

Beth Webb

The witch and her dog have guarded the cave for centuries. But only Dave and Maddy guessed that she was more than stone, that there really was a sad old woman behind the stories. Even so, they are amazed when the witch starts demanding food and clothes to keep her warm. The recent death of their own grandmother inspires them to take pity on old Hester. Soon, however, her eccentric and ungrateful behaviour makes them wish they hadn't...

An adventure about two children who become fascinated by a strange rock formation in the famous Wookey hole caves.

ISBN 0 7459 3894 9

The Dragons of Kilve

Beth Webb

One day the dragons of Kilve have a wonderful surprise when some long-forgotten dragon eggs begin to hatch. The mischievous little dragons have all sorts of adventures and mishaps: but the wise old Dragon Master is always close at hand. And, best of all, he helps them to discover three great treasures...

Twelve funny and imaginative stories about a group of wayward young dragons, which show that everyone is special and that caring for others is important.

ISBN 0 7459 4881 2

Foxdown Wood

Beth Webb

Foxdown Wood is under threat from unscrupulous property developers and Matt and Cathy are determined to save the ancient wood and its wildlife. Then they are unexpectedly summoned to the Other World – a place that is somehow familiar, but also very unlike their own. It seems that each world's struggles between good and evil are linked in some way – but can the children do anything to help?

A time-slip adventure with strong environmental and family themes.

ISBN 0 7459 3848 5

The Magic in the Pool of Making

Beth Webb

The River Planet is in danger. Its life source, the Lightwater River, is dying, poisoned though centuries of pollution and misuse. Manny, a starving and mysterious Sand boy, is the only person who knows how to put things right. Now, through a simple act of kindness, Johin is entwined in his dangerous quest.

As they cross the drought-stricken land, Johin realizes that the River offers life in more than one way. But clearing its source won't be enough. She and Manny also have to defeat the evil Brilliance...

A powerful allegorical fantasy showing the destructiveness of greed and prejudice.

ISBN 0 7459 2234 1

Them

Fay Sampson

Berlewen is trapped in a past she has not chosen, denied any modern technology. Honesty, her servant, longs to free her family, now enslaved in a weapons factory. Only Map, the bootboy, seems sure of the freedom promised in the ancient song. They are all prisoners of THEM.

One day a summons from THEM forces Berlewen and Honesty to flee and brave the mysterious being that guards Glastonbury. Their quest is to find the legendary Prince and free their people from the ruthless domination of THEM.

But does the Prince really exist? How will they recognize him? And even if they find him, how can anyone defeat THEM?

'[THEM] can be recommended unreservedly as a novel of quality.'
School Library Association

ISBN 0 7459 4670 4

All Lion books are available from your local bookshop, or can be ordered via our website or from Marston Book Services. For a free catalogue, showing the complete list of titles available, please contact:

Customer Services
Marston Book Services
PO Box 269
Abingdon
Oxon
OX14 4YN

Tel: 01235 465500
Fax: 01235 465555

Our website can be found at:
www.lionhudson.com